PLAY IT DIRTY

PLAYERS OF HANNAFORD U
BOOK 1

MICHELLE HERCULES

INFINITE SKY PUBLISHING

PLAY IT DIRTY © 2023 by Michelle Hercules

All rights reserved.

No part of this book may be reproduced or transmitted in any form or by any means, electronic or mechanical, including photocopying, recording, or by any information storage and retrieval system without the written permission of the author, except for the use of brief quotations in a book review.

This book is a work of fiction. Names, characters, places, and incidents either are products of the author's imagination or are used fictitiously. Any resemblance to actual persons, living or dead, events, or locales is entirely coincidental.

Paperback ISBN: 978-1-959167-26-6

PLAYLIST

Sweet Child O' Mine - GUNS N' ROSES
Let's Go To Bed - THE CURE
Kiss - PRINCE
Dynamite - BTS
If I Can't Have You - SHAWN MENDES
Hold Me Closer - ELTON JOHN, BRITNEY SPEARS
The Adventure - ANGELS & AIRWAVES
Perfect - ONE DIRECTION
11 Minutes - YUNGBLUD, HALSEY, TRAVIS BARKER
Think of You - WHIGFIELD
Head over Feet - ALANIS MORISSETTE
Obsessed - GUCCI MANE, MARIAH CAREY
Whenever, Wherever - SHAKIRA
Celebration - KOOL & THE GANG

CHAPTER 1
NOAH

My ears are still buzzing from all the shouting at the end of the game. Jesse Hartnett, the team captain, brought the place down when he sent that puck to the back of the net like he shot it from a bazooka, giving the Warriors the lead at the last second. That poor goalie didn't stand a chance. I jumped out of my seat right behind their box and banged on the glass, joining in the frenzy. Next year, I'll be on the other side, celebrating with my new teammates.

With that win, the Hannaford U Warriors guaranteed themselves a spot in the Frozen Four finals, and the next semifinal game will determine if they'll be facing Clayton U, our rival school. Suffice it to say, it's a madhouse in Tampa's Amalie Arena.

Assistant Coach LaRue, who's still in the box, looks over his shoulder and signals me to meet them in the locker room. I was invited by the school to attend the championship games since I'm starting next semester, and he gave me a pass earlier that grants me access. I turn to leave, but there are people in my way. As I wait for my row to empty, I look around. And that's when I see her, the most beautiful girl I've ever laid eyes on, exiting a row a couple of levels up from mine. Light brown hair secured into two braids, flawless tanned skin, and a face that belongs on the cover of a magazine. She's perfect.

Someone taps on my shoulder. "Are you going to move?"

"Oops. Sorry."

That girl put me in such a trance, I didn't notice there was no one blocking my way anymore. I walk quickly, hoping to catch up with her, but there are too many people on the stairs, and I lose sight of her.

When I finally reach the food court area, I crane my neck, hoping to see her in the crowd. No such luck. I bet she went to the washroom. I head in that direction. There's a line outside the women's washroom, but if she went there, she'd be standing at the end. Shit. I lost her.

I've never been more upset about a missed opportunity than I am today. I shove the disappointment aside. There will be other pretty girls.

As I head to the locker room to congratulate my future teammates in person, I pinch myself to make sure I'm not dreaming. I could hardly believe it when Derek LaRue, former NHL legend and now the assistant coach, reached out to me last year. Other schools were hounding, but it was game over when Hannaford U said they wanted me. I've always wanted to play for them.

I'm about to round a corner when I hear a female voice shout, "Ryder! Wait."

"Do *not* follow me, Gia."

I keep walking since the locker room is in that direction. But I stop in my tracks when I see the hottie from earlier grab notorious Warriors D-man Ryder Westwood's arm.

"The hell I won't. What was that crap in there?" She points at the locker room door.

Wait, what was she doing in the locker room? My gaze drops to the lanyard hanging from her neck. She has a pass like mine. I'm damn curious now.

Locked in a staring contest, they don't notice me hovering at the end of the corridor. He yanks his arm free from her grasp, and her eyes widen. Shit. She has pretty hazel eyes, and even from a distance, I can see they're swimming in pain. Future teammate or not, I already loathe him. It's crazy. I don't know them, or why he's pissed, but how dare he hurt that girl?

Logical, I'm not.

"I don't owe you any explanation. You're not my girlfriend anymore, remember?"

Her lips quiver, but instead of wincing, she lifts her chin. "I didn't forget, asshole. Do you think I'm here to beg you to take me back?"

Damn. Gorgeous and feisty. I like her. But hell, why did she date that jerk in the first place?

"What do you want from me then?"

She puts her hands on her hips. "You can't quit. The team needs you."

Whoa. He quit just after getting to the finals? What kind of bullshit is that?

He laughs derisively. "The team needs me... I didn't know you were a jokester, babe."

She squints. "I'm not your babe."

"Right. You aren't. And to answer your first question, I can do whatever the hell I want. And what I want is off this fucking team."

Now she does wince and steps back. She seems more offended by the way he addressed the team than her. She has the looks, the personality, and she's loyal—basically, she's the whole package and is quickly becoming my dream girl. I'm a second away from punching that asshole in the face when someone else walks out. Jesse Hartnett.

"Forget him, Gia. We don't need him."

Ryder scoffs. "Jesse, the golden boy. I was wondering when you'd show up and play the knight in shining armor."

He scowls. "Just go, Ryder. You've caused enough disruption."

"With pleasure." He strides away and takes the exit at the end of the corridor.

Jesse looks at Gia. "Are you okay?"

She wipes the corner of one eye. Hell, that asshole made her cry.

"I'm fine. I just need a minute."

He nods and returns to the locker room. I know she said she needs a minute, but I feel like I need to say something to her. I wait too long though, and before I can walk over and introduce myself, she disappears into the women's washroom.

Crap. I debate waiting until she gets out, but I might look like a creep. I'd better head to the locker room and find out first why Ryder Westwood quit the team. But I'm annoyed that I didn't act fast enough. Patience is not a virtue I have, especially when I want something.

And I definitely want to get to know her.

CHAPTER 2
NOAH

SIX MONTHS LATER

"How are you feeling, man?" Sean Davenport, the Warriors' new captain, asks when he catches me wincing as I walk from his truck to the bar.

"I'm sore in places I didn't know could hurt. I didn't realize Assistant Coach LaRue was a sadistic motherfucker."

He chuckles. "He's the nicest guy I know, but yeah, he'll work us until we beg for mercy. The next time he 'volunteers'"—Sean makes air quotes—"to be your gym partner, just say no."

"Yeah, right. Like I'll say no to anything that man asks."

Sean's eyes twinkle with mirth. "Aww, do you have a crush?"

"Shut up. As if you guys don't idolize him too."

"We do, but I guess we aren't as starstruck anymore."

I rub my abs. "I don't think I've ever done that many sit-ups in one go. I hope no one decides to be funny tonight. I can't afford to laugh."

"I can't promise that." He walks into The Heritage, the popular sports bar near the Hannaford U campus, and I follow him.

It's Friday night, and as usual, the place is crowded and

noisy. The Heritage is where legends hang out and memories are made. It was relatively calm during preseason training, but we're a month into the fall semester, and everyone is already feeling the pressure of keeping up with academics—myself included. Booze is a coping mechanism for many. Tonight, not only are there more people, the ratio of dudes and chicks is tipping considerably in favor of the ladies.

The girls near the entrance glance in our direction, and they're all smiles. I check them out because they're hot chicks wearing skintight clothes, but I'm not interested in any of them. There's only one girl I'm hoping to see tonight. I haven't been able to erase Gia Mancini from my mind since I witnessed her fight with Ryder Westbrook, but it's been two months since I moved to Fairbanks, Connecticut, and I have yet to meet her.

It turns out my dream girl works for the team as the social media coordinator. I didn't meet her in Tampa. She never returned to the locker room, and later I heard she cut her trip short and returned home. To say I was bummed out was an understatement.

I expected to see her around, but it seems she's been avoiding the rink. It's possible she's still upset about her breakup with Ryder, but that doesn't bother me much. I can make her forget that douche canoe. Even if I don't see her tonight, she's scheduled an interview with me next Monday. I'm counting the hours.

I've been following her on social media like a stalker. She not only manages the Warriors' social media accounts, but she's also an influencer with almost a million followers on Instagram and TikTok. Gia is a talented dancer, and her videos always go viral.

The crowd parts to let us through. Hockey is huge at Hannaford U, and everyone knows the players. Girls greet Sean like he's a king, batting their eyelashes or flicking their hair. They're flirty with me too, but with less intensity. I'm the rookie; no one has seen me play yet. That's fine by me. Sleeping around is not on my agenda.

I don't need to crane my neck to search the room. I'm not the tallest on the team—I'm only six-one, while some of the guys are six-four and six-five—but I *am* taller than most people here. My search is fruitless, though. I don't see Gia anywhere.

Sean stops ahead of me, and because I'm not paying attention, I bump against his wide back. "Oops, sorry."

He looks over his shoulder, sporting a curious grin. "Are you all right there?"

"Yeah, I'm good."

He steps aside, and the Kaminski twins come into view. They've managed to grab a high-top table near the bar. They're identical, and it took me a while to figure out who was who when they were out of uniform. It doesn't help that they have the same haircut, short on the sides and longer on top. But then I noticed Logan, the oldest of the twins by two minutes, had a small scar on the left side of his jaw.

They're both smirking at me, but it's Alex Kaminski who speaks first. "How was your training sesh with LaRue?"

"Shut up," I grumble.

His brows arch and his blue eyes widen innocently. "What?"

"I bet it only hurts when he breathes," Logan pipes up.

"Ha-ha, you guys are hilarious." I glance away once again to scan the room.

"Are you looking for someone?" Sean asks.

"Yeah, I'm wondering if Gia will be here," I reply absentmindedly.

"Ah *hell* no," Alex groans.

I face them again. "What?"

"Please don't tell me you're into her."

I would confess if I wasn't picking up a doomsday vibe from them. When they want to appear intimidating, they look like two pissed-off Viking warriors.

"What? No way. It's about my interview. I'd like to meet her beforehand, that's all."

Their stances relax, and now I want to know why I ruffled their feathers.

"Why are you acting like two protective big brothers?"

They trade a look, but it's Sean who answers. "Gia's like a sister to us, and what Ryder did was fucked up. She got hurt, it was messy, and we don't want to see that happen again."

"Besides, I seriously doubt she'd ever want to date another hockey player." Logan takes a sip of his beer. "Or a rich asshole."

My stomach drops through the earth, and it's damn hard to keep the disappointment from showing on my face.

"I'm grabbing a drink," I say. "Do you want another round?"

Sean raises an eyebrow. "You know you're not in Alberta anymore, right?"

My face becomes warm. God, they must think I'm an idiot.

"Hold on, Sean. Maybe Noah's got a fake ID," Alex interjects.

"I don't. I'm just gonna grab a club soda."

I begin to turn, but Sean puts a hand on my shoulder. "I'll grab the drinks. Everyone okay with beer?"

The twins lift their almost empty glasses in response, and I just mumble a yes before pulling up a chair.

No sooner do I sit down, resting my forearms on the table and slouching my shoulders, than Alex shouts, "Gia! Over here."

I sit up straight so fast, I almost fall off my chair. The twins laugh. My ears are burning, and I'm glad my longish hair hides them.

"Hi, guys." She smiles at them, then turns to me. "Hey, Noah. It's nice to meet you in person finally."

I open my mouth to reply, but no sound comes forth. I just stare at her like a doofus, and the longer the silence stretches, the more awkward the situation becomes.

Say something, you idiot. Anything.

"Noah? Are you okay?" She touches my arm, her brows furrowed in concern.

I shake my head. "Yeah, I'm fine. Sorry, I'm so tired I think my brain is in sleep mode already."

"He trained with LaRue today," Logan tells her, and her eyes widen in understanding.

"Oh... now I get it. No one warned you about him, huh?" She drops her hand from my arm, and I want to put it back there again.

I don't do it, obviously. I just managed to save myself from a humiliating first meeting. I won't act like a weirdo again.

"Nope." I glower at the duo, who are trying and failing to hold down their laughter.

Jerks.

"You guys are the worst," she replies, then turns her bright hazel eyes toward me again. "Anyway, I'm so excited about our interview on Monday. I sent you an email an hour ago with homework."

"Homework?" I quirk an eyebrow while my lips curl upward.

Her gaze drops to my mouth for a second, reminding me that I'm not a dumbass who can't talk to girls. For a moment, I forgot I *do* have game and my smile... it's killer.

"Yes, just some questions I'll be asking during our TikTok live. I want you to be prepared."

"Are you sure it's wise to do a live with this guy?" Alex butts in, eyes shining with mirth. "I mean, he's from Canada."

"Do you mind? I'm trying to have a professional convo here," I retort.

"Ohhh, someone's not terrified of you for a change, Alex." Gia laughs.

He narrows his eyes, and I can't tell if it's an act or if he's seriously aggravated. Alex is a notorious hothead and holds the penalty box record on our team. It's probably not wise to get on his bad side.

"Maybe he should be." He drains the rest of his beer, keeping his eyes on me.

I reward him with a droll stare. "I have two older brothers who are bigger and meaner than you, and I survived."

Logan is turning red, and I realize he's trying not to laugh.

Alex notices him and punches his arm hard. "What are you laughing at?"

"You. You're losing your touch, bro. Can't even scare the scrawny rookie."

"Who are you calling scrawny?" I ask, seriously offended now.

"Ignore them. You're definitely not skinny."

"I know that," I say, still defensive as shit because, compared to the twins and everyone else on the team, I look like a twig.

She laughs and then taps my shoulder. "I like your vibe, Noah."

At once, my annoyance melts away. It's almost an impossible task to keep my face from showing what she's doing to me.

"Hey, Gia. I haven't seen you in a while," Sean says as he returns to the table.

"Yeah, I had enough content to post this past month, and my schedule is hell. I figure I should focus on my classes before hockey season starts. By the way, I'm looking for a French tutor. If you know any, let me know."

A light bulb turns on over my head, and before I can stop to think, I blurt out, "I can tutor you."

Her brows arch. "You speak French fluently?"

"Yep."

Liar, liar. Pants on fire. My French is rough, and she'll be able to tell as soon as I try to speak it. I'm an idiot.

"I thought they primarily spoke English in Alberta." Alex gives me a meaningful look.

Yeah, he's not buying your BS, Noah.

"That's true, but my parents insisted I learn French." I shrug.

That, at least, is true. The problem is I was more interested in playing hockey than learning the language. Now I wish I'd paid more attention to the private tutor they hired to teach my siblings and me.

"Gia!" A short blonde waves at her from the bar.

Gia waves back and is already moving away from the table when she says, "I'll catch you guys later."

Fuck. I barely talked to her, and the whole French tutoring thing is up in the air. I shouldn't watch her walk away, but I can't help myself.

A paper coaster hits my shoulder, drawing my attention from her.

"What?" I ask no one in particular.

Logan shakes his head. "Not into Gia, my ass."

CHAPTER 3
GIA

I didn't realize how hard it'd be to hang out with the guys again until I saw the Trouble Twins, Sean, and the team's newest star, Noah Kingsley. I tried my best to appear like my old self, but the truth is, my heart hasn't recovered from Ryder's betrayal. When Ashley shouted my name, I thanked the heavens for the opportunity to escape.

"Girl, I haven't seen you in ages." She gives me one of her boa constrictor hugs. She's tiny, but she isn't meek.

We've been friends since my freshman year. Ashley is an art major, and I'm a film and media studies major, so we've had some classes together. She also happens to be Sean's stepsister, but we clicked way before I made the connection. Unlike everyone else at this school, Ashley isn't a hockey fan.

"I've been buried in homework and projects for my classes already."

"Ugh. Don't remind me. And I thought my days stressing about studies were behind me when I got into Hannaford U. College is supposed to be fun, damn it."

I laugh. "I honestly don't know how Sean does it. His classes are tough."

She twists her face into a scowl. "Don't remind me how

unfair life is. Sean is a fucking genius, okay, which annoys me to no end."

"Why does it annoy you?"

"Because someone that attractive shouldn't be smart *and* good at sports."

I blink fast. "Since when do you think Sean is attractive? You've always said he's a troll."

Something he clearly isn't. He could be Henry Cavill's younger brother with that square jaw, chin dimple, and all those muscles. He'd have girls lining up even if he wasn't on the hockey team.

"He *is* a troll," she mumbles, then tilts her head and studies me closely. "Enough about him. Is it hard being back here?"

My stomach twists. I don't want to answer that question, or better yet, I wish I could answer with a flat no, it isn't hard. But I can't bullshit Ashley. She'd see right through me.

"Yeah. I didn't think it would be, though."

"You're better off without him. I never liked that preppy asshole."

"I'm not brokenhearted because he dumped me."

Not a lie. I was sad when Ryder ended our one-year relationship, but things weren't working out anyway. What started great had fizzled into monotony. I got over the breakup quickly. But when he turned his back on the team, that betrayal cut deep. No one saw it coming.

"What that jerkface did was unforgivable, and that's coming from a non-hockey fan. Who quits on their team in the middle of the Frozen Four?"

My eyes burn as I remember the scene in the locker room. Ryder took off his helmet and announced in a tone cold enough to freeze the room that he was done, killing the celebratory mood in an instant. I don't want to cry over that again. We lost the championship because of him, and it was Jesse's final year to boot. That sucked. My brother, Jaime, was devasted.

"Can we not talk about him anymore?"

"Absolutely. Ryder who?" She smirks, then gives me an ice-cold Corona and takes one for herself. "Cheers to a fantastic season without assholes."

We clink our bottles, and I take a large sip of mine. I'm not a huge drinker, and I usually stick to one or two beers when I'm out. Tonight, I could use something stronger, but I won't indulge. Getting wasted while in the presence of the guys is not an image I want to portray. I consider them my friends, but I also need to maintain a professional appearance. They need to respect me so I can get them to do all that stupid shit for social media.

My phone vibrates in my pocket, and I yank it out to see who texted me.

"Who's that?" Ashley, the ever so curious asks, already glancing at my screen.

"It's Zoey. She wants to know if I'm here tonight."

Ashley twists her face into a scowl. "Why is she texting you and not me?"

I give her a bright smile. "Maybe she likes me better than you."

She blows me a raspberry before bringing the bottle to her lips.

"Oh," I blurt out when I read her the following text.

"Oh what?" Ashley peers at my phone again. "Ah… that's why she texted you first. What are you going to tell her?"

I force down the lump in my throat. "It's fine. I have no issue with Blair."

Never mind that she's given me the cold shoulder ever since her brother quit the team. Blair is Ryder's younger sister, and she used to be my best friend. I don't begrudge her taking her brother's side in the matter, but she could have at least returned my calls.

I reply to Zoey's text, repeating what I just told Ashley. I don't care if Blair comes to The Heritage. When I look up from my phone again, Ashley is no longer paying attention to me. Her gaze is trained on the guys' table, and she seems pissed.

I follow her line of sight. They're already surrounded by beautiful girls. What I don't get is why she's mad about that. That's a normal occurrence for them. I recognize Tori, a gorgeous brunette who reminds me of a young Megan Fox. She's plastered to Sean's side, shoving her cleavage against his arm. He's smiling at her, oozing charm.

"What's wrong?" I ask.

"Nothing. Ugh, that's why I hate coming here." She chugs what's left of her beer and turns to the bartender to order another round.

"Because of the guys' fans?"

"They're not fans, Gia. They're puck bunnies."

I know what they're called, but I refuse to use that derogatory name. When I got the job of social media coordinator for the Warriors, I was called that and worse. The hate stopped when I started dating Ryder. Now I wonder if the insults will resume. I get sick to my stomach thinking about it.

I'm not new to bullying. Kids used to pick on me in middle school because I wore thick glasses and was a little chubby. Then I found dance, and that became my passion. It gave me the confidence I'd never had. I stopped using food to hide my pain, and the pounds dropped. People stopped picking on me then, especially when my videos on YouTube started getting a lot of views.

A cute blonde with a pixie haircut stops next to Noah. She isn't as forward as Tori, but even a door could see she's flirting with our new star. He nods at something she says, but then he looks in my direction. Grinning, I lift my drink in salute. The thousand-watt smile he rewards me with makes my heart do a backflip. Damn. I wasn't prepared for that. It's been a while since a pretty boy had that effect on me.

I look away quickly, lest he notices my reaction. Ryder was the first and last hockey player I'll ever date. I've learned my lesson. There are plenty of cute guys on campus who aren't on the team—not that I have any desire to date anyone right now. I have enough on my plate with my job at the Warriors, school, and dance. Jumping into another relationship isn't a distraction I need.

Ashley's sour mood doesn't improve, so I decide to steer her away from the guys. We head for the back of the bar where the pool tables are. Naturally, there isn't a single one available, and the booths lining the wall are all taken. I freeze when I recognize a familiar face.

Ryder is at one of those booths, hanging out with his high-society buddies.

While his friends seem to be having a good time, he's slouched against the seat, swirling the whiskey in his glass.

Ashley sees them as well and blurts out, "Fuck a duck."

Her exclamation is loud enough that it can be heard over the background music. They all look in our direction, including Ryder. Without breaking eye contact with me, he drinks his whiskey like a shot and then slams the glass back down on the table.

I haven't seen him since Tampa, and like a volcano, all the anger from that day shoots up from the pit of my stomach. If I stay, I'll end up doing something I'll regret.

I turn to Ashley. "I'm leaving."

Her brows rise. "Because of him?"

"I can't be under the same roof as Ryder yet."

"Why is that?"

"I might punch him in the throat if I do." Unlikely, but I'd for sure tell him to go to hell. The last thing the team needs before the season starts is for their social media coordinator to make a scene.

Ashley glowers in his direction, but I don't look to see if he's still staring at us.

"Zoey and Blair will be here soon," I add, feeling guilty that I'm bailing on her.

"Yeah. Don't worry about me. I'll just hang with Sean for a bit."

I give her a quizzical look. "You're going to hang out with the guys?"

She shrugs. "It might be fun to antagonize some puck bunnies."

I shake my head. Ashley could be the poster child for "cute but psycho." I'm glad she's my friend.

"All right. Try to not stab anyone." I give her a hug and quickly make my escape.

CHAPTER 4
NOAH

I've been trying to listen to what the girl next to me is saying, but my attention is split. Gia disappeared with her friend a few minutes ago.

"So, what was it like growing up in Canada?" The blonde touches my arm, moving closer. She told me her name, but I've already forgotten.

I shrug. "I'm sure the same as growing up here."

She giggles, and the sound is as grating as nails scratching a blackboard. How long until I can go in search of Gia without being obvious about it? Alex, Logan, and Sean are distracted. I could escape now. I'm about to go for it when the petite blonde who waved at Gia earlier joins us at the table. Unlike the other girls here, she isn't all smiles. My gaze travels past her, but Gia isn't around. Shit.

"Hey, look who's here." Alex grins from ear to ear. "Sean's baby sis."

"I'm not his sister," she grits out.

Sean's expression darkens, and he works his jaw hard. "What do you want, Ash?"

"Nothing. Can't I just come and say hello?" She turns to the girl next to Sean. "Hey, Tori, if you press your fake boobs any harder on Sean, they might explode like water balloons."

The girl scoffs. "You're rude."

"Where's Gia?" I ask, and I realize immediately it was a mistake. Alex and Logan are now staring at me intensely.

"She left," Ashley replies.

"Why?" Sean furrows his brows.

His stepsister pinches her lips, and my spine goes taut. I don't like that expression.

"Ryder is here with his asshole friends."

"What?" Alex jumps up from his chair.

"Hey, take it easy, man. You're *not* to engage with him." Sean turns to Logan and me. "That goes for everyone."

I wasn't planning on confronting Gia's ex. I'm not a dumbass with anger issues, and I know Coach Bedford won't tolerate his players picking fights in a bar. I can't say the same about Alex and Logan, especially Alex.

"That's bullshit. He shouldn't be here."

"Why'd he quit the team, anyway?" the brunette next to Sean asks, curling a strand of hair around her finger.

Everyone ignores her question except Sean's stepsister, who's openly glowering at her. "That's none of your business."

"What's your problem?"

Sean pinches the bridge of his nose. "Ashley, don't start."

She crosses her arms and glares. "I didn't start anything. Do you want to tell your new friend why one of your best players quit before the Frozen Four championship game?"

They engage in a staring contest that gets broken only when something catches Alex's attention, and he curses loudly. "Great, now the clusterfuck is complete."

I look around to see what's got him annoyed. Another pair of gorgeous girls are coming our way. One has auburn hair and freckles all over her face. She looks familiar, but I can't place her. The second is a brunette with porcelain skin and big blue eyes.

"Zoey! Blair! Thank God you're here," Ashley blurts out.

Zoey waves at us and says hello. Blair remains a step behind and makes eye contact with no one. Alex, however, is openly glaring at her.

"Where's Gia?" Zoey asks.

"She left a few minutes ago."

"Because of me?" Blair pinches her eyebrows.

"No—your brother is here."

Aha. Mystery solved. She must be Ryder's sister. No wonder Alex is pissed that she's here, although his reaction seems a little over the top. Ryder is the one who fucked the team over, not her.

She shakes her head. "He's an idiot."

"Not an idiot. He's an asshole with a capital A," Alex chimes in.

"It takes one to know one," she retorts.

Okay, then. It seems I was spared all the drama during preseason training, and now everything is coming to the surface. I couldn't care less about all the feuds. My whole life I've tried to stay away from bullshit and focus on hockey only. The reason I came out tonight is no longer here, so I might as well go home.

I fake a yawn. "I think I'm gonna head out."

The girl next to me whines, "Already?"

"Yeah. I'm beat. Catch you guys later."

I'm outta there before someone decides to offer me company. I just want one girl, and her name is Gia.

CHAPTER 5
GIA

By a miracle, I didn't have to put out any fires last weekend. When I got home from The Heritage last Friday, it did occur to me that the guys could have gotten into a fight with Ryder—especially Alex, who can never maintain his cool. But I'd hoped Sean would keep them out of trouble, and he had.

I've been running errands all day and have barely had time to breathe. When Martin—a friend who sometimes collaborates with me on dance videos—calls me, I let it go to voice mail. He's not going to like it, but tough shit. He can't keep a call short, and I'm already late to meet Noah at the rink. I said I'd be there after practice for his interview and asked him to wait for me in his gear. The engagement for the videos is usually much higher when the boys are sweaty and in their uniforms.

I burst through the front doors and sprint down the corridor toward the staff offices and locker room. Then I hear male voices coming from ahead. When I turn a corner, I bump into Darren Michaels, one of our goalies, and Sean, all showered and ready to head out.

"Shit. How long since practice ended?"

They trade a glance, and then Darren replies, "Fifteen minutes or so?"

"Did Noah wait for me in the rink?"

"He didn't come to the locker room."

"He's waiting for you, Gia." Sean smiles. "I think you'll find him to be the easiest one of us to work with."

Sean is usually super serious, but there's a twinkle in his eyes that makes me curious.

"Why do you say that?"

"No reason."

"Noah is nice—a bit cocky, but we all were in the beginning," Darren adds.

"All right. I'd better go. Be on the lookout for an email from me in the next couple days. I have plans for you two."

They groan. No surprise. The hardest part of my job is convincing the guys to do stuff for the team's social media accounts. Some of them, such as the twins and CJ King, one of our D-men, are more than happy to be in front of the camera. Darren and Sean are the hardest to convince.

I look at my watch and see that I'm going to be late for my own live stream. Damn it. I don't sprint, I run, making a loud noise when I shove open the heavy door that leads to the Warriors' lounge area. Only players and staff are allowed in here. When I make my big entrance, Coach Bedford and Assistant Coach LaRue are chatting by the coffee machine. They grow silent and look at me.

"Hey, Gia." Coach Bedford waves at me. "Where's the fire?"

"I'm late for my live with Noah," I reply without slowing down.

There's a hint of amusement on his face as he shakes his head. Coach Bedford is the reason I work for the Warriors. A year ago, the competition to handle the team's social media accounts was fierce, but he went out on a limb for me and gave me the job. Not that I wasn't qualified for it, but it was unheard of for a freshman to land such a coveted position. I'm sure in part he did it because of what happened to Jaime three years ago. A year older than me, Jaime was a promising hockey star and had been given a full ride to play for Hannaford U. And then the car accident happened. He was coming home after dropping off Coach Bedford at the airport—who came to Chicago to watch Jaime's Division I championship game. Jaime got hurt really bad, and that was the end of his hockey career. It wasn't Coach Bedford's fault, but I know he feels guilty about it.

Thinking about Jaime puts a lump the size of Texas in my throat. He was supposed to be here and be part of the Warriors family, not me.

I shove those sad thoughts aside. I can't be all depressed during my live.

I head down the tunnel that leads to the rink. There's no one around save for Noah, skating on the ice.

He lifts his head and waves at me.

"Sorry I'm late," I say as I dump my duffel bag on the bench.

"It's okay. I don't mind having the ice all to myself."

I take a seat and put on my skates. I could keep my boots on, but I feel more at ease if I can move without fear of falling on my ass. When I look up, Noah is watching me with his stick resting across his shoulders. He's not wearing a helmet, and his wet, shaggy brown hair is tousled in a sexy way. Perfect. The women who follow our account are going to love him.

"Are you ready?" I stand with my phone in hand.

"Yes, ma'am."

A chuckle bursts from my lips. "Ma'am?"

Looking sheepish, he rubs the back of his neck. "Ah, sorry. I didn't mean anything by it."

"No, that's fine. Unexpected, that's all."

I join him on the ice and shiver. It seems I'm always underdressed when I come here.

"Are you cold?" he asks.

Shaking my head, I reply. "No. I'm good."

"So, what exactly happens during these lives?"

"Well, I'm going to officially introduce you to our followers and then ask you the questions I sent via email. After that, we'll take questions from the comments, if there are any."

He grimaces, and I realize that he might not be comfortable with that.

I tilt my head. "Are you nervous?"

Making an adorable face that causes my stomach to pitch, he replies, "Would you think less of me if I said yes?"

Man, Noah Kingsley is going to be the newest obsession of all the girls on and off campus. He's just too adorable for his own good.

I grin. "Of course not. I take you've never done a live before?"

"Nah, I never cared much about social media." He widens his eyes. "Nothing against what you do. I swear."

"Relax, I didn't take it as a putdown. Okay, I'm going to start now." I position the phone in front of me and then press the record button.

"Hey everyone, sorry we're a bit late to start the live. I know you're all super excited for the hockey season, and so are the Warriors. This week will be all about introducing the new members of our team to you, and to start, we have Noah Kingsley, the fastest center you'll ever see on the ice."

I move closer to him, making sure the camera captures both of us. "Hi Noah, thank you for doing this."

"No problem. Happy to be here."

"How are you today?"

"I'm awesome. How about you?" He looks at me, and it feels weird that he's staring at my face while I'm looking at the camera.

So I turn to him to answer… and realize my mistake. He's too close to me, and the way his warm brown eyes are staring with such intensity makes me flustered.

"I'm feeling good," I reply a beat too late.

God, I hope no one noticed that I lost my train of thought for a moment. I begin to fire the boilerplate questions at him. Where he's from, how many siblings he has, and so on. He answers all of them without missing a beat, oozing charisma. He might not care much about social media, but he's a natural in front of the camera. I can tell by the number of comments that are popping up on my screen. The girls are already swooning.

"Wow, you have five siblings?" I ask, legit surprised. "How was that growing up?"

"It was great. I'm the middle child, so my parents didn't notice me much. I could get away with a lot of stuff."

He's smiling, and yet I catch a glint of sadness in his eyes. I don't think his childhood was as terrific as he's claiming it was, but that's not something to unpack during a live.

I move on. "I bet. I think we should take some questions from the comments now."

"Let's do it."

I scan the newest comments, until I find one question that always pops up when I interview the guys.

"Jessica Warner wants to know if you have a girlfriend."

"Nope. Never had one."

"Why is that?" I blurt out, forgetting that I'm supposed to be taking questions from the comments section.

"Hockey kept me busy, and it wouldn't be fair to date anyone and not give them one hundred percent of my attention."

"Does that mean you'll never date?"

He looks away from the camera and pierces me with his eyes again. "Oh, when I find my dream girl, you bet I'm going to be the best boyfriend on the planet."

"Dream girl? Can you describe what she'd be like?"

"She's achingly beautiful but not in a superficial way. She's kind, feisty, and, most important, loyal. Oh, and she loves hockey."

The way he used the present tense to describe her makes me think she's not hypothetical—she already exists. Or maybe he's manifesting. Either way, I feel my cheeks getting warm. Noah

Kingsley is making me blush, and I don't know what to do with myself. I break eye contact first.

"Did you hear that, ladies? Noah Kingsley is looking for his dream girl. Let's help him find her."

The comment section explodes with heart emojis and love declarations. He'll have no trouble finding a girlfriend now. As we continue the interview, the questions from our followers become more daring and racy. I have to be careful here. It's okay to exploit our players' good looks, but I don't want them to become uncomfortable.

I skip most of the questions related to Noah's relationship status and focus on the ones about hockey. That is, until I come across a mean comment asking me what it feels like to be the team's whore. I pretend I didn't read it, but it gets to me. I was afraid those nasty comments would resume, but I was hoping they wouldn't.

I don't have the heart to continue now, so I cut it short. Noah and I say goodbye, and then the camera is off.

Without looking at him, I say, "Thank you for doing this. Did you have fun?"

"Are you okay?"

I glance at him, hoping he can't see the sadness shining in my eyes. "Yes. Why do you ask?"

"I read that shitty comment about you. I'm sorry."

My cheeks are burning up. Hell, I was hoping he didn't see it. I avert my gaze. This is so humiliating.

"Well, it happens sometimes. I'm used to them."

"You shouldn't have to get used to them. I hate internet trolls. They're a waste of space."

"Yes, they are. That's why I try to not think about them. They're not worth my time." I step out of the rink and sit down to take off my skates.

Noah remains standing in front of the bench, and I sense he's staring again. I look up. "What?"

"Are you still looking for a French tutor?"

My heart races at the prospect of spending time alone with him. But that's a stupid, crazy reaction. I'm not going there again with another hockey player. It's a recipe for disaster. Guaranteed.

"Yes, but you don't have to do it. Your schedule will be insane once the season starts."

"I wouldn't have offered if I didn't think I'd have time. Besides, it's good for me to practice."

"Oh, all right. But I'm going to pay you."

He smiles broadly, and my body reacts the same way it did last Friday at The Heritage.

Shit.

"Of course you're going to pay," he replies cheekily. "I don't work for free."

CHAPTER 6
NOAH

Out of all the "great" ideas I've had, this one is by far the dumbest. I was excited as fuck when Gia agreed to let me tutor her, but then I remembered that I don't actually speak fluent French. Of course, the notion of giving up doesn't exist in my brain, so what did I do? I spent the entire evening brushing up on my skills. Rosetta Stone app for the win.

I'm bleary-eyed when I stroll through the Percival Wallace King Memorial Library. It's a quarter past eight, but I didn't hit the sack until three in the morning. The first time I came here, I was awestruck. The Gothic architecture features a high, arched ceiling and tall windows at the front that provide extra light for the students, faculty, and staff bustling about the hallways and sitting at the tables in the middle of the open room. The vast collection of books spans the walls from floor to ceiling, the shelves like the ribs of a grand cathedral. I'm not a bookworm, but just being in this place makes me want to check out some books outside of the mandatory reading material for classes.

Instead of grabbing one of the tables in the library's atrium, I veer left. I'm meeting Gia at the Spare Time Café, the coffee shop inside the library building. Tutoring her in French requires speaking, and we can't do that in the main library.

I stop by the entrance and scan the shop. It's relatively busy, and almost all the tables are taken. I spot her sitting in a corner. Her head is down, and she has a book in her hands. My heart skips a beat and then takes off running. A rush of adrenaline spreads through my veins, the feeling akin to when I'm about to step onto the ice before a game.

As if sensing my stare, she lifts her head and then smiles and waves at me. My pulse is racing at breakneck speed now. I need to calm the fuck down, or I'll blow this meeting. Taking steady breaths, I make a beeline for her table.

I'm halfway there when someone reaches out and grabs my arm. I startle, frowning, and look down at the person who stopped me. A cute blonde with huge blue eyes is smiling at me.

"Can I help you?" I ask coolly.

"Are you Noah Kingsley?"

"Yes."

She giggles while her cheeks turn a shade pinker. "I saw your TikTok live yesterday. Have you found your dream girl yet?"

Oh God. Is she for real?

"Uh…"

"Because if you haven't, I'm free anytime you want to take me out."

"Oh, thanks. I'll keep that in mind." I step away, freeing myself from her grasp.

"Wait. Don't you want my number?"

Shit. I really don't, but she put me on the spot, and I sense people in the vicinity are watching. I don't want to be the asshole who says *thanks but no thanks*. I have a hard time disappointing people.

I shrug. "Sure."

"Can I have your phone?"

Yeah, not gonna happen, darling.

"Don't have it on me. Why don't you write it down on a napkin?"

Her face falls, but she quickly recovers and scribbles her

name on a piece of paper. "I'm free now. Why don't you join me?"

"Can't. I'm meeting someone." I take her number, and before she can say anything else, I escape.

When I glance at Gia again, she's smiling. Man, I wish she was annoyed. If she's amused about my interaction with another girl, it means she doesn't see me as boyfriend material yet. I have to change that fast.

"Hey, have you been waiting long?" I dump my backpack on the chair next to mine and sit down.

"Not really. What was that all about?"

I grimace. "She saw our live yesterday and wants to be my dream girl."

Gia pinches her lips together, but the corners of her mouth are twitching upward.

"You're amused," I add.

"Sorry. She's cute though."

I crunch the piece of paper into a ball and drop it on the table. "Not my type."

She tilts her head. "Who's your type?"

You.

The answer is on the tip of my tongue, but I still have a shred of self-control, and it remains unsaid.

"I'll know when I meet her." A yawn escapes my mouth.

"Late night?"

"Yeah. I need caffeine stat." I get up to order at the counter. "What can I get you?"

"A latte, please. But you don't have to pay for my drink." She sets her book down and reaches for her purse.

"It's my pleasure."

"Noah, come on. This isn't a date."

I place a hand over my chest. "Ouch. That hurts."

Her expression falls. "Sorry, but you know what I mean."

"Yeah. I'm just messing with you. I'll tell you what. You can get the drinks next time."

She relaxes against the back of her chair. "Okay, you win."

No. Not yet anyway.

GIA

In a daze, I watch Noah walk to the cashier. Even tired, he's cute as hell. No wonder he's a chick magnet. When that blonde stopped him to chat, it shouldn't have fazed me, but it did, and that's a problem. I can't develop a crush on another player, so I need to make sure he doesn't get any ideas about us. He's too charismatic, and I'm sure if he puts his mind to it, he can win over any girl he wants.

An uncomfortable feeling washes over me. I look around the room and sure enough, the cute blonde is glaring at me. Great. She must think I'm on a date with Noah. Receiving hate from fans isn't new to me. I had to learn to block it out, but it still sucks.

A text message from Blair pops up, making my stomach clench. This is the first time she's contacted me since the breakup. I debate ignoring it, but my curiosity gets the better of me.

I unlock the phone and read the full text.

> I'm sorry about last Friday. Ryder should know better.

I stare at the screen, not knowing how to respond. When Noah returns with our drinks, I'm still frozen.

"What's wrong?"

I put the phone away, screen down. "Nothing."

He watches me as if he doesn't believe my lie. "I hope it isn't another nasty comment by an internet troll."

The fact that he's worried about me melts some of my anxiety away. "No, it's nothing like that. Thanks for the coffee." I bring the cup to my lips, even though the drink is piping hot. I just want to hide my face.

He keeps staring for a couple beats before he takes a tentative sip of his coffee. A moan comes from him, and the sound is so damn sexy, I end up choking.

"Are you okay?"

I cover my mouth with a fist as I cough my way out of the situation. My eyes are tearing up, and my cheeks are on fire.

"I'm fine," I croak after a moment. "Wrong pipe."

"This is damn good coffee."

"Yeah. So good, I drank it too fast."

His eyes twinkle, and there's the beginning of a smile playing over his lips. I force my gaze away from his face fast lest his knockout smile hypnotizes me again.

"So, what do you need help with?" he asks.

I grab my French book, glad to have something to focus on besides my stupid reaction to him.

"Pronunciation, mainly, and remembering verb conjugations. This term, we have to write a report on one of Dumas's novels and then present it in class."

"Which novel did you pick?"

"*Le Comte de Monte-Cristo.*"

"I've seen the movie. Have not read the book."

"It's okay. You don't need to read the book. Just help me to not butcher the language."

He nods. "I can assist with that, but you know, it might help if you have something already written."

He's totally right, and I know he must be busy. I don't want to take up too much of his time, even if I'm paying for it. In hindsight, maybe I should have gotten a different tutor—someone who doesn't get me hot and bothered with one single smile.

Too late now.

CHAPTER 7
NOAH

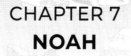

I'm tired as fuck by the time I have to be at the rink. I might have dozed off in a few of my classes. But it was totally worth it. I got to spend time with Gia, and she didn't realize yet that I'm full of shit about my French skills.

I'm in the middle of a yawn when D-man CJ King gives me one of his trademarked arrogant glances. To say I don't like him is an understatement. The asshole has gone out of his way to make me feel like I don't belong here.

"Looking rough, Kingsley. Is training too much for you already?"

I smirk. "Don't you wish?"

He scowls. "You think too much of yourself, rookie. Let's see how you handle a real game."

"Aw, that's sweet. You're worried about me?"

He scoffs. "I don't give a shit about you. I only care about winning, so try to not fuck it up."

I work my jaw, a weak attempt to stop a retort from spilling out. But hell, I can't let this asshole have the last word. "Big talk coming from someone who had to ask Daddy Dearest to buy him a position on the team."

It's a cheap shot. Coach Bedford would never accept bribery

from anyone, and if he heard me saying shit like that, I'd be in a world of trouble. My jab hits the mark though.

With his face already purple, CJ takes a menacing step toward me, his arm pulled back and his hand curled into a fist. "Say that again, I dare you."

"Whoa. What the hell is going on here?" Darren Michaels gets between us.

"The rookie has a big mouth."

He pushes us farther apart. "I don't give a damn who started it this time. Your petty bickering is childish and annoying. Get in line, or you'll be sitting on the bench."

Darren isn't the team captain, but when he speaks, we listen. If he's angry, you'd better be on his side of the argument.

"Sorry, I'll try to keep my thoughts to myself," I grumble.

"Good." He turns to CJ.

"I'll give the rookie a wide berth until he screws up, which will happen sooner rather than later." Already in gear, he stalks out of the locker room.

Darren rubs his face, then says, "You know why he doesn't like you, right?"

"Because he's an ass?"

He glares at me. "No. He was in your shoes last year. He was the star rookie, and now he feels like he's losing the spotlight to you."

"Your explanation doesn't make him less of an asshole, it just reinforces my opinion of him."

Darren taps my shoulder. "Try to look past his animosity and get to know the guy. You might be surprised."

"I'm a team player, so for the sake of the Warriors, I'll try to ignore CJ's douchey ways."

"Good. Now, I have a favor to ask."

Darren Michaels is asking me for a favor? This should be good.

"I'm all ears."

"I've heard you're giving Gia French lessons."

Ah hell. If he asks me to tutor him as well, I'm done for. I'm already skating on thin ice as it is.

"I'm just helping her with an assignment. It's no big deal." I shrug.

"But you're going to spend a lot of time alone with her, right?"

That's the plan.

"I guess… why do you ask?"

Hell, I hope he doesn't have a thing for her and wants my help in that department. That would be awkward as fuck.

He rubs the back of his neck. "She wants me to do this idiotic skit for TikTok, and I've been dodging her. She's relentless when she wants something, though. I need your help convincing her that I'm not social media material."

I laugh, relieved as hell. "I'll try, but I can't make any promises."

"Thanks, man. I appreciate it."

When practice is over, I'm ready to hit the sack. My eyes are shutting of their own accord, and I debate getting a ride with someone instead of driving. It'd be safer but super inconvenient tomorrow. I have an early class, and I doubt I'll be able to get an Uber. My roommate doesn't have a car, so he's not an option. Maybe I can rent one of those campus bikes.

"Earth to Kingsley." Alex stops next to me.

"What?"

"You have a dazed and confused look on your face. What's up?"

I shake my head. "Nothing. I'm just trying to decide if I should drive or not right now."

He squints. "Why? Did you sneak booze in the locker room?"

"No! I'm just tired as hell. I slept only a few hours last night."

He gives me a sly grin. "Already enjoying the extra perks of being a Warrior, huh?"

"You have a filthy mind, Kaminski. I spent the night studying."

"Sure, sure. I can give you a ride home, but you're on your own tomorrow. Wednesday is the only day of the week I don't have class until mid-morning, and I plan to sleep in."

"Yeah, that's the issue. I think I'll just grab an energy drink from the vending machine."

"I wouldn't do that if I were you. You'll be up all night again. How about I follow you to make sure you don't drive into a ditch?"

"Are there ditches on campus?" I smirk.

He hits my shoulder playfully, shoving me sideways. Even when he doesn't mean to be rough, he is. The guy is a menace.

We head out together, but as soon as we hit the parking lot, I spot some of my teammates clustered in front of my truck. Over the top of their heads, I can see colorful balloons swinging with the breeze. I increase my pace.

The crowd parts for me, revealing the fucking mess that's now my truck. It looks like a clown car.

"What the hell!"

Someone attached heart-shaped balloons to the side view mirrors and wrote all over my windshield with pink paint.

Noah's Dream Girl was here.

"Bro, your girlfriend is a psycho," someone in the crowd says, but I'm too busy processing what's in front of me to know who spoke.

"Hey, there's a card under the wiper," Alex points out.

I'm shaking with fury as I free the pink envelope and tear it open. I flip the glittery card, and a picture falls to the ground.

Alex bends over to pick it up while I'm busy reading the ramblings of a crazy chick.

I hope this proves I'm the girl for you, Noah. Call me.

She gave me her phone number, email address, and all her social media handles.

"She's hot." Alex shoves a nude picture in my face. "If you don't call her, I will."

I take the photo and rip that and the card to shreds.

"Oh, man. Why did you do that? What a waste," he complains.

"I don't date girls from Psychoville." I shove the confetti I made out of her card and photo into Alex's chest. "Help me clean this shit off my windshield, please."

I use my nails to try to scratch the paint off but quickly realize it will take too long like this, so I grab the ice scraper from my glove compartment and get to work. Meanwhile, my jerkface teammates simply joke around and capture everything with their phones.

"Gia's gonna love this," CJ laughs as he points his camera at me.

I didn't notice him join the fray. I throw him a glower, but then remember the promise I made Darren and keep my mouth shut.

I don't see Alex anywhere, but a moment later, he returns with another ice scraper. Together we clear the paint from the windshield. We miss a few spots, but it's clean enough to drive. I yank the balloons from the side view mirrors, and they float away into the night.

"Do you still need me to follow you?" Alex asks.

"No, man. After this shit, I'm wide awake."

CHAPTER 8
GIA

I'm catching up on homework at a table outside Ditzy Donuts while I wait for Martin to show up. I finally spoke to him last night, and we're meeting to plan our next dance video collaboration. He doesn't go to Hannaford U or any other college, but he lives close by at an amazing loft apartment, which he shares with three other people who are all into the arts. Someone he knows owns it, and he rents it super cheap. Martin is a full-time influencer, and could afford to live on his own, but he's frugal. He asked a while ago if I wanted to be one of his roommates, but I like my apartment on campus and the convenient location.

It's a rare warm day for October, and I couldn't pass up the chance to soak up the sun. My phone pings with a text message from my older brother, Jaime.

> What happened to your account?

My stomach dips, as I think immediately that someone hacked into it.

> What do you mean?

> There hasn't been a new dance video in weeks.

The anxiety releases its hold on me. Curse Jaime and his bad habit of starting convos like a newspaper headline.

> I've been busy. Meeting with Martin in a few.

> Meh. I prefer your solo dance videos.

I shake my head and drink my coffee before it gets cold. Then a notification from Instagram gets my attention. Someone tagged the Warriors' account on a post. I try to check the accounts only at certain times during the day and not every time I get a notification. Social media can suck a person into a void if they aren't careful. But when several new notifications pop up all at once, they raise a red flag.

I open the app and watch the first video that tagged our account. It's from CJ. At first, I don't know what's going on, but then Noah comes into the frame holding an ice scraper. The camera is zoomed in on Noah's face, and he looks pissed. A moment later, the camera zooms out, allowing me to see the full scene. Someone vandalized his truck with paint and balloons.

My stomach drops through the earth. Judging by what's scribbled on the windshield, the prank was prompted by Noah's TikTok live. Shit. He must be furious with me.

Someone plops into the chair next to mine, scaring the crap out of me. I jolt in my seat, holding the phone against my chest.

"Martin! What the hell. You almost gave me a heart attack."

"Sorry, darling. It's not my fault you were glued to your phone and didn't sense my approach."

"Something happened last night, and I'm just learning about it."

"Oh?" He raises an eyebrow. "Something to do with those Neanderthals?"

I pinch my lips together. I like Martin, and he's a terrific dancer, but he hates sports, especially hockey. He doesn't bitch about the guys too much, and when he does, I try to ignore it. His long, strawberry blond hair is pulled back into a man bun, and as usual, he has scruff on his face. He's a good-looking guy, though he's never given me the feels. But every time we post a video together, people always ask if we're a couple. We do have chemistry, but only when we dance.

"Yeah, someone vandalized the truck of one of our players," I reply.

"Oh, I hope it was Ryder's."

"Ryder is *not* part of the team anymore," I snap.

"Ouch. No need to bite my head off. But can you forget about hockey for a second and focus on us? I thought that was the point of meeting this morning."

"You're right. Sorry." I put the phone down.

There's nothing I can do now, and the prank doesn't put our players in a bad light. My only concern is Noah, but I can text him once I'm done with Martin.

"So what do you have in mind?" I ask.

"You're going to love this." He gives me a cheeky smile. "What if we danced to 'Flowers' by Miley Cyrus in front of the Warriors rink?"

I stare at Martin unblinking, waiting for the punch line. When he doesn't add anything, I ask, "Are you serious?"

His green eyes widen innocently. "Yes, of course I'm serious. Why would I joke about that?"

"Well, for starters, we never dance to current pop songs. Our brand is all about the 80s, 90s, and sometimes early 2000s."

"So? We can branch out. Besides, it'd send a message."

"Yeah, that's the other problem. It sends the *wrong* message. If I do that, everyone will assume I'm bitter over the breakup with Ryder, which I'm not. And even if I were, I'd never pull a Taylor Swift move. I don't do drama, you know that."

His lips become nothing but a slash on his face. "Sorry. I thought you'd be all over my idea."

"I don't hate it completely. In fact, I'm keen on the location. Maybe we can even ask a couple of the guys to make a cam—"

"Hell to the fucking no! I'm not going to help you promote the Warriors." His voice drips with venom.

When I first started to collaborate with him, he disliked sports in general. Now he seems to full-on hate everyone on the team. It doesn't make me super psyched to work with him, which is a bummer. Our video collabs are always fun to shoot. But I can't work with someone who openly loathes my friends.

I let out a heavy sigh. "Okay. Maybe we can pick a different location then. How about the…" I lose my train of thought when I see Noah walk past Ditzy Donuts. He's looking at his phone, distracted.

I jump up from my chair. "Hold on a second, I need to say hello to someone."

Before Martin can protest, I run after Noah. Thanks to his long legs, he's gotten far by the time I reach the pathway, and there are people in front of me.

"Noah! Wait."

He stops and looks over his shoulder. I'm afraid he'll be angry with me, but once again, when he sees me, a bright smile blossoms on his face. It makes me feel like the most cherished person in the world.

"Good morning, Gia."

"I just found out what happened to your truck. I'm so sorry."

His grin wilts. "Ah, don't worry about it. It wasn't your fault."

"It was in part. You got pranked thanks to the live."

He shakes his head. "You can't be responsible for what people decide to do after watching something on the internet."

"Did they damage your truck?"

"No, it was all paint, and it came off easily. I heard CJ's video got a lot of views though."

"I didn't check the stats. I was too upset about it."

He cocks his head while the corners of his lips twitch upward. "You were worried about me?"

My heart does a backflip. Noah is flirting with me, and I'm not immune to his charms.

I can't let it become a thing we do.

"Gia!" Martin calls my name, and I curse in my head. I totally forgot about him.

Noah stands straighter, and his friendly expression turns ice cold.

"Hey, Martin. You didn't have to come after me. I was coming back."

"I wasn't sure." He stares at Noah. "Who's the kid?"

Noah looks over his shoulder, then back at Martin. "Kid? I don't see any kid around."

"Martin, this is Noah Kingsley, one of our new players. Noah, this is Martin Lucero."

"Her partner," Martin adds.

"Partner?" Noah looks at me with a question in his eyes.

"Dance partner. We collaborate on videos sometimes."

"Ah... I thought you looked familiar, but when Gia is dancing, she just outshines everyone." He smiles at Martin, but his eyes aren't friendly, they're challenging.

I ignore that the guys are engaged in a testosterone contest because I'm busy freaking out about the fact that Noah watched my dance videos. My face feels hot. I never get flustered over my posts. Why is the knowledge that Noah watched them making me react this way?

Martin laughs without humor. "Aren't you cute, trying to flirt with Gia? You'd better forget it, dude. She'll never date someone like you."

Noah glowers. "What's that supposed to mean?"

"Martin meant nothing. He's just being a dick because he doesn't like jocks." I throw Martin a stern glance. He's seriously pissing me off today.

"What's to like about them?"

For a second, I fear Noah is going to punch Martin in the face. He sure is throwing daggers at him with his eyes. But he schools his expression into an indifferent mask.

"It's cool, Gia. This isn't the first time I've met a hater. Are we still on for Saturday night after the game?"

It takes me a second to process his question. The way he phrased it made it sound like we have a date, but then I remember our French tutoring lesson. It isn't set in stone, but I guess he's trying to aggravate Martin further.

"Yeah. Of course."

Well, it's confirmed now. I may have agreed just to annoy Martin, or maybe I already have a weak spot for Noah. Either way, both are terrible reasons.

"All right. See you later then." Noah walks away, leaving me alone with a fuming Martin.

"You're going out with *him*?" His voice rises to a shrill note.

My irritation turns up several notches. "What if I am?" I take my backpack from him.

"I can't believe you'd date another player after Ryder dumped you. Have you no self-respect?"

"How does dating a guy imply that I have no self-respect?"

"You know what I mean. People used to call you the Warriors' whore. If you date another player, those nasty rumors will resurface."

"People are going to talk trash about me whether I date another player or not. I'm not going to let internet trolls have a say in my life."

Not anymore, anyway. I remember the days when I used to eat lunch in the restroom at school, crying because people made fun of my looks and what I ate.

"Fine. Don't listen to the trolls. Listen to me, a friend. You'll get clobbered again if you date Noah or anyone else on the team. Jocks can't be trusted, Gia. They have women throwing themselves at them on a daily basis. They don't know the meaning of being in a committed relationship."

"Ryder never cheated on me." I cross my arms.

"That you know of."

I pinch the bridge of my nose. "I'm not having this conversation with you. If you still want to talk about our collaboration, let's. Otherwise, I'm going to the library to study."

His face softens. "I'm sorry. I know I'm being an ass." He throws an arm over my shoulder. "But I'm only like this because I care about you."

"I know."

At least... I think I know. I don't reject Martin's apology though. Despite his flaws, I do admire his talent and brilliance when it comes to dance.

"Let's order a box of donuts and then brainstorm ideas," he says in a much happier tone.

Maybe I should come up with an excuse and bail, but instead, I let him steer me back to Ditzy Donuts. I haven't been motivated to record a new video in weeks. I need someone to kick me into gear, and I know Martin can do that.

I've let the situation with Ryder and my job at the Warriors take over my life. I need to get back on track to pursue my dreams, and dance is a big part of them. That means no distractions, no boys, and most definitely, no dreamy Noah.

CHAPTER 9
NOAH

It's been days, and I'm still pissed about meeting Gia's dance partner. He was a fucking asshole. But at least I walked away without getting in trouble, and I scored a quasi-date with her. It isn't really a date—we're going to work on her French assignment, and it's after the exhibition game against Clayton U, which isn't the best time for studying. But it was the only time this week we could squeeze into our packed agendas.

Classes and hockey have kept me occupied, and I even managed to not blow up her phone with text messages. I don't want to come across as a stalker before I see her again in person.

I thought I was playing it cool these past few days until I bump into her in the Warriors' common area before the game. Her curly hair is in braids, which is cute as hell on her. She's also wearing a tight sweater and a plaid miniskirt paired with high-heeled, over-the-knee boots. She's a sex kitten, and all I can think about is getting her out of those clothes.

"Hey, Noah." She waves at me. "Ready to face off with our archenemy?"

"What archenemy?"

Of course, I had to ask that stupid question in front of CJ.

"Oh my God. Did you hit your head in the shower or something?"

"Oh, Clayton U? I was born ready." *Lame comeback, dude. So, so lame.*

CJ scoffs and walks away. Yeah, he wasn't impressed either.

"Are you all right?" Gia asks.

"Why?"

"You look a little green."

"I'm okay."

She squeezes my arm for a couple seconds. "You'll be amazing."

"Thanks."

I head into the locker room before I can embarrass myself again. I wasn't nervous until I arrived here, and then I saw her, and my brain turned to mush. Now I'm feeling the full weight of what's to come. The tie around my neck feels too tight. I yank at it, trying to loosen it a bit. I hate that we have to dress up before a game. This rule is stupid.

I didn't expect to be nervous as fuck about the game. I don't usually get jitters before I step onto the ice, but tonight the stakes are higher than usual. I've been hyped up, and if I fail to deliver, not only will it be humiliating, but I might not get to play as much during the season. This is the Warriors' first game against Clayton U after the loss at the Frozen Four championship final. Even though it's just an exhibition game, the pressure to obliterate our rivals is high.

As soon as I enter the locker room, I confirm I'm not the only one feeling the weight of responsibility tonight. All my teammates seem to be on edge. Even the Kaminski twins, who usually crack jokes nonstop, are remarkably quiet.

I drop my duffel bag in front of my locker and begin to undress. It feels good to peel off my suit jacket and get rid of the tie that, honestly, feels like a noose around my neck.

Sean steps next to me, already in gear. "How are you feeling, buddy?"

"I'm good. Ready to kick Clayton U's ass."

"They'll be gunning for you. Look out for number 28. He's a nasty son of a bitch."

"I remember him. Don't worry, I'll leave him eating chipped ice."

Sean grins and taps me on the back before continuing his round. He makes a point to talk to each teammate individually.

"Did Sean warn you about Atlas Kodiak?" Alex asks as he approaches me, half-dressed.

"Yeah. I'm not worried."

"I got your back, bro. If he tries to pull a nasty trick on you, he'll be sorry."

Hockey games at college level aren't as violent as the NHL, but fights happen from time to time. That usually means a harsher punishment for the team.

"Thanks. What kind of stupid-ass name is Atlas Kodiak anyway?"

He laughs. "Beats me. My guess is his parents were hippies. His brothers are called Eros and Orion."

I give him a droll look. "You're joking."

He shakes his head. "I swear to God."

"I'd change my name."

"No, you wouldn't," CJ pipes up. "They milk that shit and the fact they're identical triplets."

Alex scowls before returning to his locker.

"What's with him?"

"Identical triplets are more impressive than identical twins?" CJ shrugs in a relaxed stance, and I do a double take. Did he forget he was talking to me? This is the first time we've had a conversation where he hasn't sounded condescending.

"Is everyone decent?" LaRue shouts. "Gia wants to come in to do her thing."

I freeze. Of course she'd come into the locker room. It's her job. Normally, I'd use the opportunity to lay on the charm. But I already proved I'm off my flirting game tonight. I'd better give her a wide berth.

GIA

I take a deep breath before I enter the Warriors' locker room. I'm nervous, just like I was the first time I came in to interview the team before a game. Seeing the guys in their element and in different states of undress was a little intimidating. That time, Ryder noticed I was nervous and oozed charm, helping me calm down.

I shake my head, annoyed that I let that memory come to the forefront of my mind. I won't think about that asshole tonight.

The door to the locker room opens, and Assistant Coach LaRue sticks his head out. "You can come in now, Gia."

"Thanks."

Most of the players are in full gear already. I search the room until I spot Noah standing next to CJ, of all people. Both seem relaxed, so I assume they aren't once again exchanging insults. Maybe they're finally beginning to act like teammates.

Seeing Noah does nothing to calm the butterflies flittering in my stomach. I suspect he's the reason I'm so nervous tonight. He looked damn fine in his suit and tie, and I regret not capturing the moment. Next time, I'll make a video of the guys arriving in the building.

Sometimes, I do a live from the locker room, but the mood tonight is a bit tense for that. I also don't want a repeat of the fiasco that was my last live with Noah. I'll do a quick round of interviews and then post to our social channels later after I edit them. I probably won't be able to post before the game.

I don't realize I'm staring in Noah's direction until he looks straight at me and waves shyly. I force myself to give him a small smile before I shift my attention to Logan, who's closest to me. I get my phone ready and, smiling brightly through my nerves, I begin recording.

"We're once again back at it. Tonight the Warriors face off with Clayton U in an exhibition game. Let's ask Logan Kaminski what we can expect from this friendly match."

I turn the camera to him. Looking serious—and scary as hell—he says, "Friendly? That word doesn't exist when it comes to Clayton U. It's payback time."

"You got that right, bro." Alex sticks his head between his brother and me. "Clayton U doesn't know what's coming for them. Isn't that right, Warriors?" he asks the room, and roars of agreement erupt among the players.

I turn the camera to myself again. "As you can see, the Warriors are ready for battle."

Alex throws one beefy arm over my shoulder. "Not battle—we're ready for blood."

"That's enough, Kaminski," Sean retorts, dead serious.

I make eye contact with him, and he shakes his head. Yeah, I didn't think he'd be down to speak to the camera. Sean's and Darren's aversion to social media makes my job harder than it needs to be. Sean is the captain, for fuck's sake, and Darren is one of the best goalies in the league.

I keep going and chat with a few other players, and I even get a couple words from Assistant Coach LaRue, but Coach Bedford gives me a look that says don't come any closer. It's a rare occasion when he gives me any content. I need to catch him in a good mood, preferably after he's won a game. If the Warriors win tonight, I might get him to talk, but to be fair, most of our followers only care about the players, and Assistant Coach LaRue because of his high profile as an NHL legend. And he's very easy on the eyes too. Most of our social media followers are thirsty ladies or dudes.

I purposely stay away from Noah, hoping I'll run out of time to interview him. It's a shitty thing to do, considering he's so good in front of the camera, but until I can get my emotions in check, I shouldn't get close to him.

Coach Bedford calls the attention of the room, and that's my cue to put the phone down. I move away from the circle and find a corner where I'm less noticeable. Usually, I tune out during coach talk, but tonight, my attention locks on Noah. His back is to me, and he's close to Coach Bedford, so I can stare at him without running the risk of getting caught. I should look away, but for some inexplicable reason, I can't. This is getting annoying. I'm better than this.

What's going to happen when I meet with him after the game? I'd cancel if I didn't really need his help with my assignment. The only course of action is to cease all flirtation and make sure nothing ever happens between us.

Friend zone for the win.

CHAPTER 10
NOAH

When Sean warned me that Clayton U would be gunning for me, he wasn't kidding. My teeth rattle as I'm pushed against the boards. I almost lose my stick from the impact. I shake it off and chase after the douche who thinks he can steal my puck. Speed is on my side. When he makes a pass, I intercept and take off toward the goal. It's me and the goalie now. He knows what's coming. I take the shot, but I don't see if it hits the mark because I'm shoved from behind and fall face-first on the ice.

White-hot pain flares, front and back, and I don't get up right away. The buzzer tells me I scored. At least I have that satisfaction.

A pair of gloved hands lift me up. I'm surprised to see CJ's face behind the mask.

"Are you okay?"

"Yeah."

From the corner of my eye, I catch a commotion. Alex is in Kodiak's face. He shoves him against the boards, and the maniac laughs. Fuck. I don't want Alex to get in trouble because of me. A ref steps between them, but Alex doesn't care. He shouts more insults at Clayton U's D-man. Sean has to haul him away before he can punch the asshole.

We're in the third period, and we're leading the game 5-4. But the ref doesn't issue a penalty to Kodiak—it was a clean hit, according to him. Yeah, clean hit my ass. Alex, however, is sent to the sin bin, granting Clayton U a power play.

The game continues, and I channel my frustration into trying to score another goal. The puck drops, and Sean gains possession. He speeds toward the goal, but Kodiak and another D-man box him in. I follow in the middle, only to be cut off by Daniels, Clayton's center. Sean can't get a clear shot. The puck hits the board behind the goal. Logan goes for it, but he overskates and loses the puck to Kodiak.

Fuck.

They're on the counterattack now. I fly over the ice. We can't let them tie the score. Daniels has the puck, and his wingers are flanking him. I see when he finds an opening, but I'm coming in hot behind him and use the momentum to fuck up his perfect angle. He shoots, but he can't elevate the puck high enough, and Darren defends.

I gain possession of the puck on the rebound and take off. If I miss this chance, I'll hang my head in shame. I'm in the perfect position to take the shot, but then something drops in front of me on the ice. It looks like a piece of red fabric.

What the hell?

It gets in my way and screws up my shot. The goalie defends it, but then everything comes to a sudden halt. There's more shit scattered on the ice.

With his stick, Kodiak lifts the piece of fabric that fucked up my shot. It's a red thong. What the fuck! A quick scan of the ice tells me it rained sexy lingerie on the rink.

Sometimes at a game, the crowd does throw things, but not during a play, and never so much at once unless it's the teddy bear toss during Christmas time. We have to return to the bench until the ice is cleared of all the shit that has fallen on it. Besides the lingerie, there are teddy bears, cards, confetti, and to my dismay, a T-shirt with my face photoshopped next to a girl I don't know, which Coach Bedford is now holding in front of me.

"Care to explain this, Kingsley?"

My mouth drops open. "I have no idea."

I look over my shoulder for Gia. She usually sits right behind our bench, but she's not there.

"We'll talk later." He turns the T-shirt into a ball and lobs it to the side.

My ears are ringing. If it wasn't for that piece of lingerie getting in my way, I'd have scored. Man, I wanted that goal so badly.

"What the hell happened?" I ask Alex.

"I don't know, man. It's like Victoria's Secret exploded onto the ice."

"Coach is pissed at me."

"Well, it was *your* face on that T-shirt."

I remove my helmet and swipe my hair back. "First my truck, and now this. I didn't realize the puck bunnies at Hannaford U were insane."

"I've never seen them go to that extreme to get anyone else's attention. You're special." He bumps my arm with his, smirking.

"I don't want to be special. I just want to play hockey in peace."

"It'll blow over. You're the shiny new toy. They'll move on if you start to date someone."

I stare at him without blinking. Is he serious?

"Don't give me that look. I'm not suggesting you get a girlfriend. Going on a few dates with the same chick should do it."

If only he knew getting a girlfriend is exactly my plan.

GIA

My eyes are glued to Noah as he breaks away from the defending zone and speeds like a bullet toward Clayton U's goal. My pulse is racing. There's no doubt in my mind he'll score, and what a big deal that'll be for him to earn an unassisted, shorthanded goal. Then my eyes notice a huge balloon floating above the rink. It's being steered by a drone.

I don't think much about it until I hear a *pop*, and a second later, stuff falls onto the ice. It takes me a moment to identify the colorful rags as pieces of underwear. One of them drops in Noah's way and messes up his shot.

It's complete chaos. The ref stops the game so the ice can get cleared of everything that fell from the balloon. My mind is racing. The crowd knows better than to throw things onto the ice during a game. When someone hands Coach Bedford a T-shirt with Noah's face on it, my blood runs cold. It's another prank prompted by my live with Noah.

I jump out of my seat and run to find Security. Whoever was responsible for the balloon needs to be removed from the rink immediately. I have my phone out when it rings. It's Ashley calling, but I can't talk to her right now. I have to put out this fire. Coach Bedford looked fucking pissed, and with reason.

My phone vibrates, and Ashley's message pops up.

> Call me ASAP. It's about the game.

I'm back in the common area, so I skid to a halt and call her back.

"What do you know?"

"It seems there's a challenge going on around the sororities."

"I thought you had information about who fucked up the game just now."

"I don't know who the culprit is, but most likely, it's some crazy bitch from a sorority."

I pinch the bridge of my nose and begin to pace. "How do you know that? You aren't Greek."

"Blair told me. She would have called you herself, but since you haven't spoken in so long, she didn't think you'd take her call."

I want to snap and say, *Whose fault is it that we haven't spoken?* But I bite my tongue. I can't get angry at Ashley. She's just the messenger.

"I'll call her later to get the details. Right now, I need to make sure the lunatic is removed from the rink."

"I wish I'd come to the game tonight. I could help you."

"You never come to the Warriors' games. But don't worry. I'll handle this."

"Okay. Call me later."

"Sure."

I run to the security office, and no sooner do I enter than I catch on their monitor two security guys escorting a girl out.

"You got her. Thank God."

Jonas, the head of security, looks over his shoulder. "Yeah. She'll be banned from the rink for life."

"How in the world did she get that balloon inside?"

He scratches his chin. "We're still trying to figure that out."

"You need to figure it out fast. Coach Bedford is *not* happy."

Jonas grimaces. "Yeah, I wouldn't be either. Kingsley was about to score."

"What's the tally now?" I move closer to the monitor showing the game.

"Clayton U tied. It's over."

"Shit," I blurt out. "Sorry."

"No need to apologize. I share your sentiment."

"All right. I need to do damage control."

Not that he cares. He has a hot potato in his hands too. I head to the office I share with the team's logistics assistant. It's empty now, and I get to work. Naturally, there are several amateur videos on Instagram and TikTok already showing the incident from different angles, and the media didn't waste any time posting it on their channels. No one has mentioned the sorority challenge Ashley told me about, but it's only a matter of time. These pranks are getting too much attention, and everyone will want to capitalize on them. It'd be all fine and good if this latest prank didn't affect the result of the game. We should have won.

A knock on the open door jars me. I jump in my seat and turn to find Assistant Coach LaRue standing there.

"Coach Bedford wants to see you in his office."

I swallow the huge lump in my throat. LaRue's expression is serious, which means I'm in a world of trouble.

Inside Coach Bedford's office, I find the man pacing in front of his desk, while Noah and Sean sit, dejected, on his couch. LaRue follows me in and shuts the door.

I try to catch Noah's gaze, but he keeps his eyes turned toward the floor. Sean looks pitiful, and he doesn't hold my stare for more than a couple beats. I focus on Coach Bedford, who's now standing like a statue with his arms crossed in front of his chest.

"Care to explain this nonsense about the Finding Noah's Dream Girl challenge?"

"It wasn't meant to be a challenge, but I take full responsibility for it. It's not Noah's fault."

Noah jumps from the coach. "I can't let you take all the blame. I was the one who went on and on about what my dream girl would be like."

"I see." Coach Bedford narrows his eyes.

"Sir," Sean interjects. "You can't blame Noah or Gia for what happened. It seems the problem originated in one of the sororities on campus. It has nothing to do with them."

How does Sean know about that? Maybe Ashley told him already.

"I don't care how it started." He stares pointedly at me. "I want this handled, or I'll be shutting down all social media accounts for the team."

My stomach dips. How am I going to stop the crazies from hounding Noah?

"Yes, sir. May I leave? I'd like to get to work on it right away."

"Yes, you can go now." He waves me off.

I rush out of his office, lest everyone see the tears in my eyes. I've never been scowled at by an employer before, but I can't blame Coach Bedford. I totally screwed up. A couple of tears have already rolled down my cheek, so I keep my gaze down. I almost make it to my office without anyone noticing me until Noah calls after me.

"Gia, wait!"

Shit. I don't want him to see me bawling my eyes out. I hastily wipe the corners of my eyes before I turn to him.

"Are you okay?" he asks before I can say anything.

"Not really. I feel awful about what happened tonight."

"It's not your fault. You couldn't have predicted this stupid challenge would happen."

"Right. I'm not sure how to make it stop though."

"I think I may have a solution."

My brows scrunch together. "You do?"

"Yeah. Alex said that the craziness would stop if I dated someone for a while."

My heart clenches in a painful way. I don't like the idea of Noah dating anyone, which is crazy when I'm dead set on putting him on the friends-only list.

"That could work, but I don't want you doing something you don't want to just to help me out."

"The way I see it, I'm helping the team too. You create great content, you bring attention to Hannaford U hockey, and, most importantly, you boost the team's morale. The Warriors need you, Gia."

Warmth spreads through my chest. Noah's heartfelt statement soothes the sting of Coach Bedford's ultimatum.

"I don't know what to say."

"Let me help you."

I shake my head. "It's not fair for you to date someone just to save my ass."

Hell, maybe it's not a sacrifice after all. Maybe he's already met someone and he's just planning on making it public.

"I'm not going to date a random girl. I'm going to date *you*."

I stare at him without blinking or breathing. "What? I can't date you."

Noah seems hurt by my outburst for a second, but he recovers in the next moment with a half smile. "Not for real. I know you've sworn off hockey players for life."

"Wait, are you proposing we fake date?"

He shrugs. "Yeah."

"Noah... I don't know."

"Come on. You know that stupid challenge won't go away until I find my *dream girl*." He uses air quotes.

I look over his shoulder, focusing on nothing as I weigh the pros and cons. He's right about that. The pranks and dares will only get more elaborate. Fake dating him would be the easiest and fastest way to deal with the problem. But it comes with a handful of other complications. If I jump into another relationship with a hockey player, my reputation will take a hit. I'm already being called nasty names online. Dating the new hotshot will put an even bigger target on my back. There's also the issue that Noah is a charmer, and without any effort on his part, he's already reeling me into his orbit.

How am I supposed to keep our relationship platonic if we have to pretend to be boyfriend and girlfriend?

Ugh. This is a nightmare.

"You don't need to decide right now," he says.

I focus on him again. He's covered in sweat, and his wavy hair still holds the shape of his helmet. Coach Bedford pulled him straight from the ice for the talk down. This is serious. I don't read any mischief in his warm brown eyes, though, only the desire to help me. I'm already leaning toward saying yes, but

I shouldn't make a hasty decision. There's gotta be a better way to deal with this situation.

"I think we should both sleep on it and also postpone our French lesson to another day."

"Yeah, I think that's for the best."

"Thanks for offering to help with the problem, though."

"I'd do anything for y—I mean, for the team."

"You're sweet." I step closer to kiss him on the cheek.

It's an impulsive decision—and damn stupid. But it wouldn't have been a big deal if Noah didn't turn his head at the last second. My innocent kiss lands on his lips, and it's a like a jolt of electricity goes through my body. I jump back quickly, embarrassed to the nth degree.

"I'm so sorry," I say.

He smiles wolfishly. "I'm not. See you tomorrow."

CHAPTER 11
NOAH

I'm on fucking cloud nine when I return to the locker room, and I can't erase the grin from my face. I turned my head on purpose so Gia's kiss would land on my lips. It wasn't exactly a smart idea, because damn if I didn't want to kiss her for real. But she jumped away from me too fast, blushing furiously. It's okay though. It's gonna happen sooner rather than later if I have something to say about it.

Sean is the first to see me. "What are you smiling about?"

I shake my head. "Nothing."

"Riiight. Weren't you just with Gia?"

Shit. I forgot that he knows I stormed out of Coach Bedford's office to go after her.

"Yeah, so?" I turn my back on him and peel off my jersey.

"Whatever you're doing, I'd suggest you stop and think about it. Gia is not a random girl you can hook up with and then ditch."

I turn around, pissed that he'd make that assumption about me. "Who said anything about a meaningless hookup?"

Darren and CJ are nearby and must overhear Sean because they're now paying attention to us.

"Then what exactly are you doing?" Sean stares at me intensely as if he's trying to read my mind.

I just proposed to fake date the girl of my dreams, no biggie. I can't tell him that for obvious reasons.

"How was the meeting with Coach?" Alex asks as he returns to the locker room fresh out of the shower.

His interruption couldn't have been timelier.

"He wasn't happy, but everything is under control," I grumble.

Sean glowers in my direction, but he doesn't call me on my bullshit. Nothing will be under control unless we can put a stop to this crazy challenge, and the only way to do that is if Gia agrees with my plan.

Do I feel bad for using all the tricks I know to get her to fall for me? Not in the least. I know the attraction isn't one-sided. I just need to get past her reservations about dating another hockey player, and the best way to do that is if we spend a lot of time together.

"I say we need copious amounts of alcohol to forget tonight's game. Who's in?" Alex asks.

No surprise, we all want to go out and drown our frustration in booze. The Heritage it is.

I just wanted to blow off some steam with my teammates. Instead, I'm dodging random chicks who are acting like I'm a teen heartthrob. I've been at The Heritage for an hour, and so far, I've been given five pairs of panties, posed for a million selfies, and been asked to hook up in the washroom by three different girls.

I'm annoyed and grumpy, and I have a headache to boot.

"What the fuck is your problem?" CJ slurs as he stumbles forward, sloshing his beer all over me.

He's utterly wasted and can barely stand up straight.

"Right now, *you* are my problem." I push him off me.

He staggers back, and I'm afraid he's going to fall on his ass, but he manages to regain his balance.

"You should enjoy the attention. It'll be gone before you know it," he tells me, all serious.

The conversation with Sean comes to the forefront of my mind. I don't want to get into an argument with CJ tonight, not while he's so drunk. He probably won't remember a word of it anyway.

Logan throws an arm around my shoulders. "Come on, rookie. Just pick one chick and the others will back off for a while."

I finish my drink instead of telling him there's only one girl I want. I wish she was here. God, I'm such a sap. I can't stand to be in my own head right now. I need something stronger than beer.

"Who wants a shot?" I ask.

CJ is the first to raise his hand. He's the one who should drink only water from now on. His eyes are so glazed, I doubt he can see anything.

"Tequila?" Alex asks, already going to the bar.

Everyone grunts in agreement. The whole point of going out tonight was to forget what happened earlier, but it seems the mood hasn't improved at all.

"Are you fucking kidding me?" Darren stands straighter.

I follow his line of sight and see Kodiak and Daniels walking toward us. My entire body becomes tense. I haven't forgotten the illegal check from Kodiak.

"Good evening, fellas." The asshole smiles from ear to ear.

"What the fuck are you doing here, punk?" Logan stands at his six-four height, projecting a do-not-fuck-with-me attitude.

Grinning, Kodiak lifts his hands, palms facing us. "Relax, Kaminski. I'm not here to fight, just came for a drink, that's all."

"There are plenty of other bars nearby," Darren retorts.

"But none of them are The Heritage—" he scans the open

room "—or have this assortment of thirsty girls."

Alex returns with a tray of shots. Before he can set it on our high-top table, Kodiak and Daniels snag two and toss them back.

"Those weren't for you, asshole." Alex takes a step forward, but Sean pulls him back.

"It's fine. I'll grab more."

Unfazed, Kodiak looks at me. "I'm looking for the owner of that pair of red panties. Have you seen her, Kingsley?"

I give him a droll stare. "Why? Do you like the unhinged type?"

Laughing, he shakes his head. "No. I just want to thank her for fucking up your play. She must be a Jackals fan."

I narrow my eyes. Does he seriously think I'm going to fall for that cheap barb?

"It's sad that you need to resort to sabotage in order to tie a friendly game." I take a shot of tequila, hoping it'll help turn this evening around.

My retort wipes the smugness right off his face. "You think you're some hotshot, don't you? How did the ice taste?"

He's really testing my patience. I'm beginning to see red, and now that the tequila has hit my system, there's less chance of me reining in my anger. If he wants a fight, I'll give him a fight.

"All right. That's enough, Atlas." Daniels pushes his friend away from our table.

"What a tool." CJ shakes his head.

"He's a dirty player," Sean replies, glowering in Kodiak's direction. "You all need to watch your backs when he's on the ice."

"He needs to watch his back when he's *off* the ice," Logan chimes in.

Sean levels him with a glare. "Don't get any ideas, Kaminski. Fighting with Kodiak while they're visiting our school will piss off Coach even more."

Sean didn't mean to take a stab at me, but I felt his piercing words just the same. "I need more tequila."

CHAPTER 12
GIA

I lose track of time as I try to figure out how to fix my big-ass problem without lying to everyone around us. I adore Noah for offering to help me, but I can't pretend I'm his girlfriend just for the sake of appearances. There's gotta be another way.

All the players and coaches have long left the rink. I check the time. It's almost midnight. I can't believe Jonas hasn't come in yet to kick me out. Shit. Maybe he forgot about me, and I'm now trapped in the building. That'd be my luck.

My phone rings, the noise too loud in the silence. I jerk in my chair while my heart jumps up my throat. Pressing a hand against my chest, I look down and see Blair's name flashing on the screen. It makes me grimace. I don't really want to talk to her right this second, but she knows the deal with the sorority challenge.

"Hello?"

"Hey. It's me. Blair."

"I know." I let out a sigh and sag against the back of my chair.

"I can't believe you answered my call."

"I only did because I'm desperate."

Silence. Is she going to hang up?

"I guess I shouldn't be upset you said that. So you spoke with Ashley?"

Straight to business. My chest feels tighter. It seems I'm not getting an apology or an explanation for her radio silence. It's better this way. I don't have the bandwidth to deal with all the things left unsaid between us anyway.

"She told me the chaos tonight was caused by a sorority challenge?"

"Are you still at the rink?"

My brows furrow. "Yeah, why?"

"I'm outside the building. Meet me out here?"

I have a million questions for Blair, starting with how she knew I was still at the rink. But I guess I can ask her in person. I quickly collect all my things and turn off my office lights. As I rush past the security office, I see that Jonas is there.

"Good night, Jonas."

"Girl. You're still here? You were five minutes from getting locked in."

Shit. I don't know if he's kidding or not. Usually, Security does a final round before going home for the night, but maybe he was planning on skipping that today. Normally, getting locked in at the rink wouldn't be the end of the world, but tonight it would be.

Blair is standing in front of the building with her back to the door, hands shoved in her coat pockets. In usual Blair fashion, she's dressed like she's going to attend a royal tea at Buckingham Palace. Her baby-blue coat is tailored, and she's wearing high-heeled Mary Janes that cost a small fortune, judging by the red color of the soles.

At the sound of my heels on the ground, she turns. "Hi."

"How did you know I was still inside?" I don't bother with polite greetings.

Blair's expression remains neutral. "I stopped by your dorm first, and Harper told me you hadn't come home yet. I thought maybe you'd gone to The Heritage, but Ashley didn't think you would."

I cross my arms. "Okay. You found me. Are you going to tell me what's going on with this stupid challenge, or do I need to shake it out of you?"

She pinches her brows together. "It started in my sorority. Our president thought it'd be a fun challenge for our pledges to try to get a date with Noah. But then other sororities got wind of it, and it became a widespread thing with all the sororities competing."

"I can't believe this. Noah is not a fucking prize. He's a person with feelings."

"I know. I'm disgusted by the whole thing. A lot of us aren't happy about it, but we were outvoted. It's not even about getting a date with Noah anymore. It's about the gesture. The more outrageous, the better."

I pinch the bridge of my nose. "That balloon tonight cost us the win. Coach Bedford is threatening to close all social media accounts for the Warriors."

Blair's blue eyes, which are the exact same shade as her brother's, turn as round as saucers. "What are you going to do then?"

"What do you think? I'm out of a job if that happens."

"I'm so sorry, Gia. Truly."

"I know." I press a hand against my forehead, trying to rein in my irritation. It's not Blair's fault. "Can you think of a way to stop the challenge?"

"Noah finds a girlfriend?"

I throw my hands up in the air. "Why does everyone keep suggesting that?"

"Because that's the whole point of the challenge. When he finds his dream girl, it's over."

I rest my hands on my hips and stare at the ground. It seems I might have to agree with Noah's crazy plan.

"Why are you still here and not at The Heritage? I know

some girls are planning more stupid shit tonight. If you want to protect your guy, that's where you need to be."

I whip my face to hers. "What are they going to do now?"

She shrugs. "I don't know."

"Hell. I so didn't want to go there tonight."

"If it's because of my brother, he's out of town."

God, I haven't thought about Ryder at all until tonight. This clusterfuck tops what he did last semester.

"I guess I have no choice but to go." I begin to walk toward my car.

"Can you give me a lift?"

I look at her. "Where's your car?"

"I had the driver drop me off once I knew you were here."

I shake my head. I forgot that Blair rarely drives, especially at night. It's not that she's a bad driver, she just chooses not to. I suppose when you have a driver at your disposal, why bother getting behind the wheel and worrying about traffic and parking?

"I'm not going to take you home, Blair. I'll wait until you call your driver back."

"I was hoping to come to The Heritage with you if that's okay."

I let out a resigned sigh. "Fine."

I'm acting grumpy about it, but in reality, I'm glad I don't have to go alone. Ryder isn't the reason I don't like going there. Bad shit always happens to me at that place.

"I don't remember this place ever being so packed and loud," Blair shouts so I can hear her over the music.

She wraps her fingers around the back of my jacket and holds on to me in the crowd while I carve a path for us and search for the guys. They usually sit at a table near the bar, but they aren't at their usual spot. Maybe they've all gone home with their respective hookups. My stomach twists as I picture Noah with a girl.

The accidental kiss is still imprinted in my mind. It was nothing, just a peck on the lips, but I can't help but wonder what it'd be like to kiss him for real.

"I don't see them anywhere." I turn my face so she can hear me.

"Maybe they're playing pool."

Clenching my jaw, I continue my slow trek toward the back of the bar. Mercifully, I spot Alex and Darren. I don't see Noah though.

Alex grins broadly when he sees me. "Gia! You made it."

He opens his arms and engulfs me in a bear hug. I wrinkle my nose and step back. "How much did you drink? You smell flammable."

He waves me off. "Just a few shots of tequila." He looks over my head, and his gaze hardens. "What's the Blair Witch doing here?"

"Bite me, Alex," Blair retorts.

Ugh. I forgot that these two don't get along, and that was before Ryder screwed over the team.

"Just tell me how hard, darling."

"Whoa, why don't you two get a room?" Darren pipes up, slurring a little. "No one needs to witness your foreplay."

I can't believe he's in this state too.

Alex twists his face into a scowl. "Foreplay? Are you out of your mind?" He looks at me. "And you say *I'm* wasted."

"Where's Noah?" I ask.

"Beats me. He was here a second ago."

"I think he went to the restroom, that is if he didn't get himself kidnapped on the way there."

He must be referring to girls going crazy to get Noah's attention.

"How bad has it been since you got here?"

"Nonstop. I'm surprised he hasn't hooked up with anyone yet. Some of those girls were hot," Alex chimes in.

"Maybe he's not a horndog like you," Blair replies.

"It's better to be a horndog than a frigid bitch."

"Alex!" I blurt out.

Blair's cheeks turn bright red, and her hands curl into fists. Shit. I think she's a second away from punching Alex.

"Who's a frigid bitch?" Logan asks as he walks into the conversation. If he were sober, he wouldn't need to guess who his brother was talking about.

"No one." Blair grabs Logan by his shirt and pulls his face down to steal a kiss. Not just any kiss, a hot and heavy one.

My jaw drops. Blair is kissing one of the Kaminski twins on purpose. The world is about to end.

"What the fuck!" Alex shouts.

Blair ends the kiss and storms off, leaving Logan with a dazed look. I start after her and freeze. Shit. I'm torn between following her and waiting for Noah to reappear. I came here to make sure he's okay, but Blair is—or was—one of my best friends.

"Man, little Blair sure knows how to kiss," Logan says with a goofy grin. "I wonder what other secrets she's hiding under all those preppy clothes."

Alex punches his shoulder. "Dude! Stop lusting after that witch. She's the enemy, remember?"

"She's not *my* enemy." He laughs and then steals the cue stick from his brother.

"Ah, here comes Noah. His clothes are still intact. That's a good sign," Darren pipes up.

When I see that he's solo, relief swamps me, but it's short-lived when a group of barely clad girls blocks his way. The music changes to Beyoncé's "Crazy in Love," and they begin a choreographed number. The entire bar stops to watch the show. Any guy would eat that shit up, but Noah looks like he'd rather be anywhere but here. He glances over the crowd until he finds our group. When his eyes connect with mine, they seem to scream, "*Save me.*"

"Ah hell." I go to him, not caring who I shove and elbow out of my way.

I'm no longer annoyed about this insanity; I'm downright pissed. I should be home, watching a stupid movie on TV, not dealing with drunk idiots and spotlight whores. I plow right through the group of dancing girls, messing up their routine because there's no other way to get to Noah.

I couldn't care less. Their antics ruined our game.

"Hey!" someone complains. I ignore them.

Before I can say anything, Noah pulls me into a hug and hides his face in the crook of my neck. "Oh my God. You're here. Thank you."

Great. He's drunk too, and I'm guessing tequila.

"Ugh. The Warriors' babysitter is here to ruin our fun," I hear someone in the crow whine.

I turn, glaring at the group of idiots who aren't dancing anymore. At least they didn't call me something worse, like *whore*.

"That's right. You'd better stop with this ridiculous challenge. It's too late."

"What do you mean it's too late?" The petite redhead at the front glowers at me.

"It means Noah's found his dream girl."

I turn to him, questioning my sanity for a brief second before I kiss him in front of everyone. Not missing a beat, Noah pulls me closer to him, and with his tongue, he coaxes my lips open. Heat spreads through my body, which is now shaking. My heart is thumping so fast, I can almost hear it. I wasn't planning on making out like this, but the moment his tongue touches mine, I can't stop kissing him back. His mouth is addictive, and it's making my head spin. I don't think I've ever had a first kiss that made me feel like this, and it isn't even a real one.

"Get a room!" someone shouts, and it's only then that Noah leans back.

I'm dizzy, and judging from how warm my face is, I must be blushing. Noah is smiling from ear to ear as he stares at me with a glint of pure adoration in his eyes. I can almost believe this moment is real.

"Wait. She's dating Kingsley now?" one girl asks.

"Is she gonna go through the entire team?" someone else adds.

Those are just some of the comments that I hear before I tune them out. It serves as a cold dose of reality. I knew fake dating Noah would come with repercussions. My name will be smeared across social media within hours. The haters were just waiting for an opportunity to crawl out of their hidey-holes.

Noah pulls me close and whispers in my ear, "Don't listen to them, babe. They're just jealous."

"Right. I guess my job here is done. I'm going home now."

"But you just got here. Why won't you hang a little longer?"

I look closely at his bloodshot eyes. "I think maybe I should take you home. You look pitiful."

"Aww, you're already taking care of me, babe? I'm touched." He traces my face with the tips of his fingers.

I hate dealing with drunk boys, but his caress sends shivers down my spine.

"Yes. As a matter of fact, I'm driving everyone home. Come on." I take his hand and return to the pool table.

Only Darren and Sean are there. The twins are gone, and I don't know where Blair went.

"That was quite the show." Darren smirks.

"I know," Noah replies enthusiastically.

Sean doesn't look happy. His arms are crossed, and he has his big-brother scowl on his face.

"You're working that jaw pretty hard there, Davenport," Noah points out.

"I'm not getting into it tonight. We should all go home."

"That's what I came here to say," I butt in. "But I need to find the twins and Blair first."

"Ah, you're too late for the twins. They left with a couple of girls. And I haven't seen Blair since she made out with Logan," Darren replies.

Man, he sure likes to blabber when he's drunk. Such a contrast to when he's sober.

Sean turns his face to Darren so fast, one would think he's a cobra about to strike. "Say what?"

"Never mind. It was just a revenge kiss," I reply, already calling Blair on my phone.

"Hey," she answers on the third ring.

"Where are you?"

"On the way home. My driver just picked me up."

I've known Blair awhile, and I notice her choked voice.

"Are you okay?"

"I'm fine. Just tired. I heard the news. Quick thinking."

She also knows me well. She realizes my kissing Noah wasn't real. I dated Ryder in secret for months before I agreed to go public because I was so afraid of people's reactions. "You already heard about that, huh?"

"Oh yeah. My group chat has been blowing up. Some girls are pissed. I think they genuinely believed they had a shot with Noah."

"It's for the best. Now they can concentrate on more productive things. I can't believe they had time for those stunts with the workload we have at this school."

"I know, right? Anyway, sorry to bail on you. Could we maybe grab a coffee sometime next week?"

I hesitate. Blair hurt me more than she knows when she stopped talking to me after Ryder and I broke up. But maybe I owe it to our friendship to hear her out.

"Yeah, I'd like that. Talk later."

When I turn, Noah and Darren are playing pool, and Sean is trying to keep CJ upright. I didn't even know he was here.

"Is he okay?" I ask.

"No. I need to get his ass home ASAP."

"I'm fine," CJ slurs, but he's so wasted I don't even think he knows where he is.

"Let's go. I'm driving you lot home."

"I'm okay to drive," Sean contests.

"I'll feel better if I do. Don't argue with me, okay? Not tonight."

He pinches his brows. "Fine. Good luck getting those two to stop their game halfway, though." He looks at Noah and Darren.

I smirk. "What do you take me for? An amateur?"

With a smile, I sashay over to Noah while he's lining up his cue. He misses the shot, but it's not like he cares.

"Hey, babe. What's up?" He smiles lazily, awakening the butterflies in my stomach.

Hell. I need to keep in mind this is just pretend.

"We're leaving and stopping at Taco Bell. Are you coming?"

He drops the cue stick on the table without care. "Taco Bell? I think I love you."

I look away quickly. I know that's drunk talk, but why the hell does my heart skip a beat?

CHAPTER 13
NOAH

My mouth tastes like ashes, but it's the pounding in my head that makes me afraid to open my eyes to find out where I am. I know I'm not lying in my own bed. The surface is too rough, I'm still wearing last night's clothes, and there's noise in the background that doesn't belong to my roommate, Terrance.

"Goddamn it, CJ. I thought I was rid of those guys after Ryder quit the team."

"You weren't supposed to be home," CJ grumbles.

At the mention of CJ's and Ryder's names, my body becomes as alert as if caffeine shot straight through my veins. I open my eyes and, with effort, sit up. My body aches in places it shouldn't, but no surprise there. I slept on the floor—the rough surface I felt earlier was a rug.

I take stock of my surroundings. I'm in a loft-style apartment with a high ceiling and wooden beams across the length of the room. Top-to-bottom heavy curtains keep the space dark, save for the light coming from the open kitchen, where CJ and another guy are glaring at each other. My guess is that's CJ's older brother, Preston King, a notorious asshole—so I hear. If he's friends with Ryder, it must be true.

The living room has two massive brown leather couches that are currently occupied by Darren and Sean. Both are snoring soundly. I guess I got the short stick in the lottery for a better sleeping arrangement.

I stretch my arms, trying to work out the kinks in my neck, then rub my face. A yawn escapes me. I need coffee STAT, but not before I use the bathroom. I jump to my feet and wince as my legs protest.

"Oh good. One of the sleeping beauties is up." Preston sneers at me.

"You think I'm pretty? Thanks. I don't swing that way though."

CJ chuckles, earning a glower from his brother.

"I'm going to the gym. Your guests had better be gone before I come back." Preston hoists his duffel bag over his shoulder and strides out of the front door, shutting it with a loud bang.

I massage my temple as the throbbing increases. "I'm guessing that was your brother."

"Yep. I'd better get Sean and Darren up."

I notice several empty Taco Bell take-out bags on the counter and remember Gia offering to stop there on the way home. Everything after that is foggy.

"Why did we come here last night?"

CJ scratches his head. "Don't know. I was shocked to wake up in my own bed this morning."

"Lucky you. I wish I was in *my* bed. Where's your bathroom?"

"Down the hallway, second door to your left."

I'm not completely awake yet, but even in my semi-zombie state, I notice the lavish decor in CJ's apartment. From the hardwood floors to the wallpaper on the walls, everything screams *wealthy*. My parents have a lot of money, more than they know what to do with, but they never show off like this.

I take care of business, and when I return to the living room, Sean and Darren are up and looking worse for wear. Darren's hair is sticking out at odd angles, and his usually tanned skin is on the paler side this morning.

"God, how much did we have to drink last night?" He rests his elbows on the kitchen counter and drops his head between his shoulders.

"My headache tells me a lot. Thank God Gia insisted on driving us here," Sean replies.

My memories of last night are hazy, especially where it concerns her. I have the impression something epic happened, but for the life of me I can't remember what, and it's driving me insane.

"Why did she leave us here though?" I ask.

Darren and Sean look at me as if I'm crazy.

"You don't remember?" Darren asks.

"I wouldn't be asking if I did."

"Because you passed out, dumbass." Sean gives me a droll look.

"I did? On the floor?"

"Yep." Darren nods. "We tried to put you on the couch, but you wouldn't let us. In the end, we decided to let you spend the night there."

I run my fingers through my hair. "Oh God. On a scale of one to ten, how much of an embarrassment was I?"

They trade a look, then Sean answers, "A solid eight. You insisted on teaching us how to speak with a Canadian accent, and that was on the way to Taco Bell. Then when we got here, you wanted to do a dance video with Gia and to convince her, you showed her your moves."

I groan. "Fuck."

I can't dance to save my life, and if I was drunk, then it was much worse. She'll never agree to fake date me now. I blew it.

"I can't believe I missed that," CJ grumbles.

"We got a video of it," Darren replies, pulling his phone out.

I confiscate the device before CJ can get to it. "Give me that."

The video was already loaded on the screen. I can stomach only a few seconds before I press the delete button.

"What the fuck did you do?" CJ complains.

"Got rid of the evidence. If there's no video, it didn't happen," I deadpan.

Sean snorts. "Oh, it did happen. Anyway, we should get going. I don't want to be here when Preston returns."

"I need to call Gia and apologize."

"Yeah, about that." Sean turns all serious, and I fear I did more than try to pull a John Travolta last night.

"What now?" I ask.

"Care to explain that kiss?"

My heart skips a beat. "What kiss?"

"You and Gia kissed at The Heritage last night," Darren replies. "You don't remember?"

I can't breathe, and my pulse is now going a hundred miles per hour. Shaking my head, I say, "No way. You're fucking with me."

"Actually, they aren't." CJ shows me a grainy picture on his phone.

My stomach dips. I can't believe I kissed the girl of my dreams, and I don't fucking remember. That's it. I'll never drink tequila again. "I have to go."

Phone already glued to my ear, I book out of CJ's apartment like a bat out of hell. Gia's phone rings until it goes to voice mail. I don't leave a message, nor do I text her. I have to see her in person. Like a creep, I found out which student hall is hers a long time ago. I don't know her apartment number, but I can find that out when I get there.

CHAPTER 14
GIA

I couldn't sleep much last night, so at the break of dawn, I get out of bed and put on my running clothes. A jog is exactly what I need to clear my head. A quick glance at my phone shows I have several notifications. Yeah, the phone is staying home.

The apartment is quiet, and I tiptoe so as not to wake Harper, my roommate. Knowing her, she stayed up late last night studying. She's the best roommate I could have hoped for. Quiet, organized, and doesn't care one lick about hockey. She has time only for school and her various internships.

The weather is pitiful. Gray and windy. The blast of cold air sends chills down my spine. I zip my hoodie all the way to my neck and after a quick stretch, I take the long way toward the center of campus by running around all the student halls. On a good day, I can make the loop in under an hour, but I haven't run in weeks, and I didn't have a good night's sleep.

When I have about two miles to go, I'm out of breath, but I push through. The exertion has made me forget the cold, and if I slow down, I'll be freezing my ass off in no time. Plus, I smell rain in the air. I look over my shoulder and sure as shit, I spot a curtain of water behind me and approaching fast. If I don't make it back to my place before it reaches me, I'll get drenched.

I run as fast as I can, pushing my legs to their limit. My lungs burn with the effort, and they're about to explode. And that was before the wind cranked up a notch, blowing against me. It creates more resistance, and I begin to slow down. The familiar scent of wet grass fills my nose. I usually love the smell, but not today. A few seconds later, the rain catches up with me, thick, ice-cold droplets drenching me in seconds. I could take cover under a building awning, but I'm close to my student hall, and I'm already wet. I might as well get home.

I slow down further—there's no point killing myself now that the sky is falling over my head. Besides, I don't want to slip and twist an ankle. In another five minutes, I see my building in the distance. The cold has seeped through my wet clothes, and my teeth are chattering.

There's a guy standing in front of the building's door, and by the looks of it, he's completely wet as well. His hoodie covers his head, but the wind is blowing too hard, and the awning offers little protection. He might be waiting for someone to buzz him in. I usually don't let strangers into the building, but at this hour, I doubt he's someone who wants to commit a crime.

"Do you need to get in?" I ask as I run up the steps.

He turns, and when I see it's Noah standing there, my heart stops beating for one second, only to restart faster than before in the next.

"Oh my God, Noah. What are you doing here?"

"Looking for you."

My eyes widen. "Shit. How long have you been standing outside in the rain?"

He shrugs. "A couple minutes."

I doubt that. His lips are turning purple. If he buzzed my apartment, there's no chance Harper would have let him up without me there.

"You must be freezing. Let's get you inside."

I open the door and urge him to walk in first. He pulls his hoodie back and runs his fingers through his wet hair. Besides the purple lips, he's pale too, and there are dark circles under his eyes. When I left CJ's apartment last night, Noah was passed out on the floor. I wonder if he came here straight from there.

The poor guy is shivering. I wish I could help him, but I'm a human popsicle myself. Plus, I don't dare get too close to him, not after last night's kiss. If we're going to fake date, then we need to establish rules. Cuddling when there aren't witnesses around is *not* a smart idea.

"Did you come here from CJ's?"

"Yeah. I had to talk to you, and you didn't pick up your phone." He sounds anxious and I wonder what's up.

"I left it at home. I wasn't ready to deal with everything that happened last night."

"Do you mean our kiss?"

I wince, then look away. "Yeah."

"You're regretting it already," he replies in a subdued tone.

I want to clarify it has nothing to do with him, but he keeps talking.

"I don't blame you, especially after what you witnessed at CJ's apartment."

My brows arch, and then a small smile tugs at the corners of my lips. "Your dance moves?"

His cheeks turn pink. "Oh my God. You're laughing just remembering them, aren't you?"

Giggles go up my throat. I cover my mouth, trying to keep them inside. "I'm sorry. You were too funny."

He faces the elevator, clenching his jaw. "Great."

Feeling bad, I touch his arm. "I don't regret kissing you, Noah."

He looks at me, hopeful. Oh man. He'd better not be harboring any ideas of turning this ruse into a reality.

"I have a confession to make." His eyes drop to my lips.

Please don't say anything that'll make me hurt your feelings.

He rubs the back of his neck, looking sheepish. "I don't remember kissing you last night."

My jaw drops, and so does my stomach. I didn't expect that confession and truth be told, I'm a little upset he was too drunk to remember.

"Oh…" I shrug, breaking eye contact. "That's fine. It wasn't memorable anyway."

"Ouch. Did I suck that hard?"

"What? No!"

"But it wasn't memorable."

"I didn't mean anything by it. I was just trying to make you feel better for not remembering it."

He doesn't reply and remains sullen during the elevator ride. I don't even blame him for acting like that. It was a poor choice of words on my part. I'd feel bummed if someone told me my kiss was meh. Noah's kiss was far from boring, but I could never tell him how it made me feel. Trouble lies that way.

Before I open the door to my apartment, I warn him, "We need to keep it quiet. My roommate is probably still asleep."

"Okay," he whispers.

I seriously doubt she is, especially if Noah buzzed the apartment. But I bet an arm that Harper is still in her room, and for some reason, I don't want her to meet Noah yet—at least not before we have our stories straight about our fake relationship.

I close the door softly and then take off my wet shoes. Noah does the same. In silence, he follows me to my bedroom. The hardwood floors creak a little, but not so loud that it would bother Harper. After Noah walks in, I close the door with a soft click, and then I place my wet sneakers by the window.

"Nice room," Noah says.

My heart takes off in a mad run again, a reaction to being alone in my room with Noah. It just sank in.

"Thanks. I got lucky."

"I'll say." He glances at my desk by the window and then

stares at my bookshelf for a couple beats before focusing on my queen-size bed. Is he imagining himself there with me?

God, what am I thinking?

"I'm dripping all over your floor." He looks down at his clothes.

"You need to take them off. I'll find something for you to wear."

He twists his face into a scowl. "I'm not wearing anything that belongs to your douche ex."

"Don't worry. I got rid of all his clothes. You can use my bathroom." I point at the door.

His brows arch. "You have your own? Sweet!"

"Yep." I turn to my closet and pull out the box of merchandise I received a couple weeks ago.

When I turn back to Noah, his hoodie and shirt are off. *Holy shit.* My eyes widen as I take in his shredded abs and chest. He's on the leaner side, but… damn, I can't stop the desire to run my fingers over all those hard ridges and smooth skin.

"What are you doing?" I squeak.

"I'm really cold."

"Well, get in the bathroom already. There are clean towels under the sink."

"What should I do with this?" He lifts the bundle of wet clothes in his hands.

"You can hang them in the bathroom."

"Okay." He takes a couple steps forward, stopping when he's in front of me. "What about you? Aren't you cold?"

Is it me, or did his voice turn huskier?

"I'll change while you're in the bathroom. Just give me a couple minutes before you walk out."

He doesn't move. Instead, he keeps staring at me with those warm brown eyes as if he's trying to read my mind. His intense stare makes my pulse quicken and wakes those butterflies in my belly that have no business reacting to him at all. My face is burning, but I don't break eye contact.

"What?" I ask.

"You're blocking my way to the bathroom."

Mortified, I step aside. "Shit. I'm sorry."

He chuckles. "Two minutes, you said?"

"Better make it three."

CHAPTER 15
NOAH

My heart is pounding as I close the bathroom door, and I can't stop the smile that spreads across my face. Maybe taking off half my clothes in Gia's room was a dirty move, but it paid off big time. She isn't immune to me, and that's all I need to know.

My jeans are disgustingly wet, and it's a relief to peel them off my legs. My boxers are also damp, but I don't know what kind of clothes Gia's going to give me, so I keep them on for now and wrap the clean towel I found underneath the sink around my waist.

I check the time on my phone and realize only a minute has passed. The temptation to walk out of the bathroom before my three minutes are up is huge, but doing so wouldn't be cool. I can play dirty, but I won't disrespect her like that.

I look around her bathroom. It's small, but way better than having to share with an entire floor. It's also nice to be in a tidy space. Curious and with time to kill, I snoop around. The first thing I do is to check what brand of shampoo and conditioner she uses. I'm that lunatic who will buy the same brand so I can smell her scent whenever she's not around. Both are a mix of vanilla and coconut. I open the shampoo bottle and take a big whiff of it. Heaven.

She knocks on the door, startling me and making me drop the shampoo bottle on the tiled floor. Fuck. My heart is beating furiously now. Luckily, the plastic bottle didn't crack.

"Is everything okay in there? I got your clothes."

"Yeah." I hastily put the shampoo back on the shower caddy, and open the door to find her standing there, still in her wet clothes. "Why didn't you change yet?"

"I wanted to get you dry clothes first. Besides. I'm not that cold."

Did I make you hot, sweetheart?

The thought pops in my head unbidden, but I don't voice it out loud.

I take the folded clothes from her. "Thanks. Now take off those wet clothes."

She quirks an eyebrow. "Are you bossing me around, Noah Kingsley?"

"I sure am. Don't want you getting sick on my account."

I close the door before she can offer a retort. Then I inspect the clothes she gave me. It's a sweatshirt and sweatpants combo. They're new and from an expensive sports brand. The tags are still on. I don't need to wear my damp boxer shorts with these pants, so I take them off too. And what do you know? My new clothes fit me perfectly.

I wait a couple minutes before I ask, "Can I come out now?"

"Yes."

Gia's wearing tight black leggings paired with an oversize Warriors hoodie. What wouldn't I give to see her wear my jersey instead.

Soon, very soon.

She gives me an elevator glance, then smiles. "Those fit you nicely."

"Yeah, they do. Where did you get them?"

"I'm a brand ambassador for the company."

"So, they pay you to wear their stuff?"

"Yeah, pretty much."

"That's cool. But why did they send you guys clothes? Don't tell me they were meant for Ryder Douche Face."

She wrinkles her nose. "No. They sent me a box only a couple weeks ago. They always include guys clothes in hopes that some of the Warriors will wear them too."

"But we can't get paid to promote companies, right?"

"No, that's against Hannaford U's policy. But if you so happen to be wearing one of their hoodies when someone snaps a picture, then you're not breaking any rules."

"Oh, so they're being sneaky." I smile.

Her luscious lips curl into a grin, mimicking mine. "Yep."

"Well, thank you for the freebies."

"You're welcome."

We don't speak for a couple beats. I'm not sure what she's thinking, but I'm busy admiring her beauty, her full lips that beg to be kissed, her big hazel eyes that are framed by long eyelashes, and the small cluster of freckles on her nose I just then noticed. Then the fact that I don't remember our first kiss comes back to haunt me. It doesn't sit well with me that not only do I have no memory of it, but Gia thinks it wasn't memorable. I don't want to brag, but I'm a damn good kisser.

"What did you wanna talk to me about?" she asks, breaking the silence.

"For starters, you let me sleep on the floor at CJ's apartment. That wasn't very girlfriendly of you."

She drops her gaze to the floor. "I'm sorry. I didn't know what else to do. The other guys weren't being helpful either. And I couldn't carry you to the car by myself."

She looks so adorable right now, I want to pull her into my arms and kiss her senseless.

I laugh instead. "Oh my God. I'm just yanking your chain."

"Noah, you suck," she says with a smile, so I know we're okay.

"Are we really going to do it? I mean, are we really going to fake date?"

"Yep. No turning back now. I already wrecked my reputation because of that kiss."

My brows furrow. "What do you mean?"

She waves her hand dismissively. "Never mind."

I take a step closer. "Don't 'never mind' me. What's going on?"

She turns around with her arms crossed and looks out the window. "It's nothing, Noah. Don't worry about it."

I close the distance between us and place my hands on her shoulders to make her look at me again.

"Come on, Gia. Tell me. For all intents and purposes, you're my girlfriend, and I need to know what's going on with you. Is someone giving you shit?"

"It's not a big deal, just the usual trolls talking crap about me. I'm used to it already."

I'm quickly becoming angry—not at Gia, of course—but at all those assholes who love to talk shit about people on the Internet.

"I already told you, no one should *ever* have to get used to being bullied."

I catch a hint of sadness in her beautiful eyes, and it kills me.

"It'll blow over. It's just a knee-jerk reaction. I mean, I did ruin that stupid challenge. Some of those girls aren't happy with me."

I clench my jaw, knowing that Gia is trying to downplay how bad it is for my benefit. But I won't push it now. I can find out what's going on on my own, and whoever is harassing her can expect a world of pain from me.

She walks around me, increasing the distance between us. I guess this conversation made her uncomfortable, and that's not what I want.

"You shouldn't have come here so early, but I'm kind of glad that you did." She sits on the edge of her bed, pulling one of her pillows across her lap. "If we're going to fake date, then we need to establish some ground rules."

"Sure." I lean against her desk, crossing my legs at the ankles. "I take it you've already thought about them."

"Some, yeah. The most important one is that we need to keep our relationship strictly platonic."

I knew this was coming, and it's a setback, but I try to keep my face neutral. "Of course."

"That means no PDA when there's no one around."

I frown. "Are you suggesting that we just kiss in public?"

She blushes. "What would be the point of kissing when there's no one to see? Noah, this is a fake relationship remember?"

"I get that, but there's a small problem with your plan."

"And what's that?"

"You told me yourself our first kiss wasn't memorable. Do you know what that tells me?"

She pinches her eyebrows together. "What?"

"It means we aren't comfortable with each other yet. How are we supposed to convince everyone that we're madly in love when our kisses are boring? We need to sell our chemistry, or no one will believe we're together."

She watches me through narrowed eyes. "It sounds like you're just trying to find excuses to make out."

Fuck, she has me. Still, I try to pretend that my master plan has nothing to do with making her fall in love with me. "I'm not. I swear it."

She jumps from her bed and walks out of her room. Is she running away? I follow her to the kitchen, where she's already busy with her state-of-the-art coffee maker.

"Do you want some coffee?" she asks without looking at me.

"Uh... sure."

I pull up a counter chair and sit across the kitchen island to watch her do her thing. I don't need to be a genius; I know she's avoiding the topic of our conversation.

I should give her time to process whatever is going on with her, but I've never had any patience, so after a moment, I get out of my chair and walk closer, crowding her space. Touching her arm, I make her look at me.

"What is it, Noah?"

"We don't have to kiss, cuddle, or so much as hold hands unless someone is around, okay? I never meant to make you uncomfortable. It was just a suggestion."

She drops her gaze to the hollow of my throat. "I think it's the safest course of action to avoid physical contact as much as possible. I don't want us getting confused." She looks up. "We can only be friends."

I hear a door open in the apartment, and guessing we aren't alone anymore, I sneak my arm around her waist, pull her body flush against mine, and claim her lips.

Fuck the friend zone.

She tenses for a second, obviously not expecting my sudden attack after I told her I wouldn't kiss her unless there were witnesses. But the thing is, there is one now, and I won't waste that opportunity. I need to prove to Gia that my kiss is not only memorable as fuck, it's the only thing she'll be thinking about for years to come.

I cup her cheek, deepening the kiss. A groan forms in my throat when she leans into me as if she's trying to meld her body to mine. An explosion of senses rushes through my veins, and a fire as hot as lava ignites in the pit of my stomach, melting my very bones. I'm burning for this girl, and I can't help it, so I pivot her around and push her against the counter while I grind my hips against hers. My cock is as hard as a rock, something that I should have foreseen when I pulled this stunt.

A throat clearing behind us forces me to step back. Gia's cheeks are a delicious pink shade, and her breathing is out of sync. Man, I want to kiss her again and again, but instead, I turn around to greet her roommate. "Oh, hi there."

Her eyes are bugging out of her skull, cartoon style. When

her gaze drops to my crotch, and she blushes, I realize I'm pitching a tent. Without the extra barrier from my underwear, my erection is pretty obvious under my sweatpants.

"Hi," she says shyly. "I didn't mean to interrupt."

Gia walks from behind me. "You didn't. Uh… this is Noah Kingsley, my boyfriend. Noah, this is my roommate, Harper Fisher."

Harper's eyebrows shoot to the heavens. "Boyfriend?"

"It's new," I reply. "Nice to meet you, Harper."

"Yeah, nice to meet you too. How do you know Gia?"

"Noah is our new center." When the girl gives us a blank stare, Gia continues. "He's new to the team."

Harper's green eyes widen. "Oh, he's a hockey player. That makes sense."

"Why do you say that?" I ask, legit curious. I also want to know if Gia's roommate is one of those judgmental people who's been giving my girl a hard time.

"Because Gia doesn't have a life. Where else would she meet a new guy?" She smirks.

"Shut up. As if *you* have a life." Gia's tone is light, so I guess Harper is all right.

"I do have a life, and I don't need a boyfriend in it. But anyway, I just came out because I smelled coffee. I'll leave you two lovebirds alone after I get a cup."

"Oh, Noah's just leaving."

"I am?" I turn to her, worried. Man, did I screw up already?

She gives me a pointed look. "Yes, you are."

"What about my clothes?"

"I'll give them to you later."

"My shoes are still in your bedroom." I remind her.

"Fine." She strides back to her room, body all stiff now. Meanwhile, Harper watches the scene with a confused gleam in her eyes.

"I think she's embarrassed that you caught us making out," I tell her.

"Yeah, probably. She never brought Ryder here."

That information makes me crazy happy. "Is that so? Why?"

She shrugs. "I don't know. Maybe she didn't want to impose his presence on me. I never liked him, and she knew it. But *you* are more than welcome to hang out."

I give her a bright smile. "Thanks."

Gia returns to the living room with my shoes in hand. But instead of letting me put them on, she ushers me out the front door.

In the hallway, I ask, "What's going on? Are you mad at me or something?"

"Yes, Noah, I *am* mad. You kissed me a second after you told me you wouldn't."

"No, I didn't say that. I said I wouldn't kiss you if there weren't any witnesses, but Harper was there."

She narrows her eyes to slits. "Fine. Just go, okay?"

"Not before you tell me something."

She crosses her arms. "All right."

"Is my kiss memorable now?"

She flattens her lips and doesn't reply.

"I'm not leaving until you answer that, Gia." I might be pushing my luck here, but she looks equal measures mad and turned on, and I'm choosing to see that as a good sign.

She raises her hands in the air. "Yes, Noah, your kiss was unforgettable. Happy now?"

I grin broadly. She has no idea.

"Very much so. See you later, sunshine."

CHAPTER 16
GIA

I'm still hot and bothered when I return to the apartment. I close the door and lean against it, shutting my eyes. That kiss wasn't supposed to happen. Noah caught me completely by surprise. I knew my comment about our first kiss not being memorable bothered him, but I didn't expect him to attack my mouth like that and in front of my roommate. He set my body ablaze.

And I know it didn't only affect me. He was also aroused, big time—emphasis on big. I had to get him out of my apartment ASAP lest we obliterate the rules of our arrangement completely. As soon as he walked out of the bathroom wearing those sweatpants, I knew he wasn't wearing underwear. I tried my best to not stare at his package, but when he leaned his body into mine during the kiss, I could feel every inch of the erection pressing against my belly.

"What was that all about?" Harper asks, spooking me.

I jump on the spot, and to hide my reaction from her, I turn to the coffee pot waiting for me. "What do you mean?"

"Why did you kick Noah out? I hope it wasn't because of me."

"No, of course not. I have a lot of things to do today, and he's a distraction." I fill the mug to the brim, forgoing adding creamer. The coffee tastes bitter as hell without it, but I need the shock against my tongue to erase the effect of Noah's kiss.

I turn around and find Harper smiling knowingly. "Oh, I bet he's a distraction. You sure have a good eye when it comes to boyfriends."

I tilt my head. "I thought you didn't like Ryder."

"Just because I think he's an entitled prick doesn't make me blind to his looks. But I like Noah way better."

"Really? You talked to Noah for a minute, and you already like him better?"

She nods. "For sure. He's not only easy on the eyes but there's something about him. He feels wholesome."

That's the perfect description for Noah. Wholesome *and* devilish because no saint kisses like that.

"He's from a small town in Canada."

Harper gives me a look that's hard to decipher. "Trust me. I've met plenty of Canadians who were assholes. Noah is just special. You'd better keep him."

She veers toward the front door, and I realize she's carrying her backpack. "Where are you going?"

"I'm meeting with my study group in the library. How's the French assignment coming along?"

I press a palm to my forehead. "Shit! I totally forgot about it."

"Did you find a tutor?"

My face warms again. Harper's going to love this. "Noah is my tutor."

Mirth shines in her green eyes, and the corners of her lips switch upward. "My oh my. Gia falling for her teacher. Classic."

"Right. That's me, a walking cliché. First, I fall for the cocky asshole, and then I start dating my tutor."

"I see nothing wrong with that. I'd better run. I don't wanna be late. What are you doing tonight? You know you can bring Noah here, right?"

Hell. I totally forgot about the logistics of our ruse. Of course,

Harper will expect me to bring Noah here since most freshmen don't have an apartment like ours. They share a room.

I debate telling her the truth, but she's a stickler for rules. I'm not sure how she would react if I told her that I'm fake dating a hockey player so I don't lose my job. Besides, the fewer people who know this is all a lie, the better.

"I didn't have any plans, but now I have to work on that French assignment."

"Have fun. See you later."

After Harper leaves, I head to my room and take off my clothes. I need a shower ASAP. Not only because I was running before I bumped into Noah, but I'm still horny as hell after that kiss. Maybe I should use one of my toys, but that could backfire. I don't want to climax thinking about Noah.

On the sink, I find Noah's wet clothes. Maybe I should have let him take them with him. They're a reminder that Noah is walking around not wearing underwear under those sweatpants. I put his clothes in the laundry hamper so I can get them washed later today.

X X X

The shower works to douse the fire coursing through my veins, but it doesn't erase the memory of that kiss. I wasn't lying when I told Noah his kiss was unforgettable. I'm not sure what making out with him again will do to my self-control.

I sit at my desk and try to not think about it. I need to focus on all the assignments I have for school, and I have to deal with social media bullshit. I've neglected my notifications for too long. If there's anything that needs to be taken care of or dealt with, procrastinating only makes it harder to solve a problem. But before I read the comments tagging me, I call Ashley.

She answers on the first ring. "I cannot believe you did that."

Straight to business. That's why I love her. "I had no choice."

"Sure. Somebody forced you to kiss the cute new guy on the team."

I rest my head against my hand. "You saw what that challenge did at the exhibition game. Coach Bedford threatened to fire me."

"Come on. He wouldn't fire you over that prank. You can't control what crazy people do."

"Oh, you weren't at the meeting. Even Sean was terrified of him. Coach Bedford was pissed."

"I don't want to talk about Sean," she grumbles. "But is this thing with Noah for real?"

The fewer people who know about my fake relationship with Noah, the better. But I cannot lie to Ashley. Besides, I'm sure I'm going to need her help at some point.

"It's not real."

"You're *fake dating* him?" Her voice rises to a shriek, making me wince and worry.

"Please, tell me you were not out in public."

"Relax. My roommates aren't home."

I let out a sigh of relief. "Okay. To answer your question, yes, I'm fake dating him. After the meeting with Coach Bedford, Noah came up with the idea."

"He did, did he?" She chuckles. "I think he has a crush on you."

The butterflies in my stomach begin to flutter their wings. *Settle down, stupid bugs.*

"I think he feels bad and he's trying to help."

"I don't buy it. Look, any of those guys would be thrilled if they had a bunch of girls trying to get their attention. Noah is new to the team. He'd be sleeping his way through Hannaford U."

I get annoyed by that comment. "Not all jocks are dogs, Ashley."

"Fine. Maybe Noah wouldn't be sleeping around, but he'd be taking advantage of all the female attention for sure. He not only didn't care about any of those puck bunnies throwing themselves at him, but he's also okay with having you as his fake girlfriend. Trust me, that boy wants you."

I was afraid of that, but I'm not going to admit to Ashley that I already suspect Noah has a crush on me. "That's too bad. I've already told him we can't be more than friends."

"And why is that exactly?"

"Come on, Ash. Do you really need to ask?"

"Just because you were burned by a hockey player doesn't mean Noah will do the same to you."

"Why are you pushing this? I thought you hated all hockey players."

"I'm not pushing anything. I'm just saying you shouldn't put Noah in the friend zone permanently yet. Maybe keep the option open? I mean, you'll be spending a lot of time together. Actually, how long are you planning to fake date him?"

"We haven't discussed it yet."

"Oh my God. That's the first thing you should have talked about! If your fake relationship doesn't last at least a few months, your reputation will be in ruins."

My heart sinks. "It's already in tatters."

"If you're referring to the nasty comments about your announcement last night, don't worry about it. Some of those girls were only pissed that you snagged another hockey hottie. But if you and Noah break up too soon, then everyone will be saying you're the team's whore."

I slouch in my chair, feeling dejected. "What am I gonna do? I can't date him for that long. It isn't fair to either of us."

"That's why I'm telling you to not put him in the friend zone. If there's real chemistry, I think you should let it play out."

"What if it doesn't work out, Ash? I don't want to get hurt again, and Noah certainly won't quit the team. If we become a real couple, and the relationship ends, someone will get hurt."

"You said the same thing about Ryder, and you dated him for a year. I know he fucked up, but do you regret dating him?"

I want to say yes, but I can't. Once upon a time, I believed Ryder and I were in love. I don't regret the memories we made.

"It's because I dated Ryder that I need to be more careful now."

"Why are you being so pessimistic?"

"I'm not. I'm just… I just want to protect myself."

There's a pause and then an audible sigh. "Okay, I won't say another word. Maybe he doesn't like you that way and he truly only wants to help."

That kiss begs to differ. No one who wants to be only friends kisses like that. But I can't tell Ashley about it. She'll never let it go.

"Reasons aside for why you had to jump into another relationship to save your job, there's a poetic beauty about it," she adds.

I laugh. "And what's that?"

"Ryder doesn't know it's a ruse. He must be eating his heart out."

"In the grand scheme of things, he's the last person I'm concerned about."

"Sure, but it's nice to know that you were the first to move on, even if it's not real."

I try to imagine Ryder dating another girl and wait to feel something, anything. But there's nothing, not even the tiniest flare of jealousy in my chest. I'm sure he's hooking up; he was never a saint. But I haven't heard or seen anything.

Since we're already speaking about the dead, I decide to tell Ashley about Blair. By some miracle, she lets me speak without interrupting until I finish telling the whole story.

"And how does that make you feel?" she asks, acting like a veritable shrink.

"I don't know yet. I barely had time to talk to her last night. But I promised to meet her this week for coffee."

"I think you should give her a chance. Imagine being in her shoes, torn between her big brother and her best friend."

"Believe me, I tried. I'm willing to hear her out."

"Good, because I'm tired of having to juggle my friendships. We need the gang back together."

"It's not only up to me, you know? But circling back to my deal with Noah. No one can know."

"My lips are sealed."

"I mean in it, Ash. Not Zoey, and most definitely not Blair."

"Do you even need to ask? Of course I'm not going to say anything to them. I'll take your secret to the grave. Unless you end up getting married to him, and you pick me to be the maid of honor, then for sure, I'll tell your love story during my speech."

I shake my head, but a smile tugs at the corners of my lips. "Yeah, keep dreaming. Call me or text me if you see or hear anything that you think I should know right away."

"You mean if you think we need to kill a bitch?"

"Not that extreme, but yeah. You know the drill."

"Sadly, I do. People suck. That's why I don't like them."

I usually contradict Ashley when she says stuff like that, but after reading some of the comments on social media about me dating Noah, I have to agree.

CHAPTER 17
NOAH

It turns out there's no better medicine for a hangover than making out with the hottest girl on campus—*my* girl. That kiss not only blew my mind, but it also it ruined me for the rest. Gia is endgame. I know it's crazy to think like that, but when you know, you know.

I have to be careful now. I'm not out of the danger zone, a.k.a. the dreaded friend zone. There's still a risk that Gia will change her mind and call off our fake-dating arrangement. She was upset about the comments on social media. One more reason to find the source—or sources—and make them stop. Most people believe you can't stop online bullying. I beg to differ.

My phone is about to die, so I don't start my investigation until I get home. I'm in dire need of a shower and food, but the first thing I do is log on to my laptop. It doesn't take long to find the nasty comments. What I read makes my blood boil. There's so much vitriol that I could choke on it and die.

I pull my hair back, yanking at the strands. I never considered the consequences of Gia dating another guy from the team. Guilt sneaks into my heart. I didn't force her, but it *was* my idea.

The only thing I can do now is protect her from the nastiness on the Internet. Replying to the trolls won't help, that much I know. They live for that shit, and they'll twist my words to serve their purposes. As much as I'd like to save the day on my own, I recognize I'll need assistance.

My first choice is Sean. Not only because he's our captain, but he's already figured me out. He knows I'm into Gia, and I'm certain he suspects our relationship is fake.

I have a ton of homework, but I can't concentrate to save my life. And my dorm room is too small. I'm already getting cabin fever. I decide a good workout is what I need to clear my head. Time on the ice would be better, but the rink is occupied at this hour by the figure skaters.

I text Sean and Darren first, and both say no fucking way they're working out right now. Sean tells me he's going to sleep all day. Weaklings. I text the twins next. They live at the gym, and a measly hangover won't keep them away. When I don't hear from them after fifteen minutes, I head out. I can go solo.

The rink has its own gym, but I'd rather work out at the gym near my student hall. It's still fairly early for a Sunday, so it's not busy yet. There are only a couple guys hogging the leg press machine.

I put on my headphones and begin my training, but after a while, I sense somebody's watching me. I look over my shoulder and see the two guys staring. I remove my headphones and ask, "Is there a problem?"

"Aren't you Noah Kingsley?"

"Yep."

I take my time now to properly look at them. My guess, they're freshmen too.

"Man, you are one lucky dog."

I pinch my brows together. "Is that so?"

"For real. You're dating Gia Mancini," the shorter one with the shaved head says.

I don't like hearing her name come from his mouth. Yes, I'm annoyed that these idiots know who she is and probably drool over her.

"You're right, I *am* lucky."

"How did you manage that?" the second guy asks.

I'm done with this conversation. It never occurred to me that Gia could have her own fan club. Now I'm wondering how many dudes watch her dance videos and fantasize about her like I did.

"Sorry, I don't share my secrets."

"I didn't think anyone on the team would dare to date her after she went out with Ryder Westwood."

That piques my interest. "Why do you say that?"

They stare at me as if I'm dense. "Because he's a Westwood. You should see how he was with her when they started dating. He would have murdered anyone who even looked at her funny," shaved head guy replies.

"Never mind those rumors, he sure put a stop to them."

My spine becomes tense in an instant. "What rumors?"

They trade a look, but before they can enlighten me, Alex and Logan stride into the gym like they fucking own it.

"Look who's here," Alex says with a smile, but it contradicts the murderous glint in his eyes.

It dawns on me that I made a huge mistake by texting them. The conversation I had back at The Heritage about them being like two protective big brothers to Gia comes to the forefront of my mind. They're going to kill me. Shit.

"Hey, what's up, guys?" I ask, pretending to be unfazed.

They corner me at the chest machine I'm using, looking menacing as hell.

"We heard the news," Logan says. "Care to explain how that happened?"

For a split second, I debate telling them the truth, but we aren't alone, and I don't think I can trust the twins to keep their mouths shut. I guess I have to go with a different type of truth.

"What happened is I like Gia and she likes me, in case you didn't know how dating works."

Alex narrows his eyes. "I find it hard to believe that Gia would agree to date you."

I scowl. "Why is that? You don't think I'm boyfriend material? Or is the real problem here that *you* have a thing for her?"

A vein throbs on his forehead. I never stopped to consider that might be the case.

"I don't have a thing for Gia." he grits out.

"If you're worried about it, you don't need to be. I like her a lot, and I have no plans to hurt her like that motherfucker Westwood did."

"That better be true, rookie," Alex replies in a tone cold enough to freeze the entire gym.

I hold his stare, not backing down. "Now do you mind? I'd like to finish this sesh."

They both grunt and step away, but they don't leave the gym. They're actually here to work out too.

When I look over my shoulder, the other guys have moved to the other side of the gym, and now I can't ask them what they meant without getting the twins' attention. But maybe I don't have to. I can probably get the story from the Kaminskis, although not today. I don't think I'm out of the woods with them yet, and it's perhaps better if I don't ask about the rumors in public.

Twenty minutes into my workout, a notification interrupts my soundtrack. I check my phone, and my heart skips a beat. It's a message from Gia.

> Hey, sorry to bother you. I still need help with my French assignment. I know you said you had to study today, but can you meet me tonight? Pretty please?

My heart kickstarts. If she'd asked me to drop everything and meet her now, I would have. Giddiness makes me stupid. I don't stop to consider the issue that I have to pretend once again to speak French before I reply.

> Absolutely.

I was wondering when it'd be okay to ask to see her again, and she just gave me the perfect opportunity. I can't let her fail her class because of me, but telling her the truth could be catastrophic.

There's only one solution to my problem. I have to call the thorn in my side.

My brainiac younger sister, Nicole.

CHAPTER 18
GIA

After the first influx of nasty comments about me dating Noah, the haters settle down. Maybe Ashley was right, and it was just a knee-jerk reaction from the girls who'd really wanted to date the new hotshot on the team. God knows everyone at this university is too busy with academics, clubs, and internships to waste their time obsessing about nonsense. That's Ivy League life for you.

After an hour of looking through all the notifications on the social media accounts for the Warriors and my own, I deem it safe to ignore any new ones that pop up.

I planned in today's schedule to work on new dance routines, but the time slipped by and my priority is my academic work. I love the extra cash that my gig as an influencer brings, but I don't know how long it will last. I don't see it as a long-term career. I want to work in movies, but not in front of the cameras —I want to direct and write screenplays. Most of my influencer friends want to be Hollywood stars.

I make a list of things I need to prioritize. I have an assignment due for my film editing class tomorrow, so I work on that first, which takes hours. I remember now why I didn't think I'd have time to meet Noah today, hence why we decided to meet after the game yesterday. I couldn't have foreseen how the evening would end. Now I have to make up for lost time.

The pressure is weighing on me, spiking my anxiety. I don't want to see Noah so soon after our kiss, but when I finish the rough draft of my French assignment, I know I needed rescuing. My essay sucks. So I ask him to meet me at my place at seven p.m. Ideally, we would've met in a public place again, but considering we're a hot topic of gossip, I think it best if he comes over. I try not to worry about it for most of the day, but twenty minutes before he's supposed to arrive, I'm nervous as hell. No, that's not the right emotion. I'm giddy with anticipation. *Crap on toast.*

Harper is not around— she texted me earlier to say she's having dinner with her parents and most likely will stay over. They live an hour from campus. That means I have the apartment all to myself, which would have been perfect if I wasn't battling all these feelings I shouldn't have. The silver lining is that I can set up our workstation in the living room. Way less dangerous than having Noah in my bedroom. He would have to sit on my bed, and I definitely need to keep him away from it.

When my intercom buzzes, I almost jolt out of my skin. My pulse skyrockets and the jitters make me shake. I haven't felt like this since I had my first crush in middle school. If it's Noah, he's ten minutes early.

I jump from the couch, wipe my sweaty palms against my jeans, and walk to the kitchen to answer the intercom mounted on the wall.

"Hello?"

"Hey, it's Noah."

"Okay."

I press the button to buzz him in, and instead of returning to the couch, I pace the living room. My heart is pumping so fast inside my chest I can almost hear it.

A couple minutes later there's a knock on the door. I don't

bother looking through the peephole. I do, however, take a steadying breath before I open it.

"Hey." Noah smiles, triggering the same reaction as always—a fluttering in my stomach from the butterflies that won't settle down.

"Hi. Thanks for coming." I open the door wider to let him through.

"It's no problem."

As soon as he walks in, I smell something delicious wafting from the greasy bags he's holding.

"What's that?"

"Oh, I didn't know if you'd eaten already so I stopped at a burger joint on the way here and got us dinner."

The fact he thought of that gives me fuzzy feelings. Why does he have to be so adorable?

"You didn't need to do that. I would've ordered us something."

He shrugs, then sets the bags on my kitchen counter. "It's no big deal. Are you hungry now, or should we work for a bit first?"

My stomach grumbles in response, making him laugh.

"I guess dinner first," I say.

"Thank God. I'm starving." He walks to the sink and washes his hands, while I get paper plates out of the cupboard.

"By the way, I've got your clothes. They're clean."

He lifts his brows while he dries off his hands on the dishrag. "You washed my clothes?"

"Of course."

A blush spreads through his cheeks. "You shouldn't have."

"Why are you blushing?"

He breaks eye contact first and focuses on getting the food out of the bags. "My underwear was in that pile."

"I didn't notice," I lie.

He gives me a look that tells me he does not believe me. "Well, thanks for doing it."

"My pleasure." I smile. "Thanks for dinner."

His eyes dance with amusement. "Look at us, acting all domestic. I bring dinner... you do the laundry...."

"Don't get used to it. Doing your laundry was a one-time deal." I take a seat at the counter and inspect what's in the bag closest to me. Curly fries. Yum.

Noah hands me a burger that's seriously almost bigger than my face.

"Man, I'm not sure I can eat it all," I say.

"I'll finish it if you can't." He takes a big bite of his.

"Oh, I bet."

He chuckles and chokes on the food.

"Are you okay?" I ask, trying not to laugh.

He hits his chest with a closed fist and swallows before replying. "Wrong pipe," he croaks.

I get out of my chair. "Let me get you some water."

"Thanks."

"Do you want ice?"

"Sure."

I grab a glass for myself too. Noah drinks half of it in one go. Then he sets the glass on the counter and stares at me in a peculiar way.

"What is it?" I ask.

"Why did you make that comment about my appetite?"

My brows arch. "Oh that. I have an older brother. And I've been around hockey boys for a long time. You guys are always hungry."

"Didn't know you had a brother. What's the age gap?"

It's always difficult when someone asks me about Jaime. I never know what to say.

"He's only a couple years older than me."

"Cool. Are you close?"

"Yeah."

"Is he the reason you know hockey players so well?"

I take a bite of my burger before I reply. I'm not sure what to tell Noah. In the end, I decide to go with the truth. Everyone on the team knows about Jaime anyway.

"He was supposed to come here. He got a free ride to play for the Warriors."

Noah's eyes widen. "For real? Why didn't he come in the end?"

I drop my gaze to my plate. "He got into a car wreck. Broke his legs and hips. It was a career-ending injury."

The change in Noah's face is instantaneous. With a crestfallen expression, he sets his mostly eaten burger on the counter and says, "That's awful. I'm so sorry, Gia."

"Thanks for saying that. It was heartbreaking. Hannaford U was always our dream school. I almost didn't apply. Jaime pushed me to do it, and when I got a scholarship, I felt so damn guilty. But Jaime convinced me to come. He said that if I didn't, then he'd feel guilty, and it'd be a never-ending cycle of remorse."

"He's right. I'm glad he convinced you to change your mind. I hope I get to meet him one day."

My heart reacts. It skips a beat, then overflows with emotion so potent, it robs me of air. Ryder had not been keen to meet Jaime. He confessed once that it made him uncomfortable. And here's Noah, looking forward to it.

"You will," I reply through the lump in my throat that I hope Noah doesn't notice.

CHAPTER 19

NOAH

After dinner, we move to the couch to work on Gia's French assignment. One of the hardest things I have to do is sit next to her and pretend I'm not affected by her nearness. I'm still reeling from the story she told me about her brother. I noticed a change in her voice and expression when she explained why he wasn't playing for the Warriors. That's a wound that hasn't healed, and I wish there was something I could do to help her.

"Ready to work?" She opens a Word document on her laptop and slides the computer toward me.

I'm nervous now. The lie I told her sits heavily on my mind. Nicole agreed to help me, but only after I promised not to give her shit if she's accepted at Clayton U, her first choice of college. She's always dreamed of living in New York City.

I crack my knuckles. "Let's do it."

"It's a little rough. Please be gentle."

Looking into her eyes, I reply in my smoothest voice, "I'll do it nice and easy, babe."

Deep satisfaction spreads through my chest when I catch her blush. She hits my arm playfully. "Will you quit it? There's no one around. You don't need to put on the moves."

I chuckle. "Just practicing. Your reaction was on point, though."

"Just read the essay, please." She sinks against the back of the couch with her arms crossed.

"All right."

I relax against the couch as well, but I lean my body toward the corner so she can't see the screen. Then I log on to my email account and send the doc to Nicole. She promised she'd be on standby.

"What are you typing there?" Gia tries to see the screen.

I turn the laptop away from her prying eyes. "Hey, you'll read my notes when I'm done."

"I thought we could go through the draft together."

"We will, but after I make my revisions."

"Fine." She jumps from the couch and disappears into her room.

Perfect. Now I can text Nicole without having to come up with an excuse or tell Gia who I'm texting.

> I sent you the file. Did you get it?

Nicole doesn't reply right away but she's seen my message. A minute later, the three dots appear on my phone screen.

> Got it.

> How long do you need?

> How many pages?

> No clue. I just forwarded it to you

Curious, I open the document again. It isn't too bad, only ten pages. My sweet sister thinks otherwise.

> IT'S FUCKING TEN PAGES!

>> Get cranking then. But how long do I need to pretend I'm working on this?

> Don't know yet. It depends on how terrible it is.

>> It might not be terrible. You're making assumptions.

> She hired YOU to be her French tutor. Need I say more?

>> Just get to work.

Gia returns to the living room, and I put my phone away quickly.

"So?" she asks.

"Sorry. I didn't read anything yet. I was just replying to a text from Sean."

I notice then that she changed her outfit. Before, she was wearing a baggy pair of jeans and a sweater. Now she has leggings on that leave nothing to the imagination paired with a snug T-shirt. I can't help but stare.

She lays a yoga mat on the floor and puts her long curly hair up in a ponytail using a colorful scrunchie.

"What are you doing?" I ask.

"Optimizing my time. I was supposed to work on a new dance routine today, but I didn't have a chance. My body needs to move, so I'm going to do some stretches while you work on the manuscript."

I swallow hard. How am I supposed to pretend I'm working while she stretches in front of me wearing *that*?

"Oh," I say.

She tilts her head. "Is that okay?"

"Yeah, of course. I won't get distracted."

"I'll be quiet."

I force my eyes to return to the laptop screen. But they don't stay there long. Maybe two seconds tops before I look up. Gia is facing me but bent over and touching her toes. At least she didn't give me a view of her sweet ass.

When she returns to an upright position, I quickly lower my gaze.

Then she drops to the floor, opens her legs wide, and leans forward, pressing her upper body against the mat. Oh my God, I'm going to die. My dick stirs, pressing against my jeans. This is absolute torture. I can't move, and I don't dare breathe. I'm busy focusing on not jizzing in my pants.

I'm so preoccupied with my crotch situation that I don't avert my eyes fast enough when she sits up straight and catches me staring.

"Are you done?"

"No." My voice is tight with need. "Sorry, I kind of spaced out."

"If I'm distracting you, I can stretch in my room. It's just there's more space here."

I shake my head. "No, you're fine. I was just thinking about hockey."

"If you're sure, then okay."

She moves on to different positions, and I do my hardest to keep my eyes on the laptop. When I can't resist a peek, I don't stare for too long. After ten minutes or so, I receive a text from Nicole, letting me know she's done.

Boy, that was fast. I download the file she sent me, and then I move it from the download folder to the document folder in Gia's computer. Then I save it as Noah's revision. She'll never know.

I'm relieved when I see there weren't a lot of mistakes. But there are comments that I never typed. I need to write, or Gia will suspect something is off.

> She's not as dumb as I thought.

> She's an academic scholarship student at an Ivy League school. Of course, she isn't dumb, dumbass.

> I can't wait to attend Clayton U and wear Atlas Kodiak's jersey when they're playing against the Warriors.

> Take that back.

> Never.

> You didn't get into that stupid school yet.

> But I will.

She's right. She can get in anywhere she wants. I don't bother replying and put my phone away.

This time Gia doesn't comment on my texting. I don't think she noticed. I pull up a new note doc and start to type random shit. I do that for a few minutes before I say, "Done."

Gia looks at me. "That was fast."

"There weren't a lot of issues."

"For real?" She gets up from the floor with a small smile tugging at the corner of her luscious lips and sits next to me on the couch.

"See it for yourself." I slide the computer toward her.

I scooch closer because, one, I'm taking every chance I can to innocently touch her. And two, I have no idea what Nicole did. Maybe I should have checked first that she didn't pull a prank on me. If she did, she's dead meat.

"Oh, that makes total sense," Gia says after a moment.

I look over her shoulder to read what she's referring to. I understand the sentence, but I don't get what changes Nicole did. "Right."

If I had revised her manuscript for real, I'd probably have a better response than that.

"How do you pronounce this word?" she points at the screen.

Fuck me. I have no idea, so I do my best.

She looks at me with her brows furrowed. "That doesn't sound very French."

"It's Canadian French. Honestly, you shouldn't ask me about pronunciation if they expect French from France."

"I didn't think about that. Anyway, I can always Google. The grammar is the most important part."

"I'm glad I could help." I spread my arms, resting them on the back of the couch as I relax my stance.

"I was going to ask you to stick around so I could practice my presentation, but since you're not very good at pronunciation, maybe there's no point?"

I jolt in my seat. "I can stick around."

"Don't you have homework to do?" She quirks an eyebrow.

"Just some light reading for an elective. Maybe we could watch a French movie after you practice your presentation."

She squints at me as if she thinks I'm crazy. "Do you want to watch a French movie? For real?"

"Why not? I heard they don't shy away from their sex scenes." I give her my trademark wolfish smile.

"Yeah, nice try, Noah." She looks away quickly.

"It was worth a shot. Don't you know that men live in hope and die in despair?"

She shakes her head, but there's a hint of a grin on her lips. "You're impossible. I'm going to say pass on the French movie."

Leaning against the couch, I link my hands behind my head. "All right. I'll just listen to you speak the language of love, then."

"Stop flirting with me. We aren't going to become more than friends."

I press my hand against my chest. "Ouch. Tell me how you really feel, why don't you? Don't worry, I know all we'll ever be is friends only."

That is until I change your mind.

CHAPTER 20
GIA

I have a busy morning, and that keeps me from worrying about my deal with Noah. I had to kick him out yesterday because he was weakening my resolve with his charms. If he keeps up with the flirting and the sneaky kissing, I'll be done for.

After my first two lessons in the morning, I receive a text from Blair asking if I want to have lunch with her today. I had agreed to coffee, but what difference does it make if it's coffee or a quick lunch? She suggests a small café just off campus, which works for me. I don't want people who know us overhearing our conversation.

When I arrive at the café, she's already there waiting for me at a table in the corner. Her long brown hair is secured with a hair band that matches her yellow coat. Blair and her love of pastels.

She smiles at me as I walk over.

"Hey, have you been waiting long?" I pull up a chair.

"No, I got here two minutes ago. I'm happy you came." She gives me a tentative smile.

"I said I would."

She lets out a heavy sigh. "You're still angry with me, aren't you?"

"I'm not angry. Just hurt and disappointed."

She links her hands together over the table and stares at them. "I know. I didn't mean to ghost you."

"Ryder didn't ask you to stop talking to me, did he?"

She shakes her head. "No, he'd never do that. It was my stupid decision. I was so confused. I knew something was up with him. He wouldn't have broken up with you just like that or quit the team."

"I'm not surprised he broke up with me. We weren't…" I drop my gaze, trying to gather my thoughts. "I don't know how to explain it. I think we knew we weren't right for each other."

"What about Noah?"

Oh no. She's not going to change the subject now.

I level her with a hard stare. "We're talking about why you disappeared on me."

She gives me a wry smile. "I guess we are. Anyway, I knew something was up with Ryder, and I wanted to figure out what was wrong. I didn't think I could do that and still be your best friend."

"Why is that?"

"Because then I'd have to lie to you."

"I'm not following your thought process."

A shadow crosses her blue eyes, making me tense on the spot. I expect her to elaborate. Instead, she just shakes her head.

"It doesn't matter now. My investigation came to nothing. If something is going on with my brother, he'll take his secret to the grave."

She's not telling me the whole story; that much I can tell.

"I wish you knew why he quit the team. That was so out of character for him. He loved being a Warrior." My chest feels heavy suddenly. I guess I'm still upset about that.

"I know. I hope you can forgive me for being a sucky friend."

She stares at me with those big round eyes that have gotten her out of trouble more times than I can count. When Blair needs to, she can look like an angel, but I know she has a dark side too. I'm not even annoyed she's trying to manipulate me using her tricks. I don't think she does it on purpose, it's instinctual for her.

"I suppose I can give you a second chance, but regaining my trust will take time."

She nods. "I know. I'll do my best to prove to you that I'm your friend. To start, I can tell you that Ryder is a little mad that you're dating the rookie."

"He is?" I'm legit surprised that he cares.

"Yup. He's been in a foul mood since Preston showed him the picture of you kissing Noah at The Heritage last Saturday."

"Preston is such a dick."

"Tell me about it. I'm surprised CJ's not more of an asshole."

"You know that shit doesn't fly with Sean." I grab the menu because I'm hungry and my time is limited.

"I'm not sure about that. Alex is hateful." She glances at the menu as well.

"He's only like that with you, but we both know you aren't a saint when it comes to him either."

"Whatever."

I chuckle. "I can't believe you kissed Logan to spite Alex."

She laughs. "I can't either. I think that was a new low for me."

"Was it a good kiss, at least?"

She looks up from the menu to give me a droll look. "The kiss was just for show. I was too angry to enjoy it. How about Noah? Is he a good kisser?"

My face warms. *Shit.* Why the hell am I blushing? This is Blair. Maybe it's because I'm not supposed to feel anything when I kiss Noah since this is all supposed to be fake. "Yes."

She narrows her eyes as she studies me. "You're blushing, so I guess you aren't lying."

"Why would I lie?"

"Because three days ago there was nothing going on with you and Noah. And then the whole thing with the challenge blew up. Dating him is mighty convenient, and an easy solution to the problem."

"Just because it worked out for the best in the end, doesn't mean it's a lie. Maybe Noah and I have been dating in secret for a while, just like Ryder and I did."

God, I hate that I'm lying to her face when this lunch is supposed to help us rebuild trust. But I can't let anyone else know my relationship with Noah isn't real. Blair already hung me out to dry once; she hasn't earned my honesty yet.

She shrugs. "I didn't think you'd date another hockey player."

"Me neither."

"Do you think Noah could be the one, then?" She cocks her head, studying me.

"I don't know, Blair. I just started dating him."

"Yeah, but I know you. You're the most cautious person I've ever met when it comes to opening your heart. Ryder had to work hard to convince you to give him a chance."

Speaking about my past with Ryder unsettles me. I did lower my guard with him, and to use Martin's word, I got clobbered.

"Can we not talk about your brother, please?"

Her eyes fill with guilt. "Of course. Ryder who?"

I grab my phone from my bag when I hear it vibrate. It's a text message from Martin. Freaky. Maybe I summoned him by just thinking about him.

> I can't believe you're dating another dumb jock.

My heart clenches. His text feels like a blow. I can almost hear his condescending voice saying that. It hurts at first, but then it infuriates me. I set my phone screen down on the table.

"What's the matter? Who texted you?"

"Martin."

Blair twists her nose as if she's smelling something bad. "He's a creep."

"I don't think he's a creep, but he's been acting super annoying lately. He was rude as fuck to Noah the other day."

"I don't know why you put up with him."

"He used to be fun. Now he's just irritating." I downplay my feelings because I don't want Martin to become *the* topic of our lunch.

The waitress finally comes over to take our orders, interrupting the conversation. I get a club sandwich, and Blair opts for the house salad and soup of the day combo.

Once we're alone again, she says, "I think he has a thing for you. As a matter of fact, I'm certain of it. Didn't he become a pain in the ass when you started dating my brother?"

I guess we aren't dropping the topic anytime soon.

"I'm not sure. Maybe."

"What did he say in the text?"

I sigh. "He's giving me shit for dating Noah. Called him a dumb jock." Anger swirls in my gut. I'm very protective of all the guys, not Noah specifically.

Blair gives me a knowing look. "He's jealous. I'd stop hanging out with him."

"I think I may have to. I don't need the drama."

My phone vibrates again but I ignore it.

Blair stares at it. "Aren't you going to check that?"

"Nope."

A minute later, the phone starts to ring. I press the side button to stop the call.

The waitress returns with our drinks, but Blair keeps her eyes on my phone. It must be killing her that I didn't answer the call. It's one of her quirks. She always answers calls and texts, no matter what. I think that's why she prefers to be chauffeured around. One time when she did drive us somewhere, she pulled over to answer a text she had received because she couldn't wait.

Feeling bad, I ask, "Do *you* want to see who called?"

"No, I'm good," she replies in a tight voice.

Pinching my lips together, I flip my phone over. "The text was from Martin."

Her stance relaxes and relief is clear on her face. "What did the douche say?"

"He's pissed that I ignored his first message."

"And who called you?"

I squint. "Not him. They left a voice message though."

"Aren't you going to listen to it?"

I roll my eyes. "If you insist. Shall I put it on speaker?" I asked jokingly, but Blair nodes emphatically.

First, there's heavy breathing and then a voice that's been modified by some device. "I knew you were a whore. I bet you got your job by sucking Coach Bedford's dick."

"What the fuck?" Blair blurts out.

The voice message ends. I set the phone down, stunned by those hateful words.

"Let me see the number." She grabs my phone.

"It was an anonymous call."

"Hell. Who would do such a thing?"

My eyes sting from the tears welling up in them. "I don't know. I was afraid this would happen again. Some people were really annoyed that I got the job with the Warriors."

"I know, but this is next-level crazy. I can't believe they're still holding a grudge. You're doing a tremendous job."

"Maybe that's the problem."

"We need to find out who called you."

"I don't want anyone to know about it."

She frowns. "Why not?"

How can I tell Blair that those words made me feel so small and unworthy? I'm ashamed and don't want anyone to know about the nasty voice message.

"I just don't want to bother anyone with my problems."

"Are you saying you're not going to tell your boyfriend either?"

"Especially not him. He can't know. I don't want him distracted by this nonsense. Hockey season is about to start."

Blair flattens her lips, a look of pure disapproval on her face.

"I do *not* support your decision, but I'll respect it."

"Thank you."

The waitress returns with our lunches, but I can't eat my sandwich. I've lost my appetite.

CHAPTER 21
NOAH

Coach Bedford worked our asses hard today. It was drill after drill. He wants us in top shape for the first game of the season, which will be an away game, but not too far from home at least. We're playing in Boston.

The first thing I do when I return to the locker room is check my phone. I sent Gia a text before practice just to ask how her day went. It remains unread.

The last time she ignored her phone, she was trying to avoid internet shit.

> Hey, gorgeous. Just finished practice. Coach Bedford was in a mood.

I wait on pins and needles for a sign that she's not ignoring me. After she cut our tutoring session short, I was a little concerned I had flirted too hard.

"What's got your undivided attention there, Mr. Dance Moves?" CJ asks, already laughing.

"Nothing," I retort. "Mind your damn business."

"Oh, someone is grumpy. I bet Gia already dumped your

sorry ass. I mean, who can blame her? She can't take you anywhere."

"What are you blabbering about?"

CJ proceeds to move like he's a zombie being electrocuted—a.k.a. me when I try to dance.

A few of the guys laugh. I toss a dirty towel in his direction. "Fuck off."

He laughs harder and then uses the damn thing as a prop. I'm a second away from wiping off his amusement with my fist when a *ping* alerts me to a new message. Immediately, I forget about CJ.

> Why was he in a mood? Was he upset about us dating?

> Doubt it. He only has one thing in mind, winning games.

> Oh good.

> Are you busy?

> Why?

Not an immediate yes, that's good. If she wanted to get rid of me, that's what she'd say.

> I'd like to take my girlfriend out on a date.

> It's Monday.

> Are dates exclusive to the weekend?

> I don't know. I'm a bit tired.

> I promise we won't stay out late. I think it's important for us to be seen together.

"Hey, Noah. We're going to that Korean restaurant you like," Sean tells me. "Wanna come?"

"Eh, I'll tell you in a sec."

> You're right. What do you have in mind?

I'm about to reply when Logan slides next to me. "Why are you telling Gia it's important for you to be seen together?"

I shove him off me. "Do you mind?"

"What? So, what's the deal, Kingsley?"

Think fast, Noah.

"Why do you think? I wanna make sure all psychos get the message that I'm off the market."

He stares at me with narrowed eyes, then he shrugs. "Makes sense. Tell her to join us."

"No way, man. I want to be alone with my girl."

"Fine. It's your funeral." He heads to the shower.

I turn to Sean. "What the hell is he talking about?"

"Gia loves that restaurant. You should at least tell her about it."

The last thing I want is to go on my first fake date with Gia in a group. But on the other hand, if we have an audience, then we have to put on a show. It might not be a bad idea after all.

> The guys are going to the Korean restaurant on 2nd street. You want to go?

> Yes! I love that place.

> Cool. I'll pick you up.

> I can meet you there.

Yeah, like I'm going to pass up the opportunity to get Gia alone in my truck.

> Nonsense. I'll be at your dorm in 10.

GIA

I'm a little concerned about going on a fake date with Noah, even though the whole point of the ruse is for people to believe we're a couple so they'll leave him alone. But I also need a distraction. That anonymous phone call rattled me, and even though I try to not let it ruin the rest of my day, I can still hear that nasty voice message in my head.

When Noah mentions going out in a group, I feel a little better. It's not until I have to decide what to wear that it sinks in—going out with his teammates means a lot of pretending.

To avoid him coming up to the apartment, I wait for him in front of my building. When I see his truck, I start toward it. He pulls up to the curb, but before I can reach him, he gets out and opens the passenger door for me.

"My lady," he says making a flourishing gesture with his arm.

"Aren't you the gentleman?"

"Always."

It's the first time I've been in his truck, and it smells nice inside. Not the new car scent that Ryder's SUV had, but a pleasant blend of sandalwood, lemon, and leather. I take a deep breath, because it's deliciously addictive. When he slides behind the wheel and the scent becomes stronger, I realize it's coming from him. Of course his aftershave has to be as intoxicating as his smile. Crap. I'm in *big* trouble.

"How was your day, sunshine?" He glances at me.

My stomach twists into knots. I'd rather not talk about it, but I really can't do that without making him worried something is up.

"Busy. I met Blair for lunch."

His brows arch. "Ryder's sister?"

I'm a little surprised he knows who she is. I've never mentioned her before, but maybe the guys did.

"Yeah. We used to be friends before I started dating him."

"Let me guess. She got weird after the breakup."

"Pretty much. How do you know about Blair anyway?"

Noah's lips twitch upward. "Alex might have mentioned her a few times. He sure doesn't like her."

"Yeah, they're academic rivals."

He laughs. "He skipped that part. I heard she kissed Logan last Saturday to annoy Alex. Is that true?"

"Yep. Caught everyone by surprise."

He shakes his head, still sporting a grin. "Man, I wish I witnessed that. She sounds fun."

I stare at his profile, trying to judge if he's being serious or sarcastic. "You really mean that, don't you?"

He looks away from the road for a second. "What? Did you think I'd automatically dislike her because she's related to Westwood?"

"Most guys in your shoes would."

"I'm not like most guys. I'd rather make up my own mind about her. If she was your friend before, I'm sure she's all right."

"She is. Anyway, we had lunch, and I think there's hope for our friendship after all."

"That's good news, right?" He peeks at me again.

"Yeah, I suppose so."

"Did you have time to work on your new dance routine?"

His question reminds me of Martin's nasty text message and the call that followed. I look out the window, not wanting Noah to see my expression in case I'm not doing a good job masking my feelings. Martin was a shithead, but that call was much worse.

"Sadly, no."

"I'd offer my assistance, but you already know I'm not a good dancer."

His comment disperses the anxiety swirling in my chest. I smile, remembering his dance moves. "I could teach you."

"Would you?" he asks in a chipper voice.

Way to go, Gia. Offer to teach Noah how to dance. It's like my subconscious *wants* me to succumb to the temptation. "Yeah. I won't be able to take you anywhere otherwise."

He grins but keeps his eyes on the road. "If you're up to the challenge..."

"Trust me, Noah. If you can skate around your opponents, you can dance."

"I can't wait, then."

The all-too-familiar sensation of euphoria spreads through my body. Noah is making me giddy, and even though I'm afraid to let him in, I can't help but chase the feeling.

We get a large round booth to fit everyone. Sean, the twins, and Darren came and have already eaten their weight in food. Naturally, Noah is sitting next to me. His arm is around my shoulder, and I'm flush against his body. He's taking every chance he gets to touch me. It's a kiss on the cheek, a hand on my thigh, little gestures that are innocent enough but are wreaking havoc on my body. I don't know what to do with myself.

The guys are watching, especially Alex and Logan, who have decided to take on the older brother role with me. I can't squirm away from Noah—not that I really want to.

"Man, I'm stuffed," Sean declares.

"Me too, but it was so worth it," I reply.

Noah squeezes my thigh. "One hundred percent worth it."

My face becomes hot—I know he's not talking about the food. Since no one can see his hand under the table, I push it away and give him a meaningful glance. He rewards me with a toothy grin.

"I have to use the washroom," he announces.

"Again?" Logan complains as he stands to let him out. "You have a tiny bladder."

"No. I drink enough water."

I watch Noah walk away, and since we're pretending to be together, it's okay if I drop my gaze to check out his ass. He has a nice tush.

"So," Logan scooches closer. "How's it going with the rookie? Is he treating you well?"

"Yes, you don't have to worry."

No one knows why the Kaminski twins are so protective of me, and I made them promise to take that secret to the grave. Last year, just after I started dating Ryder in secret, they saved me from an unsavory situation at The Heritage. Three assholes cornered me in the dark hallway that leads to the restrooms, and things could have gotten bad if they hadn't shown up. I didn't want Ryder to know because I was afraid he'd go after the men and get in trouble. Since then, Logan and Alex have kept an eye on me, and they take their protective role seriously.

Logan nods. "Good. I like Noah. I'd hate to have to rearrange his face."

"Don't say stuff like that. I really like his face."

Not a lie. Noah Kingsley checks all my preferences when it comes to men. He's sweet, attentive, funny, plus he has that gorgeous face and mischievous smile. He's the perfect combination of nice and wicked. I shouldn't be thinking about him in those terms when I'm afraid to jump into another relationship with a hockey player, but I'm quickly realizing he might be my kryptonite.

"He's not being harassed anymore, is he?" Sean asks.

"If he is, he hasn't told me."

"Oh, I think we have our answer," Alex says as he looks beyond our booth.

I follow his line of sight and catch a pretty girl making a beeline toward Noah as he returns from the restroom. She's a petite blonde with chin-length hair and big boobs. He smiles when he sees her, but not his polite grin. He gives her the same smile that knocked the air out of my lungs the first time he aimed it at me. My body tenses and an ugly feeling spreads through my chest. This is jealousy, plain and simple, and it catches me by surprise. My gaze hardens as I watch the scene unfold.

"I don't think he's minding that interaction," Logan says in a dangerously low tone.

"He's not," I grit out, more annoyed than I should be.

He's not my real boyfriend. Why am I reacting as if he was?

CHAPTER 22

NOAH

I'm shocked when Maxine, my old neighbor and former babysitter, blocks my way back to the booth.

"Surprise!" She beams from ear to ear.

"Holy shit, Max. What are you doing here?" I pull her into a hug.

"I'm in town for a wedding. George's side of the family. I was planning to call you so we could meet."

I ease back and look over her head for her husband. "Where is he?"

"Oh, poor thing caught a stomach bug. He's at the hotel. I'm here with some of his cousins." She points at a large table where a group of people are chatting animatedly. "How have you been?"

"You know, busy as hell. Hockey season is about to start."

"Oh my God. I saw that video with the underwear explosion." She laughs. "You're like a celebrity."

I groan. "Please don't remind me of that game."

"Okay."

"Hey, Maxine," someone at the table calls her. "The food is here."

"Oh, I'd better go. Come say hello before you head out."

"Sure thing. And say hi to George for me."

I return to the booth, still amused that I bumped into Maxine here of all places. My good humor evaporates when I find Logan and Alex glaring at me, and Gia is gone.

"Where's Gia?"

"She went to the restroom. Who was that woman, rookie?" Logan asks.

Shit. He only calls me rookie when he's pissed.

"That's Maxine, my old neighbor."

"You looked pretty chummy with her," Alex pipes up.

Heat surges through my neck and my ears as my irritation grows. "Are you for real? I've known her my whole life. She's like a big sister to me. Besides, she's married."

"Oh." Logan relaxes against the back of the booth. "You'd better tell Gia, then. I think she got upset."

A spark of excitement shoots down my spine. "She did?"

"You don't know that," Darren retorts. "Stop stirring the pot."

Logan twists his face into a scowl. "I'm not."

I turn around and head back to the washroom. If Gia got upset because I was friendly with Maxine, then it's possible she was jealous. I can totally make that work in my favor.

GIA

I'm such an *idiot*. Why did I let that interaction between Noah and that woman affect me so much? I knew the twins were paying too much attention to me, so I had to leave the table. I don't really need to pee, so I just reapply my lipstick and then wait a bit until I can get my emotions under control.

I don't expect to find Noah waiting for me outside the

restroom, leaning casually against the wall opposite the door with his hands in his pockets.

"What's up, Noah?"

Without replying, he walks over until he's invading my personal space. I take a step back, meeting the wall behind me. I crane my neck to maintain eye contact while he rests his forearm next to my head.

"I heard you got upset."

"I didn't."

He leans down, bringing his lips to my ear. "Are you saying you didn't get jealous seeing me talking to a pretty girl?"

My pulse accelerates, and I have a hard time answering him. "No. You're not my boyfriend, remember? You didn't need to come after me."

"It's what a real boyfriend would do. Besides, I don't buy it." He kisses my neck, sending chills of desire down my spine.

"You don't buy what?" I whisper.

"That you didn't get jealous."

"Well, I didn't."

He keeps placing open kisses down my neck and then my collarbone. I should make him stop, but I don't want to. It feels too good. I close my eyes instead, arching my back, and flattening my palms against the wall.

"I think you're lying, sunshine." He places a hand on my hip. "You don't need to be jealous, though. I only have eyes for you."

"Noah..."

He captures my lips, cutting off my protest, which was going to be weak anyway. His fingers press harder against my skin as he destroys all my barriers with his tongue. He nudges my legs apart with his, leaning into my body and pressing his wide chest against mine. He shouldn't be kissing me like this when we're alone, and I shouldn't be letting him. We're only meant to pretend, but this feels like the real deal.

Seconds before I'm about to combust on the spot, he steps back and stares at me through hooded eyes.

"What was that?" I breathe out.

"Proof that fake boyfriend or not, you have nothing to worry about."

"You… I don't expect you to turn a blind eye to every attractive girl that crosses your path. Our deal has an expiration date."

It kills me to say that, but it's the truth. This relationship isn't meant to last.

He tilts his head. "Does it?"

"Yes, Noah," I reply more firmly. "I told you, we can only be friends."

His lips curl into a grin. "Friends can have fun."

That's a recipe for disaster. "Until someone gets hurt."

He bumps the tip of my nose with his index finger. "Has anyone ever told you that you're a little pessimistic, sunshine?"

"I'm not. I'm realistic."

He moves closer again, making my breath catch. His lips are dangerously close to a sensitive spot on my neck. "Let me give you a dose of reality. Whenever you're feeling horny, I can make you come just by whispering dirty words in your ear. And if you let me touch you, you'll never need any other man."

I want to call him on his bullshit, but I believe him. My panties are already soaked through, and he hasn't done anything but talk to me in his whiskey-poured-over-ice voice.

"We'd better get back to our booth." I make a motion to walk around him, but he takes my hand.

"In a sec. I want to introduce you to someone."

Still under the "Noah effect," I let him steer me back into the restaurant and toward a group of people sitting at a long table. Immediately, I spot the pretty girl he was talking to earlier. Now that I see her up close, I notice she isn't as young as I thought she was. I'd say she's in her late twenties.

"Good evening, everyone." He waves at the group.

"Noah!" the woman from before says. "Are you leaving already?"

"In a bit. I came by to say hello and introduce my girlfriend, Gia."

Being introduced as such to strangers does things to me. It makes me happy in a way that shouldn't. It's one thing to pretend at school, quite another to be Noah's girlfriend outside our bubble.

"Your girlfriend?" Her brows shoot to the heavens. Then she's out of her chair. "You little turd. Why didn't you say you had a girlfriend and that she was here?"

"Your stomach got in the way. You went after food."

She shakes her head and then focuses on me. "Oh my God. You're gorgeous."

Blushing furiously, I reply timidly, "Thanks."

"I'm Maxine, Noah's old neighbor and former babysitter."

Relief washes over me. I really didn't have anything to worry about. He wasn't flirting with her before.

"Nice to meet you. So you babysat Noah, huh? What was he like as a child?" I glance at him, smirking.

"A terror. Boy, do I have stories to tell!"

"Hey, hey. I didn't introduce you to Gia so you could poison her against me," Noah interjects.

Maxine wrinkles her nose. "I'm pretty sure she already knows that you're the devil."

She has no idea.

"I hate you," he replies in a fake annoyed tone.

"How long are you in town?" I ask.

"Until Monday. We have a wedding on Saturday."

"Maybe you can come to the Warriors game this Friday. It's in Boston, though."

"Oh, that'd be great," Noah pipes up.

Maxine pouts. "I wish I could. Friday is the rehearsal dinner. I hope there aren't any more panty explosions."

Oh man. She saw that too. I should already be resigned that everyone who follows hockey got wind of that fiasco.

"The craziness should be over," I reply.

"The only panties I want to see tossed at me during a game are Gia's," Noah adds.

My jaw drops. "Noah!"

Maxine laughs. "Ah, there's the no-filter Noah I love. Anyway, you probably want to get back to your friends. I won't keep you."

"If you're not too hungover, maybe we can hang out on Sunday," he says.

She gives him a droll stare. "Don't you know me anymore? I'll probably still be drunk on Sunday. That never stops me from doing things. I'll text you. It was nice to meet you, Gia. You take care of this one, okay? He's special."

"Don't worry. I will." It's what a real girlfriend would say, but there's nothing fake about my statement. I know it the moment the words leave my lips.

Noah tosses his arm over my shoulder, and we walk like that, side by side, back to our booth.

"Where have you been?" Logan asks.

"Going at it like rabbits in the washroom," Noah deadpans. "Why do you care?"

I elbow him in the stomach. "Noah, come on."

"I was just joking, sunshine."

"So, you've met Noah's old nanny?" Alex asks innocently, but I read the mischief in his eyes.

"Yes, she's so nice."

"She's hot," Logan adds.

"Dude, I already told you she's married," Noah retorts.

"That's never stopped me before." Logan grins like the cat who ate the canary.

"Yeah, we all know. You're a dog," Darren chimes in. "Well, shall we get the check? I have an early class tomorrow."

"Yeah." Sean raises his hand, signaling our waiter.

Noah pulls a wad of cash from his wallet and drops it on the table. "That should cover our portion of the bill."

I open my mouth to tell him he shouldn't pay for me, but then I remember that we're on a date, even if it's fake.

"What? Are you in a hurry or something?" Alex asks.

"As a matter of act, yes." He glances at me. "I'm ready for dessert."

CHAPTER 23
GIA

"Man, I can't believe we bumped into Maxine. What are the odds?" Noah says as soon we're on the road.

"She sounds like a super fun person to hang out with."

"Oh, she is. My oldest brother had such a crush on her." He laughs.

I'm glad that the topic of conversation is Noah's family and friends and not another attempt to seduce me. Once again, he unraveled me with kisses and naughty promises, weakening my resolve to keep things platonic between us.

"What's the gap between you and your older brother?"

"Nathan is five years older than me. Then there's Nixon, who's a couple years older than me."

"Do all your siblings have names starting with N?"

He bobs his head up and down. "Yep. Nicole is a year younger than me, and then there are the twins, Neve and Nash. They're my parents' big 'oops.' They just turned ten."

"Wow, your parents have been busy. Why did they choose names starting with N, though?"

"Because they thought it'd be fun. Nancy and Nick are their names."

"They sound like my kind of people," I say with a smile.

The traffic light turns red, and Noah switches his attention to me. "If they come to one of my games, you'll meet them. They'll love you."

His eyes have turned wishful again, so I work hard to keep the subject on his family and not us. "I can't imagine what your house must have been like when you were a kid."

"Oh, it was complete chaos. Our place was the spot where all the kids in the neighborhood hung out. So instead of six, there were always twenty kids running around. How about you? Any other siblings besides Jaime?"

"Yes. My father was married before he met my mother. I have two much older sisters, Tina and Robyn. They're in their forties."

"Wow. That's quite the gap."

"It was great. They spoiled me rotten. They're also the reason I love pop songs from the eighties and nineties so much."

He chuckles. "Ah, now your music choices for your dance videos are explained. They basically brainwashed you."

"In a way. What? You don't like the classics?"

"Oh, I like the classics, but I'm not a fan of pop."

Folding one of my legs under me, I turn in my seat so I can really look at him. "Why not?"

He glances at me quickly. "In case you forgot, I can't dance to save my life."

"Oh, right. We'll change that. I swear."

"I'm holding you to that." He gives me a look that promises many dirty moments.

Shit. We've entered the danger zone. Abort. Abort.

I clear my throat. "So, what's your favorite song from that era?"

"'Sweet Child O' Mine,'" he answers without hesitation.

"That's a great song."

"It makes me think of you."

I swallow hard and quickly look away. "Noah, please don't start."

"Sorry. I'll just pretend there's absolutely no chemistry between us."

I sigh. "Okay, you do that."

By a miracle, he doesn't offer a response. Instead, he turns on the radio and tunes in to an eighties station. During the ride back to my dorm, it plays some of my favorite songs, but they don't make me relax. I'm too aware of Noah and how my body reacts to him. If it were only physical attraction on my end, it'd be easier to deal with, but I think there's more, and I'm terrified.

When he parks the truck, it takes me by surprise.

"We're here," he announces.

"Wow, I didn't notice."

"You were awfully quiet during the ride. Are you upset about something I said?"

I glance at him. "No. Anyway, thanks for the ride."

"I'll walk you to your front door."

"You don't need to."

"I insist. It's dark, and it'll make me feel better knowing I delivered you safe and sound to your apartment."

I narrow my gaze. "How chivalrous. You're not coming inside."

His eyes widen. "I wasn't expecting an invitation. I heard you loud and clear. You're not interested. I'm not going to keep trying to get into your pants. Although I think we're missing a great opportunity here."

He's giving up, and I should let him, but instead, I say, "Is that so?"

"I understand your reservations about dating another hockey player. But the thing is, for all intents and purposes, you're already dating one. Why not reap the benefits? We'd have a great time."

"Oh, like your promise to make me come by whispering dirty words in my ear?"

He smiles broadly. "That'd be one of the perks."

"I think you're full of it." I get out of the truck before things escalate.

I'm such an idiot. I should have just kept my mouth shut, not led him on.

"Gia, wait." I keep walking at the same pace, and he catches up in the next second. "What if I prove to you that I'm not kidding? Would you agree to the benefits part?"

My pulse skyrockets, and the damn insects in my stomach fly around wildly. I force my expression to stay neutral. "What? Are you going to make me come with dirty talk?"

"Yes," he replies in a smooth voice.

Sweet baby llamas. How can he make one simple word sound so sexy? I don't answer right away because part of me—the horny part—wants to see if he can do it. Noah seems to guess my conflict, so he remains quiet until we're standing in front of the elevator. I wasn't supposed to let him come into the building. Now I'm going to be trapped with him in a metal box while wondering if he's that skilled with words.

"A penny for your thoughts," he says.

The elevator arrives. We walk in, and when the door shuts, Noah invades my personal space, crowding me into a corner.

"What are you doing?"

He brings his mouth to my ear. "I'm giving you a taste. You love when I'm near you, don't you, sunshine?"

The goose bumps that form on my arms and on the back of my neck can't deny the truth. "Maybe."

He chuckles, fanning hot air against my sensitive skin. "There's no need to be shy. I know you do. I bet your nipples are already as hard as pebbles. Imagine my tongue circling them, making them even harder right before I suck them into my mouth. Will you arch your back and whimper softly when I do it, or will it be a loud moan?"

I close my eyes and picture him doing that to me. I can almost feel his tongue playing with my nipple, teasing me beyond reason. My breathing is shallow, and tendrils of desire curl at the base of my spine.

"I'd say it'll be softer at first, then gradually, the sounds coming from your sinful lips will get louder, wilder. You're going to beg for more. And do you want to know what I'm going to do?"

"Yes," I hiss.

"I'm going to explore your body slowly, drawing my tongue down your belly until I reach the edge of your panties. They're already soaked through, aren't they?"

Shit. They are. I'm saved from blurting out the truth when the elevator pings, announcing we've arrived at my floor.

Noah steps back, sporting a shit-eating grin. "Ladies first."

CHAPTER 24
NOAH

I've never been hornier than I am now. Playing seduction games with Gia has consequences that are pushing against my jeans and not in a pleasant way. I let her walk ahead so I can adjust myself. Unfortunately, her apartment isn't far from the elevator, and we get there before I can solve the problem.

There's an obvious solution, but I know when to advance and when to retreat. It's time for the latter. I ignore my erection and pay close attention to her. Her cheeks are flushed, and her hand is shaking when she unlocks the door. She doesn't meet my eyes, though. But most importantly, she makes no motion to enter her apartment.

"Gia?"

"Yes?"

"Are you going to open that?"

She takes a deep breath before she turns her face to me. "Would you like to come in?"

Fuck yes! The thought is loud in my head, but I have enough self-control and don't blurt it out. "You know I do."

She swallows hard, and it's audible. "Okay."

My plan is to push her against the wall and claim her lips the moment we walk in. But when we cross the threshold, I know the evening won't end as I hoped. There are boxes scattered everywhere, and in the middle of them, we find Gia's roommate in a panic.

She turns to us with wide eyes. "Oh, thank God you're here."

"What happened?" Gia walks farther into the apartment and sets her purse on the kitchen counter.

"Adrian fucking Steele happened."

I furrow my eyebrows. "Who is that?"

Gia pinches her lips together before she replies. "He's one of Ryder's friends."

"Of course he is," I mutter.

"I didn't know you knew him, Harper," Gia continues.

The girl looks legit on the verge of crying. "I'm working with the asshole. Do you remember the internship I got this semester? It's at Steele Entertainment Corp. I'm working with Adrian on a very important project."

"And what did he do?" I butt in.

She opens her arms wide. "This! We have a big event tomorrow, and he was in charge of the welcome boxes. When I asked him for an update a week ago, he said he had everything under control. Then I came home only to find all these boxes waiting for me downstairs."

"How did you get them up here?" I ask, trying to count the number of boxes. There's gotta be a couple hundred at least.

"I paid some guys to help me bring them up. But the biggest issue is, if I don't have the boxes prepped for tomorrow's event, then I can say goodbye to my job."

"Why? If Adrian is responsible, why would *you* be penalized?" I ask, earning a funny look from them. I sense I said something stupid.

"His father owns the company. Who do you think will get fired?"

Ah, nepotism... I almost forgot that's pretty common in wealthy circles.

"What's the plan?" Gia asks.

"I have to prep all the boxes tonight. There's no other way. I can't miss my classes tomorrow. Besides, they need to be at the venue first thing in the morning."

I give the room another cursory glance. She'll never finish it in time by herself. The solution is simple to me. "What can we do?"

She shakes her head. "It's late. I don't expect you to help me."

"Nonsense. Of course we're helping you," Gia replies.

Harper begins to shake her head, so before she can refuse our assistance again, I add, "You have no choice, darling. You're stuck with us. What's the first step?"

She takes a deep breath before answering. "There are several items I need to put in each box. We should create an assembly line, and each of us will be responsible for a few items."

"Sounds good. The first order of business is to unpack stuff, right?" Gia says.

"Yes." Harper reaches for the box closest to her and rips the tape off with enough fury that I suspect she's imagining it's Adrian Steele's head.

"I'll move the boxes out of the way," I tell them.

We begin to work fast, and twenty minutes later we have our assembly line. Only then do I pay attention to the material in front of me and realize these are boxes promoting the latest blockbuster starring a household name in action movies.

"Holy shit. Is this promo for Gordon Montana's newest movie?" I ask.

"Yeah. Usually, the events take place in LA. However, because the movie is set in Fairbanks, Marketing decided it would be fun to hold an event for influencers here. Gordon will be there."

"No way! Man, I'd love to meet him."

"It starts at six—if you can make it, I'll add your names to the list."

I turn to Gia. "What do you say, babe?"

"Don't you have hockey practice?"

"I do, but it starts early. It should be over by then. Besides, we can totally shoot some videos for the team's page. How awesome would that be?"

She frowns. "I'm not sure if that'd be allowed."

Gia and I turn to Harper.

"I can find out," she replies.

I step closer to Gia, pulling her into side hug. "Will you come with me? Pretty please?"

"Oh, all right."

I kiss her cheek soundly. "And that's why you're my dream girl."

She steps away from me, but her cheeks are bright red now, so I keep my smile in place.

"I don't get it," she says. "If this event is so important, why didn't the marketing department hire someone to do this job?"

"Because my boss is a sadistic ass. He likes to test his employees. My mistake was trusting his son."

"I'm surprised Adrian is working for his dad. Ryder once told me he never wanted anything to do with the business."

And now my good mood evaporates. If we could stop bringing that douche's name up, that'd be great.

"He's being forced to. And because his father is making Adrian work with me, he's taking his anger out on me."

"Another jackass. I'm not surprised he's Ryder's friend. Like calls to like," I chime in.

"Oh, he is a certified jackass," Harper replies. "And he wants to see me fail."

"Well, we're not going to let that happen, are we?" I grin, suddenly energized by the prospect of pissing off one of Ryder's asshole friends.

"Definitely not." Harper smiles back.

Gia claps her hands together. "Okay. Let's get cracking. We need some music to get us going. Any suggestions?"

"I'm good with whatever," I say.

"You know me. I'll listen to anything that's not guttural screaming."

"All right. I have the perfect playlist, then."

No surprise, Gia's perfect playlist is a compilation of songs from the 80s, 90s, and early 2000s.

"I'll make a fresh pot of coffee." Harper veers for the kitchen.

Once we're sufficiently caffeinated and at our designated workstations—the girls on the couch and me on the floor—work begins. Soon, I lose track of time. I guess that's what happens when you do repetitive tasks. But toward the end, tiredness seeps into my bones, and keeping my eyes open becomes difficult.

When the final box is assembled, I lean against the couch, tilting my head back and closing my eyes. "It is *done*."

"I can't believe we pulled it off," Harper says.

"It only took us five hours," Gia replies.

My eyes fly open. "Five *hours*?" I jump up from the floor, and every muscle in my body screams. I stayed in the same position for too long and now I'm paying for it. "I'd better get back to my dorm."

"You're half-asleep. Why don't you stay?" Harper suggests.

I glance at Gia. When she invited me to come in, I had one plan in mind, but I think the moment has passed, and I don't want to impose my presence on her. Plus, I'm dead tired, and I'm sure if I try to seduce her, it'll backfire.

"You're not going anywhere," she tells me.

I try to suppress a yawn and fail. "Are you sure?"

"Positive." She offers me her hand. "Come on. Let's go to bed."

I let her steer me into her bedroom, and the excitement of finally being alone with her is making my heart pump like a factory. I close the door behind me, then tug Gia into my arms.

"Alone at last," I say before I kiss her slowly and gently.

She opens her lips for me, surrendering to the moment, to the feeling that has wrapped around us. I want to lift her into my arms, fall into bed and take my time worshiping her, but she leans back, ending our connection too soon.

"It's late. We should sleep."

"Do you think I'll be able to shut my eyes when you're lying next to me, sunshine?"

Her gaze drops to my mouth. "You have to. Otherwise, you're sleeping on the couch."

"Harper will think we had a fight."

"Harper is already in dreamland." She walks backward until she disappears into the bathroom.

Since I'm not planning to sleep in my jeans, I take them off, and then my sweater and T-shirt for good measure. But I don't want to scare Gia, so I get under the covers to wait for her. Without her near me, and now lying in a comfortable bed, my body betrays me and begins to shut down. My eyelids turn heavy, and like an idiot, I allow them to close, thinking I'll be able to open them again when Gia comes to bed.

Fucking colossal mistake.

CHAPTER 25
GIA

The process of waking up in the morning is slow for me. I usually stretch like a cat and roll to my side, pulling the cover over my head. This morning is a little different. The moment I become aware of Noah's body next to mine, I'm wide awake.

His arm is wrapped around my waist, and one of his legs is slung over mine. At first, I tense. Last night I was close to falling for his charms and breaking my own rules. I could say Harper's emergency saved me from an unwise decision, but if I'm honest with myself, it only delayed the inevitable. My shield against Noah has cracked in so many places already. A little bit of pressure will shatter it to pieces.

Last night, I took my time in the bathroom, wrestling with all my contradictory emotions. I knew I was in trouble when my heart refused to slow down. But when I returned to my room, I found Noah sound asleep. The poor guy was exhausted. I didn't join him in bed right away, just stared at him for a moment. He offered to help my friend without hesitation, even though that messed with his own plans. And he didn't do it to score brownie points with me either. I know when someone's trying to manipulate me.

Carefully, I reach for my phone on the nightstand. My heart jumps into my throat when I see the time. Fuck! It's half past seven. I have class in thirty minutes.

I push Noah's arm off me and jump out of bed, not bothering now to be quiet.

"Noah, wake up," I say as I run to the bathroom.

I just have time to brush my teeth, wash my face, and pee, which I do in record time. Back in my room, I expect to find Noah already out of bed, but he hasn't budged.

I lean over him and shake his arm. "Noah, we're going to be late."

"Huh?" he mumbles with his eyes closed.

"It's already seven thirty in the morning."

"No way. I just closed my eyes."

"Way. Now get up."

He finally opens his eyes and smiles lazily. "Good morning, sunshine."

My stomach does a backflip, and my heart jump-starts. It's not fair how gorgeous he is after just waking up.

"If you don't get up, I'll leave you behind."

"Okay, okay."

He flips the bed cover out of the way, revealing what I already suspected. He slept in his underwear, and the tight fabric allows me to see *everything*, including his raging erection. My mouth goes dry. He throws his legs off the side of the bed and gets up. But I can't stop gawking.

He must still be half-asleep because he doesn't say anything about me staring at his package.

"Is it okay if I use your shower?" he asks through a yawn. "I can't wake up properly if I don't shower in the morning."

"Yeah, of course," I croak. "But be fast. And if you want, help yourself to the new toothbrush in my drawer."

"Thanks."

While he's in the bathroom, I change clothes, choosing the simplest outfit I can find, which is a pair of jeans, boots, a T-shirt, and a sweater. My curly hair is a tangled mess, but there's nothing I can do about it while it's dry, so I just make a messy bun on top of my head.

Noah walks out of the bathroom a few minutes later with a towel wrapped around his hips. His hair is wet, and droplets of water cling to his wide chest. It takes every ounce of self-control I have to not jump into his arms. I still remember the naughty words he whispered in my ear last night, and now I regret I didn't get the chance to experience everything he plans to do to me.

"What's up, sunshine?" He grins while his eyes dance with mischief. It's like he can read my mind.

"Nothing. I'll leave you alone so you can change."

"Or you can stay and watch." His grin turns into a full-blown smile.

I swallow hard. "Better not."

I run out of my bedroom faster than a bullet train. If I stayed, there's a high chance I'd jump him. And I really can't afford to be late for class.

Harper is in the kitchen eating a sandwich while she waits for the coffee to brew.

"Good morning," I say.

"Hi. Did you sleep well last night?"

"I slept like a baby." I grab a mug from the cupboard.

"Really? I thought for sure you'd be up for a little bit longer." She smirks.

So did I. "Noah passed out as soon as he hit the mattress."

"We worked the poor guy until his last drop of energy." She chuckles. "And he didn't even get a reward. It *is* a hard-knock life."

Not wanting to keep talking about Noah, I grab that reference like a lifeline. "I can't believe we didn't sing that song while working."

"Yeah, we missed our chance. Oh, coffee's ready."

I fill my cup and hers, and then we fall silent as we savor our "fast" juice. I drink mine with milk, but Harper prefers hers black.

"I have to say, you hit the jackpot with him." She breaks the silence. "He's adorable, and so into you. Don't let him get away."

A warm and fuzzy feeling spreads through my chest. I want to believe so bad that her observations are correct, but so far, I'm certain only that Noah wants to fuck me. Don't get me wrong, the feeling is mutual. The guy is a walking wet dream. But if I let my guard down around him, I'll be the one left with a broken heart. He's young and popular. Guys his age don't usually want to jump into a serious relationship. This could be nothing but a chase. The moment he gets what he wants, it'll lose its appeal.

Noah walks out of my bedroom looking like a fucking rock star. I try to hide my reaction, but I have never been good at concealing my emotions. Mom always says my face is an open book.

"Good morning," he says in that sexy voice of his. He's not even trying.

"Good morning. Did you sleep well?" Harper asks.

"Yeah, a little too well." He gives me a meaningful glance that makes my insides all mushy. "Oh, is there enough coffee for me?"

"Yeah, plenty," I say.

"Do you have a to-go cup? I need to stop by my dorm before I head to class."

"I think I have a thermos you can borrow." I look in the cupboard and pull out a Warriors thermos that I never use. "How do you like your coffee?"

"Just black is fine."

I fill the cup to the brim, completely aware that Harper is observing the whole interaction. She's going to say something about it as soon as Noah leaves.

"Here you go."

"Thanks." He sets the thermos on the counter and looks over

my shoulder at Harper. "Now, excuse me, but I need to say a proper goodbye to my girlfriend."

He pulls me flush against his body and slants his lips over mine for a possessive, toe-curling kiss. It's scorching, demanding, and leaves me breathless.

When he leans back, I'm a little dizzy. Smiling like a fiend, he takes his coffee and walks backward until he reaches the front door. "I'll pick you up at five thirty."

My lust-infused brain can't process his words. "Uh?"

"Did you already forget the reason we went to bed at three in the morning?" He laughs.

"Oh right."

"You'd better pick her up at five. There'll be traffic," Harper chimes in.

"Good call. I'll be here at five, then."

"Yeah, sure, I'll be ready."

He turns to Harper. "Actually, what should I wear?"

"Cocktail attire."

"Perfect." He looks at me again with his hand already on the doorknob. His eyes are sultry... and full of promises. "See you later, sunshine."

Still reeling from his goodbye kiss, all I can do is nod.

I'm in so much trouble.

CHAPTER 26
NOAH

I've never showered and gotten ready so quickly after practice in my life. I skipped the usual chitchat and ran out of there faster than The Flash. I had the foresight to bring my date clothes with me, which resulted in curious glances from my teammates. We usually don't dress up in slacks and a jacket unless we have to. I managed to leave before any of them could interrogate me—and only because the twins and CJ were in the shower when I got dressed.

I knew I'd be cutting it close when I agreed to pick up Gia at five. I text her to let her know I'm running late, so when I arrive at her place at ten past five, she's already waiting for me in front of her building.

I don't know what she has on underneath her black coat, but she's wearing fuck-me heels that only serve to emphasize her gorgeous legs.

I park by the curb and get out of the truck to open the door for her. Before she gets in, I curl an arm around her tiny waist and pull her close so I can kiss her. I'll never get sick of this—she's the best thing I've ever tasted. I don't care that there's no one around. In my mind, I'm done with the fake-dating part, and

I think she is too. My heart is beating so fast it's on the verge of bursting out of my chest.

"You smell nice," I murmur against her lips, dying to kiss her deep and hard.

She leans back and looks into my eyes. "Thanks, you too." Her voice is tight and breathless. I love that I have that effect on her. "Shall we go? We're already running late."

"Yeah." I step aside to let her into the truck.

Once I'm behind the steering wheel and on the way off campus, she asks, "Are you excited to meet Gordon Montana?"

"I was super excited about the idea last night, but today I'm not so sure."

"Why is that?"

"You know how they say it's better to never meet your idols—what if he turns out to be a jerk? I'll never be able to enjoy his movies again."

"That's true. Maybe we can avoid him. I'm sure it'll be a fun event nonetheless."

"I'd have a good time anywhere with you by my side." I smile at her.

"So we're starting it already," she replies, but her tone is light.

"I never stopped." I look at her again so I can read her face.

"That's true."

No hard-set brows or clenched jaw. I'm still good, but I decide to change the subject just to be safe. "Do you think the guy who fucked Harper over will be there?"

Now her expression changes. Her lips flatten before she replies, "I'm sure he will."

"Good." I return my attention to the road, but when I sense her stare burning a hole through my face, I look at her again. "What?"

"You're not going to do anything, right?"

"I won't go looking for trouble if that's what you're worried about. But… if the opportunity presents itself…" I shrug.

"I doubt Harper wants any drama. So, please don't say anything."

"All right. I won't. I guess he's another person we need to avoid, huh?"

"I'm afraid so."

I don't like the direction this conversation is going. I'd much rather focus on her. "How was your day, sunshine?"

"Oh my God, it was brutal. It was so hard to concentrate on my classes. I never drank so much coffee in one day."

"I hear ya. I was mainlining caffeine the whole day." There's a lull in the conversation, so I continue. "How's everything in the social media world? Did things calm down?"

"Everything's fine." Her voice becomes tight and cold, making my stomach twist with worry.

I haven't had a chance to ask Alex or Logan about the rumors Ryder put a stop to, or discuss the situation with Sean. And thanks to classes and hockey practice, I didn't get a moment to search social media for clues. It's frustrating me.

"So no more nasty comments aimed at you?" I glance at her again. Gia doesn't have a good poker face, so I'll be able to tell if she's hiding something.

She lets out a loaded sigh. "To be honest, I'm not checking the comments sections on my page or the Warriors socials right now. I've asked Ash to keep an eye on it. But please don't tell anyone. It's my job, after all. I just don't have enough spoons to deal with negativity online."

I already know she's been the victim of internet trolls before. If I keep asking about it, it will only sour her mood. But I hope we'll get to a point in our relationship where she'll trust me with her problems.

"Hey, a thought just occurred to me. Do you come to our away games?"

"Not always. It depends on my schedule."

"Are you coming this Friday?"

"Yeah... it's actually my birthday."

Shit. I knew that. When I realized that she was my dream girl, I learned everything about her, including her birthday. I can't believe I forgot it was coming up. The days have been a blur and I spaced out.

I'd better pretend I had no idea. "No way! We have to celebrate."

"Oh, don't worry about it. Just focus on the game."

"No, this is serious. I'm a firm believer that we should always celebrate birthdays, especially birthdays of someone we care about." I look at her quickly to gauge her reaction and have the satisfaction of seeing her cheeks turn pink. "Besides, what kind of boyfriend would I be if I let your birthday go by without a fuss?"

"My girlfriends are coming to Boston too."

"Is that so? Who?"

"Ashley, Zoey, and maybe Blair if I can convince her."

"Do you think Blair wants to be around her brother's former teammates?"

Gia bites her lower lip, distracting me to the point that the car swerves slightly to the left. Luckily, the left lane was empty.

"Well, she usually avoided them even before all the drama. And you know she doesn't get along with Alex."

"Alex can be such a big baby. I hope she comes. What about Harper?"

"I invited her, but she isn't coming, which isn't a surprise. She's always too busy to do anything fun."

"That's sad."

Gia shrugs. "I used to think so, but now I believe she's happy the way she is. She's miserable when she has downtime."

Until she's on the verge of a breakdown, like yesterday. I keep the thought to myself though. I don't want Gia to think I'm judgmental.

"I know that Ashley doesn't like hockey. Is she coming to the game?"

"Hmm... that I don't know."

I reach for her hand and bring it to my lips so I can kiss her knuckles.

"What was that for?" she asks.

"I was already super stoked about Friday, and you just made it ten times better." I keep our fingers interlaced, pleased with myself when Gia doesn't pull away. "So... what's the plan?"

"Not sure yet. Maybe clubbing after the game."

"Oh, boy, that means I'm going to need my lessons soon."

"Wait. Do you want to come dancing with us?"

I give her a droll look. "Darling, there's nothing in the world that's going to keep me away from you on your birthday. I mean, unless you don't want me to come."

"No, of course I want you to come. This isn't a girls' night out, although I'm pretty sure Ashley wishes it was."

"Why is that?"

"If you come, then that means some of the guys might as well, including Sean."

"True. What's the deal with her and Sean anyway? Why don't they get along?"

"I don't know. Now that you mention it, she gets irritated whenever I talk about him in a positive light."

"I really don't know what she could have against him. He's the nicest guy I know."

"Right? Anyway, Ashley is a bit complicated. But it'll be fine. There'll be lots of people there, and I can keep them separated."

"We can stick Ashley with Alex, and if Blair decides to come, she can keep Sean company. That way we avoid Armageddon."

She laughs. "I like the way you think."

GIA

I don't tell Noah, but I'm pretty excited about Friday too, and not only because I get to celebrate my birthday with my friends in Boston. He's the reason the butterflies are going crazy in my belly. Going out with our friends means really putting on a show that we're together. Although to be fair, it feels like we're a real couple, even when we're alone.

Traffic isn't as bad as Harper predicted, and we arrive at the Five Diamonds Hotel—where the event is taking place—just in time. Noah lets the valet take care of parking and then links his arm with mine before we walk through the automatic doors.

The hotel lobby is the size of a large atrium, but it feels like we're in a palace worthy of King Louis XIV. The high domed ceiling has classic paintings of angels, the beige marble floors shine, and the golden light fixtures tie the whole place together in a decadent bow. I'm surprised this is the location Steele Entertainment chose to host an event for a Gordon Montana movie.

We follow the signs pointing to the event, and just before we enter the ballroom, Noah asks if I want to check my coat.

"Oh yeah, I guess I should do that instead of carrying it around."

Because he's wearing a suit jacket, he skipped the coat. My dark-purple dress has long sleeves, but it's backless and form-fitting. It was a gift from Ryder, but I never got to wear it while we were dating. It's sinfully hot and yet comfortable thanks to the soft velvet material, which has a bit of stretch. Maybe it's silly of me, but I purposely wanted to wear it on this date with Noah. Let him reap the benefits.

Noah's eyes bug out when he sees it, and I can't help my satisfied grin. He gives me an elevator glance that feels like a caress. The memory of him talking dirty to me in the elevator comes to the forefront of my mind, and now I'm turned on as hell.

"Wow," he blurts out. "Is that all for me?"

"Do you like it?" I do a quick spin so he can see the back.

"Do I *like* it? You're kidding me, right? I have half a mind to forget the event, take you back to your place, and finish what we started last night."

My pulse skyrockets and heat spreads through my cheeks. It's pointless to put up a fight. I can't deny the chemistry between us and how badly I want him to do all those naughty things to me.

"Now behave," I say.

"Behave? If you truly wanted me to behave, you shouldn't have worn *that*." He takes my hand and pulls me flush against his body. Leaning closer, he whispers in my ear, "As a matter of fact, I think you're doing it on purpose. You want me to lose control, don't you?"

I pull back and look into his eyes. "Of course not."

Liar, liar, pants on fire.

He narrows his eyes, letting me know he's seeing through my ruse.

"Hey Gia, Noah. You're here!" Harper says from the ballroom door.

I turn, but Noah doesn't let go of my hand. "Hey, Harper. We just got here."

"Awesome. I'll walk you in."

"How's everything? Did the boxes arrive in time?" he asks.

"Oh, yeah. The courier picked them up this morning."

"What about Adrian Steele?" he continues.

I give him a warning look, and in turn, he widens his eyes innocently as if to ask, *What did I do?*

"He's not here yet. But I'm sure he'll show up eventually, probably drunk."

I'm sure Noah wants to comment on that, but I squeeze his hand harder and ask her, "So besides, Gordon, who else from the movie will be here?"

"Gretchen McCoy and Philip Williams."

I expect Noah to be enthusiastic about meeting Gretchen. She was voted one of the sexiest actresses in Hollywood several years in a row, and in every movie she's been in, they've exploited her sex appeal. But Noah doesn't make a peep.

Harper excuses herself because she has work to do, and we

head toward the open bar. The room isn't busy yet, and the few people here are standing in small clusters talking. I spy the boxes we put together lying prettily on a long table by the wide windows in the room, and I shiver.

"I don't know about you, but if I never see another box like that, it'll be too soon," Noah jokes.

"Ditto. I'm surprised you didn't want to meet Gretchen."

"Why would I want to meet some actress when I have the most beautiful girl in the world with me?"

The bartender laughs. "Good answer, buddy."

"It's the honest truth. Look at my date. Actually, scratch that, don't look at her."

The bartender grins and shakes his head. "What can I get you to drink?"

"I'll have club soda," Gia replies.

"Me too."

The guy chuckles. "You guys party hard."

"Oh yeah, we're party animals." Noah looks at me, giving me that mischievous smile that makes me forget all the reasons I shouldn't fall for his charms.

"My, my... look who's here."

My stomach dips and my blood runs cold. I turn and come face to face with Ryder, who's smiling at us in a chilling way.

I know that look well, and he usually saves it for his enemies.

CHAPTER 27
GIA

I don't need to look at Noah to know he's as tense as a board and staring daggers at Ryder.

"What are *you* doing here?" he asks before I can say anything.

Oh boy. Here we go. I don't even blame him for his reaction. Ryder is projecting an aggressive stance too.

Ryder looks at him as if he's an insignificant insect. "Excuse me?"

"What do you want, Ryder?" I butt in before things escalate.

"What?" He arches his brows innocently, softening his facial expression. "I just came to say hello. Am I not allowed to greet an old friend?"

"We aren't friends," I grit out.

He looks me up and down. "I see you're wearing the dress I gave you. It looks nice on you; like I knew it would."

I can't believe he mentioned the dress was a gift from him. Fucking jackass.

Noah cuts me a look that tells me he feels betrayed, but he schools his expression into a cold mask in the next second. I'm not going to explain myself to him while Ryder is watching. That's exactly what he wants.

Instead, I step closer to Noah, linking my arm with his. "Yes, now someone special gets to reap the benefits."

Ryder twists his face into a scowl, and the animosity returns to his eyes. Before he can offer a retort, Harper comes in to run interference. "Is everything okay?"

He turns to her. "Why wouldn't it be? I haven't seen Adrian yet. Is he here?"

Harper flattens her lips. "I'm not his babysitter, Ryder. Why don't you call him?"

"Jeez, what's with everyone today?" he asks like he's not acting like an asshole.

She shifts her attention to us. "Do you want to meet Gordon Montana now?"

Shit. I didn't have a chance to tell her that Noah changed his mind about meeting Gordon, so I'm surprised when he says, "Sure."

"Follow me, then."

"Hey, I want to meet him too." Ryder opens his big mouth, reminding me that he's also a fan.

Harper gives him a nasty glance. "Sorry. You don't have VIP privileges. You can meet him when everybody else does."

Amusement bubbles up my throat, but I manage to keep it bottled. Noah doesn't care to restrain his glee and snorts loudly.

Ryder narrows his eyes, his jaw working hard. A second later he mutters "Whatever" and walks away with his phone already glued to his ear.

"What a fucking douche," Noah blurts out.

"You can say that again," Harper pipes up.

I can't deny that Ryder acted like a jackass, but the whole interaction made me feel like shit. I dated the guy for a year. Was he always like that? Was I an idiot for not seeing it?

We follow Harper across the room and through a set of doors until we reach the greenroom. It's like a second party is taking place here. There's a huge spread of food on a long table, another bar, and several couches and chairs that look super comfy.

Gordon Montana is sprawled on one of them, holding his phone in one hand and a glass of whiskey in the other. He looks exactly as he does in his movies, with the trademark bald head and lips that are curled into a perpetual smirk. He's in his late fifties, but he's still damn fine and in top shape. I can see his biceps bulging underneath his jacket.

Harper walks toward him with confidence, her high-heeled shoes tapping rhythmically against the floor. I glance at Noah to see how he's doing. He seems relaxed. I'm not even a fan of the guy, and I'm a little nervous.

Gordon looks up when he senses our approach.

"Hi, Mr. Montana. These are the friends I mentioned before. Gia Mancini and Noah Kingsley."

"Harper, I already asked you to call me Gordon." He smiles kindly, putting me at ease.

He stands and shakes hands with Noah and me. "Nice to meet you, Gia and Noah. Thanks for coming."

Noah doesn't say anything, only stares with his mouth agape and a starstruck gleam in his eyes.

"We're so excited to be here and can't wait to see the movie," I reply even though I have no clue what the movie is about.

"You'll get the chance to see it tonight."

"We will?" Noah blurts out finally. "That's awesome. I'm such a huge fan."

Gordon smiles, making the creases on the corners of his eyes sharper. "Harper told me you play for the Warriors."

"Yes, sir. Center."

He leans closer, almost as if he's about to tell us a secret. "Did you know that I played hockey in high school?"

"No, I didn't. Although perhaps not knowing that fact disqualifies me as a huge fan."

Gordon waves his hand. "It's a detail no one cares about. I wasn't good enough to get a scholarship and play in college. Fate would have it that I'd end up in Hollywood instead. I still love the game though. Your team is pretty good, huh?"

"Yes, sir."

"They went all the way to the Frozen Four," Harper chimes in.

That's a sore spot I wish she hadn't brought up. I wasn't part of the team then, but it pains me just the same.

"Season's started already, right?" Gordon asks, thankfully not making a comment about the Frozen Four. "When is your next game?"

"Actually, the first game is this Friday in Boston. We're playing at Ballard College."

Gordon's eyes light up. "Fantastic! I might be able to see you guys then. I'm planning to stick around the area for a few days."

"That'd be amazing."

"And we can get you a pass to visit the locker room and say hello to the players," I add.

"I'd appreciate that very much. Now, would you like a picture?"

"Absolutely!" Noah replies, unable to hide his excitement.

Seeing him this happy gives me more satisfaction than I expected. I'm usually joyful when my friends are, but this is different, and I can't explain why.

We take our places on either side of Gordon, and Harper takes pictures with Noah's phone, my phone, and hers. After that, Gordon signs promotional postcards for the entire team. I should watch more of his movies. I like to support nice people. When he's done, it's time for him to make his appearance at the party.

From the corner of my eye, I see Gretchen McCoy enter the greenroom. She's wearing a skintight catsuit and stilettos. Her long blonde hair cascades down her back in luscious, golden waves. She's gorgeous and one hundred percent worth the hype.

"Do you want to talk to Gretchen?" I ask Noah.

He spares her one quick glance, then turns to me. "No, I'd rather get out of here and get you out of that dress."

"What about the movie?"

"We can watch it later. I'm no longer in the mood for that."

The heat in his eyes tells me exactly what he's in the mood for, and I'm so on board with that.

CHAPTER 28
NOAH

I might be acting like a caveman here, but there's a primal need in me to rip Gia's dress off her body. Yes, I'm fucking annoyed that her ex bought the dress, but I also love the fact she never wore it while she was dating him. It's the type of clothing designed for *un*dressing. I almost lost my mind when she did that little pirouette for me. Now I'm in a hurry to get the fuck out of here so I can finally get her alone.

"Noah, slow down. It's hard to run in heels."

"Sorry, sunshine."

We stop by the coat check first, but the girl who took Gia's coat isn't around. I press the bell, then lean against the counter. "Hello, anyone back there?"

Nada.

"Maybe she went to the restroom," Gia pipes up.

"I guess we'll have to look for your coat ourselves." I brace my hands on the counter, then jump to the other side.

"What are you doing?"

"Going on a treasure hunt." I smirk. "Are you coming?"

She shakes her head and laughs. "You're crazy."

"Crazy for you."

She looks over her shoulder and then follows me to the other side of the counter. Her snug dress rises up her thighs, giving me a nice view of her toned legs. Man, I want those legs wrapped around my shoulders while I eat her out.

"I think she stuck my coat all the way in the back," she tells me.

"You'll have to help me because all black coats look the same."

"I know. Maybe I should adopt Blair's style and wear bright outerwear."

She continues checking the racks, but I'm no longer interested in locating her coat. I wanted to get her alone, and alone we are.

"Found it," she declares triumphantly, holding the hanger with her coat in her hand.

Before she can put it on, I push her against the cluster of coats and jackets, and slant my mouth over hers, coaxing her lips open with my tongue.

Something drops to the floor, and I realize it's her coat. She let go of it to hold my upper arms while I devour her mouth and lean against her, removing any space between us.

"I've been dying to do this since I saw you in this dress," I whisper against her lips.

"We're going to get caught. We should go."

"Relax, sunshine. No one can see us." I switch my attention to her neck, leaving a trail of open kisses on my way to her ear.

Gia arches her back, pressing her breasts against my chest. "The coat-check girl will probably return soon."

Probably, but I'm caught in a fever, and I'm beyond having smart thoughts. I run my hand down her naked back, making her shiver. Then I squeeze her sweet ass before my hand disappears underneath her dress.

"I thought the deal was for you to make me come with dirty talk first before I agreed to the benefits."

"Babe, we're beyond that. But don't worry, I'll dirty talk to you while my fingers are deep in your pussy." I reach for her panties, finding them soaked through already.

"Noah, this is insane," she breathes out.

"If it is, I don't want to be sane." I press my thumb against her clit through the fabric of her panties, and Gia moans against my lips. "You like that, don't you, sunshine?"

"*Yes.*"

I move the fabric to the side and slip one finger inside her pussy.

"Oh my God," she moans.

She's so wet that my finger slides in easily. I insert another finger and begin to pump in and out of her while pressing my thumb over her clit.

She clenches her legs together while her internal walls flex against my fingers. "That's it, babe. Work my fingers. Pretend it's my cock that you're milking."

"I need more."

I add another finger, and Gia lets out a loud gasp. "I love how wet you are for me, sunshine. I can't wait til it's my cock buried deep inside you, stretching you to the max."

"Faster, *faster*," she demands with her eyes closed.

I shove my tongue into her mouth, kissing her with the hunger of a starving man, while I fuck her with my fingers without mercy. When she tightens around them, I know she's close.

Instead of pressing my thumb against her clit, I flick it left and right. Her body jerks, and then she's coming all over my hand. I swallow her moans of pleasure, but her addictive sounds are making it hard for me to not follow her into *O* town. My balls tighten, forcing me to clench my butt cheeks to prevent an accidental spill. My dick is pressing against my pants in a delirious agony.

I don't stop moving my hand until Gia relaxes against my

body. I break the kiss, but only to rest my forehead against hers. We're breathing hard in sync.

"Are you okay, sunshine?"

"More than okay."

I chuckle, pleased to the max.

"Hey! You can't be back there," someone shouts, probably the coat-check girl.

Gia tenses in my arms. I pull my hand from under her dress and fix her skirt, which rode up. Then I pick up her coat from the floor and help her into it.

"Did you hear what I said?" The girl is closer now.

I turn to her with my most innocent expression, hoping my jacket covers the situation down my pants. "You weren't here, and we needed her coat."

She's openly glowering at us. "I need to see your ticket."

Gia retrieves the piece of paper from her purse. "Here."

The girl takes the ticket in a huff, but we don't wait for her to check the number. I take Gia's hand and steer her out of the coat-check room, this time using the door.

We don't speak as we speed walk through the hotel lobby. I do look at Gia briefly to make sure she's not mad at me. She doesn't seem to be, but her face is beet red.

While we wait outside for the valet to bring my truck, I throw an arm over her shoulder and pull her into a side hug. "Are you okay, sunshine?"

"I'm fine."

"Don't tell me you're embarrassed."

"We almost got caught."

"But we didn't." I lean closer to her ear. "And can I say that the sound you made back there was the hottest thing I've ever heard in my entire life?"

"You're impossible." She pouts, making me want to kiss her again. I refrain from doing it now, but I can't help the bright smile that splits my face.

✕ ✕ ✕

GIA

I can't believe I let Noah finger fuck me in a coat-check room. If that woman had come a minute earlier, she would have seen me in the midst of a mind-blowing orgasm. I've never done anything like that in my life. Never mind that I recklessly crossed that line with Noah. I don't know if it was the situation or the fear of getting caught at a moment's notice that made the experience so exhilarating. I've never orgasmed so fast. I don't have an ounce of regret in my heart, but the fear of getting hurt is there, more ominous than ever.

I have to keep this under control. There's no turning back now, and I don't want to return to our platonic status. My clit is still throbbing from the onslaught of Noah's expert fingers. I glance out the window and try to think of anything besides how much I want him to touch me again.

"You're awfully quiet," he says.

"I'm tired."

"Are you sure you're okay?"

I could lie and say everything is peachy. But for some reason, I feel comfortable sharing what's on my mind. Maybe because we aren't dating for real, and even though we added benefits to the equation, he's still my friend.

"Honestly? I'm a little nervous."

He looks at me. "Nervous? About what?"

"You know. Us. I haven't changed my mind about the nature of our relationship."

So why does it hurt to say it?

"You mean the fake nature of our relationship?"

"Yes."

"I see." He clenches his jaw.

"You're upset."

"I'm not upset."

"Your furrowed forehead says otherwise. Why do you want to date me so badly? You could have any girl you want."

He switches his attention to me again. "I don't want any girl. I want you. I'll just have to work harder to prove to you that I am *real* boyfriend material."

"I don't have any doubt about that, Noah. And that's the problem. I don't think you'd understand. It's hard to explain."

"You're afraid to get hurt again, aren't you?"

I bite the inside of my cheek and look out the window. I was determined to not have this conversation with him. What's the point of being friends with benefits if you can't do it without thinking too much about the consequences?

"I don't want to talk about it."

"Hey, we don't need to talk about anything. We're just having fun. Just know that I'd never *ever* hurt you."

I turn to him, and our eyes meet. I believe him wholeheartedly. Then why am I so afraid of what's happening between us? Oh yeah, he's only nineteen and surely doesn't really want or need a serious girlfriend right now. I don't believe he just wants to seduce me and ditch me, but young guys are fickle by nature.

"I believe you."

"And to prove that I'm not a jerk with a one-track mind, I'll drop you off at home and head back to my dorm. There's no need for you to reciprocate anything."

My eyebrows furrow. "That's not fair."

"It's okay, sunshine. I don't want to push you into anything you're not comfortable with."

"I think I can decide for myself what my limits are."

He smirks. "Oh yeah? And what do you have in mind?"

"You'll see."

He groans. "Man, I'm trying to be a nice guy here, but you make it so difficult. Do you have any idea how hard my dick is right now?"

"Maybe I can help you?" I reach for his crotch, but he covers my hand with his.

"As much as I want you to touch me, I need to keep my focus on the road."

My face bursts into flames. "Right... sorry."

He swallows hard, and I can hear it. "You have no idea how much I want to pull over and let you have your way with me."

"I'm pretty sure you'll be more comfortable at my place."

"Do you know all the dirty things I want to do to you?" His voice turns lower, huskier.

"No. Why don't you tell me?"

He narrows his eyes. "You're trying to make me lose control again. You're playing with fire, sunshine."

Suddenly the truck accelerates, and my spine presses against the back of the seat. We hit the highway, and Noah seems intent on getting us back to my apartment as fast as he can.

"Somebody's in a hurry to get to campus."

"You have *no* idea."

We do make it back in record time. Noah doesn't tell me what he plans to do to me, and it's driving me insane. The suspense is also turning me on.

He parks the truck in the visitors' lot in front of my building, and then tries to get to my door before I get out, but I'm faster than him. He pushes me against the side of the truck though, and claims my mouth. His tongue is possessive, but the kiss isn't rough. It's tender and lazy. I get light-headed, almost delirious. Never mind what his kiss is doing to my pussy. My clit is throbbing, and if I were to cross my legs and move a certain way, I could probably climax again.

My body melts into his, and I don't know if I'll be able to walk to my building with the way my legs have turned to jelly. He pulls back, ending the kiss, and stares at me with eyes filled with desire.

"Shall we?" he asks in a tight voice.

I nod, unable to utter a single word. My ears are buzzing, and my heart is beating at breakneck speed. My skin tingles, hot and alive. We're really doing this. As terrified as I am of getting hurt, I'm jumping off the edge.

We're about to cross the street when I hear a soft whine from the direction of the recycling container on the side of the lot to our right. The school installed the units near all student residence halls.

"Did you hear that?" I ask.

"I did."

We stop and wait. The whine comes again, but this time, it sounds like two distinct noises.

"There's something there," Noah says, already steering me in that direction.

On the other side of the container, we find a cardboard box that's closed on top but has small holes in the sides. Now the whining is pretty obvious.

"What do you think is inside?" I ask.

Noah drops into a crouch in front of the box. "Only one way to find out. Can you hit me with your flashlight, babe?"

I take my phone out of my purse and aim the beam at the box.

Noah flips the lid open carefully, and then gasps. "Son of a bitch. I can't believe this."

I can't either. Inside the box, we find puppies. They're so small and still have their eyes closed—they must be newborns. My eyes fill with tears. Who would do something so cruel?

"Oh my God. I can't believe someone would do that."

Noah closes the box again and picks it up. "We need to bring them inside."

"Shouldn't we bring them to a vet?"

"Yeah, but I want to get them warm first. Who knows how long they've been here?"

"Good thinking."

We hurry across the parking lot, and then we wait impatiently for the elevator to arrive. Noah opens the box again. "It's okay, little guys. We're going to take care of you."

I'm still upset about finding those puppies left in the cold to die, but seeing the sweet way Noah talks to them makes warmth flood through my chest.

I didn't want to fall for him, but I think it might already be too late.

CHAPTER 29
GIA

As soon as I open my door, Noah rushes inside and places the box of puppies on my coffee table. I hurry to my room and grab a couple of thick blankets to wrap around them.

"How many are there?" I ask when I return to the living room.

"Seven. I think they're Dalmatians." Noah takes one out of the box, and it makes an adorable sound. "Hello, little guy. Don't you worry, you and your siblings are safe now."

Every time I think Noah can't become even more adorable and irresistible, he proves me wrong. My heart is melting again.

I sit next to him on the couch—butterflies fluttering in chaos in my belly—and give him one of the blankets. "Here."

"Thank you."

"He's so tiny."

"He's the smallest of the bunch." Noah puts his index finger close to the puppy's mouth, and the pup immediately tries to suck it. "I think he's hungry."

"We need to get them warm before anything else. If we wrap the blankets around them and hold them against our bodies, it'll be faster."

He nods. "That's what I was thinking."

I open the blanket over my lap, and Noah places three puppies on it. They whine and squirm but at least they're moving. One tries to roll off my lap, but I push it closer to the other two. "Where do you think you're going?"

"You got a runaway?" Noah laughs.

"Yeah. They're restless. I guess that's a good sign."

"For sure. If they were lethargic, that'd be a red flag."

He sets his share of puppies over his lap, and like me, he covers them with his blanket before picking up the bundle and holding it to his chest. I do the same. If someone walked into my apartment right now, they'd think we're cradling two babies.

"They're so stinking cute." Noah stares down at them, smiling softly. "I want to keep one."

"They don't allow pets in student halls."

He turns to me. "Even here?"

I hate to tell him that the rule applies to all student halls, especially when I'm smitten with the puppies and would love to keep one too. "I'm afraid so."

"That sucks." He looks at the puppies in his arms again and then says, "What if we don't tell anyone?"

"How do you plan on hiding a Dalmatian in your tiny dorm room?"

"I was hoping we could adopt one puppy and keep him here?"

The way he's looking at me now, so eager and hopeful, takes my breath away. It also plays keep-away with my intelligence. I should say a flat no to the idea because it's insane, but that's not what comes out of my mouth.

"You want to get a puppy together?" I squeak.

"Yeah."

My heart does several cartwheels and takes off skipping into the sunset. "That goes beyond being friends with benefits."

He quirks an eyebrow. "Does it? I think friends can share a pet."

"I don't even know if Harper would be okay with it."

He turns his bundle toward me. "Do you think she's going to say no to this cuteness overload?"

I shake my head. "We can talk about that later."

He smiles impishly. "Are you saying you're going to think about it?"

"Yes. Now let's focus on getting these puppies fed. I have some milk, but I'm not sure if they should be drinking that. Are they like human babies? Would they need formula?"

He furrows his brows. "I don't know. I'll google it."

After a couple minutes of searching the Internet, he says, "Yup. They need to drink a special formula."

"Makes sense. Now that they aren't in danger of freezing to death, we should take them to a vet."

"Agreed." Noah glances at his puppies. "What do you say, guys? Are you ready for a road trip?"

A smile tugs the corner of my lips. He really needs to stop being swoony when he talks to the pups. It's making him so much more irresistible, and he's not even trying to get into my pants now.

He glances at me and catches me staring. "What?"

I shake my head, hoping I'm not blushing. "Nothing."

His wicked smile tells me he knows exactly what I was thinking. Curse my inability to hide my emotions. "It seems our plans got derailed again."

"Maybe that's a sign that we should remain friends without all the benefits," I reply, not really meaning it.

His eyes widen. "Please tell me you're joking."

I jump from the couch and place my puppies back in the box, but this time with the blanket underneath them. "We should go. We don't know how long they've been without food."

"Nice evasion, sunshine. I'll let it slide this time because, you know.... puppies need our help."

"Do you think I can change out of this dress? I'll be quick."

His face falls. "I was hoping to have the pleasure of helping you out of it."

I smirk. "You'll have another chance."

"Hell no. I don't want to see you wearing that dress ever again."

My eyebrows arch. "Why? Because it was a gift from Ryder?"

"Damn straight."

I usually don't like guys acting overly jealous, but seeing Noah behave like that sends a rush of guilty pleasure through my veins.

"But I love this dress." I tease, opening my coat then running my hand over my stomach. "It fits me like a glove."

He narrows his eyes and clenches his jaw so hard his cheeks hollow. "Do you know what else will fit you like a glove?" he grits out. "My cock, deep inside your pussy."

"Wouldn't it be the other way around?" I arch an eyebrow.

He makes a deep sound in the back of his throat that's pure male. "Careful, sunshine. You're playing with fire."

Hell and damn. If sweet Noah was dangerous when he talked dirty, angry Noah is ten times more lethal to my self-control. I swallow hard, and then close my coat hastily.

"I won't change. Let's go."

CHAPTER 30
NOAH

I'm not one to let jealousy overwhelm me, but Gia teasing me with that damn dress her ex gave her did the trick. I saw red, and if it weren't for the puppies needing our help, I would have jumped from the couch and ripped the dress to shreds before I followed through on my intentions.

At this hour, the only place we can go is the emergency vet, which, luckily, isn't far from campus. Gia rides in the back seat so she can keep an eye on the puppies, which results in a very silent trip. But at least she can't see me pouting, which I totally am like a damn child.

Noah, get your act together.

Ten minutes later, I park the truck in front of the vet's office and help Gia with the box. I don't make eye contact with her lest she see I'm still in a foul mood. Instead, I open the lid and peer at the puppies quickly.

"Some fell asleep," she tells me.

I feel a little pinch in my chest. "I hope that isn't a bad sign."

We go inside the building together and take turns explaining the situation to the lady behind the counter. She asks to see the puppies and then purses her lips.

"I can't believe someone would leave these poor babies out in the cold."

"We're lucky we heard them," I reply.

"Yes, they were very lucky."

I don't correct her. I meant to say *we* because I can't help but feel we found a winning lottery ticket. I've always wanted a dog, but my parents are allergic to them.

"You'll need to fill out this form. The vet will see you shortly."

Gia takes the clipboard and pen, and I carry the box. We sit next to each other, but there's a new tension between us that I don't like.

"I'm sorry," I say.

"About what?"

"About the dress. It was stupid. I don't know what came over me."

Instead of agreeing with me, she smiles. "It's okay. I get it. I wouldn't like to see you wearing something an ex-girlfriend gave you."

"You already know I never had a girlfriend before."

"True, but if you did, I'd hate that."

I perk up in my seat while a jolt of adrenaline makes my heart beat faster. "Why is that, Gia? I thought we were only friends."

A blush spreads through her cheeks. It's like a punch to my chest, releasing all the pressure. I love making her face go red like that.

She turns her attention back to the form on her lap. "I need to fill this out."

One of the puppies begins to whine, so I put a pin in the conversation and focus on them. It turns out it's the smallest one who's awake and making a fuss. I fish him out of the box and bring him close to my face.

"What's the matter, little guy? We don't want to wake your brothers and sister."

From the corner of my eye, I notice Gia stops writing to watch us. I don't look at her this time but keep my attention on the little bugger that I already know is mine.

"I think he's the one," she says after a moment.

Now I turn to her. "Yeah, how did you know?"

She tilts her head. "The look on your face. You're in love."

I reach for her, tucking a loose strand that fell out of place behind her ear. "Yeah, I am."

She blinks fast before leaning back. That was a loaded declaration, and she must know I wasn't only speaking about the puppy. I probably said too much, and now she's freaking out. I'm an idiot.

I don't have time to try to save the situation. The vet assistant tells us we can bring the puppies to the examination room. I place my guy back in the box and close the lid so the bright light won't bother them.

Gia returns the form to the front desk clerk, then we follow the vet assistant down the hallway until she stops at an open door.

"Dr. Mitchell will see you now."

I expect a young vet who's working at this hour to pay his dues, but instead, we get a skinnier version of Santa Claus. Dr. Mitchell's hair is as white as snow, matching his trimmed beard. At the end of his nose sit wire-framed glasses, which he fixes when we enter the room.

"Good evening. It seems someone left behind a box of little wonders."

"Yes. We tried to keep them warm, but I'm afraid they're starving," I reply.

"Let's see what we have here. Just set the box on the examination table, please."

He takes the puppies out of the box one at a time to examine and weigh them. It's a slow process since there are seven. My little guy is the last one to be checked, and he's the one making the most fuss.

"This one is feisty." The vet laughs.

"Yes. That's mine."

He looks up. "You're keeping one? Good for you. What about the others?"

"We don't know yet," Gia replies. "We just want to make sure we can take care of them properly until we figure it out."

"They're newborns, so they'll need intense care for the next weeks."

I trade a glance with Gia, trying to read her thoughts on the matter. Taking care one of one puppy is already a big deal, but seven? I don't want to turn my back on them though.

"We can foster until we find forever homes for them," she replies.

My heart expands and overflows with emotion. I didn't think I could fall harder for her, yet she keeps proving me wrong. An overwhelming desire to hold her tight in my arms hits me. If we were alone, I wouldn't contain myself.

"Are you sure?" the vet asks. "That's a lot of work. They need to be fed every three to four hours for the first two weeks, then six to eight hours between two and four weeks of age."

"We can handle it," I reply with confidence, which I'm mostly faking.

"All right. They'll need their first shots around six weeks."

"Besides that, they're okay, right?" I ask.

"Yes, you must have found them soon after they were left behind. They're just hungry now. I have formula samples and small bottles for you. If you're determined to foster them, I need to show you the ropes."

Dr. Mitchell calls his assistant in, then shows us how to prepare the formula and feed the puppies. We each feed two puppies at a time, besides the vet, who's holding my little guy.

"Now, be careful to not overfeed them. It can give them diarrhea. Just follow the instructions to calculate the correct amount," he tells us.

"Yikes, we definitely don't want that." I chuckle.

"It's late, so I'll give you enough formula to last you through the night until you can get to a pet store."

"Thank you so much," Gia replies.

After the feeding sesh is done, we put the puppies back in the box, and then I take care of paying the bill. It's more than I expected, and I have to use the credit card I have for emergencies. My parents won't care, but I don't like to abuse their generosity. I'm a firm believer that I'm not owed anything just because *they* are well-to-do. I make a mental note to put the amount in the spreadsheet I've kept since hockey started. I vowed to pay back my parents for every cent they've invested in my career.

"Noah, that's too much. Let me pay for half," Gia says.

"It's okay, sunshine. I got this."

She pinches her lips. "Taking care of the puppies will be expensive. I don't expect you to pay for everything. I volunteered to foster them with you."

"Only because you read my mind. I was about to do the same."

"Still. It's only fair that we share the financial burden."

The hard set of her brows tells me she's not going to back down. I feel bad letting her contribute. Scholarships don't cover everything and living in Fairbanks is expensive. But I have to respect her decision.

"Okay. Let me cover tonight's vet bill, and you can buy the formula. I'm sure it won't be cheap."

Her expression softens, and I notice a hint of surprise in her eyes. "Oh, okay. Thank you."

On the way out of the vet's office, I ask, "You didn't think I'd agree with you, did you?"

"Honestly, no. I thought you'd be a pigheaded about it."

"I can be stubborn, but not at the expense of your happiness. Would you get the door for me?" I stop next to my truck.

"How did you know sharing the costs of fostering the puppies would make me happy?"

I set the box in the back seat and then look at her. "Because I know you, sunshine."

The parking lot is not well lit, but she's standing close to me, and I notice her beautiful eyes turn rounder. There's a tug in my chest, and a second later, it accelerates. The air between us seems to crackle with electricity. This would be a prime opportunity to steal another kiss from her, but I just drink her in instead.

"We should go." She slides into the back seat, breaking the connection.

I close the door after her and walk around to the driver's side slowly. My body is shaking, filled with raw emotion. Something just happened between us, and it was monumental. I think that maybe she's finally beginning to see me as more than a fake boyfriend with benefits.

CHAPTER 31
GIA

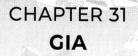

We ride back to campus in silence again, but this time, the atmosphere is heavy for a different reason. There's no misplaced jealousy toying with our emotions. It's something far more powerful—the truth about us. The one I've been trying to deny all along. I'm hot and cold at the same time. When he said he knew me, I felt it. The goose bumps that formed on my arms attest to that.

I'm thankful for the puppies. They provide a distraction. I need to get my thoughts in order and decide. Do I jump head-first into this new relationship with Noah, or do I end the charade for good?

He parks in the same spot as before, but everything is different. It's like months have passed, not only a few hours. When we returned from the party, I was horny and certain I wanted to get railed by him. Now there's so much more.

Like before, Noah takes the box, and I walk by his side, not daring to make a sound. My heart is making plenty of noise though, and it seems to increase in speed every time I sense Noah's stare. The first two instances, I pretend I don't notice him looking at me. The third time, we're waiting for the elevator in the lobby, and I lose my nerve.

"Tired?" I ask.

He smiles, then shakes his head. "No. You?"

I swallow hard before answering. "No."

We exchange only a few words, but the silence that stretches between us is loud and poignant. I'm trying to keep my balance on the tightrope and failing. There's no avoiding the fall. Will I crash against the solid ground or develop wings and fly?

"Good. I think these guys will keep us up all night."

He's not wrong about the puppies, but his sexy voice tells me other things will keep us up all night long.

"Right."

I'm a hot mess by the time we're finally standing in front of my apartment door. My hand is shaking as I insert the key, and I hope the box is blocking Noah's view. It's past ten, but inside, it's quiet and Harper's bedroom door is open. She's not back yet. I have a feeling the party will run late.

"Do you have another container for the puppies?" he asks.

"I do, but it's plastic, and I'm not sure if that's the best for them."

"I think we need a crate. I hate the sight of this box." He twists his face into a scowl as he stares at it.

"What if we switch them to a different box?"

He nods. "Yeah, I think that would work."

I go to my room and pull a big box out of my closet, emptying its contents all over my floor. I need to find another place to put the merch, but I can do that later. I grab a pair of scissors from my desk, and when I return to the living room, all seven puppies are clustered together on the living room rug. Noah looks up, sporting a guilty face.

"What happened?"

"Tiny puppies, small bladders. They made a mess out of the blankets."

A small smile tugs at the corners of my mouth. "You seemed so panicked I thought something worse happened, such as losing a puppy on the way here."

He widens his eyes, twisting his face into something I can only describe as sheer horror. "Don't even joke about that."

Laughter goes up my throat. "Okay, I won't. But did you count them to be sure?"

He squints. "Now you're just being mean."

I sit across from him, keeping the puppies between us. "I'm just teasing. Now that I know it's so easy to get you riled up, be prepared."

"Two can play at this game, sunshine. Let's see who can tease harder."

This is full-on flirtation, and the fluttering in my stomach says so. But I can't stop. I don't want to stop. As nervous as I still am, it seems I've already decided.

"Is that a challenge, Noah Kingsley?"

His face splits into the broadest grin. "You betcha."

"You're on."

One of the puppies decides to move away from the group, and no surprise, it's the one Noah is adopting.

"Your son is running away."

He picks him up and cradles him against his chest. "*Our* son."

I snort. "Our?"

"Am I wrong?" He quirks an eyebrow.

I stare at him for a couple beats just to fill him with doubt. I wasn't kidding when I declared the teasing session open.

"I'm not sure I want to co-parent with you. Maybe I'll get a puppy of my own."

His jaw slackens. "Aww. For real?"

I cover my mouth with my hand, trying to hide my amusement.

"Are you yanking my chain? You are, aren't you?"

No point keeping the laughter contained. I have a terrible poker face anyway.

"You're the devil, woman."

"You just make it too easy. But anyway, sure, I'll co-parent with you. But only if you do your share of the work."

"Of course. I won't let you do it all by yourself, but that means I have to spend a few nights here, you know, to help while they're young." His voice cracks a little. Is he afraid I'm going to back down?

"I'm okay with that."

I don't get a smile; I get a smoldering look that melts my bones and makes me want to yank the clothes off my body.

"What time do you think Harper will get home?"

"I'm betting late."

We don't speak for a couple beats, then Noah glances at the new cardboard box I brought. "Let's get these puppies into their new bed."

CHAPTER 32
NOAH

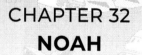

Standing together in the living room, we watch our puppies sleep in their new bed. The soiled blankets have been put away in the laundry basket, and our hands are scrubbed clean, but the thoughts in my head couldn't be dirtier. I'm all too aware of Gia and how my body is being pulled into her magnetic field.

"Should we bring them to my room?" she whispers.

"No," my voice comes out like a growl.

She turns to me with her electrifying gaze, and I'm in flames in an instant. Then it happens. The invisible cord restraining us snaps and we collide. I grab her face between my hands and fuse my mouth with hers in every way possible way—lips, tongue, and teeth. I don't want her to escape before I can satiate my hunger for her.

She flattens her hands against my stomach, then slides them down and under my shirt. Her hands are a bit cold, but even so, they can't douse the fire coursing through me. She runs her finger up and down my abs, leaving a trail of goose bumps in their wake. I wish she'd travel south because I'm already dying here. My cock is as hard as a rock, pressing against my slacks. If I don't find release tonight, it'll be a very miserable evening.

But she reads my mind and grants my wish. Her fingers make quick work of the button and zipper, then she slides her hand through the opening. I groan, letting go of her face and grabbing her ass instead.

She frees my cock, curling her fingers around it and drawing a guttural sound from deep in my throat. Easing back a little, she whispers against my mouth, "Bedroom."

Propelled by a brand-new urgency, I pick her up and toss her over my shoulder, keeping my arms wrapped firmly around the back of her legs.

"Noah! What are you doing?" She tenses, working to keep from diving headfirst. Like I'd ever drop her.

"Getting you to bed." I reach her room in three long strides, and by a miracle, my pants don't slide down my legs.

"You're crazy," she says through laughter.

"For you."

I set her down instead of tossing her on the mattress like a caveman—although that would be hot as hell. Next time. As much as I'm burning for Gia, I'm determined to take my time. Fucking this up is not an option. I have promises to keep. I told her I'd ruin her for other men, and I intend to prove that.

I kiss her again, deep and hard, pulling her tight against my chest. She melts into me, circling her arms around my lower back. Then she squeezes my ass and says, "I was dying to do this."

"You can squeeze me anytime, sunshine."

She pushes me back, creating a gap between us. I begin to frown, but she drops to her knees and, keeping her eyes on my face, pulls my slacks and briefs down to mid-thigh. My raging erection pops up, hitting my belly.

I inhale deeply, fighting to keep my heart from hammering out of my chest. "What are you doing, babe?"

"I'm returning the favor." She curls her fingers around my length and presses her thumb over the top, spreading precum over the sensitive skin.

I jerk forward, my balls tightening immediately. "Gia, babe, you're killing me."

"Your cock is beautiful, Noah. I bet it tastes amazing too."

Holy shit. My girl likes to talk dirty. I'm in heaven. I run my fingers through her curls, ruining her pretty hairdo, then I twist my fingers around a lock of her hair and yank a little. "You're a naughty girl with a filthy mouth."

Her lips curl into a devious grin, making me even harder. "I'll show you how filthy my mouth can be."

She licks my length from the bottom to the top slowly, making me shiver. It's delirious torture. When she stops and makes lazy circles with her warm tongue over the head, I almost lose my mind completely.

Tightening my hold on her hair, I groan, "Fuck."

"In a minute," she replies, watching me with those big and mischievous hazel eyes. Then she sucks my cock into her mouth until the head hits the back of her throat.

"Holy fucking shit," I blurt out, trying my best to let her set the pace instead of pistoning in and out of her mouth.

Keeping her fingers wrapped around the base, she sucks me in and out while working her tongue at the same time. I've never experienced a blow job that felt like a real pussy, and I'm quickly spiraling out of control.

Unable to stop, I pump my hips, fucking Gia's sweet mouth. Tendrils of desire have a vise hold at the base of my spine, and my balls are stretched tight, ready to explode. In all my wildest fantasies about Gia, I didn't imagine the first time I'd come would be in her mouth.

"That's it, babe. You're so good at sucking me."

With her free hand, she plays with my balls, squeezing them gently. Jesus fucking Christ. That's my undoing.

I move faster, chasing the orgasm that's around the corner. Gia takes everything I give her, all of me, and the sight of her down on her knees, working my cock like that—it's the most erotic thing I've ever seen.

"I'm gonna come," I say just before I empty myself into her mouth. I keep pumping my hips and Gia keeps drinking every single drop.

I give a final thrust before awareness returns to my body, and I realize maybe I took things a little too far in the heat of the moment. Letting go of her hair, I pull out, then I cradle her face with my hand. "Are you okay, sunshine?"

She sits on the back of her legs and wipes the corner of her mouth. "I was right. You do taste amazing."

I help her back onto her feet and then kiss her hard. The wave of pleasure has not withdrawn yet, and my body is still shaking from it. She places her hands on my forearms and lets me worship her mouth. But I'm still burning from her, and now it's my time to have some fun.

Leaning back, I look into her eyes. *"You're* amazing."

A blush creeps up to her cheeks, but she holds my stare. "Ditto."

Her response makes me chuckle. "Now it's my turn for a taste."

I nudge her back, making her sit on the edge of her bed, then I drop to my knees and hike up her skirt until her lacy panties are exposed. I don't stop there, though, I push the fabric all the way up.

"Lift your arms for me, sunshine."

She does so, and when the dress is off, her perky breasts become a distraction that makes my mouth water, but I have other priorities. I twist the velvet fabric, turning it into a rope, and then bind her wrists together before she has the chance to lower her arms.

"What are you doing?"

I reward her with a crooked grin. "Just relax, babe. Do you trust me?"

Her eyelids drop halfway as she stares at my mouth. "Yes."

"Good girl. Now lie down and spread your legs wide."

She swallows hard before following my instructions. She's

shaking though, so I add. "There's no need to be nervous. I'll make you feel good. Promise."

"I'm not nervous."

"Good." I place my hands on her inner thighs and her hips buck. "Shhh. It's okay."

Slowly, I run my fingers toward her pussy, but I just toy with the edge of her panties at first.

"Noah, why are you torturing me like this?" she breathes out.

"Patience, sunshine."

"I don't have any."

"Is that so? Tell me how badly you want my mouth on your pussy."

"I'm sure you can tell."

"I want to hear you say it."

"Just eat me out already."

Fuck if that doesn't feel like she's fisting my cock right now. I have a raging boner again, and I can't wait to sheathe myself in her heat.

Not moving my fingers from the edge of her underwear, I lean closer and blow hot air against her clit.

Gia squirms again, and her legs tense. "Noah, please…"

I could torture her a bit longer, but she's not the only one without patience. I slide two fingers under the sheer fabric and press them against her clit.

"Oh fuck," she blurts out, lifting her hips again.

"Soon," I reply, repeating what she told me earlier.

She's already slick, so I slide my fingers left and right over her clit, making her moan loudly. My cock twitches, begging to be allowed to play.

Not yet.

I pull away so I can get rid of her panties. I almost weep when her pussy opens up for me, all pink, glistening, and bare, ready for the taking.

"Oh, babe. You're so beautiful."

"You talk too much."

I laugh. "But I thought you liked it when I talked."

"I do, but…"

I insert my index finger into her pussy, and she arches her back.

"You were saying?" I tease while curling my finger inside her, looking for her sweet spot.

She flexes her legs, trying to close them. "Oh my God, Noah."

"You like that, don't you, my sexy girl?" I insert another finger and then rotate them.

She brings her bound wrists to her lips and mumbles something I can't hear. I decide then that I tortured us both enough, so I place her legs over my shoulders, lean closer, and suck her clit into my mouth.

Gia cries out against her binding, sending an electroshock of desire straight to my balls. I want to fuck her so badly it's not even funny. But I also want to make her come all over my tongue. I alternate licking and sucking her clit while I finger fuck her. She tastes like the nectar of the gods, and I can't get enough.

I'm lost in the moment, focusing on making my girl feel damn good. Then I feel her fingers in my hair. I didn't tie her hands to the headboard, so she can still reach me. She yanks my hair at the strands, and the bit of pain spurs me on. It becomes harder to keep from spilling my cum all over her floor, but I concentrate on it. The next time I come, it will be inside her pussy.

"I'm close, Noah. Don't stop."

Not a chance of that happening, sunshine. Everything fades besides us, and the only sound I can hear is of my tongue working her bundle of nerves and the delirious moans coming from her mouth.

She jerks suddenly, shouting my name. Her body convulses, and her clit throbs in my mouth. I keep eating her until she relaxes against the mattress. Then I jump to my feet and fish a condom from my jacket pocket, which I never bothered to take off. I get rid of it now, and my shirt.

Gia has her eyes closed and her breathing is uneven. But when I tear the condom wrapper, she looks at me.

"I need to be inside of you, babe. But if you tell me to stop, I will."

She furrows her brows together. "Tell you to stop? Are you out of your mind? I've never wanted to be railed by anyone more than I do right now."

Relief washes over me. "Thank fuck."

I roll the condom down my length, then I join her in bed. Gia brings her knees up, opening her legs wide for me.

"Are you going to keep me tied like this?"

I bring my nose to her neck and my cock to her entrance. "Yes."

She loops her arms around my shoulders and crosses her ankles behind my ass. The shift makes my cock slide into her slick heat a little.

"Damn it. You feel so good."

"I need all of you, Noah."

"Don't need to tell me twice, sunshine." I bury myself in her to the hilt, and then I don't move for a beat or two. I need to focus so I won't come too soon.

"Are you okay?" she asks.

"Yeah, babe. I'm good, so *so* good."

I pull back almost all the way only to hammer into her again hard. She tosses her head back and cries out.

"Look at me, beautiful." I frame her face with my hands.

We lock gazes and don't speak for a moment. I want to memorize every detail of her face while I fuck her. But when I'm in serious danger of telling her how I truly feel about her, I kiss her and then surrender to the desire wrapped around us.

CHAPTER 33
GIA

While Noah pounds into me, I work to free my wrists from the improvised rope he made from my dress. What he did can't be good for the material, although maybe that was his wicked way of making sure I never wear this dress again. It was too hot of a gesture for me to complain. But now, I'm dying to unbind my wrists so I can touch him everywhere.

Noah is too focused on fucking me into oblivion to notice what I'm doing. To be fair, it's hard to concentrate on the task when he's making me feel so good already. His cock is stretching me in the most pleasant way, and he's hitting me in just the right spot.

Finally, the fabric slackens, and with another pull, I untie the knot completely. It's only then that Noah notices what I'm up to.

He leans back to give me a stern look. "Hey, who said you could remove the binding?"

"I did, so I could do this." I run my long nails down his back, scratching him a little.

He kisses the corner of my mouth and whispers, "You're one devious kitten."

"I know. You aren't the only naughty person in this room, babe."

He jerks back, eyes as round as saucers, and stops fucking me for a second. "You called me babe."

I quirk an eyebrow. "Yeah, so?"

Slowly, his lips spread into his panty-melting smile. "I love it."

"Good."

He curls his arm under my right leg and hoists it over his shoulder, lifting my hips off the mattress in the process. When he pistons into me again, I cry out, loving this new angle.

"That's it, babe. Show me how much you love my big cock filling you, stretching you to the max."

He's kneeling on the mattress now, hovering over me and away from my hands. But he's already turning my brain into fluffy clouds, so I close my eyes and press a closed fist against my forehead while clutching the sheet with the other.

"Fuck me harder."

"As you wish." He digs his fingers into my hips and begins moving at breakneck speed. The headboard bangs against the wall, making a god-awful noise.

Not a moment later, there's a loud knock on the wall. The neighbors are complaining. Noah stops for a second, but I tell him, "Ignore them."

"Good, cause I don't want to slow down."

I know we aren't being very neighborly, but I'm beyond being nice. I'm about to see stars, and nothing is going to keep me from them.

Noah groans, "I love the way your pussy milks my cock, sunshine. Tell me you're close."

I'm about to reply that yes, I'm close, but it's too late. The orgasm hits me like a tsunami, dragging me under and into a whirlpool of mindless bliss. I tumble, losing all sense of direction, before I break into pieces, floating away in a vast ocean.

He gets harder right before his cock throbs inside of me and a string of incoherent words leaves his mouth. With a final thrust, he sets my leg down and crashes his lips against mine.

Finally able to touch him again, I hold his face between my hands and let myself drown in him. My heart is beating at the speed of light, and not because of sex. It's pumping with euphoria, and I want to grab on to this feeling and never let go.

He rolls onto his side, pulling me with him. He's no longer inside of me, but it's like we can't quite let go of each other. Eventually, Noah pulls back.

"I should get rid of the condom."

"Right."

He tosses his legs to the side and jumps out of bed. "Be right back."

"Okay." I face the ceiling, then close my eyes.

Every nerve ending in my body is alive and tingling. My clit still throbs with the aftershock of another obliterating orgasm. I never doubted Noah would be good in bed, but he surpassed all my expectations. I'm slick with sweat and should definitely shower, but I'm currently boneless.

I hear the faucet turn on and then off before Noah returns to the room and slides into bed next to me. He touches the side of my face. "How are you feeling, sunshine?"

"Amazing. Thank you."

"No, thank *you*." He kisses my cheek, sending the butterflies in my stomach aflutter.

I turn my face to him. "Where did you learn all your tricks?"

He makes a face. "I'm not sure it's safe to answer that."

I laugh. "Relax, I'm not trying to get you in trouble, and I swear I'm not one of those girls prone to retroactive jealousy."

His brows arch. "Really? So you aren't jealous at all?"

"I wouldn't say *that*..."

"You did get jealous of my former nanny before you knew who she was. Confess."

I shake my head. "Never."

He runs his fingers over my collarbone, dropping his gaze. "I'll confess then. I got jealous tonight."

"Of Ryder? Noah…"

"I know I'm only your fake boyfriend, but I couldn't help it." He lifts his eyes to mine again. "You wore the dress he bought, and he probably imagined undressing you."

"He undressed me plenty of times. He's my ex."

His face falls. "If that's your way of making me feel better, you're not doing a good job, sunshine."

I rub my finger between his brows, trying to erase the crease there. "You have nothing to worry about. I'm with you."

"But it's not real."

I bite my lower lip. "Why do you want it to be real so badly?"

"How can you not know it by now? I'm crazy about you, sunshine. I have been since I first saw you."

"At The Heritage?"

He rolls onto his back and stares at the ceiling. "No, that wasn't it."

I rest on my elbow so I can peer at his face. "Where did you see me then?"

"At the Frozen Four semifinal." He looks into my eyes. "I saw you in the crowd. Then, on my way to the Warriors' locker room, I caught your argument with Ryder."

My stomach dips. "You were there?"

"Yeah."

"And did you witness the whole thing?"

He nods, remorse shining in his eyes. "I'm sorry. I know I shouldn't have spied, but I didn't know what to do, and… are you mad?"

Am I mad? No. That's not the emotion swirling in my chest. "I'm embarrassed."

I sit up, turning my back on him.

"Why? You have nothing to be ashamed of. The one who should feel that way is Ryder Fuckface."

How can I make Noah understand? That was a low point in

my life. I felt raw, vulnerable, and not because I was heartbroken about the breakup. I felt betrayed. I thought I knew who Ryder was, but I was staring at the face of a stranger that night.

"It doesn't matter." I stand up, feeling cold and bereft in an instant. I want to return to the warmth of Noah's arms, but my walls have re-formed, and my fear of trusting him and his feelings for me is back with a vengeance. "I should go check on the puppies."

I put on my oversize hoodie and walk out of the room. I'm running away from Noah and his big feelings, and I'm a coward for it, but knowing he was there that night is messing with my head, and I need to process not only that, but everything.

I should have known he would follow me. Before I can check the box, he hugs me from behind and rests his chin on my shoulder.

"I know there are things you're keeping close to your chest, and that's all right, babe. I'll be here if you decide to tell me in whatever role I have—friend, fake boyfriend… love of your life." He chuckles, melting my anxiety away.

I laugh with him. "Love of my life? Aren't you getting ahead of yourself?"

He spins me around and gently caresses my face with the tips of his fingers. "Am I?"

With the way he's staring at me, I almost believe he's serious. But the sound of a key makes me jump apart from him.

Harper walks in a second later. Her eyes widen, and she turns away quickly. "I'm so sorry."

"Oh shit. No, I'm sorry." Noah runs back to my room in all his naked glory.

My face is burning up. How did I not notice he followed me without bothering to put on clothes?

"Is he gone?" Harper asks.

"Yes. I'm sorry. That won't happen again."

"It's okay. I barely saw anything. You were blocking most of him."

Her face is redder than a tomato, so to change the subject.... "How was the event?"

"A great success. Gordon was happy, which means my boss was happy."

"Did Adrian show up?"

Her lips flatten. "Unfortunately, yes."

Before she can elaborate, Noah returns to the living room, wearing his slacks and shirt. "Did you show her the puppies?"

Harper's brows shoot to the heavens. "What puppies?"

"Does that answer your question?" I smirk.

Noah walks to the box and opens the lid. "*These* puppies."

Harper walks closer and leans forward. "Oh my God. They're tiny. Where did you find them?"

"Abandoned by the recycling bin."

Her spine straightens. "What kind of monster would do such a thing?"

"A heartless one."

She crouches next to the box. "But we can't keep them. It's against the student hall rules."

"We aren't planning on telling anyone while we're fostering them."

"There's a girl in one of my classes that has a secret pet. It's a cat though, so a bit easier to hide." Harper counts them. "There are *seven* puppies in there. You guys are insane."

"I'm hoping we can find other foster parents," I say.

"We are?" Noah looks at me, surprised.

"Yes. I'll bring them to the arena tomorrow. Maybe some of the guys will be interested."

"But not Marshall—he's ours."

"Wait, since when did we decide on that name?"

"I just did. You know, after Marshall from *Paw Patrol*. Marshall Kingsley has a nice ring to it, doesn't it?"

I cross my arms. "Why not Marshall Mancini? I think it sounds even better."

I'm teasing, but it goes right over his head. He pouts, turning his lips even more kissable. "But I like Marshall Kingsley."

When he acts like that, it reminds me he's only nineteen. Although the things he did to me in the bedroom are a contradiction to that.

"I'm just yanking your chain. Marshall Kingsley sounds great."

Harper unfurls from her crouch. "I'd better get to bed. You guys are too sweet, and it's already giving me a toothache."

"What about the puppies?" Noah asks.

"I'm okay with one puppy in the apartment, but not seven. I'm assuming Marshall has to stay here, right?"

"Yeah. Noah can't have a dog in his tuna-can-size room."

She watches me intensely for a couple beats. "Things are getting serious between you two."

Shit. Why did she have to say that in front of Noah?

"We're just co-parenting a dog. No big deal," I say without looking in his direction.

She narrows her eyes. "Sure. Well, good night then. I'll see you tomorrow."

"Good night, Harper," Noah replies.

I finally glance at him, but he's distracted. He's holding Marshall now, and the puppy has his undivided attention.

"You shouldn't play with him this late. It's not time for their feeding yet."

"I know, but I can't resist."

"I'm going to bed."

"I'll be there in a sec." He doesn't meet my eyes, and it makes me feel like a bitch.

I hurt his feelings, but I don't know what to say to fix things without lowering my barriers again.

CHAPTER 34
GIA

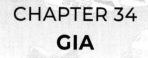

I toss and turn, waiting for Noah to come to bed, and after an hour alone, I decide to check on him. I find him sleeping on the couch with Marshall lying across his chest. His arm is keeping the puppy from falling. I melt at the sight, and at the same time, guilt pierces my heart. Noah is amazing, and he's given me proof time and time again that he's into me. Why am I still hesitating?

Maybe because he's too good to be true.

In the box, the puppies are whining. I realize it's time for them to eat again. Instead of waking Noah, I head for the kitchen to prepare their formula. I warm it up in the microwave and then split the mix into the small bottles the vet gave us.

Without his help, I can feed only two puppies at a time, but he looks so peaceful sleeping I don't want to disturb him.

I get comfortable on the floor and fish two puppies out of the box. Their eyes are still closed, so I have to place the bottles against their little mouths, but then they take over.

"Why didn't you wake me?" Noah asks in a groggy voice.

I lift my face. "I wanted to let you rest."

He sits up and covers his yawn with a fist. Marshall is also awake and moving in his hand.

"You shouldn't have to do this all by yourself. They're my responsibility too."

"I know. It's okay. I already prepped their formula. Now we just have to feed them."

Noah sits crossed-legged on the other side of the box facing me and takes two bottles from the coffee table where I set them. He feeds Marshall and another puppy first.

We work in silence, and I can't tell if he isn't talking much because it's late or if he has something on his mind he isn't telling me.

"I'm sorry about what I told Harper," I blurt out.

He scrunches his brows together. "I don't follow."

"About us co-parenting Marshall not being a big deal. I didn't want her getting ideas about us."

Noah smiles. "It's okay, Gia. It didn't bother me."

"Are you sure? You didn't come to bed."

He cocks his head, watching me in amusement. "You missed me, sunshine?"

"As a matter of fact. I did. I like to cuddle."

His smile broadens. "You won't go without cuddles while you're with me."

The *while* gets me. I'm the one who told him this is temporary, but it hurts when he says it. Ugh. Why am I such a mess?

"What's wrong?" he asks. I must have shown the turmoil on my face.

I shake my head. "It's nothing."

"Talk to me, babe."

My heart twists, and it hurts so much I can't breathe properly. I don't want to burden him with my problems. If he finds out I'm not the self-assured person I portray, will he care less about me? And then comes the next question—why would it bother me if he did?

"I'm just tired… and cuddle deprived." I smile, hoping he believes me.

He watches me for a couple of beats, and I can almost see the gears in his head turning furiously to figure me out. "All right."

We fall silent again and concentrate on getting the puppies fed and back in their box. When we finally make it back to bed, it's past three in the morning.

I don't change out of my oversize hoodie, but Noah undresses down to his briefs and slides in next to me, immediately pulling me into his arms for the promised cuddling. His nearness makes me hot and bothered again, but exhaustion wins. I fall asleep almost instantly.

My alarm jars me awake from a pleasant dream. With my eyes still closed, I reach for my phone on the nightstand to make the noise stop. I'm more than happy to go back to sleep, but Noah's arm across my belly tightens, then he kisses my shoulder.

My brain isn't completely awake yet, but my body sure is. I purr like a kitten and melt into his embrace. His arm slides down my belly, and then his hand is under my hoodie and between my legs.

A soft moan escapes my lips when he finds my clit and starts to play with it. I'm completely awake now. My folds are slick, and Noah uses that to his advantage, alternating between teasing my clit and fucking me with his fingers.

His erection is pressing against my ass. I reach back and guide it to my entrance. He's not wearing protection, so he just rubs his cock against my pussy while he keeps playing with my clit.

"Hmm, this feels good," I murmur.

"I need to be inside you, sunshine."

"Hold on."

I stretch my arm and pull my nightstand drawer open. It

takes me a moment to locate the box of condoms I have there. I finally pull one packet out of the box and tear it open.

"Here."

"Thanks, babe."

He needs his hands to put the condom on, so that means he deprives me of his expert fingers for a few seconds. But when he returns, it's with a vengeance. He enters me with a precise thrust while his fingers resume working their magic against my core. His movements are fast and hard, which is fine by me. We only have time for a quickie, and I'm so turned on that the tension has already reached the tipping point. The first tendrils of orgasm overtake me, and all I can do is ride the wave and try not to scream too loud.

Noah's pace increases, and then he blurts out, "Gia... babe, fuck."

He keeps moving at the same speed until the tremors in his body subside. I cover his hand with mine, forcing him to still his fingers too. There's such a thing as too much stimulation.

Noah kisses my shoulder, wrapping his arms around my waist. He remains sheathed inside me though.

"Good morning," he whispers.

"Yes, a very good morning, indeed," I reply with a smile.

"I could stay like this forever."

"I wish we could."

A knock sounds on the door. "Gia, are you up?"

"Yeah."

"Well, your puppies are too. I'm heading out."

"Okay."

Noah releases me, pulling out of me. "We should get going. Why don't you shower while I clean the mess in their box?"

"Are you sure?"

He kisses my cheek. "Yeah, babe. I'm sure. I just need to get rid of the condom."

He jumps out of bed and disappears into the bathroom. I get up too, and collect the clothes scattered on the floor. Noah's pants, shirt, and jacket are a little wrinkled. If he's going to be spending the night, he needs to leave some clothes here.

Fake boyfriend or not, we are getting serious, despite my reluctance to admit it. I grab another pair of sweatpants and a T-shirt from the pile of merchandise that's sitting in the corner of my room now since I gave the box to the puppies and lay them on my bed.

Noah walks out of the bathroom, smelling like toothpaste. "Oh, I'm getting new clothes? Sweet."

"Yeah, but that's the last pair in your size. You should leave some clothes here," I reply without making eye contact.

I expect him to make a big deal out of my statement, but all he says is, "Okay."

"I'm going to shower now."

He smirks. "Okay."

He's amused about something, but I'm not going to ask what. I smell like a sex dungeon and have morning breath. I take refuge in the bathroom before he decides to kiss me.

I lock the door and rest against the hard surface for a bit, trying to get my emotions in check. Then I'm horrified by my reflection in the mirror. I look like a Tasmanian devil. My curly hair is a tangled mess, resembling a bird's nest. Maybe that's what amused Noah.

Kill me now.

This was supposed to be a quick shower, but it's going to take forever to work through the knots. I might not be able to help Noah with the feeding, but I'm confident he won't mind and will do it all gladly.

CHAPTER 35
GIA

While I showered, Noah took care of everything—he cleaned the puppies' box and fed them all. Now it's his turn in the shower, and we have a little time before we need to head out, so I'm making us breakfast. The coffee is freshly brewed, and I'm already sipping my first cup. I have a stack of pancakes ready. I just finished flipping the last one onto the plate when my doorbell rings. I wonder if Harper forgot her keys.

I open the door without looking in the peephole and I'm shocked to find Martin standing there, his eyes red and puffy.

"Martin, what happened?"

He engulfs me in a bear hug and begins to cry in earnest. I forget that I'm mad at him for sending me that rude message. He's in distress, and I still consider him my friend.

"The worst happened," he sobs.

I pull back, untangling myself from his embrace. "Come in."

He wipes his tears with the sleeve of his jacket and, without being prompted, pulls up a chair by the kitchen island.

"I'm sorry to drop by without calling first. I know you have class, but I didn't know what to do."

"Tell me what happened, please. You're scaring me."

He swallows hard, then rests his forearms on the counter, hunching his shoulders forward. "My cousin Rob got into a car wreck. He's in bad shape."

"Oh no, Martin. I'm so sorry." I walk over and put my arm around his shoulder. "Is this the one that lives in Europe?"

"Yeah. He's in Germany."

"How bad is it?"

"He's currently in a coma. We'll know more later."

"Are you going to see him?"

He shakes his head. "No, my aunt doesn't want anyone to travel right now, you know… in case we have to be there for the fu…" He shudders. "I can't even say it."

I get teary-eyed, not only to see Martin in this state, but I'm also thinking about Jaime. His accident hit our family hard, especially in the first few hours, when we didn't know how bad his injuries were.

"If there's anything I can do, I'm here for you."

"Thanks, hon."

"Babe, have you seen my—" Noah, who just came out of my room, stops short when he sees Martin.

I step back, and Martin's spine becomes taut in an instant. His sorrowful expression twists into a scowl as he glares in Noah's direction.

"Is everything okay?" Noah asks, looking more concerned than annoyed.

"Martin received some bad news."

"I'm sorry to hear that."

"Right," Martin mutters.

Noah's eyebrows pinch, but mercifully he doesn't respond to Martin's sarcastic reply. The last thing I want is an argument.

"I have coffee and pancakes. You're more than welcome to stay, Martin."

He stands up. "No, I'd better go. I don't want to intrude."

I feel terrible that he doesn't think he's welcome here because of Noah. "You aren't intruding."

"Nah. We can hang out later when you aren't busy. This Friday for the big two-one celebration?"

My stomach falls through the earth. Shit. I never told Martin I'd be in Boston. It didn't occur to me to invite him since he hates the guys so much. And then he pissed me off with that text.

"Gia is coming to our away game on Friday," Noah chimes in.

Martin narrows his gaze. "Is that so? You'd rather work than celebrate your birthday?"

Noah walks over and pulls me into a side hug. "Who said she isn't celebrating her birthday? But you should totally come."

His brows shoot to the heavens. "To a hockey game? Pass."

"We're going clubbing after. You need to come. Please?" I add, feeling guilty that I didn't invite him.

"Is this a pity invitation?"

Fuck. It totally is.

"No, not at all. Everything was up in the air until yesterday," I lie.

Martin works his jaw for a moment, glances at Noah fleetingly, then back at me. "I'll be there."

"Great!" I say in a high-pitched tone that sounds fake to my own ears.

"Thanks for listening to me. I'll call you later." He veers for the door and walks out without saying bye to Noah.

"He didn't like seeing me here, did he?" Noah asks.

"Don't take it personally. You know Martin doesn't like hockey players."

"Nah, his problem isn't that he doesn't like hockey players. I think he just likes *you* a little too much."

"He doesn't have a thing for me." I turn toward the coffee pot so Noah can't see my face.

I'm beginning to suspect Martin does have a crush on me, but if I acknowledge that to Noah and keep hanging out with Martin, that could create tension I don't need.

"If you say so. I wouldn't blame him if he did."

I glance over my shoulder. "You're not jealous?"

He gives me a wolfish smile. "Nope. Not of that weasel."

So only of Ryder then. I keep the thought to myself.

"Are you okay with him coming to my birthday party?"

"I am, but are you? I'm sorry if I overstepped."

I shake my head. "No. I'm glad that you did. His cousin is in a coma and Martin is in bad shape as you could see."

"That's awful. I'd be a mess as well if that happened to any member of my family."

"Yeah. The story reminded me of Jaime's accident." I turn away, getting misty-eyed, and not wanting Noah to see it.

"Where's Jaime now?"

"Chicago. Now that he can't play hockey, he's studying to be a physiotherapist."

"Really? That's awesome."

I smile, my chest swelling with pride "Yes. My brother is the best. Do you want coffee?"

"Sure. Hit me." He glances at the stack of pancakes. "Those smell divine."

"You might want to warm them up in the microwave. I reckon they're cold already."

He grabs one and takes a bite, closing his eyes as he does so. A moan comes from deep in his throat, sending a shot of libido to my core. How can he turn eating breakfast into something sexy?

He opens his eyes and locks his gaze with mine. "This is fucking amazing. Not as good as your pussy, though."

Heat rushes to my face. "That's too bad. You're only getting pancakes now."

He pouts. "That's sad."

"Keep whining and I'll take away the pancakes too."

He pulls the stack of pancakes closer to him and curls his arm protectively around them. "No, they're mine."

"Here's your coffee." I set the cup in front of him. "And you aren't eating them all." I fish two pancakes from the stack because I'm sure he could scarf them all down in the blink of an eye.

"You're lucky I like you," he grumbles.

"Ditto." I take a bite of my pancake, loving the way a simple word makes his eyes twinkle with joy.

"How's your schedule today?"

"I have a two-hour class in twenty minutes. Then I'm shooting a video for the brand of clothes you're wearing. I've procrastinated on that for too long." I glance at the puppies. "I don't feel good leaving them alone though."

"I'll take them. I have hockey this morning. I'm sure if I ask nicely, someone at the arena will keep an eye on them while I practice."

"That works. I was planning to swing by the arena before lunch. I should probably hit the pet store before though. We're out of formula."

"Great. How about after lunch?"

I remember that I'm presenting my French assignment today and tense on the spot. "Shit. I have my French presentation. I'm so unprepared for that."

Noah's expression softens. "You'll be fine. Your paper hardly had any issues. Do you want to practice now?"

I glance at the microwave clock. "I have to leave in five minutes, or I won't find parking. But I could practice during lunch?"

"Sounds good."

"What about the puppies?"

Noah shrugs, unfazed. "If you buy a crate, I'll bring them with me to my afternoon classes."

"Do you think your professors will allow it?"

"I'll sit in the back. No one will notice."

I bite my lower lip. "If you're sure."

His gaze drops to my mouth, and when he replies, it's a little gruff. "I'm sure."

Just one smoldering look and a husky reply send my heart racing. If it weren't for our busy schedules, I don't think we'd leave the bedroom.

Harper is right. Noah is a keeper. I just have to convince my insecurities of that.

CHAPTER 36
NOAH

I'm smiling from ear to ear when I enter the arena. I had the most amazing night and morning with the girl of my dreams, and if I could dance, I'd be doing it to Pharrell Williams's "Happy". The first person I bump into is CJ, and judging by his sourpuss expression, he's not having a good morning. He's also fighting with the vending machine and cursing under his breath.

"Good morning," I say in a chipper voice.

He turns his irate gaze on me. "Why are you talking to me?"

"I'm being polite. What's with you?"

He faces the machine again. "This piece of shit junk ate my breakfast."

No wonder he's in a foul mood. I set the box down and pull a granola bar from my duffel bag. "This is yours if you want it."

He stares at the wrapper in my hand for a couple beats. "Sure."

I toss it to him, but Alex intercepts my throw. "Oh, granola bar. Thanks."

"That's mine, jackass," CJ complains.

"Is it? Since when do you accept snacks from Noah?"

CJ pries the bar from Alex's hand. "Since he offered. Don't start with me. I had a shitty evening and a shittier morning."

He lives with his jackass brother, so I believe him.

"What happened?" Alex asks.

"I don't want to talk about it." He tears the wrapper with his teeth and bites off a big chunk of the granola bar.

"What's in the box?" Logan stops next to me.

Alex shakes his head. "You're doing it wrong, bro. It's *what's in the box*!"

CJ gives him a droll look. "If you're trying to sound like Brad Pitt in *Seven*, you're doing a terrible job."

"Bite me, punk."

For fuck's sake. It's not even eight yet, and these dumbasses are already bickering. CJ really needs to learn to suffer in silence.

"Circling back to Logan's question. This is something Gia and I found last night," I reply.

Logan twists his face. "Why is the box whining?"

I drop into a crouch and flip the lid open. "Ta-da!"

"Puppies? You guys found *puppies*?" His voice rises an octave.

"What?" Alex walks over, followed by CJ. "Holy crap. They're tiny."

"They look like rats," CJ pipes up.

"What are you guys looking at?" Sean asks, joining us.

"Noah found puppies!" Logan replies.

"And you brought them here?" Sean looks at me, his brows pinched together.

I shrug. "I couldn't leave them alone, and Gia has class now."

"And we have practice." He gives me a meaningful glance.

"What's going on here?" Coach Bedford asks.

The guys take a huge step back, leaving me alone to explain myself to Coach. Shit. I was hoping to find a babysitter before he found out I brought the puppies here.

"Gia and I are fostering these puppies we found abandoned last night, and I had to bring them here because they need to be fed every three hours and I couldn't leave them alone in her apartment." The words roll off my tongue like an avalanche.

Frowning, Coach bends over and peers inside the box. "Dalmatians. They're just a few days old by the looks of it."

"Yes, sir."

He looks up. "You can't keep them here."

My stomach drops. "They have no one. Who's going to take care of them?"

He stares me down. "You have a big heart, Noah, but explain how you're going to reconcile taking care of newborn puppies with your schedule. Even if you split responsibilities with Gia, there's no possible way you can make it work."

"Besides, we have an away game this Friday, dumbass," CJ pipes up, earning a glower from Coach.

My heart sinks. I don't want to give the puppies up, but I might not have a choice. I pick up Marshall and cradle him against my chest.

"I was planning on keeping this one. I already named him and everything. Marshall Kingsley."

CJ snorts. "How original."

Assistant Coach LaRue, who was watching from afar, comes closer. "My parents have a farm thirty minutes from Fairbanks. They're used to dogs. I think they'd be okay fostering the puppies until they can be placed in their forever homes."

Hope flares in my chest. "That would be amazing. And I could come visit Marshall until he's ready to come home with me."

Coach Bedford gives me a look that says he believes I'm insane. "Son, you can't keep a dog in your dorm."

"Only if the school finds out."

Coach flattens his lips, then shakes his head. "Then I never heard of this."

"If Noah is keeping a secret puppy, I also want one."

"Oh, they can be team mascots!" Logan adds.

"We already have a team mascot. It's the guy who wears the warrior costume every game," CJ interjects.

"Would it kill you to be nice?" I ask him. "I just fed you, for crying out loud."

He huffs and then spins on his heels and heads to the locker room.

"You can discuss puppy allocation on your own time. Now get ready for practice," Coach Bedford grumbles.

"Can I at least bring the puppies into the locker room?"

"No." He strides away.

Man, who knew Coach Bedford was a cold-hearted grump?

"Give them to me," Assistant Coach LaRue chimes in. "I'll ask Security to keep an eye on them during practice."

"Thank you. Do you think your parents will be keen on the idea of fostering them?"

"I think so. If not, we'll think of something. Don't worry. Just focus on hockey."

"Yes, sir. And thanks for helping."

He nods, showing a hint of a smile. "I like dogs. I might keep one puppy myself."

I beam from ear to ear. "That'd be so cool. Even better if all the puppies were adopted by members of the Warriors family."

He taps my shoulder. "Don't get ahead of yourself."

GIA

I rushed to class this morning for nothing. Right before I stepped into the building, I received a text message saying it was canceled. Both the professor and his assistant are sick.

Since Noah already took the puppies to hockey practice, I go to the pet store instead. There's a superstore ten minutes from campus, and this early in the morning, it's an in-and-out situation. I bet if I'd come with Noah, we'd have spent an hour in the store buying things we don't need.

I got the formula—damn expensive—a crate, toys, and cleaning supplies. Once the puppies switch to solid foods and water, I can get more accessories. I need to post more videos and get more sponsorships, or I won't be able to afford any of that.

I don't text him on the way to the arena, because I want to witness the look on his face when he sees me there earlier than expected. I'm giddy with anticipation, acting like a teenager going to surprise her first boyfriend.

On the way to my office, I stop by Security, guessing that's where Noah left the puppies. I was correct. Jonas and one of his coworkers, Bill, are busy playing with them.

"Hi guys," I greet from the door.

Jonas turns. "Hey, Gia. We're babysitting your kids while Noah is on the ice."

"I can see that. I hope they aren't bothering you."

"Not at all." He gives me an assessing look. "You don't usually stop in at this time. No class this morning?"

"The professor and his assistant are sick. So I went to the pet store and got supplies." I lift the two large plastic bags I have in my hands.

"Oh you got a crate! That's smart. The cardboard box won't last long with them pissing all over it."

"I know."

"The boys just stepped onto the rink. Maybe you want to shoot some videos of their warmup? I'm sure that will get a lot of views."

He's not wrong. I haven't shot any videos of their training this season.

"I thought they'd be done with warm-ups by now."

"Nah, they started a bit late," Bill chimes in. "You know, on the account of our visitors."

My stomach twists with worry. Coach Bedford hates when things don't start on schedule. "Was Coach upset?"

Jonas shrugs. "Eh, no more than any other morning."

"Is it okay to leave this here with you?" I set the crate down.

"Sure. Do you want us to transfer them?"

"Only if you have time."

Jonas looks at Bill and then back at me. "We have time."

"Okay. Thank you."

I sprint to my office to drop off my bag, and with only my cell phone in hand, I head to the practice rink. I make sure I'm stealthy as I find a good spot to shoot some videos of the guys on the ice. Mainly, I'm avoiding Coach Bedford. I'm not out of the woods yet with him, thanks to that prank.

Immediately, my eyes find Noah. He's in the middle of the ice, on one knee and doing hip-thrust motions. I've seen the guys do that stretch exercise a million times, but all I can think about today is how Noah did similar movements last night, impaling me on his cock. My clit throbs as desire awakens in my core, and I feel hot despite the low temperature in the rink.

I have my camera poised to start recording, but I change my mind. I don't need to be drawing attention to Noah's sex appeal when just a week ago, girls were going out of their way to get him to notice them.

He's mine.

The thought shocks me. It's the first time I've thought of him possessively. I lower my phone and watch him finish his exercises, already dreaming about tonight. Now that I've had a taste of him, I want more.

Noah jumps to his feet and spins, facing me now. He stops when he notices me. Then he starts in my direction, but Sean skates in front of him and points at Coach. He nods and then waves at me instead of skating closer to say hello. Thank God Sean was there to save him from getting Coach more aggravated.

Logan and Alex, however, do skate toward me, and I decide to take a shot of the twins' approach.

"I thought you had class," Logan says.

"It got canceled." I stop recording and lower my phone.

"Should you be talking to me? I don't want to get yelled at by Coach."

"We came to tell you we want one puppy. You'd better keep one for us," Alex adds.

"Sure. Boy or girl?"

They trade a glance, then shrug. "It doesn't matter. I guess we'll see which one likes us best."

"Sounds good. Now you'd better go before you get *me* in trouble."

They skate away, and that's when I sense the weight of Coach's glower. Maybe today isn't such a good day to be around him. I leave the training rink and go check on the cuties responsible for his foul mood.

Jonas is back at his desk working, and Bill is gone, but the puppies are already in the crate.

"They're sleeping now," he tells me.

"Good, I'll bring them to my office. Thanks for keeping an eye on them."

"No problem."

I return to my office with the puppies. It's once again empty. My schedule and the logistics assistant's schedule rarely collide; we usually each have the office to ourself.

I do some work for the Warriors, answer emails, and reply to comments. The number of nasty ones is low, which means either Ashley already cleaned out the bad ones for me—she has the password—or people are done being terrible.

I have to work only a few hours a week on Warriors stuff, and after an hour, I'm caught up with everything on today's to-do list. Now I can study without guilt.

As soon as I open my laptop to do another read-through of my French essay, my phone rings. It's an anonymous call. My heart shrinks inside my chest and my body shivers. I freeze and watch my phone ring and ring until the call goes to voice mail. A moment later, a text tells me whoever called left another message.

I don't listen to it. Instead, I call Blair. As it rings, I realize it's kind of big of a deal that my impulse was to call her instead of Ashley. Maybe that's because she was there when I received the first nasty call.

She answers on the third ring. "Hello?"

"Hey, Blair." My voice is shaky.

"What's wrong? Did something happen?"

I rest my forehead on my hand. "Yes. I got another anonymous call."

"Son of a bitch. What did they say this time?"

"I don't know. I was too chicken to answer it, and I haven't listened to the voice mail yet."

"What did Ashley say?"

"I haven't told her."

There's a noticeable pause. "You called me first?"

"Yes."

"Okay."

I let out a shuddering breath. "I didn't tell her about the first call either. And you were there when it happened."

"Right."

She sounds dejected, so I add, "And I do want us to mend the bridge."

"Me too. Where are you? I can come by, and we can listen to the message together."

"Would you?" I feel like such a coward for accepting her offer.

"Of course. My schedule is wide open this morning, and sadly my mother is aware of that. She wants to discuss my future, which is code for, 'Who am I going to marry?'"

"Oh, Blair. I thought she stopped trying to play matchmaker."

She snorts, something that's completely unlike her. "Have you met my mother?"

I grimace. Sadly, I have. Awful woman.

"I'm sorry you're still going through that bullshit."

She sighs. "The story of my life. But we're focusing on your problem. Where are you? I don't mind coming to the rescue, and it'll give me an excuse to avoid seeing Mother Dearest."

"I'm at the arena. My morning class was canceled."

"I'll meet you there," she says without hesitation.

"Are you sure?"

"Absolutely. Unless you think there's a risk Security won't let me in."

"You're not banned from the arena, Blair. But you might bump into Alex."

"I see that jackass plenty in the classes we share. I'm not afraid of him. Besides, seeing me in his domain will probably piss him off. It's a win-win situation for me. I'll see you in ten."

CHAPTER 37
NOAH

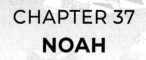

Because I know Gia is already in the building, no sooner does practice end than I'm the first one out of the rink and into the locker room, which means access to the shower stall before anyone else. I've never rinsed and lathered so fast in my life. I'm dying to know what she's doing here instead of class. I would have asked her when I saw her, but Sean saved me from making that mistake and pissing off Coach Bedford further.

Regardless, Coach was extra hard on me, yelling more than usual, which pleased CJ to no end. I thought we were getting over his animosity, but I guess once an asshole, always an asshole.

When I return to the locker room, all showered and wrapped in a towel, Logan smirks at me. "My, aren't you in a hurry?"

"Wouldn't you be as well if your hot girlfriend was waiting outside? Oh, that's right, you don't have one."

He laughs, shaking his head. "You think that dig bothers me? I don't have a girlfriend by choice."

"That's right. Having a girlfriend is a pain in the ass," Alex chimes in. "You can't expect us to pick a favorite flavor of ice cream when there are hundreds we haven't tried yet."

"I'm more of a believer that once I taste something fucking amazing, there's no need to keep trying other flavors."

"Suit yourself. More for us," Logan replies.

I roll my eyes. "I'd love to stay and chat, but my girl is waiting for me."

"Are you leaving the arena now?" Alex asks.

"I'm not sure. I thought Gia had class this morning, but it seems something changed. I promised I'd help her with her French assignment. Why?"

"I want to choose our puppy before LaRue takes them to his parents' farm."

My eyebrows shoot to the heavens. "Are you really serious about adopting?"

"Hell yeah."

"But just one though," Logan interjects. "It'd be crazy to commit to two dogs."

"I haven't figured out yet how to get permission to have a dog in the student hall. You know that, right?"

"I'm not concerned," Logan replies. "School administration goes out of their way to make us happy. The hockey team brings a lot of revenue to Hannaford U. It'll be fine."

Darren approaches, already out of his jersey and protective gear. "If you think they'd be okay with dogs on campus, I might keep one too. I love dogs."

"You guys are a bunch of dumbasses," CJ pipes up from across the room. "Who's going to dog-sit your puppies when we're at an away game?"

"Have you ever heard of dog-sitting services, jackass?" Logan retorts.

"Whatever." He heads for the shower without glancing in our direction.

"What crawled up his ass?" Alex asks.

"Ignore him," I say. "I think it'd be awesome if each puppy went to a Warrior. LaRue already said he wants one."

Alex lifts his hand. "Wait a second. Too many people are

interested in getting a puppy, and I said I wanted one first. That means I get first pick."

"You can pick first. I don't care," Darren replies.

"Yep. Besides I already got the best one." I add.

"Yours is the smallest." Logan gives me a droll look.

"So?" I turn to Alex. "I'm heading out to meet Gia, and I don't know how long we're going to stay. If you want to choose your puppy, you'd better come now."

GIA

Despite Blair's bravado that she doesn't care about anyone's opinion or the possibility she's going to receive nasty glances when she comes into the arena, I decide to do the right thing and wait for her by the entrance.

Today she's wearing a light-pink knee-length coat, yellow tights, and white ankle boots. She looks like an Easter egg, but she makes it work. It's a gift. As usual, her hair band matches her coat, and her dark-brown hair is styled to perfection in soft waves down her back. I've always envied her ability to look put together no matter what. With the way my hair curls so wildly, it's a struggle to do anything with it. Most of the time, I don't bother and just put it up in a messy bun or ponytail.

"You didn't have to wait for me," she tells me. "Unless you didn't think they'd let me in if not accompanied by you."

"The building is open to the public, but it's easier if I'm with you when you cross into the Warriors zone."

"Is the jerkface still there?"

She's obviously referring to Alex.

"Yeah, they haven't finished training yet."

"How much longer?"

I give her a curious glance. "Are you actually looking forward to bumping into Alex?"

She rewards me with her most innocent look. "I'm not looking forward to *seeing* him. I'm looking forward to *annoying* him."

I shake my head, laughing. "There's a fine line between love and hate, Blair, and I think you're toying with it."

She gasps. "Take that back right now."

"Relax. I was just messing with you. Besides, I wouldn't wish the twins on any of my friends. I love them to death, but they're manwhores."

Her nose wrinkles. "Disgusting."

No one gives Blair a second glance as we walk from the entrance to my office. It'd be a different story if it was her brother. He's banned from the premises. It's a good thing too, because coming to a game would be some shit Ryder would do. No one will care that Blair is here—well, besides Alex.

"You haven't listened to the voice mail yet, have you?" she asks me.

"No, and I'm now debating if I should. You know it's going to upset me."

She stops in her tracks and touches my arm, making me stop too. "You did not make me come all the way here only to drive me insane. You know that if we don't listen to that voice message, it's going to bug me for weeks. It'll be all I think about."

Subconsciously, I knew that, and maybe that's why I told Blair about the voice mail. Like then, I wouldn't have a choice but to listen to it.

I take a step forward but then see Noah and Alex coming toward us. Noah's face splits into the biggest smile, which is the opposite of Alex's expression. He sends a death glare in Blair's direction. Noah breaks into a run and picks me up in his arms. "I can't believe you're here early. This is the best surprise."

I laugh. "Put me down, silly."

"Yes, put her down, man. What's wrong with you?" Alex pipes up, amused.

"Somebody's jealous of other people's happiness," Blair retorts.

"That was a joke, but I guess you wouldn't understand since you always have a stick up your ass. What the hell are you doing here anyway?"

"Not your damn business."

Noah shuffles so that now we're standing between Alex and Blair. "Why are you here early, babe?"

"My morning class got canceled. So I went by the pet store and got the formula and the crate."

Blair interrupts her stare-down with Alex to glance at me. "Formula for what?"

Oh, right. I never got a chance to tell her about the pups.

"We found Dalmatian puppies last night near Gia's student hall, and we're fostering them now," Noah replies.

Her pretty blue eyes turn rounder. "Are they here?"

"Yeah, in my office," I say.

"I want to see them." Her voice rises in pitch. Blair rarely gets excited about anything, but not because she's a cold bitch like Alex believes. Joy was never encouraged in her household. She's learned to suppress it.

Alex lifts his hands. "Whoa. You ain't getting a puppy."

She narrows her eyes, putting her hands on her hips. "Excuse me?"

"Yeah, Alex. Who made you the lord of the puppies?" I ask.

"It was Noah's idea to keep the puppies in the Warriors family."

Noah glares at him. "Way to throw me under the bus, dude. If Blair wants a puppy, she can have one. There are seven."

She crosses her arms and smirks at Alex. "I bet my puppy will be cuter than yours."

"We'll see about that."

I pinch the bridge of my nose. "Really, guys? Are you going to compete about puppies too?"

Blair and Alex don't reply, but they maintain their staring contest.

Noah throws an arm over my shoulders. "Come on, sunshine. I'm pretty sure they're up and hungry."

He's right. The pups are making a fuss inside their crate. Noah and Alex crouch next to it, ignoring us. Noah opens the crate and pulls Marshall out, but Alex just observes the rest for a moment. While he's distracted by the pups, Blair leans forward, getting into his personal space so she can reach inside the crate and take a pup out.

"Oh, you're a cutie pie. You're coming home with me," she coos.

Alex turns to her, shooting daggers with his eyes. "You can't take him home yet."

"Are you my daddy now? You can't tell me what to do."

Alex's eyes widen, and then something mischievous sparks in his gaze. I know exactly where his perverted mind went. Shit, if it's bad now while he views Blair as a rival, it'll be ten times worse if he starts to consider her as a potential hookup. Mercifully he doesn't comment about her poor choice of words.

"He's right though," I say. "They'll need a lot of care in the next six weeks. And they haven't gotten their shots yet."

"But you're fostering them. I can help! I'm very responsible."

"Actually, Assistant Coach LaRue offered his parents' farm as a potential place for the pups until they're ready to go to their forever homes."

"Really?" I blurt out.

Noah nods. "Yep. I'm a little sad that I won't get to see Marshall every day, but with hockey season starting and our crazy schedules, it'd be almost impossible for us to take good care of them."

Relief washes over me, but at the same time, I feel guilty about it. We really didn't think things through when we agreed to foster the puppies.

"Yeah. Coach Bedford wasn't happy that I brought them here. And he also didn't think we'd have time to foster them."

"As much it as saddens me to say it, he's right. We're in way over our heads. And we have the away game this Friday."

"And your birthday," Blair adds. "I'm really looking forward to going out in Boston."

"Wait, *you're* coming?" Alex pipes up again

Blair gives him a droll look. "It's my best friend's birthday. Of course I'm coming, dumbass."

Alex grinds his teeth. "You're also coming to the game?"

"I haven't decided yet. Why do you care? I won't be there for you."

"Maybe you're going to curse us. You are a witch, after all."

"I don't even know how to respond to that stupid remark."

If I don't put a stop to it, they'll bicker until tomorrow. But it's Noah who speaks first.

"Dude, didn't you want first dibs on a puppy? It seems Blair already has hers."

"I don't want the one she chose anyway." He opens the crate and picks up the chubbiest of them all. "This is the one."

"That's the only girl in the litter," I point out.

"Is that so? Then I already know what I'm gonna call her." He smirks.

Oh boy, here we go. Please don't say it, Alex, please don't say it.

"What?" Noah asks, clearly not picking up on Alex's mischievous vibe.

"Blair." He glances at my friend. "It seems an appropriate name for the only bitch in the litter."

Hell. He went for it.

Blair twists her face into a scowl, and her cheeks flush. If she punches Alex in the throat, I won't blame her.

But she takes a deep breath, straightens her spine, and replies calmly, "Your obsession with me is getting pathetic, Alex. Have some self-respect."

Her reply wipes the smirk from his face, and it's now his turn to flush beet red.

"All right. That's enough. Blair, are you sure you want to keep that puppy?" I ask.

She nods. "I'm sure."

"What are you going to name him? Please don't say Alex." Noah laughs, but his joke doesn't amuse anyone.

"I'm not going to name him Alex. Come on. I have to think about it but in the meantime..." She fishes a golden ribbon from her purse and ties it around the puppy's neck. "There. Now everyone will know this one is taken."

"Why did you have a ribbon in your purse?" Noah asks.

"Oh, it's for my hair. I always carry extra accessories."

Alex watches her in disgust but at least he doesn't say anything.

"You know what? You two should help us feed the puppies," I suggest.

I don't say it's a test. I want to see how they fare. Alex and Blair look at each other, and now both seem uneasy.

"It'd be great training for when you have to take care of your puppy twenty-four-seven," Noah adds.

Blair breaks eye contact with Alex first. "Sure. Just tell me what to do."

CHAPTER 38
GIA

I'm so preoccupied with keeping Alex and Blair from killing each other while they help feed the puppies that I don't notice when Noah disappears. He's sitting right next to me one second, and then I turn around and he's gone.

"Where did Noah go?"

Both Alex and Blair give me blank looks.

"Maybe he went to the restroom," she replies.

"Considering Noah has a tiny bladder, that's probably where he went," Alex adds.

Blair raises her eyebrows. "You're agreeing with me on something? The world must be ending."

Alex pinches his lips then looks at me. "See what I have to deal with?"

I smirk. "Like you're a saint."

His eyes widen, and a glint of betrayal shines in them. "I can't believe you're taking her side."

Blair tosses her perfect hair back and stares at Alex with her trademark smug expression. "Queens before peens."

He squints. "I'd correct your statement, but out of respect to Gia, I won't."

I roll my eyes, then focus on putting Marshall back in the

crate. He's the smallest, but he's also the most energetic. In a sense, he reminds me of Noah, which makes him the perfect pick for us. A warm sensation flutters across my chest. Every time I think about Noah, I feel it.

A couple minutes later, Sean, Darren, Logan, and CJ find us. They give Blair a double take, but no one makes a comment or asks why she's there. Logan, however, does give her a come-hither look, which she notices.

"What are you staring at?" she snaps.

His lips curl into a grin. "Just wondering if it's safe to be near you or if you're going to attack my mouth again."

Alex groans, and Blair glares at Logan through narrowed eyes. "Don't let that go to your head. There won't be a repeat."

"Like my brother wants to kiss you again," Alex retorts.

Logan shrugs. "Meh, I wouldn't be opposed to a make-out sesh. But it's your loss, sugar."

"Here comes your boyfriend." Blair points with her head.

Tired of Blair and Alex's bickering, I walk away from the group and meet Noah halfway. "Hey, we're almost done here. Are you ready for French?"

"Yep. I had to get something in the locker room." He gives me a folded jersey—his jersey. "You know… for the game this Friday."

An uneasy feeling settles over my shoulders. I never told Noah about my stance on jerseys.

"Is this your jersey?" I ask like I didn't already know.

He nods. "Will you wear it on Friday?"

I sigh, "I would love to, but I can't."

His eyebrows furrow. "Why not?"

"I have a rule that I never wear jerseys from anyone on the team. It's because I work for the Warriors. I don't want to show favoritism. I don't think I should wear yours."

His face falls, and his reaction makes me regret my stupid rule. I never wore Ryder's jersey even though he bugged me about it constantly. If I changed my rules for Noah, I might as well declare to the world he's special to me, and even though that's true, I don't trust that our relationship won't crumble like a sandcastle. It's too soon to be having all these strong feelings for him.

"If it makes you feel any better, I never wore Ryder's jersey either."

He grimaces. "No, it doesn't make me feel better."

I try to give the jersey back to him, but he shakes his head. "No, sunshine. The jersey is yours. One day I'll convince you to break your rule."

By the time we rejoin everyone crowding the crate, almost all the puppies have been assigned to an owner. Darren's taking one, and Sean's taking another. There's only one pup left.

"Man, I feel bad for this poor guy," Logan says then turns to his brother. "Are we sure we can't take two?"

"Be realistic, bro. We can barely take care of one. Do you know how much work just Blair will be?"

Darren and Sean stare at human Blair, who's sporting a tomato face.

CJ walks over and stares at the remaining puppy. "What's wrong with this one? Why doesn't anyone want him?"

"He's very shy and doesn't want to interact with anyone," Darren replies.

"So, he's the runt of the litter?"

"There's no runt in this litter," Noah retorts.

CJ watches the puppy for a couple beats, then, in a surprising turn of events, he says, "I'll take him."

"You?" Noah blurts out. "You said they look like rats."

"Well, they do."

"I'm not sure I want you taking one of the puppies." He crosses his arms.

CJ matches Noah's stance. "Why? You don't think I can take care of a dog?"

"I think you're more of a cat person. You know, because you're an ass."

It's time for me to run interference—*again*. It seems that's all I do these days. If it's not Blair and Alex, or Sean and Ashley, it's CJ fighting with everyone on the team.

"CJ, if you're really sure you want the last pup, then you can have him."

Noah leans into me and whispers in my ear, "Are you sure about that? I don't think he's qualified to take care of a fly."

"Oh, and you are? You're barely out of diapers," CJ chimes in.

"Enough!" Sean blurts out. "CJ, a word alone, please."

"Why? I did nothing wrong."

"Don't argue with me," Sean grits out and heads to the locker room.

Sean rarely loses his temper and the mood shifts in the common area. CJ follows his captain without his usual arrogant swagger.

"I hope Sean can figure out what's wrong with CJ," Darren says.

"Yeah, his assholery today was off the charts," Logan agrees.

Blair catches my gaze and then looks pointedly toward my office. Shit. I forgot about the anonymous phone call and voice mail.

"I have to get my stuff in my office," I tell Noah, and then Blair and I walk together down the hallway.

"I can't believe he didn't follow you. Noah is like the eighth pup in the litter."

"He's not a puppy."

"He stares at you with lovesick puppy eyes."

I shut the door to my office, regretting telling Blair about the phone call. I'm sick to my stomach, and my hands are clammy.

"Jesus, you look as white as a ghost. Do you want me to listen to the message first?"

"No. I have to know what I'm dealing with here."

"A nasty piece of shit."

I press my code to access the voice mail and then put the

phone speaker. Blair and I huddle together with our backs to the door since the office has windows facing the hallway, and I don't want anyone catching our facial expressions by chance. I know mine will show everything.

First comes the creepy, heavy breathing, then the robotic voice. "Does your new boyfriend know how big of a whore you are, Gia Mancini? I bet that little idiot doesn't know you're having threesomes with the Kaminski twins behind his back or that you like to suck Assistant Coach LaRue's cock while Coach Bedford watches."

My heart is thundering, but at least I don't feel like crying when the message ends.

"What the *fuck* was that?" Noah asks from the door.

I pivot, clutching the phone to my chest. One look at Noah's horrified expression makes me want to cry. I swallow the lump in my throat and try to answer him, but I can't make my tongue work.

"Gia?" He enters the office and closes the door. "What's going on? Is someone harassing you?"

"She's receiving anonymous phone calls, and they're leaving those lovely voice messages," Blair replies when I can't.

His horror morphs into rage. "How long has this been going on?"

"Not long. There were only two calls."

"Why didn't you tell me?"

"Okay, I think I should leave you two alone," Blair says before walking out of the office.

Tears roll down my cheeks. "I was embarrassed."

Noah shortens the distance between us and pulls me tight to his chest. "That's crazy. Whoever is leaving you these messages is the one who should be ashamed, not you."

"I know, but I can't help how I feel."

"Has anything like this happened before?"

I tense in his arms, and he obviously notices. He's already heard the latest nasty message, so there's no point hiding what happened before. "Not to this extent. No one ever left me anonymous phone messages."

"There's gotta be a way to find out who's calling you."

I take a deep breath of his soapy scent, my fingers clutching his shirt. "I doubt it. I shouldn't have listened to the message."

"Why did you?"

I lean back and look into his eyes. "Maybe because I'm a glutton for punishment."

He wipes the moisture from my cheeks. "Please, babe, do me a favor and don't listen to those messages anymore. What if you change your number?"

"That would be such a hassle, and I'm pretty sure whoever is calling me would be able to get my new number. The best thing I can do is ignore it."

Noah's gaze hardens. "The next time they call you, if I'm around, I'll answer it."

"And do what?"

"Give them a piece of my mind."

"I think I should be the one doing that. I could have today. I saw when the call came, and I chose to ignore it. I'm such coward."

"You're not a coward. Don't ever repeat that."

I take a breath to argue, but Noah stops my argument with his mouth. He coaxes my lips open, then his tongue dances with mine softly and unhurriedly, making me melt into him. The heaviness in my chest wanes, and although it doesn't leave me completely, it's far better than it was before.

He pulls back and stares at me with heat in his gaze. "How long do we have until you need to be ready for your French class?"

"A couple hours."

"Plenty of time for more French things besides literature."

"Like kissing?" I smile.

"Among other things."

CHAPTER 39
NOAH

I'm totally using sex to make Gia forget that fucked-up message, and I don't feel an ounce of regret when she gyrates her hips, increasing the friction against her clit while I worship it with my tongue. I love everything about her, but eating her pussy is one of my favorite things. Her fingers are in my hair, pulling, and when her hips buckle and her body convulses, she yanks it hard, shouting my name.

I suck her clit into my mouth, swallowing all her juices, and fuck her faster with my fingers. She's slick with my saliva and her own arousal, making it easy for them to slide in and out fast. When she begins to relax against the mattress, I lean back and flip her over.

"Noah," she squeaks.

"Lift your pretty ass for me, sunshine."

She kneels on the mattress, opening her legs wider. Her pussy is glistening, ready for more. I grab the condom wrapper from the nightstand and make quick work of tearing the package and rolling the rubber down my erection. I slide into paradise in the next second, closing my eyes for a moment as I get used to her tightness again. She fits so perfectly around me it's insane.

Grabbing her hips, I start to move slowly, pulling out almost completely, and then hammering all the way in hard. She cries out, biting the bedsheet to muffle the sound.

"That's it, babe. Scream for me."

"I'm trying not to."

"Why? Are you concerned about the neighbors? Let them hear how well I take care of my girl."

"You don't live here. I'm the one who has to bump into them in the hallway!"

"Oh, they'll be seeing plenty of me, babe." She moans, getting tighter around me. "Fuck, you take me so well."

I grab a fistful of her hair and pull back while I lean forward to meet her halfway. "Talk to me, sunshine. Tell me what you want me to do to you," I whisper in her ear.

"I want you to fuck me faster, and harder, and I want you to..."

"You want me to what?"

"I want you to wrap your hand around my neck and squeeze."

Damned if those words aren't a double shot of desire straight to my cock. I do as she asks and apply pressure around her throat for a couple seconds before releasing it. She's getting even more worked up, and so am I. I'm ready to come, at the edge of the abyss, but I hold on, waiting for her to take the plunge with me.

Her body shakes, sending waves down my shaft. I release her neck to wrap my arm around her middle and flatten my chest against her back. My own orgasm is intense as hell, and I can't help but shout her name over and over again until she milks every single drop of cum out of me.

I shudder into the final thrust before I pull out and stagger back. Damn. That was intense. Gia collapses on the mattress, face hidden from me. I get rid of the condom before I join her, lying by her side. Her wild hair is scattered everywhere and covers most of her face. I part her curls so I can look into her eyes.

"There you are," I say.

"Hi." She smiles lazily.

"I have to say, this is the best lunch date I've ever had."

"Same here."

"I'm glad your class got canceled."

"Me too." She closes her eyes and sighs. "If only my French class had the same fate."

"Are you nervous? You don't need to be. You sounded great, better than me."

I don't add that she was always better than me. The guilt about lying to her returns, but she's already anxious about her presentation; coming clean now won't do anything but make her more nervous. I do have to tell her the truth eventually though. Maybe fifty years from now, when we're a couple of retirees relaxing in the South of France.

"I should hop in the shower and get ready for class." She sits up.

"Yeah, I need to get going too."

"Are you sure you're okay bringing the puppies with you?"

"Absolutely. Alex reminded me that the school administration wants their star athletes to be happy. Besides, all my professors are hockey fans. I don't foresee any issues."

"Okay, then." She relaxes her stance, but her hazel eyes remain troubled.

I was hoping a couple of mind-blowing orgasms would make her forget that nasty voice message. It seems I was wrong.

I cup her cheek. "Are you all right, sunshine?"

She nods, then turns her face to kiss my palm. "I'm fine. I'll be quick."

She disappears into the bathroom, but I keep staring at the closed door. My chest is heavy again. I have to find out who's harassing Gia and teach the motherfucker a lesson. If only I knew a hacker.

I remember the conversation with those two guys at the gym. Ryder put a stop to the trolls before, but I won't go to him for help. For all I know, he's the culprit. I wouldn't put it past him. If it's him, he'd better fucking run.

Gia's phone rings, immediately drawing my attention to it on the nightstand. When I see Martin's name flash on the screen, my mood turns darker. I work my jaw, fighting the urge to answer the phone. It rings and rings until it goes to voice mail. I relax a little but get pissed in the next second when he calls again.

My self-control snaps. If a person doesn't answer the phone, it's because either they don't want to or they're busy.

"Hello," I say.

"Who is this?" Martin asks, sounding annoyed.

"This is Gia's boyfriend."

"Does she know you're answering her calls?"

"She can't come to the phone right now, and you were pretty insistent. Where's the fire?"

"What?"

"I take it you're having an emergency, hence why I answered her phone. So what's the problem?"

"I'm not having an emergency. I just wanted to invite her for lunch."

"Sorry, we already had lunch. Better luck next time." I'm about to end the call, but he continues.

"You think you're something special just because you play a stupid game, don't you? But you're nothing but a little boy, and sooner rather than later, Gia will see that. You'll screw up like Ryder did, and I'll be there to pick up the pieces."

I laugh in derision. "That's your grand plan, isn't it? Circling around the edges like a vulture, hoping to catch a scrap of affection. I hate to break it to you, buddy, but I'm not going anywhere. I'm her endgame, and all you are is white rice, always a side, never the main dish."

I end the call before the douche can offer a retort. Gia walks out of the bathroom then, wearing a robe and drying her hair with a towel.

"Who were you talking to?"

"No one." I jump from the bed and walk over, pulling her flush against my naked body to steal a glorious kiss.

She drops the towel and clutches my biceps. My cock springs awake, and I press it against her belly. She moans against my lips, quickly making me lose my mind. Hell, she puts my libido in overdrive. I want to take her again, but I know there isn't time even for a quickie.

Reluctantly, I step back, my eyes blazing with hunger. "I'd better get in the shower."

Her hooded eyes focus on my lips. "Yes, you'd better."

CHAPTER 40
GIA

The rest of the week is a blur. I recorded several dance videos and now I have enough content for a couple of weeks. I shot videos for the Warriors and with Noah's help, I got Sean and Darren in a few of them. I didn't suck at presenting my French assignment to the class. On the contrary, the professor was actually pleased with me. Naturally, I rewarded my tutor accordingly.

Noah stayed at my place every single night, which resulted in a lack of sleep but more orgasms than I can count with my fingers. He's insatiable, but who am I kidding—so am I. I've never experienced such consuming desire for anyone before, and the hours we spend apart are torture. He's an addiction I didn't see coming.

Assistant Coach LaRue took the puppies to his parents' farm, which was a relief, but both Noah and I miss them.

Noah's alarm clock goes off too early, making me groan. I pull my pillow over my head, hoping I can fall back asleep. He turns the alarm off but then runs his fingers down my back.

Still half asleep and grumpy, I bat his hand away. "Too cold."

He chuckles. "Good morning, birthday girl."

"It can't possibly be morning. I just fell asleep."

Noah moves, and the sheet makes a rustling noise. Then his warm tongue replaces his cold fingers, drawing a scorching path down my back. I close my legs, rubbing them together as I try to ease the sudden ache between them. I'm wide awake now and panting like a dog in heat.

When he reaches the curve of my ass, he stops, and then he smacks one of my buttcheeks hard.

"Ouch! What was that for?"

"You're not moving fast enough. Come on, babe."

He jumps out of bed, leaving me horny and annoyed. I rub the sore spot and scowl in his direction. The room is too dark, so he can't see my face, but I bet he can feel the weight of my death glare.

"Is this how you treat me on my birthday?"

Noah stops by the door and looks over his shoulder. "Yes. Hurry, we don't have much time. The bus leaves for Boston in an hour." Then he walks out of the room.

Grumbling, I toss my legs out of bed and get up. A yawn escapes my mouth as I trudge to the bathroom and go through my morning routine like a mindless robot. Since I don't think I'm having birthday sex this morning—sad times—I hop into the shower. Now I'm awake.

I get ready in ten minutes, so my only expectation when I walk into the living room is to smell freshly brewed coffee. Instead, there's a spread on the kitchen island of croissants, baguettes, and other pastries, a charcuterie board, and assorted fruits.

My jaw drops. "When did you have the time to do all this?"

"I've been up for a few hours. Happy birthday, sunshine."

"You made me a French breakfast! I don't know what to say." My vision is already blurred from the tears welling up in my eyes.

He walks around the kitchen island and reveals a small box in his hand. "This is for you."

My heart is thundering in my chest. Small boxes usually

mean jewelry. That was Ryder's go-to gift of choice. He never realized I'm not a girl who cares for expensive bling. I rarely wear anything besides earrings.

"Thank you."

With shaking hands, I untie the bow and open the lid. Inside, I find a silver charm bracelet with a few charms already dangling from it.

"Do you like it?" Noah's voice cracks, and he's watching me expectantly.

I remove the bracelet from the box and inspect the charms. "It's gorgeous."

"I know you don't wear a lot of jewelry, but when I saw that at the store, I couldn't resist. See, I added an American flag, a Canadian flag, a Dalmatian puppy…"

"And a hockey stick and…" I squint. "Is this supposed to be a dancer?" I point at the figurine with an arm and a leg extended.

He rubs the back of his neck, looking sheepish. "She's a dancer from the seventies, I guess. It was that or ballet slippers."

"This is the most thoughtful gift I've ever received. I love it."

"Really?"

"Yes. Can you help me with the clasp?"

I extend my arm, and Noah fastens the bracelet around my wrist. "They had other cool charms, but I didn't know what else to get."

"These are perfect." I rise on my tiptoes and kiss him on the cheek. "Thank you."

"You're welcome." He stares at me with eyes that twinkle with happiness. I hope mine show the same.

The air around us becomes supercharged with electricity, and I don't know about him, but I'm a second away from dragging him back to bed so I can thank him for the gift properly. Wow, I've become a one-track-mind woman.

But our moment is interrupted when Harper joins us. "Hey, good morning, guys."

Noah steps back and glances at her. "Good morning, Harper. I hope I didn't make too much noise earlier."

"Earlier? Didn't you just wake up?"

"Nope."

"Then I heard nothing." She turns to me and pulls me into a hug. "Happy birthday, sweetie."

"Thank you."

"I have your gift in my room. I'll give it to you once Noah hits me with that coffee I smell."

"Yeah, sure." He walks around the island and grabs a few mugs from the cupboard.

"How do you take it?" he asks her.

"Black is fine."

He doesn't ask how I want mine; he's already memorized my preference, just like I've memorized his. We've been fake dating for a little over a week, but we've reached an intimacy level I honestly never had with Ryder or any previous boyfriend. Is it because we're just friends who have amazing sex together, or is it more?

"Boy, that's quite the spread." Harper stares at all the food.

"You're more than welcome to join us," Noah tells her.

"Oh no. I don't want to be the third wheel on your date."

"You wouldn't be a third wheel," I say.

"No, no. I just want coffee and a croissant." She reaches for one of the flaky pastries and then disappears into her room again.

"Should I make you a plate?" Noah asks.

"It's fine. I can make my own plate, but thank you."

He passes over a paper plate because he already knows I rarely use the ones that I'll need to wash later.

"There's a lot of food here. You probably should bring some to share with the guys on your bus ride."

"I'm sad you aren't coming with us on the bus."

"It would be weird now that we're dating."

His lips curl into a grin. "You didn't say fake before dating."

I drop my gaze to my plate and pretend to be one hundred percent interested in tearing my croissant apart. "It's a mouthful. But you know what I mean."

I'm not sure why I'm still insisting on the fake part of our relationship. It's like the last shield of protection in my arsenal. My pessimistic mind is waiting for something horrible to happen.

"One day you'll be my real girlfriend, Gia. Mark my words."

I don't contradict him. Instead, I shove a piece of croissant in my mouth and take my time chewing it. "One day you'll realize you're wasting your time with me and find greener pastures," I reply, half joking, but the fear is real.

His brows furrow. "Sunshine, that's never going to happen. Do you wanna know why?"

"Why?"

He doesn't answer right away, just stares at me with those intense brown eyes. "You're not ready to hear it yet." He brings his cup of coffee to his lips and takes a tentative sip.

"Are you serious? You're not going to tell me?"

"Nope."

Pouting, I reply, "It's my birthday. You have to tell me."

"I'll tell you if you wear my jersey to the game."

I flatten my lips and stare at him through narrowed eyes. "That's blackmail."

He raises an eyebrow. "Is it?"

"Yes," I hiss. "It's not going to work on me. I already told you why I can't wear your jersey."

He shrugs, unfazed. "Then I can't tell you my secret either."

I set my cup down and sashay toward him. "I bet I can make you spill all your secrets."

Satisfaction spreads through my chest when his Adam's apple bobs up and down. "Is that so?"

I invade his personal space, craning my neck to maintain eye contact while I wrap my arms around his waist. "Oh yeah, babe."

The intercom buzzes, interrupting my seduction moves. I stare at the offending machine.

"Who's bugging me at this hour?"

"It must be Sean. He's giving me a ride to the arena."

Disappointment floods my chest. "Oh, you have to leave already?"

Noah glances at the clock on the microwave. "Shit. I actually do."

He kisses me quickly on the lips, then rushes to the bedroom to grab his duffel bag. A morose feeling descends upon me, and I don't know how to shake it off.

Noah returns to the living room, ready to walk out the door, but he pulls me into his arms and gives me a proper goodbye kiss. It doesn't help that it just makes me miss him that much more when he leaves.

Stop being stupid Gia. You'll see him in a few hours.

CHAPTER 41
GIA

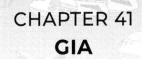

For my birthday, the girls take me out to lunch, and I'm fashionably late thanks to answering calls from my parents, my sisters, and Jaime. Jaime talked my ear off, more than usual, and he kept asking me questions about Noah even though I never told him I was dating him. Surprisingly, he didn't give me shit for that.

The girls and I are in the same café where I had lunch with Blair before, which Ashley objected to until she checked the menu online and confirmed they sell alcohol.

"What time do you need to be at the arena?" Ashley asks, then takes a sip of her mimosa.

"I probably should head out soon. The game is at seven thirty, and there'll be traffic."

"I don't have any classes this afternoon. I could ride with you," Zoey says.

"Oh, that'd be great. I hate driving alone."

"Why didn't you go with the team?" Ashley asks.

"I had a morning class I couldn't miss. Plus, you know I avoided traveling with them when I started dating Ryder."

"You did? I guess I never paid attention when you went to an away game. It didn't happen often."

"True. It's rare that I get to go because the games often clash with my schedule. And I work for them part time. Usually, my coworker Paul is the one going to the away games."

"Who's that?" Blair furrows her brows.

"He's the logistics guy. He's actually on the bus and shooting some videos for me."

"I get it," Zoey pipes up "You're trying to maintain a professional relationship with the team. Traveling with them now that you're Noah's girlfriend is a different dynamic."

I nod. "It worked out for the best. We get to go on a road trip together."

"Hey! Why aren't Blair and I invited?" Ashley complains.

"I didn't say you weren't, but you never said you wanted to come to the game. I just assumed we'd meet up later."

"I don't care about hockey, but knowing that my presence will annoy the crap out of Alex is enough incentive. Count me in." Blair smiles wickedly. "That is, if you can get us tickets."

I smirk. She sure is going out of her way to get into Alex's path. Maybe there's more than hate going on between them. I hope I'm wrong. Not that I don't believe her feelings can change from hate to love, but Alex isn't boyfriend material. Actually, neither twin is, but Alex is definitely the worst of the duo. And Blair, despite her sharp tongue, doesn't have a lot of experience dating.

"I have extra tickets. I got them just in case you changed your minds," I reply.

"Where are the seats? Are they close to the ice?" Blair asks.

"Not this time. They aren't bad though. We're right in the middle and have a good view of the puck."

"Who's favored to win?" Blair takes a sip of her mimosa.

"The Warriors, right?" Zoey looks at me.

"Yeah, they're the favorite, but you never know with hockey."

"They'd better win." Ashley twists her face into a scowl. "I don't want their loss to mess up your birthday celebration."

"I'm pretty sure Noah will do everything he can to make it happen. That boy is *seriously* in love with you," Zoey says.

Ashley perks up in her seat and gives me a meaningful glance. She's the only one who knows that my relationship with Noah is fake. God, I can't even think about him in those terms anymore. What we have is real, and I think it's about time I let him know.

"Really?" Ashley arches her eyebrows.

Blair nods. "You should see the way the guy looks at her."

"I can't wait to witness that for myself." Ashley brings her drink to her lips and smiles before she takes a sip. "Did he get you anything for your birthday?"

My cheeks warm. I know she'll have a field day when she sees my bracelet.

"Yes. This." I lift my hand and show them.

"Aw, he gave you a charm bracelet. How adorable," Zoey coos.

"How is he in bed?" Blair blurts out, earning everyone's attention.

"How many mimosas have you had?" Ashley laughs.

"Shut up. I'm not drunk."

I drop my gaze and don't answer.

"I don't think our girl has slept with her new boy toy yet." Ashley's statement is loaded.

"Hmm... I think you're wrong," Zoey pipes up. "Gia's face is beet red now."

Ashley narrows her eyes. Hell. I haven't told her anything, and now she's going to give me so much shit.

I push my chair back and stand up. "I'm going to the restroom."

"I'll come with you," she says.

Since Zoey and Blair were just there, they don't offer to tag along. No sooner do I enter the women's restroom than Ashley corners me.

"You slept with Noah and didn't tell me?" Her voice is high-pitched.

"No, because I knew you were going to make a big deal out of it."

"It *is* a big deal. I thought your relationship was supposed to be fake!"

"Well... it was until the benefits were added to the table."

She crosses her arms and levels me with a hard stare. "I know you're not *that* stupid. Sleeping with a guy you were supposed to fake date is a recipe for disaster. And if it's true that he's into you, you're going to break his heart."

Guilt twists my stomach painfully. "I know, but I have a confession to make. This relationship is beginning to feel real."

She throws her hands in the air. "Duh, of course it is. You're going on dates, adopting a puppy, and now you're fucking his brains out. It doesn't get more real than that. My only question is, why do I sense hesitation from you?"

I take a deep breath, looking away from her intense stare. "Because he's a sweetheart. The best guy I've ever dated, and I'm afraid he's too perfect to be real."

"Let me get this straight. You're just going to keep things as is because you're afraid he's not who you think he is?"

"Yep." I glance at her again.

"Noah isn't Ryder, Gia. I know that jerk blindsided you, but that doesn't mean Noah will do the same thing. If you care about him, then you have to take the leap."

"I know that, and I've been close to telling him how I feel, but... I always end up choking."

She smirks. "What you need is some liquid courage. You're telling him tonight."

My heart speeds up. "I was planning to."

"You should wear his jersey to the game."

I shake my head. "I'm not ready for that yet. Besides, you know my rule."

She rolls her eyes. "Oh yeah, you don't ever wear any guy's jersey to the game because you wanna remain impartial."

"Exactly, and I *just* started dating Noah. It's a monumental gesture that I'm not ready for."

Ashley rubs her chin. "True. You should save that for later. But you *will* tell him how you feel at the club. Deal?"

"Deal."

"Also, now that I know that you're banging the hot rookie, you're getting your own room at the hotel."

I should want to be with my girlfriends, but I'm looking forward to the prospect of spending the evening with my not-so-fake boyfriend.

I smirk. "If you insist."

"Like you weren't already thinking about it."

When we return to the table, Zoey tells me, "Your phone was ringing."

My stomach falls through the earth. Is it another anonymous call?

Blair adds quickly, "It was Martin. His name popped up on the screen."

Relief washes over me, and I send her a silent *thank you* with my eyes.

"Oh yeah. He's coming to Boston too."

Ashley twists her face. "Why did you invite him?"

"I didn't. It was Noah."

"Really?" Her eyebrows shoot up.

"Martin showed up at my apartment the other day, crying his eyes out because his cousin was in a bad accident. He mentioned that he was looking forward to spending time with me on my birthday. I think Noah could tell I was feeling guilty for not inviting Martin, so he did."

"I'm shocked. Didn't you say Martin was rude to him the other day?" Ashley asks.

"Yeah. I was surprised too."

"He probably invited Martin because he knows the guy is

important to you. Noah is so dreamy." Zoey sighs. "I want my boyfriend to be just like him."

"I thought you didn't have time to date," Blair chimes in.

Zoey's face turns serious. "I don't right now, but one day I will. It sucks that most likely, I'll have to go to Jesse and Riley's wedding without a date."

"Holy crap!" Ashley smacks the table. "I totally forgot about that. When is it again?"

"During Christmas break."

"Oh yeah, the invitation is on my fridge," I say. "He invited the entire team, even the new guys, so they wouldn't feel left out. That's a couple months away, Zoey. I'm sure if you want, you can find a date."

She wrinkles her nose. "I don't wanna go with just any guy."

My phone rings again. It's Martin calling back. "I should answer this."

I begin to stand up.

"You don't need to go outside. You can answer the phone here. And put it on speaker so we can all hear." Ashley smiles wickedly.

I'd rather take the call outside, but now I can't without looking suspicious.

"Hey, Martin. What's up?"

"Happy birthday, gorgeous. How's your day going?"

"Great. I'm out with my girlfriends having lunch."

"Oh... where at? Maybe I can stop by to give you your gift."

They all shake their heads.

"We're about to head out. What time are you coming to Boston?"

"It depends. What time are you leaving? I was hoping to catch a ride with you."

Blair trades a glance with Zoey while Ashley just twists her face in disgust.

"I'm driving with the girls."

"Oh..." He sounds disappointed. "Is there any room for me? If you don't mind? Unless it's a no-dicks-allowed situation."

Ashley bobs her head up and down as she mouths *no dicks*.

I try to tell her with my eyes that I can't simply tell him to drive by himself. Martin is a mess thanks to the unfortunate situation with his family.

"If we take the Escalade, then there's room," Blair replies.

"Am I on speaker?" he asks.

"Yeah, sorry. I should've told you."

"It's fine. Ladies, I promise I won't be a jerk and you can listen to whatever you want."

"We're leaving in a couple hours. Can you make it?" Ashley asks, not hiding her annoyance.

"Yep. I'm all ready to go."

"You're going to chill at the hotel by yourself while we're at the game," I tell him.

"Actually, I was hoping to get a ticket to the game. Do you think it's possible?"

Ashley's jaw drops to the floor. Mine too.

"You want to come to a *hockey* game? Who are you, and what have you done to Martin?" I ask through a nervous laugh. I'm not really keen on him tagging along, but I also don't want to be a dick and tell him I don't have an extra ticket when I do.

He laughs. "This is a one-time deal, babe, and only because it's your birthday. All I care about spending time with you. It doesn't matter where."

Ashley sticks her finger in her mouth and pretends to be vomiting. It's hard to keep a straight face.

"I have an extra ticket for you. So that's settled, then. Meet me at my place at three?"

"Sounds good."

As soon as I end the call, Ashley blurts out, "What the fuck were you thinking?"

"What?"

"You're bringing Martin to a hockey game. He's the guy who openly hates everyone on the team," Zoey replies.

"I feel bad for him. He's going through some family stuff. Did you want me to tell him he couldn't come?"

"Yes!" they reply in unison.

"You'd better keep Martin hidden so the guys don't see him while they're playing," Ashley says.

"How am I supposed to do that? Martin's red hair is like a beacon."

"Don't sit next to him if you don't want Noah getting distracted." Blair shrugs.

"Noah isn't the jealous type. He wouldn't have invited Martin otherwise."

"Trust me, Gia. All guys get jealous. If he sees you sitting next to Martin, he won't be happy about it," Ashley replies.

An uneasy feeling settles in the pit of my stomach. Maybe she's right and I didn't think this through. "It's too late now. Martin is coming. So please stop making me feel bad about it."

CHAPTER 42
NOAH

I have jitters just like I did before the exhibition game against Clayton U, but the vibe in the locker room is much different than before. The excitement is palpable; I can feel it in the air and underneath my skin. Even CJ has put his assholery aside and is acting like a team player.

I expect to see Gia in the locker room, but she doesn't come. In her place is Paul Samuels, the team's logistics assistant. He came on the bus with us and has been taking a ton of video footage.

I've already changed into my uniform, so I pull up my phone to text her.

> You're not coming to interview us?

> No. Coach asked me not to.

> Why?

> I don't know.

> Do you think it's because of our relationship?

> I hope not. Is Paul getting everything?

>> Yeah. Has not put the camera down for a second.

> Oh boy. That means lots of footage to go over.

>> Are you at the arena already?

> Yes, everyone is here.

>> Where are you seated? I'll look for you in the crowd.

> Section B, tenth row. We have signs.

>> [heart emoji]. I gotta go. Coach is about to speak.

> K. Good luck.

"You have a goofy grin on your face. You must have been texting Gia," Sean says.

"Yeah. She said Coach told her not to come into the locker room. Do you know anything about that?"

Sean furrows his brows. "No. That's strange. Maybe because it's her birthday and he doesn't want her to work?"

"I didn't think of that."

He taps my shoulder. "I'm pretty sure that must be it. Don't worry."

I watch him walk to the other side of the room to speak to CJ, but his words didn't put me at ease completely. I hope he's right though. I don't want our fake relationship to jeopardize her job. That would negate the whole point of it. True, I had ulterior motives when I came up with the idea, but getting her to fall in love with me can't cost Gia her job.

Logan and Alex are goofing around, but they stop when Coach Bedford and Assistant Coach LaRue enter the room. They take turns speaking, and the overall message is that tonight should be an easy game. We're ranked higher than the opposing team. But the message is clear—we're not supposed to slack off. I don't plan to. The last thing I want is to screw up Gia's birthday party by losing the game and having everybody be a sourpuss around her.

Ten minutes later, we head to the rink. I'll never get used to the sound of thousands of people cheering all at once, even if the majority are supporting our opponents. The energy is electrifying, and it seeps into my bones, making me feel alive. My heart is beating faster with excitement.

As soon as I step onto the ice for the warm-ups, I look for Gia. It doesn't take long for me to locate her. She's holding a sign that says *Go Warriors*, but she's talking to Ashley and doesn't see me. A slow smile begins to unfurl on my face, but it wilts when she lowers the sign and I see who's sitting next to her. That weasel Martin.

I clamp my jaw so hard it hurts my molars. I'm not jealous of the guy, but I know he's only here to piss me off. The moment I met him, I knew he had a thing for Gia, but now that he's admitted it, it's war.

Alex stops next to me and follows my line of sight.

"Who are you glaring at?" A second later he continues. "Oh, *that* guy. What the fuck is he doing here?"

"I invited him to Gia's birthday party. I didn't think he'd come to the game too."

"Why would you do that? You know he has a major crush on her."

"Yep. The douche told me so."

Alex skates in front of me. "Come again?"

"Never mind. We need to warm up."

I try to push my irritation into a dark corner of my mind as I skate around our side of the rink. I won't let that nimrod get under my skin. Besides, I have a surprise for Gia, and I can show it to her only after I score.

By the time we return to the bench, my rage has subsided to a low simmer in my gut. The announcements and national anthem take another ten minutes, and by the time the game kicks off, I'm antsy as hell, ready for action.

I'm in the starting lineup, but it's Sean who faces off with the opposing team's captain. He wins the draw and sends the puck in my direction. The moment I gain control of it, I get in the zone, more determined than ever to play the best game of my life. I want to hear Gia scream my name while that fucker sits next to her and sulks.

We easily dominate, keeping possession of the puck and staying in the offensive zone for the first thirty seconds. Ballard tries to protect their net, but eventually, they succumb. Alex shoots, and the puck bounces off the goalie's pad straight in my direction. I don't hesitate and fire a shot that is impossible to block. The goalie doesn't have a chance to react before the puck flies over his shoulder.

I let out a yell, throwing a fist in the air, then skate toward the bench to fist-bump everyone before I veer toward Gia's section of the stands. She's jumping up and down with Zoey, Ashley, and even Blair. As I predicted, Martin is glowering.

I lift my jersey, revealing the surprise I have underneath it. I ordered a custom shirt with a pattern of Gia's face printed all over it. I make sure she sees it, and then I make a heart shape with my hands. She won't wear my jersey, but I'm wearing hers.

GIA

I jump out of my seat when Noah scores, yelling as loud as I can to compensate for the silence in the arena. Warriors fans are a minority here. Even Ashley and Blair join Zoey and me in the celebration. Martin remains seated. I'm waving my sign when Noah skates by us and lifts his jersey.

My heart skips a beat and then restarts much faster than before.

"Is that your face all over his shirt?" Ashley asks.

I don't reply; too busy trying to remain calm and not freak out. Noah is wearing *my face* when I refused to wear his jersey. Then he goes and makes a heart-shaped sign with his hands. It's impossible not to swoon hard.

"Oh my God. I can't believe he did that," Zoey chimes in. "That's so romantic."

"That was so gimmicky and pathetic," Martin grumbles.

I ignore him because not even his bad mood will change the fact that my heart is overflowing with giddiness and excitement, and the butterflies in my stomach are going wild.

"You have to wear his jersey at the next game, Gia," Ashley says. "If you don't, I'm going to hit you upside the head."

I glance at her. That comment coming from the only person who knows my relationship with Noah is fake is ten times more meaningful.

"I'm serious," she adds.

"Excuse me, do you mind trading seats with me?" A familiar voice asks Martin.

"Uh, yeah, I do mind," he retorts.

I jump out of my seat and yell, "Jaime! What are you doing here?"

He's smiling from ear to ear when he replies, "Surprising you, duh." He opens his arms wide. "Do I get a hug or what?"

With Martin seated between us, we have no choice but to crowd him as Jaime pulls me into a bear hug.

"I can't believe you're here."

"You have to thank Coach Bedford. He arranged the whole thing."

"That's why he didn't want me in the locker room before the game."

"Yeah. My flight was delayed, hence why I'm late."

"Can you please sit down?" a guy in the row behind us asks, sounding annoyed.

"Yeah, sure, sorry." I look down at Martin. "Scooch. I want to sit next to my brother."

I could understand his reluctance to trade seats with a stranger, but he doesn't look happy now either. "Sure."

I return to my seat, and now that Jaime is next to me, I'm feeling a million times better. "I thought you were busy this weekend."

"Well, I had to tell you that so you wouldn't suspect I was coming." He looks over my shoulder. "Hi ladies. How have you been?"

They all say hello to him and then turn their attention to the game. I do as well when the whistle blows. Alex got himself a penalty. That must be a record for him.

"Why aren't you wearing your boyfriend's jersey?" Jaime asks.

"You know my rule."

"Your rule is stupid."

I sigh. "Everyone keeps telling me that."

"Noah is a good hockey player, but is he a good boyfriend?"

"He's the best," I reply without hesitation.

Jaime nods. "Then wear his damn jersey next time."

I elbow his arm. "Did you come here just to boss me around?"

He smirks. "I'm your big brother. That's my job."

I focus on the game, but in the back of my mind, I'm seriously reevaluating my rule. Maybe it was easier to refuse to wear Ryder's jersey because the feelings I had for him weren't this strong. The connection I have with Noah is like nothing I've ever experienced before. He's all I think about, and when I'm with him, I need to be close. I need to touch him. He makes me feel like the most cherished person in the world. And that's why it's so fucking scary to admit what's happening to me.

But I'm not going to be a coward anymore. I'm all in.

CHAPTER 43
GIA

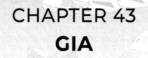

By the end of the game, my voice is almost gone. The Warriors won 6-1, and I couldn't be happier for them. It's only when we're getting ready to leave the arena that I notice Martin's seat is empty. Maybe he left to use the restroom? I'd feel bad that I ignored him for the most part if he hadn't acted like a jerk when I asked him to trade seats with Jaime.

"Are you going to the locker room now?" Zoey asks.

I look at Jaime to gauge his reaction. He hasn't been inside a locker room since he was forced to quit hockey. Sensing my stare, he says, "You can go. I'll wait here with your friends."

"I don't have a pass. Let's find Martin and head back to the hotel."

No sooner do I say that than my phone rings in my purse. My heart does a cartwheel when I see it's Noah who's calling.

"Hey," I say with a smile.

"Hello, sunshine. Did you enjoy the game?"

"What kind of question is that? It was awesome. Is Alex okay? He took quite a hit."

Noah chuckles. "Have you met the guy? He's a boulder, barely felt a thing."

"I didn't hear anything from Gordon Montana's team. I don't think he made it to the game."

"That's fine."

"We're about to head back to the hotel and wait for you there."

"Don't go yet. I want to see you."

"But I don't have a pass to the locker room."

"I'll come to you."

"Where? This place is huge, and we're already on our way out of the stands."

"Pick a location and text me. I'll see you in a few."

"Okay."

"Wow, the boys are just barely off the ice and he's already calling you. He's in *lurve*." Ashley smirks.

I give her a droll look. "Please, Ash, don't start."

"I can't wait to finally meet him in person." Jaime smiles, and his eyes twinkle with mischief. *Crap on toast.*

"What did he want?" Zoey asks. She wasn't close enough to overhear the conversation.

"He wants me to wait for him before we head back to the hotel."

"It looks like someone's marking his territory," Blair pipes up.

I frown. "He isn't like that."

"Oh darling, all guys are like that, even the non-jealous type," Ashley replies.

"Well, he doesn't need to be jealous. Martin is just a friend and not even a close one anymore."

"Good to hear," Zoey chimes in. "He gives me the creeps."

"He's *sooo* friendly," Jaime adds.

We finally make it back to the food area, and I search for a place that's not super packed. The game is over, so most people are heading out. I stop by the hot dog stand and text Noah.

"Speaking of Martin, where did he go?" Blair asks.

"I'm not sure."

"If we're lucky, he went back to the hotel," Ashley replies without looking up from her phone.

Knowing Martin, he didn't. He just wants me to look for him. But I can do that after I see Noah.

"I need to take a leak. I'll be right back," Jaime tells me.

"Okay."

My phone vibrates in my hand. It's a text from Noah saying he's on his way. Two seconds later, Martin also texts me.

> Where are you?

I tell him our location, wishing that he'd taken longer to resurface. Oh well.

A minute later, I spot his red head in the crowd. I wave at him, and when he sees me, he smiles. Suddenly, strong arms wrap around my waist and lift me off the floor. I let out yelp, but I know exactly who's kissing my neck now from behind. It tickles, and I can't help the burst of laughter that goes up my throat.

"Noah, put me down."

He does so and then spins me around in the next second. Then he traps my face between his hands and crushes his lips against mine. I don't even have time to prepare for the intoxicating assault. I melt against his body, opening my lips to allow his tongue access. I don't care that we're making out in front of all my friends.

"Jesus Christ, get a room." Martin's annoying comment pops my bubble of happiness.

Noah leans back, ending the kiss too soon, and looks over my shoulder. "*You* should get a room and stay there because you're clearly tired and grumpy and in need of a nap."

"I'm not tired," Martin grits out.

Noah switches his attention back to me and smiles. "Did you like the surprise?"

"Do you mean your shirt?"

The corners of his lips twitch upward. "Yep." He leans closer and whispers in my ear. "Unlike you, I have no problem letting the world know I'm yours."

The fluttering in my belly intensifies, and my heart beats staccato. "I have no problem with that either."

He tilts his head and watches me with an intensity that only he can muster. I realize that my statement can be taken two different ways. What I meant to say was that I don't have any issues telling the world I'm his. But did he get that?

"Hey, get your hands off my sister," Jaime says as he walks over.

Noah turns and his eyes widen. "Shut up!" I expect him to be taken aback, not hug my brother as if they're old friends. "I thought I recognized you from the ice. I didn't know you were coming."

"Coach Bedford arranged everything, but he warned me to keep my piehole shut."

I clear my throat. "Hello. What's this?" I wave my hand between them.

"What's what, sis?" Jaime asks innocently.

"You know each other?"

They trade a guilty look, then Noah replies, "Your brother reached out to me through social media a few days ago."

"Why didn't you tell me?"

Jaime hugs me, but it's an excuse to whisper in my ear. "I know all about the fake dating, sis. Don't be mad at Noah. He only told me after I threatened to castrate him. Oh, and by the way, he's so fucking in love with you, it's not even funny. I approve."

I meet Noah's stare and see the guilt shining there. My brother can be a jackass when he wants to.

Noah's phone rings, and I don't have a chance to tell him I'm not angry he didn't tell me Jaime contacted him.

"Hey, Sean. I'm with the girls. What's up?" There's a pause, and I can't hear what Sean is saying because of the background noise. "Oh, already? Okay. I'll be right there." He ends the call and looks at me. "I have to go, sunshine. They're ready to head out."

"That was fast," Ashley pipes up.

"Everybody's excited and ready to party. Do we know where we're going?"

"Yes. I'll let you know once you guys are at the hotel," I say. "We still need to change."

"Are you all sharing a room?"

"I got my own room," Jaime replies. "Obviously."

I give him a questioning look. "Why obviously?"

"Do you even have to ask?"

"Ew, Jaime."

"What? Like you and Noah aren't—" I cover his mouth with my hand.

"Shut up!" My face is on fire, and when I glance at Ashley and catch her amused expression, it only makes things worse.

I try to communicate silently, reminding her to keep her mouth shut. I don't want to tell Noah that I have my own room now, all thanks to Blair pulling some strings with the reservations department. Our hotel was fully booked, and I don't know how she managed to snag an extra room, but she made it work. Mercifully, Martin isn't staying in the same hotel as us. He's in the one across the street.

"We're sharing a room," Blair answers, and when Noah isn't looking, she winks at me.

"Cool. I'll see you, ladies, later," he says, then kisses me on the cheek. "I'll be counting the minutes, sunshine."

I watch him walk away, still in a daze from his first kiss. A slow smile unfurls on my face when I witness Noah turning heads as he goes. A deep satisfaction spreads through my chest because I know he's all mine.

CHAPTER 44
NOAH

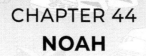

Naturally, the guys and I are ready way before the girls. I still don't know where we're going; I only know it's a place we can dance. I should be dreading it, but I'm still on a high from our win, and from knowing I get to be with my girl on her birthday.

It gives me time to get to know Jaime better though. We exchanged only a few words over DMs, and then a video call once. He's a cool guy but super protective of Gia. He has nothing to worry about when it comes to me. I'll do anything for her.

"We should do shots before the ladies get here," Alex pipes up.

I glance at the club soda in my hand and then shake my head. "You go ahead."

For starters, the bartenders are carding everyone, and I didn't bother getting a fake ID. Plus, I don't want to get trashed before Gia even makes it down to the lobby. I'm the only one who doesn't take Alex up on his offer. Jaime, Sean, Darren, Logan, and CJ are game.

While they're busy trying to decide what type of shot they want, I pull out my phone and text Gia.

> What's the ETA?

I don't expect her to reply right away, but she does.

> Zoey and I are ready. It's Ashley and Blair who are taking the longest.

> The guys are already doing shots.

> And you aren't?

> Nah. I don't need alcohol.

I hesitate before I type the next sentence. It's corny as fuck, but hell, she already knows who I am.

> I'm already drunk on you.

> I knew that line was coming. :)

Someone taps me on the shoulder—Logan. "Isn't that Martin making a beeline for the elevators?"

Son of a bitch. It is. He isn't staying at this hotel, but it's obvious he has every intention of going up to the girls' room. *Not in this lifetime, pal.*

"Yes. I'll be right back."

He's waiting in front of the elevator when I catch up with him. Forcing a smile on my face, I shout, "Martin, my man! Where are you going?"

He turns to me, eyes round as if he's surprised that I'm addressing him in a friendly manner.

"Uh, I was going to hang out with Gia."

I throw my arm around his shoulder and steer him away from the elevator. "No way. Come hang with us and let the ladies do their thing. Trust me, the last thing they want is a guy hovering while they get ready."

His body is tense next to mine. It doesn't take a genius to know the last thing he wants to do is hang out with a bunch of hockey players—and *me*. I'm not threatened by him, but I'm also not stupid. He ain't spending alone time with Gia tonight if I can help it.

Everyone turns when I get back to the bar with Martin in tow. Alex openly glares, but mercifully he doesn't make an aggravating comment.

"Look who I found lost in the lobby," I say.

"I wasn't lost," Martin grumbles.

"Hey, Martin." Sean approaches, sporting a friendly smile. "How's it going?"

"Pretty good so far."

"He was at the game. Can you believe it?" I tap his shoulder harder than necessary, before stepping to the side.

Logan's eyes widen innocently. "No way! I thought you hated hockey."

Before the douche canoe can reply, I say, "I think Gia's love for hockey is finally rubbing off on him." This couldn't be further from the truth, and I can't wait to hear what's going to come out of his mouth.

"Yeah, that must be it," Jaime adds sarcastically.

I get the feeling he's also not a fan of Martin. I think only Gia can't see he's an unlikeable ass, but maybe it's because he fakes it well in front of her. Let's hope tonight he lets the mask fall.

Unfortunately, Sean butts in before Martin can reply. "What're you drinking?"

He shakes his head. "I'm good thanks."

"Come on, man," Alex butts in, smiling wickedly. "Have a shot with us."

Before Martin can refuse, Alex puts a shot of tequila in his hand. They clink glasses—*Alex* clinks his glass against Martin's—before throwing his head back and drinking the whole thing in one go. He sets the glass back on the bar counter with a loud thud. I'm surprised he didn't break the glass.

Still holding his full shot glass, Martin looks at me. "Aren't you drinking? Oh, that's right, you can't yet."

I laugh in my head. *Is that the best you got, buddy?*

"Oh, I'll have a drink when my girl gets here."

He scowls. "She's a person, not an object you own."

My lips twist into a smirk. "It's mutual ownership. And she loves when I call her mine."

The hatred pouring from his eyes is palpable. It doesn't faze me though. I don't even consider him an adversary. He's just an annoying bug.

My phone vibrates in my pocket. I check and see it's a text from Gia telling me she's coming down.

"If you'll excuse me." I leave Martin and his hatred behind and go back toward the elevators. I'd rather meet Gia in the lobby before she sees him hanging out with us. I know she'll find it weird, and I want to reassure her that we weren't giving him a hard time.

A minute later, she steps out of the metal box, and my jaw drops. She's wearing a skintight one-piece catsuit that makes my pulse accelerate. It's black and shimmers in certain spots. The front isn't cut low, just enough to give me a hint of her glorious breasts. My head is spinning already.

She smiles broadly and asks, "What do you think?"

I can't answer right away. All the blood in my brain has traveled south and I'm having a hard time controlling my reaction.

Ashley laughs. "He can't even speak."

I swallow hard. "Wow. I'm not even sure I want to go out anymore. Let's go back up to the room."

Her face turns bright red, but it doesn't stop her from sashaying toward me and invading my space.

Her arms wrap around my waist, and with her high heels, she doesn't need to tilt her head up that much to look into my eyes. "That wouldn't be fair to our friends."

"I'm having a hard time thinking about them." My voice comes out low and tight.

"Maybe you *should* go back to the room. There's so much sexual energy here it's affecting me," Ashley complains.

Without breaking eye contact with Gia, I reply, "Then you'd better go to the bar. I'm about to kick things up a notch."

Gia arches her eyebrows, but she doesn't step away from me. I barely notice when her friends move on.

I only have eyes for my girl. "You look stunning, sunshine."

"Thanks. You don't look too bad yourself." She brings her nose to my neck and takes a deep breath. "And you smell so good."

Her closeness makes me shiver. I close my eyes for a second so I can get my head on straight. I'm on the verge of tossing her over my shoulder like a caveman and returning to my room. My hard-on is already pressing painfully against my jeans.

"You have no idea what you're doing to me right now, babe." I touch my forehead to hers.

She releases a shaky breath. "Trust me. You're not the only one affected."

Leaning back, I cup her cheek, then slide my hand to the back of her head before bringing her face to mine. The moment our lips touch, an explosion of emotions seems to go off like fireworks. I'm burning for my girl, dying to have her on her back, screaming my name as I plow into her. But there's more, the unmistakable certainty that I'm head over heels in love with her.

I want to confess, shout to the world that I'm in love with Gia Mancini, but I control myself. The fear that I'll scare her is holding me back. I pull back before I combust on the spot. Deep male satisfaction spreads through my chest as I witness her flushed cheeks and hooded eyes.

"Okay, let's join the group before we make this a party of two," I say, lacing my fingers with hers.

"Yes, we'd better."

Maybe desire is making me imagine things, but I'm almost positive she'd rather go upstairs.

I'm counting the minutes.

CHAPTER 45
GIA

The moment I step foot in the club that Ashley picked, I know I'll have a good time. It's eighties night, which means I'm in heaven. We lingered long enough at the hotel before coming here, so the place is already full and the dance floor is on fire—just like my body. Noah hasn't left my side, and now his arm is wrapped around my waist, the closeness wreaking havoc on my body. The two tequila shots I drank at the hotel bar are probably contributing to my state of horniness.

He leans closer and whispers in my ear, "What do you want to drink?"

"I should probably stick to tequila."

"I'll pass on the message to Jaime." He kisses me on the cheek and steps away to talk to the guys.

My heart is fluttering, and I'm in a daze, swooning hard over my fake boyfriend who will soon know I'm striking the *fake* out of our deal. I want him, all of him.

I'm so busy staring at Noah that I don't notice Martin's approach until he's standing right next to me. "Finally. I thought he was going to stay attached to your side the whole night like a leech."

"Martin, be nice."

"I *am* being nice. So what are you drinking? I'm buying."

"Oh, Noah is already getting me a drink."

"How? Isn't he like eighteen?"

"Nineteen. And he isn't buying it."

Martin shakes his head. "Man, doesn't it suck to be dating a guy barely out of high school?"

"No."

"He can't even drink wine on a date," Martin continues as if I hadn't spoken.

"I don't drink wine either." I shrug. "It's actually refreshing to be with someone who isn't always wasted or high."

He grimaces. "Ouch. Was that a dig at me? I'm not always high."

I roll my eyes. "I didn't mean as a dig, but if the shoe fits…"

He tilts his head and studies me for a couple beats. "You've changed, you know."

"Everyone does, Martin."

"Yeah, but…" He shakes his head. "Never mind."

I know what Martin is doing. He's been super critical of my life choices since I started dating Ryder, and now Noah. It's a shitty thing to do on my birthday, but I won't let his issues kill my buzz.

I'm glad when Noah returns with my drink and one of his own. I've barely spoken to Martin, and I already need a break from him.

"Here it is, sunshine," he says, ignoring Martin.

"Thanks."

Noah clinks his glass with mine, and then we both take our shots. He shakes his head and blurts out, "Whoa."

"First time drinking tequila, kid?" Martin smirks.

He snorts. "Absolutely not."

I turn to Noah, remembering what happened the last time he drank tequila. "I thought you swore off tequila after the dancing incident."

His eyes widen. "Shit. You're right. Short-term memory, I guess."

"Are you going to show me your moves again?" I smile.

He twists his face into a grimace. "Hmm, I might need more than one shot for that. But first I gotta visit the washroom."

"Washroom?" Martin asks in a mocking tone. "Do you mean restroom?"

"Potato, potahto."

Noah sneaks his arm around my waist and pulls me flat against his chest. I don't have time to react before his mouth claims mine. The kiss is deep and hungry, and it leaves me breathless. When he eases off, I sway a little. "I'll see you in a sec, sunshine."

"Okay." I watch him leave like a schoolgirl pining for her crush across the quad.

"Where did Noah go?" Zoey asks, joining Martin and me.

"Restroom. Where have you been?"

"I got separated from the girls on the way back from the restroom. Then I spent the last ten minutes looking for them."

I glance over her shoulder. "I take it you didn't find them."

"No, they might be on the dance floor already. Do you wanna go look for them?"

I look toward where Noah disappeared and hesitate. "Maybe I should wait for Noah."

"Oh, come on. He's not a baby," Martin chimes in. "He can find you later." He links his arm with mine. "Besides, you owe me a dance, partner."

Zoey's attention drops to our joined arms and then moves back to my face. It's dark in the club, but I can guess she's asking me if she needs to run interference.

I'm really not in the mood to get into an argument with Martin, so I say, "Sure, let's dance."

X X X

NOAH

It wasn't my intention to leave Gia alone with Martin, but I couldn't hold on any longer, or I might piss my pants. And bringing her with me and making her wait in front of the washroom would be overkill. Besides, I'm sure she would be hit on nonstop. A pretty girl like her alone in a club.... yeah, easy target. I'd rather leave her alone with Martin. The devil you know and all that.

On my way back, someone taps me on the shoulder. I turn and can't believe my eyes when I see Gordon Montana staring at me.

"Dude! What are you doing here?" I ask as if we're old friends. This is already the tequila talking.

"A buddy of mine owns the club. I was on my way to the VIP lounge."

"No shit. Small world. Did you come to the game?"

"I did. My agent got tickets. You guys kicked ass. And before you ask, I didn't have time to visit you in the locker room. I had an emergency that I had to take care of."

"I hope everything's okay now."

He waves his hand. "Yeah, sure. Don't worry about it. Where's your pretty girl?"

"I was on my way back to her. It's her birthday. We're here with friends."

"That's amazing. You should all come with me to the VIP lounge."

"For real?" My brows shoot to the heavens. "That'd be awesome!"

"All right, then. Let's go get the crew."

He gestures with his arm, urging me to lead the way. I'm having an out-of-body moment. Never in a million years did I dream that I'd be hanging out with Gordon Montana in a club in Boston.

When we return to the spot where I left Gia, I don't see her.

Alex and Logan spot me and walk over. At first, they don't notice Gordon standing next to me, but when they do, their eyes bug out and their jaws drop cartoon style.

"Holy shit!" Alex blurts out. "You're Gordon Montana."

"That I am, son." The guy smiles broadly.

"Wow! We're such huge fans," Logan says and then turns to me. "Why is Gordon Montana hanging out with you?"

I give him a droll look. "Because I'm cool as shit. What do you think?"

Gordon laughs. "He ain't lying."

"Have you seen Gia?" I ask.

Alex's face turns serious. "The last time I saw her, she was on the dance floor with Martin."

My stomach twists savagely before dropping like a rock. I'm not surprised that weasel got her alone the moment I turned my back. It isn't like I can compete with him when it comes to dancing. I suck.

"Come again?" Gordon frowns. "Your girl is dancing with another dude?"

"He's an old friend," I grumble.

"Is he gay? Otherwise, I'd be going down there right this second, buddy."

He doesn't need to tell me twice. I was already planning on it. The only guy who's going to dance with Gia all night long is me. "I'm on it."

It's surreal that I don't think twice about walking away from Gordon Montana, my idol growing up, so I can stop that jerk face from monopolizing my girl. If I were certain his feelings for her were platonic, I wouldn't mind so much. But I know he's trying to sneak back into her life.

The dance floor is on a lower level and packed. I have no hope of finding Gia if I decide to venture in blind. I need to locate her from a vantage point first. I stretch my neck and look for Martin instead. His red hair will come in handy. It takes me a good two minutes to find them, and what do you know—he's trying to pull Gia closer to him for a dance that involves a lot of grinding. Hell to the fucking no. The only person who can do that to her is me. Jealousy breaks free and courses through my veins, spreading like wildfire. Under normal circumstances, I don't get possessive like this. But I'm already under the influence, and I know Martin has no good intentions.

I dive into the sea of people, pushing and shoving without care. Luckily, most of them are drunk or high and barely notice me.

The music changes to a Prince song, the one that's sexy as hell—I can't think of the name now. I'm close enough to them that I can see Martin's ready to make a move. Neither sees me coming. Before he has a chance to trap her against his body, I step between them, giving him my back.

"Hey, babe. Miss me?"

She throws her arms around my neck and smiles. "Would you judge me if I said yes?"

"I'd judge if you said no."

"Really, dude? I was dancing with her," Martin complains.

I look over my shoulder. "Sorry, buddy. Only I can dance this close to my girl. Go find your own."

His nostrils flare, and I can only imagine what kind of violent thoughts are running through his head now. But all he does is give me the death glare before he walks away, shoving whoever's in his path.

"Now you've done it. He's going to hate on hockey players for life." Gia laughs.

"You aren't mad?"

She arches one eyebrow. "Did you want me to get mad?"

I shake my head. "Of course not. I'm sorry I was abrasive with your friend. But I meant it. I don't want to see another guy dirty dancing with you, whether you're my real girlfriend or not."

"I don't want to dance with another guy either." She touches my face and then rises on the tips of her toes to kiss me.

The world ceases to exist, and my jealousy evaporates like magic. The beat of the song wraps around us both, and lo and behold, I'm dancing with her. I probably look ridiculous, but she doesn't seem to mind my stiffness. Her eyes lock with mine, and then suddenly, I don't give a shit about hanging out with Gordon Montana, or stupid Martin and his games. I care only about the person standing in front of me, watching me like I've been hoping she would one day—as if I'm the only person that matters in the world.

My heart is thundering, and my pulse is beating so loud in my ears it's competing with the song playing in the background.

"Are you having a good time, sunshine?"

"Yes."

I tighten my hold on her, pulling her even closer to me. I'm turned on as hell, and our hips swinging to the beat of the song are creating enough friction to make me feverish.

"What happened to your friends?" I ask.

"Don't know. I think I lost them."

I lean down and whisper in her ear, "Do you wanna go look for them?"

"In a little bit. Let's finish this dance." She sighs, stretching her neck as she tilts her head to the side. It's a temptation I can't resist. I place open kisses down the column of her neck, sucking a little when she mewls like a kitten. Hell. This public foreplay is driving me wild. She grabs my forearms, digging her nails into my skin. I run my hands down the curve of her ass, then squeeze it. I'm a second away from steering her to a place where I can take care of both our aches.

"Noah..." She leans back and stares into my eyes.

"Yes, babe?"

"I..." She bites her lower lip. "I'm done."

A viselike hold tightens around my heart.

"What do you mean, you're done?" I ask through the lump in my throat.

"I don't want to be your fake girlfriend anymore or friends with benefits."

My pulse skyrockets and every beat of my heart becomes pure agony. She's going to end things. I drop my hands from her ass and take a step back, but she doesn't let me go far. She grabs my wrists and places my hands back where they were.

"I've been in denial land. What we have isn't fake, Noah. It's the most real thing I've ever felt, and I'm sorry it took me so long to admit it to myself."

The anguish slashing my heart goes away, and pure ecstasy takes over, overwhelming my senses. I capture her face between my hands and crush my lips to hers. I don't want to taste her; I want to *drown* in her, and let her feel all my love. Her tongue is sweet and matches my tempo perfectly. We are made for each other, and I'll spend the rest of my life proving to her that it is so.

I pull back so I can make sure I'm not dreaming. Her eyes seem dazed as she stares back at me.

"What is it, babe?" she asks, making me smile from ear to ear.

"I love hearing you call me babe."

She rewards me with a smile of her own. "I like calling you that."

Then she presses her face against my chest, and we keep slow dancing even though the song has changed to something more upbeat. I don't care. This feels right.

A few minutes later, Zoey, Ashley, and Blair join us. I give Gia space so she can be free to dance as she wants. As for me, I pretend to dance, which is pretty much me doing the side-step thing over and over again. It's dark, everyone is wasted, and nobody is paying attention to me anyway.

The song changes once again and this one I know. It's "Celebration" by Kool & the Gang. Two seconds later, I'm shoved from behind, and then a big hand slaps me on the shoulder.

"I can't believe you're dancing again, Kingsley," Alex shouts.

"What are you talking about? You weren't even around for my last performance."

He laughs. "Oh, but I heard all about it."

I notice then that our entire group is on the dance floor, besides Jaime and Martin. I hope the douche left the club.

"Where's Jaime?" Gia asks.

"Oh, he was a goner when Gretchen McCoy showed up. He went to the VIP room with her and Gordon," Sean replies. "Alex and Logan were in the restroom and missed her."

"Oh, they must be pissed." I laugh.

"Oh yeah." Sean smiles. "So pissed."

"Are you okay that Jaime ditched you for celebrities?" I ask Gia.

She smiles. "Hell yeah. He's lost so much in his life, let him have his fun."

The guys are drunk as fuck, and dancing as awkwardly as me. I relax completely then and try some new dance moves, not caring anymore if I look ridiculous. Gia tries to teach me, but I'm a horrible student.

I lose track of time, and the night goes by in a flash. I never have a chance to sneak out with her for a quickie in the washroom, even though that's on my mind. One thing is certain—I'll never forget tonight, even though I might have drunk a little too much.

But all good things must come to an end. The bartender yells last call, then the music stops, but we're still on a high. Nobody wants the night to be over.

"I'm not ready to sleep yet! This was such fun," Gia pipes up.

"Who said the night needs to be over?" Blair slurs.

I squint, paying attention to her now. This is the first time I've seen her with messy hair and not looking prissy.

"Did you really just say that?" Alex asks. "Isn't it past your bedtime already?"

Blair sways on her feet. "I'd tell you to bite me, but I don't wanna ruin Gia's birthday party and bicker with you."

"Aren't you sweet?" He laughs. "But I like when we bicker."

"Dude, you like it so much, you'll end up marrying her," Darren replies.

Both Blair and Alex make a face of disgust. But before either can offer a retort, Logan pipes up, "Nah... it'd be more fun if I married her, and then Alex realizes that he's been in love with her all this time, but he has no choice but to pine for her from afar."

CJ, who is also very much intoxicated, stares at Logan as if he's lost his mind. "Okay... that's not just alcohol talking. What did you take?"

Logan lifts his hands. "I didn't take anything. I swear. Don't judge me for having a vivid imagination."

I shake my head and step closer to Gia. "Do you wanna get out of here? Everyone's talking crazy."

I don't really expect her to take me up on my offer; after all, this is her birthday party, and those crazy people are our friends.

She meets my gaze. "I'd love to."

CHAPTER 46
GIA

When we walk out of the club, Noah is ready to request an Uber, but I spot a free taxi approaching and flag it like a maniac.

"What are you doing, wild girl?" Noah asks.

The taxi stops in front of me, and with my hand already on the door handle, I look over my shoulder. "Getting us a ride. Come on."

Noah runs to catch up. Inside the vehicle, he throws one arm around my shoulder and pulls me flush against his side.

"Address?" the driver grumbles.

I answer him, then giggle when Noah nuzzles my neck.

"If you're thinking about getting it on in the back seat of my taxi, think again. This isn't a motel on wheels," the driver says.

"No worries, sir. We'll behave," Noah replies solemnly.

The driver grumbles again, but at least he doesn't kick us out. I relax against Noah, resting my head on his shoulder, totally expecting him to keep his word. I should have known he wouldn't behave. A couple minutes into the drive, he begins torturing me. He runs his fingers up and down my thigh, getting closer to my pussy with each stroke. I rub my legs together, trying to make the throbbing stop.

I have to bite the inside of my cheek to keep myself from moaning out loud when his fingers finally reach their final destination. He swipes his thumb over my clit from side to side, creating a delicious friction between my legs. Desire is building fast, and if he keeps this up, I'll come in the next minute. My breathing is uneven. I want to touch him too, but I'm afraid I won't be as subtle as him. I definitely don't want to get kicked out of the taxi before we reach the hotel.

A familiar guitar riff penetrates my lust-infused brain, and I can hardly believe this particular song is playing now.

"Oh, I love this song," Noah tells the driver. "Would you mind turning up the volume?"

"Sure."

Guns N' Roses' "Sweet Child O' Mine" blasts loudly, drowning out any other noise. Noah doesn't stop his ministrations, though. He keeps working my clit, but now that the music is loud, it gives me a sense of protection. It's like there's a barrier, and if I make a sound, the driver won't hear it.

I tense when my orgasm hits, and I try my best to keep my moaning low. Noah comes closer and whispers in my ear, "That's it, babe. I love when you come for me."

I shudder, and a small whimper leaves my lips. The wave of my climax slowly recedes, and then I'm afraid I was too obvious. But the song is still playing loudly, and the driver seems oblivious. Noah's fingers move away from my throbbing clit, and then he kisses my cheek sweetly. I close my eyes again, relaxed to the point I could fall asleep. But I won't—not before I ride Noah until we both can't walk straight.

NOAH

Gia is still in a daze when we arrive at the hotel, but not from alcohol. I can tell the difference. The hotel lobby is quiet at this hour—it's past one in the morning. It will be a different story when the rest of our party arrives. I doubt those idiots will keep it quiet.

"How long do you think we have until our solitude ends?" I ask her as we wait for the elevator.

She gives me an impish grin. "Oh, we have all night, babe."

I arch my brows. "We do?"

She pulls a card key from her purse. "Blair got us a room as a birthday gift."

My jaw slackens. "She did?"

Gia nods. "Yep."

I pull her into a hug and kiss the corner of her mouth. "I have to thank her later."

A sharp *ping* announces the elevator has arrived. No sooner do the doors slide shut behind us than I push her against the wall, pressing every inch of my body against hers, and trap her arms above her head. "Do you have any idea how bad I want you right now?"

"I do. It's pushing against my belly."

I grin. "You're one sassy girl."

"And you are one naughty boy."

I run my free hand over the length of her body, taking my time when my fingers brush the undersides of her breasts. She arches her back, pressing her gorgeous tits against my chest.

"You haven't seen how naughty I can be, sunshine."

"I can't wait."

We arrive at her floor, which sits at the top. I step away from her, lacing our hands together, and we walk side by side toward the room. I stop in my tracks when I notice there are only two doors on this level—both double doors.

"Is this right?" I ask.

Gia squints at the number written on the card key sleeve. "Room 1401."

She scans the card, and the light turns green. We're at the right place. She pushes the door open and enters slowly.

I follow close behind and freeze. "Holy shit! This place is massive."

"I can't believe she got us a presidential suite."

"It's ten times the size of my tiny dorm room."

"Probably bigger." She laughs.

"Right? And look at this sleek furniture."

I eye the L-shaped leather couch, which looks inviting as hell. It's black, which is probably a good call for a hotel room.

To our right, another set of double doors open to a bedroom. I can see the king-size bed from where I stand.

We both walk to the panoramic windows that give us a beautiful view of the city. I press my forehead against the glass and look down.

"What are you doing?" she asks.

"Checking to see if I still get vertigo." When the feeling of falling out of the sky comes, I take a step back. "Yep. Still got it."

"I never tried that before."

She copies my example but lasts longer than I did. After a moment, she steps back. "Nope. I'm fine."

An idea pops into my head. "Maybe there's a way I can cure my condition." I step behind her. "Don't turn around yet."

"Okay."

I run a hand down her naked back—her jumpsuit is the backless type—and watch as her skin breaks into goose bumps.

"Where's the zipper to this thing, kitten?"

"Right side."

I locate it and slowly pull it down, and it's an exercise in self-restraint to not yank fast and rip the fabric off her body. "I love your outfit, but I'll love it more in a heap at your feet."

She gets rid of her shoes, and I help her out of it. And now she's standing in black lacy underwear that's so flimsy, I could tear it in two with just a hard pull. My cock seems to grow larger at the mere sight of it.

"Want to know why I wore it tonight instead of a dress?" she asks, already breathless.

"Why?"

"It had to be difficult to get out of. If I'd been wearing a dress, I'd have found a dark corner in that club and fucked you."

I groan, losing control. I grab her hips, digging my fingers into her skin. "You're a devious vixen. Do you know how many times I thought about doing that to you? And trust me, your sexy jumpsuit wouldn't have stopped me."

She reaches for the back of my head and grabs a fistful of my hair as she leans on me. "What stopped you then?"

"I didn't want to kidnap you from your own party." I kiss her neck. "We have some catching up to do."

I spin her around and push her against the window, then I take my time showering her with kisses on my way south.

"Noah..." She flattens her palms against the glass and opens her legs a little.

On my knees, I look up. "Yes, sunshine?"

She doesn't speak, just stares at me for a couple beats. I want to know what she's thinking, but her pussy is right in front of my face, and it's calling to me.

Without breaking eye contact, I push the lacy fabric of her panties aside and lick her clit with a long stroke.

She whimpers, running her fingers through my hair. "Why are you so good with your tongue?"

"Because I'm eating you, babe. You make me good."

I take my time toying with her clit, paying attention to her reactions. What makes her moan louder or yank my hair harder.

"Oh, this feels so good. I'm close, babe," she pants.

I know she is, and that's my cue to initiate phase two. I jump back to my feet and lift her off the floor, keeping her back pressed against the glass.

Her eyes widen. "What are you doing?"

"Finishing you off properly."

Holding her with one arm, I lower my zipper and free my erection, then I rub my cock against her wet pussy.

"Oh my God," she breathes out.

"I love how wet you get for me, sunshine." I slide into her heat and shiver. "Fuck, you're so tight."

"Wait. Did we forget something?"

I stop and then remember. *Shit.* "I'm so sorry." I begin to pull out, but she traps me with her legs.

"I'm negative, and I'm on the pill."

"Same." I kiss her but stop when she giggles against my lips. "What?"

"You're on the pill too?"

"Shut up." I kiss her harder while thrusting my hips forward, sheathing myself completely in her.

She isn't laughing now.

Without the condom, fucking her feels even more amazing—which means it's that much harder to keep from coming too soon.

I have no problem with Gia climaxing almost instantaneously. I had already brought her close to the edge; she only needed a little push.

She squeezes my cock at the height of her orgasm, and I can't stop myself from following her.

"Fuck," I blurt out, getting lost in the sensation. "You feel so good, babe."

"Don't ever stop fucking me." She grabs my face and slants her mouth over mine.

I keep moving in and out, letting her milk me dry and slow down only when she eases back and looks into my eyes.

"Take me to bed."

CHAPTER 47
GIA

Don't you hate when you're tired as hell, but you still wake up because your bladder is whining like a bitch? I open one eye and try to see the time. The bedroom is in complete darkness thanks to the blackout curtains. It's ten minutes past eight. Not that early under normal circumstances, but Noah and I fell asleep around five.

He's out to the world, sleeping on his belly and with a pillow over his head. The bedsheet covers him from the waist down, and even in the darkness, I can see the outline of his wide back. In the daylight, the scratch marks I left there will be visible. I got a little carried away last night.

I get out of bed and tiptoe to the bathroom, then close the door softly. I was planning on not turning on the light, but there's no window here, so it's pitch black. I wince when the bright light illuminates the room. Then I get nauseated.

I drop to my knees and curl my body over the toilet seat, throwing up everything I drank and ate last night.

"Damn all that tequila," I mumble to myself after I stop heaving.

Puking my guts out works against the nausea. But I still need to pee. On unsteady legs, I take care of business with my eyes half-shut. My head is already beginning to hurt. While washing my hands, I spy a set of two toothbrushes and a tube of toothpaste. I don't think twice about brushing my teeth, even though I plan to go back to sleep. Who wants puke breath? I wish I brought my duffel bag here instead of leaving it in the girls' room. Now I have to put last night's clothes back on when I leave the suite. Oh well, something to worry about later.

I turn off the light before I walk out so I don't disturb Noah and I end up colliding with him. I let out a shriek and jump back.

Placing a hand on my chest, I say. "Shit. You scared me."

"Sorry, sunshine. Didn't mean to." His voice is raspy, probably from needing to shout at the club to be overheard.

"It's okay."

I sidestep and return to bed, but being spooked worked as a jolt, and now I'm fully awake. I'll end up paying for it later if I don't sleep more. I bet another orgasm will make me tired again. I smile in the dark. It's crazy that I want to have sex after throwing up, but I do. The nausea is gone, and desire has removed the lethargy from my body. None of my previous relationships turned me into a nympho. It's the Noah effect. I can't get enough of him.

He turns off the light in the bathroom before he opens the door just like I did, and a moment later, he slides into bed next to me, pulling me closer and nuzzling my neck.

"Did you get sick? I thought I heard you throwing up."

"I did. I think the sudden bright lights didn't agree with me."

"Are you feeling better now?"

"Much better."

The scent of minty toothpaste wafts from him—he had the same idea as me. I purr like a kitten, running my fingers down his abs until I reach the tip of his erection.

"Someone isn't tired anymore." I wrap my fingers around his shaft and squeeze a little.

"No," he replies in a gruff voice. "But, babe, we can just cuddle if you're feeling hungover."

"We can cuddle after." I run my hand up and down his length.

"Okay." He kisses my neck, sucking a little.

"Are you trying to give me a hickey?"

"Not on purpose, but you taste so good."

I push him away, and before he can complain, I straddle him and turn on the nightstand light. "I think you *are* doing it on purpose, and now I have to punish you for being naughty."

He grabs my hips and moves in a circular motion. That makes my wet pussy rub against his cock, and even though I'm a little sore from last night's activities, I'm craving more.

"Noah... you aren't playing fair."

"Oh, but I am, sunshine. I'm helping you punish me."

"How is this punishment for you?"

"I'm not buried inside you yet, am I?"

I rise a little, putting weight on my knees, and guide his cock to my entrance. I hiss when I lower my hips and his fullness completes me.

"I love the sounds you make, babe," he says.

"I'm only getting started." I move slower at first, but it doesn't take long to get caught in the heat of the moment. The chase begins, and ideally, I should maintain a steady pace and prolong the journey, but this feels too good, and I'm greedy for more.

Noah jerks into a sitting position, shifting me a little. I can't go as fast, but his mouth is on my breast, adding another layer of pleasure. I can't complain about that. I find my rhythm again, getting closer and closer to another earth-shattering orgasm.

It happens when he bites my nipple, the zing of pain sending me over the edge. "Fuck!"

"That's it, babe. Scream for me. Scream my name."

"Yes, Noah! Yes!"

He kisses me hard, swallowing my cries of ecstasy, then he whispers against my lips, "You feel so good, kitten. I love fucking your tight pussy. Say you're my girl."

"I'm your girl, Noah. I'll always be your girl."

He jerks, and then he grips my hips, helping me move faster as he climaxes. The waves of pleasure are beginning to recede when another mini orgasm hits me. I don't cry out; I whimper instead as my body disintegrates into tiny pieces.

He goes still, and I hide my face in the crook of his neck. His cock is still pulsing, spewing his release inside of me.

In a soothing gesture, he runs his fingers through my hair. "Are you okay, babe?"

"I'm more than okay." I ease back and look into his eyes. "And you?"

Noah curls his lips into that smile I adore. "You have no idea." Then he traces my face with the tips of his fingers. "I love you, Gia."

NOAH

In an instant, her supple body tenses. Her eyes widen, and her plump lips make a perfect O. My pulse reaches Mach 10 as my stomach dips. I made it awkward with my big mouth. I shouldn't have confessed, not when Gia just agreed to be my girlfriend for real. I'm such an idiot.

"You don't need to say it back."

"Noah... I—" Her phone rings, cutting her off.

She slides off my lap and gets out of bed, her back toward me as she answers the phone. In a shaky motion, I run my fingers through my hair, pushing my long bangs back. I'm so frustrated with myself, I could scream.

"No, Ashley, you didn't wake me. What's up?"

I jump out of bed too and go hide in the bathroom so I can recover from this mess. I was planning on throwing some cold water on my face, but I need more time, so I jump in the shower. I'm not sure how long I stay there, but I'm certain more than five minutes pass. When I return to the room, Gia is sitting on the edge of the bed, looking down at her phone.

She lifts her face, and immediately, I know something is wrong.

"Ashley blabbered."

"What?"

"She was the only one who knew our relationship was fake in the beginning, and in her drunken state, she told everyone."

"Who's everyone? Our friends?"

"Yes, who else?"

I sit next to her and touch her arm. "Why are you freaking out? They're not going to say anything, and we aren't fake dating anymore."

"It doesn't matter. I have to tell Coach Bedford. Too many people know the truth now, and sooner or later, someone is going to open their big mouth again."

"Then we'll tell him together. And I'll take full responsibility for the ruse."

"I can't let you do that. I agreed with the plan."

"Yes, but it was my idea."

She opens her mouth to protest, but I press a finger against her lips. "I don't want to hear it, babe. We'll do this as a united front. It'll be okay. I promise."

Gia's eyes are suddenly brighter. She cups my face and kisses me softly. "Thank you for being you."

It's not the love declaration I was hoping for, but it's a start.

CHAPTER 48
GIA

The drive back to Fairbanks is a quiet one. The girls are hungover, and I have a lot on my mind. I keep replaying Noah's love declaration over and over again, wishing I had reacted differently to it. Do I love him? I think I do, but I panicked and... *ugh*. I feel horrible.

Martin isn't with us, which is a blessing. Last night, after Noah irritated him, he disappeared. I don't know if he left the club or if he just avoided us. This morning he texted me he had taken the bus home. He's acting like a diva, but today, his behavior is working for us. I don't need to deal with his drama on top of everything else.

Jaime rejoined the gang after Noah and I were already in our room, Blair told me. When I saw him at breakfast and asked about the VIP room, his only reply was that Gretchen McCoy was worth the hype. He wouldn't tell me if he hooked up with the starlet or not. It'll take more pressure to make him spill, but I'll save pestering him for another day. He had to run to catch his flight back to Chicago.

I'm driving Blair's SUV because she's in no condition to do so. She does look pitiful sitting next to me. Her skin is a little green, and she's hiding her dark circles under her ginormous sunglasses.

"It feels like we're going to a funeral." Zoey breaks the silence. "Can we listen to some music?"

"Hell to the fucking no," Blair grumbles. "My head is splitting in two. I never want to drink again."

Ashley snorts. "Yeah, I've said that before, and I never learn my lesson. My memory is shit."

"In your case, I believe you. How could you forget that you weren't supposed to reveal Gia's secret?" Blair retorts.

I grimace. I don't want to talk about that.

"Ugh! Don't remind me. I already feel like crap. I'm so sorry, Gia. I don't know what came over me."

"Copious amounts of tequila," Zoey pipes up.

"It's fine, Ashley. It'll be better if I come clean to Coach anyway," I reply.

"But if it weren't for my big mouth, you wouldn't have to. Especially now that you're dating Noah for real."

"To be fair, I never thought you were faking, Gia," Zoey chimes in. "Anyone could see the chemistry between you and Noah. That guy is crazy about you."

"And I'm crazy about him," I confess.

"You are?" Ashley asks. "I mean, I knew you were attracted to him, but I hadn't realized he'd become more."

"There was a spark between us the moment we met. I was just too stupid to realize it then."

"I don't think you were stupid," Blair butts in. "You were just hurt and afraid to be betrayed again after what my stupid brother did to you."

"Maybe..." I reply, even though she's one hundred percent correct.

I can't bring myself to admit my cowardice to them. Fear was keeping me from a great relationship—perhaps *the* greatest relationship of my life.

"Anyway... I kind of messed up already."

"What do you mean?" Zoey asks.

I let out a heavy sigh. "Noah told me he loved me this morning, and I froze."

Blair looks at me. "You didn't say it back?"

"No. He caught me by surprise. It's just happening so fast."

"Oh, somebody's afraid again," Ashley interjects.

"If you don't feel that way, then you can't lie to him," Zoey says.

"That's the thing. I think I do, but part of me thinks it's crazy to admit it. How can I have fallen in love with someone so quickly?"

"It's totally possible," Zoey continues. "Not crazy at all. When you know, you know."

Blair waves her hand dismissively. "Yeah, yeah. Everyone knows you think life is a Hallmark movie, Zoey."

"Not a Hallmark movie—a PassionFlix. I want the smut."

Ashley laughs.

"Can we get back on track and focus on my problem, please?" I say. "What should I do? I think I hurt Noah's feelings."

Blair snorts. "You think?"

"Just tell him that you love him too," Zoey replies matter-of-factly.

"It's not that simple. I can't just say, 'By the way, I love you too' mere hours after I said nothing. It won't feel genuine."

"I know how you can show him how you feel," Ashley pipes up.

"How?" I glance at her through the rearview mirror.

"Wear his damn jersey."

Zoey claps her hands. "Oh my god! That'd be amazing. And the next game is at home against Clayton U."

I slap the steering wheel. "Of course! I'm such an idiot. That's what I'll do."

"He'll be so happy." Zoey sighs.

My phone rings, and since it's connected to the vehicle's sound system, it blasts from the speakers loudly. A second later, Noah's name pops up on the dashboard.

"Speak of the devil," Blair says.

I press the button to take the call. "Hey, babe. How's it going?"

"Good. We just got our rental. We're on our way back to Fairbanks. How far are you?"

"We're making good progress. We should be home in an hour. There isn't a lot of traffic."

"Great. How's everyone feeling today?"

"Dreadful," Blair replies.

Noah chuckles. "The guys are also in bad shape. What did you do last night?"

Blair groans, looking out the window. "No comment."

"I can't comment. I don't remember what happened after we left the club," Zoey says.

"You don't remember sucking face with CJ?" Ashley asks.

"What?" she shrieks. "I didn't make out with him."

"That did happen... unfortunately," a rough voice replies in the background. CJ is my guess. What an ass.

"Way to go, Ash," Blair retorts. "Noah has us on speaker too."

"I want to die." Zoey curls into a ball in the back seat, covering her face.

"Don't worry, darling," one of the twins replies. I can't tell who. "Your bad judgment call with CJ wasn't the most embarrassing thing that happened last night. Blair takes that trophy."

Okay, that's Alex.

"Shut up," Blair snaps.

"Never." He laughs.

"All right, then," Noah cuts in. "I'd better hang up before things escalate."

"Yes, that'd be best. I'll call you when we get home."

"Sounds good, babe. Drive safely."

"You too." I press the end-call button, and then, ask, "What the hell happened last night?"

"Let's not talk about it anymore," Ashley replies.

"Agree," Blair chimes in.

"Did I really make out with CJ?" Zoey asks in a small voice. "I don't even like him."

I guess we're going to keep talking about it. It's fine. I'm damn curious anyway.

"You liked him fine last night," Ashley pipes up.

"Did I hook up with him?" Zoey's voice rises in pitch.

"No. We stopped you from making that mistake," Blair replies.

From the rearview mirror, I see Zoey sinking against the seat with a relieved expression on her face. Totally understandable. She's still a virgin, and I'd hate for her to sleep with someone all thanks to alcohol. She's a hopeless romantic and wants her first time to be special.

"I'll definitely never drink again," she says. "If my coach finds out what I've been up to, she's going to flay me alive."

"Don't feel too bad about it, hon. We've all been there and made bad decisions thanks to booze."

"Speak for yourself. I haven't," Blair retorts.

"So you challenging Alex to a tequila shot contest wasn't a bad decision?"

"That's not what I meant. A bad decision would have been if I fucked him after all those shots."

"I think one day you're going to eat those words." Ashley laughs.

Blair turns in her seat to look at Ashley. "What are you implying?"

"You know exactly what I'm saying. You guys act like you hate each other, but I think, in reality, you don't. You're just pissed that you're attracted to each other."

"I'm not attracted to that Neanderthal," Blair grits out.

"Whatever."

"Okay, I think maybe we *do* need some music." I turn on the radio before this drive turns into a trip from hell.

CHAPTER 49
GIA

I'm wearing a turtleneck today because Noah did give me a hickey. No one paid attention to it yesterday since they were all hungover, and I kept my hair loose to hide it. But this morning I'm meeting Coach Bedford, and I definitely don't want him to see it.

Noah didn't spend the night at my place. He said he was too tired and crashed at his dorm room instead. I'm not sure if he's avoiding me because of what I didn't say. I hope that's not the case. I don't want things to get awkward between us, especially when there's no reason for that. Maybe I don't need to wait until the next game to let him know what's in my heart.

Actually, I don't think I will. Why make him suffer so I can make a big gesture?

He's meeting me today at the arena so we can talk to Coach Bedford together. I could easily have done it by myself, but he insisted on being there.

I'm the first to arrive, and I make a beeline to my office to drop off my bag. By chance, Paul is there too.

He looks up from his computer and smiles. "Good morning, Gia. I didn't know you were coming this early."

"I have to speak to Coach Bedford."

"How was the party Saturday night?"

"Amazing. Too bad you couldn't come."

He shakes his head, then fixes his thick-rimmed glasses. "It was a good choice for me. I spent my entire Sunday working on an English lit assignment, and I'm still not done."

"What are you doing here then?"

"Just putting in a few hours. By the way, I uploaded the videos from the trip to Boston. Have fun sorting through them all." He smirks.

"How many are there?"

He shrugs. "No idea."

"Oh, boy. Better to have too many than not enough, I guess."

"That's what I thought. There are some good ones there. Your boyfriend is hilarious."

I arch an eyebrow. "Is he now?"

"Yeah, and it's obvious that he's so into you. Every other sentence is Gia this, Gia that."

"Everyone keeps saying that."

Paul furrows his brows. "You don't think that's true?"

"I know it's true. Anyway, is Coach Bedford already in?"

"I believe so. You don't look too happy about the meeting. Did something happen?"

I wave my hand. "It's nothing serious, but I'm glad the Warriors won Saturday. He should be in a good mood."

Paul bobs his head up and down. "Yeah, for sure."

I drop my bag on the desk. "I'd better go. See you later."

"Bye."

On the way to Coach Bedford's office, I text Noah.

> Where are you?

> I'm walking through the doors.

> Meet you in the common room.

K

I grab two cups of coffee while I wait for Noah, guessing he'll want one. I'm adding creamer to mine when I see him walking over from my peripheral. I turn, concerned about what I'm going to read on his face. Relief washes over me when I catch his smile.

"Here you go." I hand him one of the cups.

"Thanks, sunshine." He leans forward and kisses me on the lips. "Did you sleep well?"

"Eh, not really."

His easygoing demeanor changes and his eyes turn dark. "Why? Did you receive another call?"

My eyes widen. "Oh no. It's not that." I drop my gaze to the floor. "I missed you."

He sets his cup down on the counter and then takes mine away and sets it down too. I look into his warm and intense brown eyes and prepare to take the jump.

"You have no idea how happy it makes me to hear you say that, Gia. I missed you too." He caresses my face with the back of his hand.

I look over his shoulder and then behind mine to make sure we're alone before I throw my arms around his neck and kiss him soundly. His arms wrap around my waist, pulling me closer to him while he matches my passion. His tongue still tastes like toothpaste. I'm glad I didn't have a chance to take a sip of my coffee before I attacked his mouth.

He steps back and ends the kiss before I'm ready. "Wow you really missed me."

I gather the courage to tell him how I feel, but before I can, Coach Bedford joins us.

"Why are you here so early? Don't you have class?" He goes straight for the coffee machine.

"We're here to speak with you, sir," Noah replies.

Coach Bedford looks at us. "Is that so?"

"Yes, it won't take long," I add.

Unless he gets über-mad and decides to fire me on the spot. My stomach clenches painfully, and I don't even want to drink the coffee anymore. It might make me sick.

"All right. I'm all ears." He brings the cup of coffee to his lips.

"Could we go to your office?"

He raises a brow. "Sure."

We follow him down the hallway in silence. Noah takes my hand and squeezes it, showing me his support.

Once we're inside and the door is shut, nerves get the better of me. My hands are clammy, and I wipe them dry on my jeans. I'm also shaking a little.

"You look tense, Gia. Did something happen?" Coach Bedford asks.

"No." I take a deep breath. "First, I'd like to thank you for bringing Jaime to the game. It was an awesome surprise. I was so touched."

He relaxes his stance and shows a hint of a smile. "Ah, it was no problem. I know you two are close. Did you have a good time?"

"Yes, we did."

His brows furrow. "But that's not what you wanted to talk to me about, is it?"

"No, sir, I'd like to come clean about something."

He links his hands over his belly and leans back in his chair. "Go on."

"When you asked me to put an end to the sorority challenge that cost us the exhibition game, the best solution was for Noah to get a girlfriend. So I agreed to fake date him."

My face is in flames, and I can barely maintain eye contact with Coach. But I know he won't appreciate weakness.

He narrows his eyes and flattens his lips, turning them into a slash on his face. "Let me get this straight. You lied to keep your job."

"It was my fault, sir. Gia didn't want to do it," Noah interjects. "I forced her hand because I was already in love with her, and I wanted a chance to prove I could be the boyfriend she deserved."

I turn with my jaw hanging loose. I can't believe he confessed that to Coach Bedford. I won't say his confession is a surprise. He never hid that he wanted things to be real between us.

"Son, if you tell me that entire circus was your idea as well... things won't end well for you."

The blood drains from his face. "What? The challenge? No, I had nothing to do with it. I swear it. I'd *never* jeopardize my hockey career by playing silly games."

"Good." Coach turns to me. "Did you know about that?"

"I suspected he had a crush on me, so I guess in a sense I knew."

Coach rubs his chin and studies us intensely for a couple beats. "Why are you telling me this now?"

"We figured it was the right thing to do," Noah replies.

I'm glad he didn't tell Coach we're coming clean only because Ashley opened her big mouth.

"I can tell the secret has been eating at you."

"You aren't mad?" I ask.

He frowns. "Not really. And you, dear, don't seem angry either."

I glance at Noah and try to find any hint of rancor, but I can't. "I know I should, but if he hadn't done that, I wouldn't have fallen in love with him."

A blush creeps up Noah's cheeks, and his eyes turn as round as saucers. "You're in love with me?"

"Yes."

He opens and shuts his mouth, but no sound comes forth. I'm glad he's not having a word vomit moment right now in front of Coach. I look at the man and find him smirking.

My face becomes unbearably hot. It hit me that I just told Noah I'm in love with him in front of my boss. *Kill me now.*

"Well, it seems everything is sorted then," Coach Bedford says. "Now get out of here. I got work to do."

We both jump to our feet and leave his office as quickly as we can. I don't go far though before Noah touches my arm and stops me.

"Did you really mean that?"

Playing stupid I ask, "Mean what?"

He gestures with his hand. "What you said in Coach's office."

The corners of my mouth quirk up. "Do you think I'd lie to the man after coming clean about our fake dating? What would be the point?"

"But... you didn't say anything yesterday."

I step into his personal space, curling my arms behind his back and tilting my face up so I can maintain eye contact. "You caught me by surprise. I froze. I'm sorry. I do love you, Noah. And I'm glad that you were devious enough to trick me into dating you."

He cups my face and rubs his thumb over my cheek. "You have no idea how happy you made me today, sunshine."

"I can imagine. I'm feeling it right now, swirling in my chest."

I expect him to kiss me, but instead, he pulls me into a tight hug that feels like home.

CHAPTER 50
GIA

The week goes by in a blur, and before I know it, it's already Friday and the Warriors are playing against Clayton U. Noah's parents and younger sister flew in this morning for the game. I'm excited to meet them and a little nervous too. Noah assures me they're going to love me. They can't be worse than Ryder and Blair's folks. I don't consider them real people—more like marble statues come to life.

I'm heading to the arena's back entrance when I spot Clayton U's bus parking. I increase my pace, aiming to enter the building before the team exits the bus. The last thing I want is to walk in with them.

Someone calls my name and I stop, looking over my shoulder. Martin is waving and running toward me. Hell. What now? I haven't heard from him since he disappeared from the club and returned to Boston on his own. I texted and called him several times, but he ignored my efforts to reach out. I figured he needed time to figure out whatever was going on with him.

"What are you doing here?" I ask.

"Waiting for you to show up." He stops in front of me, a little out of breath.

"You couldn't have called me back?"

"Honestly, I didn't think I should."

"What made you change your mind?" *And ambush me at the most inconvenient time.*

"I've been talking with friends, and they made me realize I can't simply give up without a fight."

My stomach dips. I don't like where this conversation is headed. "What are you talking about?"

"You truly don't know?" He runs a hand through his hair in a jittery motion. "Maybe I should have been more obvious and not bided my time. I was sure you wouldn't date another hockey player after Ryder."

I glance over his shoulder and see that the players from Clayton U are now exiting the bus. *Shit.* "Martin, I really don't have time to talk right now."

"This can't wait, Gia. I've wasted enough time. And now that I know you're only fake dating Noah... well, I'm done playing it safe." He grabs me by the shoulders and pulls me toward him... then crashes his lips against mine.

I freeze on the spot, and my eyes go wide.

A couple seconds later, I recover from the shock and push him back. "What the fuck do you think you're doing?"

"Oh, it seems Kingsley's dream girl is *everyone's* dream girl," Atlas Kodiak says with a smirk.

Hell! He had to be the one to witness Martin acting like a jackass. Did he overhear Martin when he talked about me fake dating Noah? This is bad. And how the hell does Martin know?

"Mind your damn business," I retort.

"Feisty! I like girls like that. Maybe when you're finished with ginger there, I can give you a taste of a real man, since your deal with Kingsley is fake."

My stomach falls through the earth. I got my answer.

"You can't talk to her like that." Martin takes a menacing step toward Atlas, who simply shakes his head and walks away.

"You stay out of it," I tell him. "Just go home."

"But Gia—"

"No 'but,' Martin. I can't believe you'd do something like this. I'm sorry that you caught feelings. I never led you on, and even if you thought I did, that gives you no right to kiss me. And for your information, my relationship with Noah isn't fake. I'm in love with him, and he loves me."

Martin's face twists into an ugly mask. "Fine. It's your loss."

He turns around and strides away. Mercifully, the Clayton U players are already inside the building. I need to tell Noah ASAP what happened before Atlas poisons his mind.

Instead of going into the arena like I originally planned, I text Noah to find out where he is. Our players were supposed to arrive within the next ten minutes, and the original plan was for me to wait for them in the hallway and shoot videos of their arrival.

He doesn't text me back right away, so I call him. It rings until it goes to voice mail. *Dammit! Where are you, Noah?*

I call Sean next. Luckily, he answers on the second ring. "Hey Gia, what's up? We aren't late, are we?"

"It depends... where are you?"

"Five minutes from the arena."

I'm about to ask if he knows where Noah is, but the man in question pipes up, "Hey, sunshine. We're almost there. Get your camera ready. We're looking stylish. Alexander Wennberg has nothing on us."

"I just called you. You didn't answer." *Way to sound needy, Gia.*

"Oh yeah, I forgot my phone at home."

"Because you were running late," Sean rebuffs.

"Hey! It takes time to achieve perfection."

Sean snorts. "You're lucky I'm not one of the twins."

"I totally teed that up, didn't I?" Noah laughs. "Why did you call me, babe?"

I don't want to tell him about Martin while Sean is listening. "I'll tell you when you get here. I'm waiting outside."

"Okay. See you soon."

I end the call but I'm antsy, so I start pacing in front of the building. To kill time—and to help with my nerves—I call Ashley.

"What's up, girl? Why are you calling me? Aren't you busy with hockey today?"

"Yep. Martin showed up at the arena."

"I was wondering when that weasel was going to make an appearance."

"You're not going to believe this. He came over to make an 'I love you' declaration."

"You're kidding me. So first he ignores you, and then he decides to show up on your boyfriend's turf with that bullshit? He does have a flair for dramatics."

"He also knew my relationship with Noah was fake in the beginning."

"No! But how.... shit, maybe he was around when I opened my big mouth. I'm so sorry, Gia. This is all my fault."

"Don't feel bad about it. Coach Bedford already knows, and he didn't care. But it gets worse..." I pinch the bridge of my nose. "The Clayton U players had just arrived, and Atlas Kodiak not only overheard that, but he also witnessed Martin deciding that stealing a kiss from me was a good idea."

"Damn. That *is* worse. Isn't Atlas one of the bad boys of Clayton U?"

"Yeah, he has a bad reputation. He's also a dirty player. I'm sure he's going to use that knowledge to get to Noah."

"You can bet on it. What are you going to do?"

"I have to tell Noah before he hears it from Atlas."

"That will get him fired up."

"I know. I hope it doesn't affect his game. I'd hate to screw up yet another game against Clayton U."

"The first mess up wasn't your fault. Besides, Noah seems like a chill guy. I'm sure he can handle it. It'd be a different story if your boyfriend was one of the twins."

"Ugh! Thanks for putting that disturbing mental picture in my head."

She laughs. "You're welcome."

In the distance, I spot Noah and Sean approaching. "I gotta go. The boys are here."

"Boys? Who?"

"Noah and Sean."

"Oh... say hello to Noah for me."

My brows arch. "Just Noah?"

"Yep. Sean pissed me off. I'm not talking to him."

"I don't have time to unpack that now, but tomorrow, you're going to tell me what's going on."

"Don't count on it. Good luck tonight."

She ends the call before I can say another word. Belatedly I realize I should have recorded the guys walking over. They do look nice wearing their tailored suits. Sean's is dark navy, and Noah's a lighter gray. I love him in his hockey uniform, but the suit is a close second. *You're getting distracted, Gia. Focus.*

"Here we are with time to spare." Sean opens his arms wide. "Where is everyone?"

"You're the first Warriors to arrive."

Noah looks at Sean. "What did I tell you? We had time."

"I'm the captain. I have to set a good example. Shall we go in?" He looks at me.

"In a minute. I need to speak to Noah."

"Okay, see you soon."

I wait for Sean to disappear into the building while Noah keeps staring at me as if he's trying to read my mind.

"Why did you ride with Sean?" I blurt out, not quite ready yet to tell him what happened.

"Cause I wanted an excuse to go home with you." He smiles cheekily.

Under normal circumstances, I'd smile back, but I'm suddenly tense about what I have to say. Since I can't hide my emotions well, his grin wilts. "What's up, sunshine? Did something happen?"

I nod. "Martin showed up as I was walking to the building."

His entire body tenses. "What did he want?"

I take a deep breath. "He came to say he has feelings for me... and he also knows that we were fake dating in the beginning. He must have overheard Ashley."

Noah clenches his jaw so hard his cheeks hollow. "I see. So, he finally had the courage to confess."

My brows scrunch together. "What do you mean?"

Widening his stance and crossing his arms, he exhales loudly. "He told me he had a thing for you, and that he was sure I wouldn't last."

My eyes widen. "When was that?"

He waves his hand. "Before your birthday. I can't remember when exactly."

"I can't believe he said that to you. Why didn't you tell me?"

He shrugs. "I didn't want to put the idea in your mind."

I tilt my head. "Were you afraid that I'd pick him instead of you?"

With his arms crossed again, he drops his gaze to the ground. "Maybe one percent afraid."

"But you still invited him to come to my birthday party."

He looks up. "That was the ninety-nine percent part of me that was sure I had nothing to worry about."

My lips curl into a grin. "Your ninety-nine percent is correct."

He mimics my expression and steps closer, but I press my hand against his chest. "Wait, that's not all. He kissed me."

Noah's spine goes taut, and he seems to grow taller. *"What?"*

"I didn't reciprocate. He caught me by surprise, and I pushed him away immediately."

He makes a fist with his hand and presses it against his forehead. "That sneaky little bastard. He'd better not dare to cross my path."

I touch his arm. "Please don't do anything to him. I don't want you to get in trouble because of him. He's not worth it."

Noah takes a couple of deep breaths. "I know he's not, sunshine. I'm just fucking angry that he thought he could just kiss you like that."

"I'm angry too. There's something else."

"What now?"

"Atlas Kodiak witnessed the whole thing. He also heard the part about our fake dating. Be prepared for some trash-talking on the ice."

His gaze darkens. "If that motherfucker says one word out of line about you, he's going to be eating chipped ice."

"That isn't what I want you to do. Focus on the game, please."

He doesn't say anything for a couple beats as he stares at me. Then his shoulders relax, and the anger leaves his face. "Only because you're asking. You know there's nothing I wouldn't do for you."

I step into his space, wrapping my arms around his waist and rising on my tiptoes to kiss him quickly. "The feeling is mutual, Noah. Now let's get inside. My tush is already frozen."

On cue, he grabs my ass and squeezes it. "Nope, it's not frozen. I can still play with it."

Laughing, I bat his hand away and step back. "Come on. We have work to do. And we're starting with your catwalk."

CHAPTER 51
NOAH

I shove my anger aside for Gia's sake, but the rage continues to simmer low in my gut. I shouldn't have underestimated Martin, but I didn't think he'd have the balls to do anything. I was dead wrong.

In the locker room, I barely pay attention to what Coach Bedford says. I have only one thing on my mind—if Atlas Kodiak says anything about Gia, he's going to regret it. I don't care that my parents and Nicole came to watch me. They've seen me lose my temper before.

We head to the rink, and I barely notice the chanting crowd. My pulse is thrumming in my ears, a combination of pregame jitters and the desire to break things contributing to the way my heart is pumping fast and hard in my chest.

During warmup, Sean steps next to me and asks. "Everything okay, man? You seem distracted."

I shake my head. "I'm fine."

He watches me like he doesn't believe a word I'm saying. "Really? Not once did your eyes turn to the stands to look for Gia."

It's true. I don't want to look for her, afraid she'll be able to tell I'm not okay.

"I just want to focus on the game."

"If you say so."

I skate away from him, annoyed that he can read me so well. I guess that's why he was chosen to be the captain. I stick close to CJ, of all people. He's usually surrounded by a dark cloud and oblivious to other people's problems. Besides, darkness calls to darkness.

Surprisingly, I'm not in the starting lineup, which sucks. Coach told us before we left the locker room. Something about strategy, I wasn't paying attention. I'm jonesing for action. I bounce from side to side, waiting for my turn on the ice. Clayton U scores in the first minute of the game, setting my teeth on edge. That's adding insult to injury. The fire in my belly is slowly getting hotter, the flames licking up my veins. I tighten the hold on my stick, counting the seconds until I can unleash the beast.

When my turn finally comes, I'm hungry as hell. I join the fray and immediately go after the puck. Atlas is on the ice as well, and no surprise, he comes for me. We collide in the corner of the offensive zone and fight for the puck.

"Why are you so angry, Kingsley?"

I don't answer him; instead, I focus on getting the puck free. I send it toward Sean and then get in position in front of the goaltender.

The asshole follows me and continues to run his mouth. "It doesn't have anything to do with the fact that your girlfriend isn't really your girlfriend, does it? Can I hire her services? I get so horny after winning a game."

I turn my attention to him, ready to punch the smugness off his face when someone yells my name.

The puck zooms in front of me but because I was distracted, I miss it and hand the turnover to Clayton U on a silver platter. "Fuck!"

I chase after it, skating as fast as I can. Logan gets to it first, but not before he sends the puck in Atlas's direction. Red tinges my vision. I won't let that motherfucker get another puck in the back of our net. Going at full speed, I hammer him so hard against the boards he has no chance to prepare for the impact. He lifts off the ice and then falls in a heap like a rag doll. Another Clayton U player gets in my face, and I shove him away as well. Atlas gets up, then yanks my jersey back. I elbow his stomach, trying to break free, and that's when the fists fly. He gets a hit to the side of my face, dislodging my mask. I get rid of it and return the punch. I was thirsty for a fight, and now I have it. I don't even hear the whistle blow. We're down on the ice, and I have the upper hand. The asshole is curled into a ball with his arms raised to protect his face. I stop punching only when Sean and Alex drag me away.

My pulse is beating so loud in my ears it's all I can hear. My face and ears are burning, and I taste blood on my lips.

On my way to the penalty box, I make the mistake of glancing in Coach Bedford's direction. If looks could kill, I'd be dead. His face is red when he turns to say something to Assistant Coach LaRue. At least I'm not the only one being punished. I didn't give Clayton U a power play. Atlas also has to sulk in the sin bin.

I keep my attention on the game for the first thirty seconds, watching it unfold at the edge of my seat. My legs won't stop bouncing up and down. Then comes a rap against the Plexiglas. I ignore it, not in the mood to engage with the crowd. But it continues, so I turn, ready to tell whoever is annoying me to fuck off. The curse dies in my throat. It's Gia who's trying to get my attention. I was so lost in my head that I didn't realize she was sitting right behind the Warriors' penalty box. Then I see what she's wearing... and my heart skips a beat. It's my jersey. *She's wearing my fucking jersey.*

I want to hold on to my anger, but seeing her in my jersey is like a ray of sunshine punching a hole through my darkness. I smile, ignoring the sharp pain from my busted lips.

"Are you okay?" she asks.

I nod.

A loud buzz in the arena draws my attention back to the ice. While I was chatting with my girl, I missed Sean scoring.

I jump to my feet and pump my fist in the air. A moment later, my time in the sin bin is up, and I re-enter the ice. No surprise, I have to return to the bench right away. Coach doesn't even look at me. He won't chew my ass out here, but I know it's coming. Despite the score being tied in the first period, I have no regrets. I'd hit that motherfucker Kodiak again if given the chance. No one is going to talk shit about my girl and walk away unharmed.

CHAPTER 52
GIA

When the game ends and the final score shows 4-1, my voice is gone. I've never screamed and cheered as loudly as I did tonight, probably because of what happened earlier with Martin, and then witnessing Noah's fight with Atlas. I had a lot of pent-up anger, and it had to go somewhere. Once the Warriors tied the score, they found their groove and dominated the rest of the game. Winning against Clayton U is always satisfying, but tonight, victory tasted even better.

I was afraid Coach Bedford would bench Noah for the rest of the game, but he let him return after the first break. I can only imagine how tense it was in the locker room after the first period.

I don't head immediately to the Warriors' common area. Instead, I wait for Noah's parents and his sister in the food court. I couldn't meet with them before the game, and their seats weren't near mine. Noah did give his mother my phone number, so we kept in touch through texting during the game. I've seen pictures of them, so I know what they look like. They spot me first though.

"Gia!" a girl shouts my name and waves at me.

She's as cute as a button, her dark-brown hair tied up in a ponytail with a big maroon bow. She's standing next to an older version of Noah—his dad—and a pretty lady with blonde hair cut in a bob. They're all wearing Noah's jersey.

I walk over, smiling from ear to ear, hoping they can't see how nervous I am to meet them in person.

"Hi." I wave, unsure how to greet them.

Noah's mother takes a step forward and gives me a hug. "It's so nice to finally meet you. You're as gorgeous in person as you are in your pictures."

Blush spreads through my cheeks. "Thanks."

Noah's dad isn't as affectionate as his wife. He offers me his hand instead of a hug. As for Nicole, she just waves at me while keeping a Cheshire cat smile plastered to her face. I don't know what to make of that.

"How did your French assignment go?" she asks out of the blue.

"It went well. I got an *A*, thanks to Noah."

Mrs. Kingsley furrows her eyebrows. "Noah? How in the world did my son help you with French? I tried to get him to learn, but the boy only had time for hockey."

Confused, I ask, "Are you saying he doesn't speak French?"

Nicole laughs. "Noah can't speak French to save his life."

"But he helped me with my assignment. He even revised my essay, and his suggestions were on point."

Mr. Kingsley scratches his head. "Well, do you think he could have learned in the last couple months?"

His wife gives him a droll look. "Nick, please. The boy is a maverick on the ice, but learning a language in a few months is beyond his skill set."

"Then who helped Gia with her assignment?" he asks.

"Who indeed?" Nicole asks with that sardonic smile.

I narrow my eyes. "Did you help Noah?"

She flattens her lips, but the corners of her mouth twitch upward.

Her parents turn to her, but it's her mother who says, "Nicole speaks fluent French. Did you assist your brother in this ruse?"

"Maybe."

I don't know if I should get mad or laugh at the whole situation. I already know Noah isn't opposed to playing dirty to get what he wants. He did offer to fake date me in the hopes that I'd fall for him. Pretending to speak French so he could spend more time with me is right up his alley.

"He's lucky I didn't flunk that class."

"I'll say," his mother replies. "I really need to have a talk with that boy."

"Oh, please do, and could you do it when I'm around?" Nicole asks.

"You're having too much fun over this," her dad pipes up.

"Of course I am. He's my annoying older brother—it's my job to annoy him back. He's lucky I'm not wearing Atlas Kodiak's jersey tonight."

"Oh, don't ever do that," I say. "Everybody on the team hates that guy."

"Is that why Noah got into a fight with him?"

Not wanting to disclose the real reason Noah let Atlas get under his skin, I reply, "Whatever the reason, he probably deserved it."

"I guess he did. He's hot, so the fact that he's an asshole tracks. In my experience, most hot guys are."

Dying to change the topic of conversation, I say, "Are you ready to visit the Warriors' home?"

"Yes, of course. Lead the way." Mr. Kingsley gestures with his arm.

Nicole falls in step with me and links her arm with mine. "You're not going to let Noah get away with his deception, are you?"

"How come I have the feeling you asked about my French assignment so he'd be found out?"

"Because it's true. It's not my fault my brother is a dumbass." She laughs.

"Well, he's lucky that I like him."

"So his shenanigans did work. I'm impressed. I swear, I thought he would crash and burn."

"He didn't, but I do agree I can't let him get away with it. But since I'm not exactly angry with him, I don't know what the best course of action is."

"I have an idea. Just follow my lead."

I turn to her. "You're as devious as your brother."

She smiles wickedly. "Oh, I'm much worse."

I use my badge to gain access to the Warriors' area of the arena. Since tonight is game night, the common area is a little busy, with parents and girlfriends mingling around.

The first person who sees us is Logan. I guess Noah didn't come out of the locker room yet.

He makes a beeline in our direction, smiling from ear to ear. I can guess why he's so interested in saying hello to us. His eyes are glued to Nicole. I wonder how Noah would feel about Logan flirting with his sister.

"Good evening. I'm Logan Kaminski. You must be Noah's parents."

"That we are, son," Mr. Kingsley replies.

"It's very nice to meet you. We all love Noah. He's a great guy."

"Thank you." Mrs. Kingsley beams at the same time Nicole snorts.

Logan gives her a quizzical look. "And you must be one of Noah's many siblings."

"This is Nicole, Noah's *younger* sister," I reply, giving him a meaningful glance. He'd better not get any ideas about her.

"Did you enjoy the game?"

"Yes!" Nicole blurts out. "I loved it, especially when Noah got into that fight. Epic."

Logan's brows shoot to the skies. "Oh you liked that, huh?"

I clear my throat. I'm sure Noah's parents didn't pick up on the nuance in Logan's reply, but I certainly did. "Where's Noah?"

"He'll be out soon. He wants to look pretty for you." He smirks.

"Ah, there he is," Mr. Kingsley says, looking into the distance.

I follow his line of vision and spot Noah coming in our direction. I begin to smile but then remember Nicole's plan, so I keep my face neutral.

Noah hugs his parents first and then tickles Nicole before kissing me on the cheek.

"So, Noah," Nicole starts. "Gia was telling us how *great* you were as her French tutor."

The blood seems to vanish from his face. He swallows hard, and his gaze bounces frantically from his parents to me. Then he rubs the back of his neck and says, "She really didn't need a tutor."

"Not true. I totally did, and you were *so* helpful. The only thing you couldn't assist me with was the pronunciation."

"Why is that?" Nicole asks innocently.

"His French is too Canadian, according to him. I wouldn't understand a word he said."

Logan snorts. "I'd love to hear it."

Noah's parents, bless their hearts, watch our exchange in confusion.

"Why is Noah's face turning red?" Logan asks.

"I guess he's shy and doesn't want to speak French in front of you," I say, keeping an eye on Noah.

Logan crosses his arms and smirks. "Now I really want to hear it."

"Will you guys quit? I'm not saying a word in French," Noah snaps.

It's getting harder and harder to keep my laughter from bubbling to the surface. I make the mistake of looking at Nicole, who's also trying hard not to laugh. I lose the battle, and the giggles become unstoppable.

"Why are you guys laughing now?" Noah turns to Nicole. "You told her, didn't you?"

Nicole is too busy losing her mind to reply.

"Wait, what's going on?" Logan asks.

"Noah might have exaggerated his French skills," I reply.

"Gia, I don't deserve you," Noah says with his heart in his eyes. "Let's face it. I straight-up lied about my French skills. I have none."

"Dude! That's horrible," Logan pipes up. "And that's coming from me."

"It is terrible," his mother says. "Gia, you could have failed that class."

Noah hangs his head. "I know. I feel gutted. Thank God Nicole was there to save the day."

I cross my arms and stare hard at him. "Were you ever planning on telling me the truth?"

"Yeah, after we were married for fifty years or so, and I was sure you wouldn't leave me."

I roll my eyes. "You're impossible. I'll forgive you this time, but that's it. Don't ever lie to me again."

He steps a step closer. "I swear, babe. I will never lie or trick you again."

I turn to his parents. "What do you think? Can I trust him?"

They look at each other, and then they both stare at Noah. "You can trust him to never intentionally hurt you. As for never lying, I don't know about that," his father says.

Noah's jaw hangs loose. "Thanks a lot, Dad."

"You have a reputation. What did you expect?" Nicole pipes up. "Oh Gia, do I have stories to tell you."

"I want in on this too," Logan butts in.

Noah glares at him. "Go away."

He shakes his head and laughs. "Not a chance."

Taking pity on Noah, I offer him an out. "We can talk about it later. How about a tour?"

He looks at me, relief shining in his eyes. It's impossible to stay mad at him when I know his heart so well already. Yes, he lied, but there was no malice in the deception. If he hadn't done any of that, I'd never have given him a chance and gotten to know how incredible he is. It took me a while to conquer my fear of putting my heart on the line again, but he's given me proof after proof that he loves me. I can trust him. I know it in my very bones. I know it in my soul.

CHAPTER 53
NOAH

I cannot believe Nicole told Gia that I don't speak French. That could have created a lot of trouble for me. I'm the luckiest guy in the world that my girl didn't get mad at me for lying.

After the tour through the Warriors' facilities, my parents insist on taking the entire team out to dinner. Couch Bedford and Assistant Coach LaRue decline the invitation, but the usual suspects come. Sean, the twins, Darren, and surprisingly, CJ. He still acts like he doesn't care about anyone, but he's been doing things recently that make me think Sean might be right about him. CJ isn't a complete jerk—he's one maybe eighty percent of the time.

During dinner, both Logan and CJ flirt with my sister. She sits between the duo, loving all the fuss. Most guys wouldn't appreciate their teammates going after their little sisters, but the joke is on them. They don't know Nicole. Watching them fight for her attention is entertaining as hell.

I watch their interactions for only a little bit before I focus on what really matters—my girl. She's so beautiful and fun. It's clear my parents are as smitten with her as I am.

It's past eleven when we finally make it back to Gia's apartment. It was a good call to catch a ride with Sean to the arena. I wouldn't want Gia driving alone, even if I followed her with my truck.

I walk from her car to the entrance of her building glued to her side, thinking again how lucky I am. In the elevator I pounce, pushing her against the wall and flattening my body to hers while I kiss her neck.

"You're not going to give me a hickey again, are you?" she whispers, already tilting her head to the side to grant me better access.

"It depends." I place an open kiss near her ear, and she shivers.

"On what?"

"Do you taste less delicious than the last time?"

She pushes me back and tries to level me with a glare. It doesn't work. Her eyes are swimming with desire already.

"I don't like wearing turtlenecks." She pouts.

"Then don't." My lips curl into a grin.

"How about you don't nibble on my neck?"

"Are you sure? You get so turned on when I do."

She narrows her eyes. "You can nibble on something else."

My eyes widen slightly. "Oh, you can count on it, babe."

The elevator door opens, preventing me from starting the appetizer course right here. "Saved by the bell."

I throw an arm over her shoulders, and we exit the elevator together. "One of these days I'm gonna make you come in there."

"It's a pretty fast elevator."

"I have confidence in my skills."

"You have yet to make me come with only dirty talk," she reminds me.

I stop in my tracks and look at her. "Is that a challenge?"

"It's not a challenge. You promised, and you didn't deliver."

"I can deliver. It's not my fault you're an impatient kitten and always want either my mouth or my cock in your pussy."

"Maybe tonight I'll be more patient." She searches for the key in her purse and then opens the door.

I give her space, but only until we're inside her apartment. My cock is already pushing against my briefs. I expect her apartment to be pitch black—it usually is at this hour because Harper goes to bed early.

Tonight, the living room is bathed in orange light coming from the lamp next to the sofa. Harper's bedroom door is shut, though, and she has a red sock covering the handle.

"It seems Harper has a visitor," I whisper.

Gia glances at the kitchen island where there are two glasses of wine and an empty wine bottle. "Yep, it seems so. Why would she put a sock over her doorknob, though? It isn't like we'd barge into her room without knocking."

"I don't know. Maybe because she never has male visitors?" I stare at her closed door. "Now I'm curious."

Gia's phone rings, making her frown. "Who would be calling me at this hour?" She fishes the phone from her bag, and then her face drains of color, and her hands start to shake.

Without asking, I take her device and see it's an anonymous phone call. The rage I felt before when I learned about Martin and again when Atlas implied she's a whore returns with a vengeance. I press the green button and wait. First comes the heavy breathing, and then a robotic voice starts to say a bunch of awful things about her. I cut him off.

"This is her boyfriend, motherfucker! You'd better stop calling her, or I'll find you and break every bone in your body. Do you understand me?" My voice rises. "I'll pound on your worthless face until not even your mother will be able to recognize you."

"Do you think I'm afraid of you, little pup?"

"If you aren't, you're stupider than I thought."

"You can't find me, but I know where you live."

"Come on, then. Pay me a visit, you piece of shit. I dare you."

The call ends but my rage is a living thing. Harper's

bedroom door opens, and she and her companion walk out, looking startled. I don't even care anymore about knowing who he is. I'm too fucking angry, and at the same time, worried about Gia. She's staring at me with wide, frightened eyes that are brimming with tears. Dammit! I didn't mean to scare her.

"What happened?" Harper asks.

I pull Gia into my arms, and she presses her cheek against my chest, hiding her face. I run my fingers through her hair, trying to soothe her. One of us needs to calm down.

"Gia's being harassed by an anonymous caller."

The tall and tatted blond dude standing next to Harper seems shocked by the news. "How long has this been going on?"

She eases from my embrace and faces them. "A few weeks."

The blond guy clenches his jaw for a moment and then asks, "Does Ryder know about this?"

Whoa. Why is he bringing up Gia's ex?

"No, and you can't tell him, Adrian."

Son of a *bitch*. That's Adrian Steele, the guy who works with Harper and screwed her over. I glance at her, but she avoids my stare, dropping her gaze to the floor.

"Come on, babe. Let's go to bed. Sorry to disturb you guys."

I steer Gia into her bedroom and close the door. Like a robot, she sits on the edge of her mattress and hides her face in her hands. She's shaking. Maybe I shouldn't have answered the call. My altercation with her stalker only made things worse for her. Guilt sneaks into my heart, making it heavy and tight. I sit next to her and pull her close to me.

"It's going to be okay, babe, I promise. No one's gonna hurt you. We're going to find out who's harassing you and make him stop."

She turns to me. "I should go to the police. I don't want you to get hurt, or worse, end up in jail because of me."

"I'm not going to jail, sunshine. Don't worry. And if you want to report those calls, I'll be with you."

"Thank you. I don't know. This is such a mess." She releases a shaky breath.

"What can I do to make you feel better?"

"I just want you to hold me. Is that all right?"

"Of course it is, sunshine. Anything you need."

We take our clothes off and get under the covers, wearing nothing but our underwear. Sex is the furthest thing from my mind when I pull her half on top of me. She rests her head on my chest and flattens one hand over my belly.

"I wish this would stop already."

"It will." I pause, not knowing if I should mention what's running through my head or not.

"You must be wondering why Adrian asked if Ryder knew about the calls."

"Psychic. It *did* cross my mind."

She runs lazy circles over my abs, leaving a trail of goose bumps behind. I don't want to sex her up, but my cock doesn't care. It's gone rogue. I ignore the erection pushing against my underwear and focus on her voice.

"There were rumors about me when I started working for the Warriors, and they got worse when I made my relationship with Ryder public. Somehow, he put a stop to the rumors. For the entire duration of my relationship with him, no troll dared to speak ill of me."

"I wonder how he managed that. Maybe I should give him a call."

She lifts her face and looks at me. "You aren't bothered by it?"

"Bothered that he took care of you when you needed his help? Not at all. And if he has the means to find out who's harassing you now, you bet I'm going to ask for his help."

"That's the most romantic thing anyone has ever said to me."

I laugh. "Really? Begging your ex for help is romantic to you?"

"Yes. Not many guys would put aside their pride and do

that. They'd rather try to figure it out on their own, prove they're the better man."

"I'll be the better man when that stalker is dealt with for good. If it means dealing with Ryder, so be it. I want you to feel safe again."

"I feel safe now with you." She rolls on top of me, straddling me and rubbing her pussy against my shaft. Her panties make the friction even better. Keeping things mellow is starting to become damn hard.

"Sunshine... I thought you just wanted to cuddle," I say in a tight voice.

"I changed my mind." She runs her thumb over my lower lip while gyrating her hips.

I grab her wrist and suck her thumb into my mouth. Her eyelids lower halfway, and her eyes fixate on my mouth. With my free hand, I slide her panties to the side and guide my cock to her entrance. Not needing any coaxing, she lifts her hips and slowly impales herself on my rock-hard erection. My balls are already tight as hell, and when she begins to move, I have to concentrate in order to not come prematurely.

I release her thumb so I can grab her hips with both hands. "I love the way you move, babe."

She flattens a palm against my right shoulder and increases her pace. Her breasts dangle in front of me, a lush temptation I can't resist. I angle my body upward and capture her left nipple in my mouth, sucking it hard.

"Noah... fuck."

I release the pressure, then run lazy circles over her tight bud with my tongue. She moans like a devious kitten, driving me wild with need. I need more—more skin, more kisses, more pussy. I roll to the side, taking her with me and switching positions.

She yelps, but before she can object, I slant my lips over hers and lift one of her legs, placing it over my shoulder. This new angle heightens everything for me and, most important, for her.

She clenches her internal walls, milking me as I plow into her without mercy. The bed frame bangs against the wall, and I know her neighbors are going to complain. The rattling knocks over the nightlamp, and the light goes off, submerging us in the dark. I don't stop. We usually don't fuck hard like this when her roommate is around, but Gia and I need it tonight. So much has happened; I have to connect with her on this deep and raw level.

She screams against my mouth while her body jerks underneath me, and when she scratches my back, the sharp pain makes my control snap. My cum shoots into her heat fast, filling her up, and violent tremors wreak havoc on my body. A primal groan scratches its way up my throat. Nothing matters in this moment but the sounds of us falling apart together.

Her body goes limp beneath mine, and then she sighs against my lips. I thrust my hips forward one last time before I collapse next to her with my heart going a hundred miles per hour. For a while, the only noise in the room is our heavy breathing. In the darkness, I find her hand and link our fingers together.

"Thank you," she whispers.

"For what?"

"For loving me."

I turn my face toward her, and even though I see only her silhouette, I can feel the emotion in her eyes. "Thank you for letting me." I pull her into my arms and kiss the side of her head. "You'll always be my girl, Gia. Always."

CHAPTER 54
NOAH

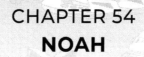

Gia and I spend the weekend holed up in her apartment. We watch movies, order takeout, and fuck like rabbits. My goal is to make her forget the ugliness of Friday night. That's possible only because my parents and Nicole aren't around anymore. They came for my game and then left early Saturday morning to go to New York City. That's my folks, doling out attention to their many children in small doses.

Until I find a way to deal with the asshole harassing her, there's no reason to keep reminding her he's out there. I don't broach the subject, even though I haven't stopped thinking about it. But Monday comes, and Gia and I can't pretend anymore that the ugly world doesn't exist.

On the way to my dorm, I text Alex. I know he has a class with Blair. Maybe I can head over and talk to her. I tried looking her up on social media, but all her accounts are private. Waiting for her to approve a friend request might take too long.

I could have asked Gia for Blair's phone number, but even though I told her I wasn't opposed to contacting Ryder to ask for his help, I don't want her to know that I'm following through. There's no need to remind her that he once was her knight in shining armor.

Instead of texting me back, Alex calls me.

"Hey, man. Thanks for getting back to me," I say.

"What the hell do you want with Blair?" he barks in my ear.

Jesus, someone must have had a bad weekend.

"I need to ask her a favor."

"You want to ask the witch a favor? Are you out of your mind?" The volume of his voice is still high, making me wince.

"Probably, but not for the reasons you think."

"Oh, is it a surprise you're planning for Gia?" he asks in a more normal tone. "If that's the case, you can call Ashley or Zoey. You don't need to talk to Blair."

I pinch the bridge of my nose. "Can you please just tell me when you have class with her?"

"Fine. It's this afternoon at two o'clock in the economics building. I'll text you the classroom number."

"Thanks. Does she usually get there early?"

"I don't know. She's always there when I arrive, but I'm always running late."

"What time does the class end?"

"Three forty."

"It's probably easier if I talk to her after."

"Yep, probably. But what exactly do you want with her?"

"I can't tell you, but thanks for the info."

He snorts. "Fine. Keep your secrets. I'll find out eventually."

I roll my eyes. "Whatever."

It's providential that Blair's class schedule doesn't clash with mine. I can't miss any of my classes. The issue is I have the whole day to wait and obsess about things. I text Gia more than normal just to check how she's doing, not caring that I'm acting like a needy boyfriend.

I ask her to have lunch with me, but she's meeting with her study group in the library. She doesn't mention it, but I suspect crashing her study group wouldn't be a good move on my part.

To kill time, I go to the gym, hoping to work out the tension. But I keep looking at the clock and counting the minutes until it's time to head to the economics building. It's no surprise that when midafternoon rolls around, I'm wound tight. I arrive twenty minutes early and do nothing but pace in front of the lecture hall.

My spine goes taut when the double doors finally open and students start pouring out. Alex is one of the first to exit and sees me right away.

He walks over, smirking, his intentions clear. If he lingers, he might find out what I want with Blair.

"You look tense, Kingsley. How long have you been waiting?"

"I just got here," I lie. "And I'm not tense."

I look over his shoulder, not wanting to miss Blair walking out.

"Relax. She's usually the last one to leave. She always likes to chat with the professor. She's such a teacher's pet." Alex twists his face in disgust.

His phone rings, distracting him. He doesn't look happy about the call. Before answering it, he looks at me and says, "I have to take this. Good luck with the witch."

I'm relieved that he doesn't stick around. He's a pest; it'd be hard to get rid of him.

A minute later, Blair walks out. She's distracted, looking at her phone, and doesn't notice me.

"Hey Blair," I call.

She stops in her tracks and turns. Her blue eyes widen in surprise. "Noah? What are you doing here? Did something happen to Gia?"

I pay attention to our surroundings, not liking that there are so many people milling about. "Can we talk someplace private?"

"Sure. Follow me."

I follow her down the hallway, and after a few turns, we reach an empty corridor. She faces me, mouth pinched and eyes shining with concern. "What's going on?"

"Gia got another anonymous phone call last night. This time I answered."

Her brows shoot to the heavens. "Holy crap. What did you say?"

"I told the caller that if he didn't stop harassing her, I'd break all his bones."

"But you don't know who he is."

"No, but I have the feeling that your brother might be able to help me find out."

Her jaw slackens. "You want *Ryder* to help you?"

I widen my stance, crossing my arms. "Look, I'm not keen on asking him. But I'll do anything to keep Gia safe. If that includes involving Ryder, so be it. I understand this isn't the first time she's been harassed, and he made it stop before somehow."

"I don't know anything about that. I mean, I knew some jerks were being extra mean to her online, but I had no idea Ryder got involved."

"He did, and now I need your help setting up a meeting with him."

Her eyebrows pinch. "He won't agree to meet you. I don't think he's over Gia yet."

"He's the one who ended things." Not that it negates her statement.

"True, but not because he stopped caring about her. My brother is complicated."

My stomach twists. *Great*. Another jerk in love with my girl. I shouldn't be surprised. She's special. But too bad for him. He had his chance.

"I guess I'll have to ambush him too."

She flattens her lips and doesn't speak for several beats. "If you really want to talk to him, your best shot is looking for him at the Gentlemen's Club on Main Street."

I scowl. "What's that? A strip club?"

She shrugs. "Who knows? I'm not allowed inside. Possession of a dick is a main requirement. If it's a strip joint, it's the upscale kind. He goes there to play poker."

"What time?"

"I'm guessing around nine."

"Is it a members-only club?"

"They allow non-members who are willing to dish out a lot of cash. Go prepared, and dress like you belong there."

"You mean dress rich." I raise an eyebrow.

"No, dress wealthy."

CHAPTER 55
GIA

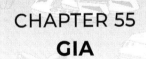

Noah did his best to distract me last weekend. It was nice to pretend there was no ugliness in the world, no stalker trying to make my life hell. But we couldn't hide in my apartment forever. We both have lives outside our safe bubble.

Harper didn't spend the weekend at home. In fact, I didn't see her Saturday morning at all, and later, when I texted her, she said she was spending the weekend with her folks. My guess is that she didn't want to talk about her late-night guest. I'm not going to judge her over who she sleeps with. Maybe Adrian apologized for being a dick to her. Despite his bad-boy persona, he never acted like an ass toward me when I was dating Ryder.

I've been so busy with classes and my job at the Warriors that I've been neglecting my own social media account. I didn't post any new dance videos last week. Maybe I'll shoot a video in front of the arena after all and ask the guys to make a cameo appearance, or maybe I'll just ask Noah to participate.

Thinking about dance makes me feel a little bit better. I'm still shaken, but I can't dwell on the negative, or it'll swallow me whole.

During the day, I go through the motions, fighting to pay

attention to my classes. I can't allow my problems to distract me to the point that they affect my grades. I need to maintain a high GPA, or I'll lose my scholarship.

Noah wants to meet me for lunch, but I can't bail on my study group in the library. I'm glad that's happening today. Studying with other people is always better, and the chances that my mind will wander are less.

After an hour of intense studying and discussion, I feel energized. But my improved mood dips again when I find Ryder waiting for me in front of the library. It's not a chance encounter. He walks over with determination.

Immediate annoyance spreads through my veins. "What do you want?"

"I heard you're getting harassed again."

"Adrian has a big mouth."

"He's worried about you, and so am I."

My brows arch. "You don't need to be worried about me. I'm not your concern anymore."

His blue eyes darken. "Just because we aren't dating doesn't mean I don't care about your well-being."

"I don't want you to care."

"I don't want to fight with you. So please, tell me about the calls."

I cross my arms, glaring. "Why? What are you going to do about it? They're anonymous."

"I know. What did the person say?"

"I'm not going to repeat the insults to satisfy your curiosity."

He runs his fingers through his hair, pulling it back in a nervous gesture. "This isn't curiosity, Gia. It's important."

He's rattled, and it's making me nervous. "What's going on? Do you know who could be behind the calls?"

"I can't tell you."

"You can't *tell me*?" I shriek. "It's my life, Ryder. I'm the one who's being harassed! I'm the one being called the nastiest names. So, if you know or suspect who's behind it, you'd better tell me right now."

His nostrils flare, and he grinds his teeth so hard I can hear it. "Trust me. I'm keeping you in the dark for your own good. I'm trying to protect you, just like I was trying to protect everybody else, no matter the cost."

"What the hell are you talking about? Does this have anything to do with why you quit the team?"

He looks away, clamping his jaw. "Forget I said anything. Coming here was obviously a mistake."

"You're just going to walk away and not give me any explanation at all?"

"That's right," he deadpans, staring at me with an unyielding expression.

"I guess I shouldn't be surprised. That's your MO, isn't it? Walking away without a care in the world no matter who you hurt in the process."

Guilt shines in his eyes. "I never meant to hurt you. Trust me, Gia. I never wanted to walk away from the team or you."

My stomach twists painfully, making me a little sick. "Why did you?"

His face becomes a cold mask again. "Because it was the only way."

"The only way for what?"

He shakes his head. "Stop asking questions I can't answer."

"Can't or won't."

"Fine. Won't. And tell your boyfriend to stay out of it."

Fear pierces my chest, and my eyes fill with tears. "Why?"

He doesn't answer for a couple beats, and I can see his jaw working hard. "Because you love him."

My jaw drops, and I don't know what to say to that.

"I'm sorry I'm scaring you," he adds. "I just want you to be safe, and the best thing is for you two to do nothing."

A tear rolls down my cheek. Ryder's gaze zeroes in on it. He swallows hard, then stares into my eyes again. "I'll fix this."

He walks away, carrying all his secrets with him. My mind is spinning as I replay all the moments we were together right before he broke up with me and then when he quit the team. I was too angry to look beyond his assholery. Now I'm filled with guilt that I didn't look further.

NOAH

I'm getting ready when my roommate, Terrance, comes in. He gives me a sideways glance. "Do you have a game tonight?"

"Nope. It's Monday."

"Date night, then?"

"Wrong again. I'm meeting friends at a fancy place downtown."

"You at a fancy place?" He chuckles.

I frown. "What's with the surprised tone?"

"I just never figured you were the type. Aren't you from a small town in Canada?"

"So? I'm not in Canada anymore. I was invited, and I'm curious."

"What's the name of the place?"

"Gentlemen's Club. It's on Main Street."

"Oh, that place." He shakes his head. "Definitely not your scene."

"Have you ever been there?"

He gives me a droll look. "No, but I've heard about it. It's where the elite of Hannaford U hang out."

I want to point out that most of the students at Hannaford U are considered elite, including him. But I bite my tongue. It's not worth making a comment.

"I'll let you know how it goes." I put on my jacket and fix the sleeves.

He plops down on his mattress with a vape already between

his fingers. "Whatever. Are you sleeping here, or are you staying at your girlfriend's?"

"I'm not sure yet."

"Maybe you could tell me when I have the room to myself. You know... so I'm aware when I can bring a girl here."

"Sure. Tonight, I might come back."

"I'll probably be passed out by then. Classes are kicking my ass." He takes a drag of his vape, making a weird sound in the back of his throat.

"I'll be quiet."

He puts on his headphones and focuses on his laptop. The conversation is over. I grab my coat and head out. I don't know why I said I'll come back here. I don't want Gia to be alone, but at the same time, I'm not sure what shape I'll be in after my conversation with her ex.

On my drive to the Gentlemen's Club, I run scenarios in my head. I don't know what I'm going to tell him. He's not only Gia's ex; he's the asshole who fucked over the team. Those guys are my family now, and I'll do anything to protect my people.

My GPS warns me I'm a minute away from my destination. The place is downtown, which means parking could be a problem. But as I approach the building, I see that they have valet. It makes sense. Rich people like things to be easy. I'm a little *un*easy when I hand over the keys. Maybe I should have done more research about the place. If my roommate knows about it, I'm sure a simple Google search could have helped me.

Too late now. I'll look like an idiot if I just stand here and look at my phone. I square my shoulders and walk through the sliding doors with the confidence of someone who belongs. Fake it till you make it. I've used that motto my whole life, and it's always paid off.

The interior screams wealth. Rich jewel-tone accents contrast with the dark wood paneling on the walls and the reception desk in front of me. A pompous young man wearing a suit I'm sure was custom made for him gives me an appraising glance. I'm wearing my best suit, the one my mother insisted I pack. I haven't worn it since moving to Fairbanks because it feels too tight. That's the problem with designer clothes, in my opinion.

"May I help you?" he asks in a flat tone.

"Yes, I'm meeting a friend. I wonder if he's arrived yet?"

"What's the name?"

"Ryder Westwood."

The arrogant man looks over my shoulder. Someone is standing behind me now; I can feel his presence, but I don't turn.

"Yes, he has arrived," the guy behind me says. "And I didn't realize we were friends."

Son of a bitch. I do turn now and come face to face with the man Gia wasted a year dating. He's studying me in a cold and calculating manner. I've dealt with worse stare-downs in my hockey career. A snobby asshole won't intimidate me.

"You're right, we aren't. Unfortunately, I need to speak with you."

He narrows his gaze and doesn't respond.

"Mr. Westbrook, do you wish me to escort this person out?"

"No, that won't be necessary. Put him on my guest list. Noah Kingsley." He walks through another set of mahogany double doors, and guessing I'm supposed to follow him, I do.

On the other side of the doors, I find an open room that follows the same opulent, ostentatious theme of brass, leather, and old money. Persian rugs cover hardwood floors, and dark furniture, wood-paneled walls, and oil portraits of figures I don't know seem to close in on me. I've never cared for this kind of grotesque display of wealth. The sense of uneasiness takes hold of me again, and I try to shake off the feeling that everyone is staring at me.

Ryder takes a seat in a deep-red velvet chair, looking right at home. I try to imagine him in the Warriors locker room, goofing around with the twins or listening intently to Coach Bedford, but I can't picture it.

I sit across from him and open my mouth to get straight to

business, but he signals the waiter and says, "The usual." He looks at me. "What are you drinking?"

"Just water is fine."

He quirks an eyebrow, looking smug as shit. "They won't card you here."

"This isn't a social visit," I grit out. "And I only drink with friends."

"Suit yourself." He waves the waiter away without even glancing in his direction. His arrogant behavior sets my teeth on edge.

"How did you know where to find me?" he asks.

"I'm friends with your sister."

"*You're* friends with Blair." He laughs. "Good one."

"I'll cut straight to the chase. Do you know who's been calling Gia?"

Ryder's relaxed stance changes in an instant. He sits straighter in his chair, and his eyes become darker, dangerous. "Why do you ask? Did she tell you about our meeting?"

His question takes me by surprise. They *met*? When? Unfortunately, I'm not quick to hide my emotion.

His lips curl into a malicious grin. "She didn't tell you, did she?"

"What did you want with *my* girlfriend?"

His haughty mask returns. "Gia and I were friends before we became a couple. I heard about the calls and wanted to check on her."

I stare at him through narrowed eyes. "Right. I'm not one hundred percent convinced it's not you who's been calling her."

His brows furrow. "Why would I bother my ex when I was the one who ended things?"

"Maybe you don't like that she moved on. Or maybe you're just a deranged fuck who enjoys wrecking people's lives."

He chuckles. "Wow, you have a lot to get off your chest."

"You have no idea."

The waiter returns with Ryder's drink, an amber liquid—

scotch or whiskey—neat, and my water, which comes in a fancy glass with a slice of lemon.

"Thank you," I say. Ryder doesn't acknowledge the man.

He brings his drink to his lips and takes a sip before speaking again. "So, you tracked me down to accuse me of being Gia's stalker? Is that it?"

Hell, this conversation has already gone off course.

"I know this isn't the first time she's been targeted. I understand you made it stop before. If you're not the one placing those calls, then I'm guessing you have the means to find out who's harassing her."

"Are you saying that you came here to ask for my help?" His tone denotes incredulity. I don't blame him.

"Yes."

He rubs his chin and studies me intently. I have no idea what he's thinking. He has a good poker face. All I know is that I've now given him a lot of ammunition to use against me later. I'm the guy who can't protect his girlfriend without asking for help.

"Does Gia know about this?"

"Of course." Technically, it's not a lie. She knows about my intention to ask Ryder to help.

But for some reason, he seems to know that I'm stretching the truth. Maybe it has something to do with his earlier meeting with her. I'm operating blind here, but I won't back down or show weakness.

"I already have my people looking into it. She may not want my interference, and I for sure don't want to help *you*, but I care about Gia. Even if we aren't together anymore, I'll never let anything happen to her."

His confession feels like a punch to my gut. It's not only his words, but it's the fire I see burning in his eyes. Yes, he ended things with Gia, but my instinct tells me he never stopped loving her.

CHAPTER 56
GIA

I get home late, and Harper is already in her bedroom. I texted Noah earlier, and he said he'll most likely crash in his dorm. The apartment feels hollow and forlorn without him, but maybe we do need a little break. We've been spending so much time together that it's beginning to feel like we can't function without each other.

I need to know that I can be by myself and handle anything life throws at me without boyfriends coming to the rescue, but I can't stop thinking about what Ryder told me. Blair did mention something was off with him—why didn't I ask more questions? He's clearly keeping her in the dark too.

He seems to believe whoever is behind the phone calls is connected to the reason he quit the team. But if that's so, why start to harass me six months later? It doesn't make any sense.

I call Blair, but the call goes straight to voice mail. Strange. I think that's the first time since I've known her that it happened. I send her a DM on Instagram instead, but if her phone is off, it might take a while until she sees it.

I'm going to drive myself crazy if I keep thinking about Ryder's enigmatic answers. I'll have a better chance of coming up with a plan tomorrow when I'm not this tired. I take a shower, get into my comfy PJs, and microwave a bowl of popcorn. A good romcom movie is exactly what I need.

No sooner do I get settled under my cover and *Legally Blonde*'s opening credits fill my TV screen than the intercom buzzes.

"Who the hell is annoying us now?"

I choose to ignore it, but it buzzes again. I hear Harper's door open. Maybe she's expecting Adrian. Although, if she had made plans with him, she'd have let me know. I have a feeling last Friday night was an impromptu hookup.

A moment later, she knocks on my door. "Gia, are you awake?"

"Yes."

"Noah is coming up."

"What?" I toss the duvet aside and get up.

Harper is almost at her bedroom door when I walk out of mine. She looks over her shoulder. "Weren't you expecting him?"

"No. I would have answered the intercom if I was."

"Maybe he wanted to surprise you." She smiles, then vanishes inside her room, closing the door behind her.

I walk to the front door and wait, pressing my ear against it. When I hear the *ping* of the elevator down the hall, I open the door a sliver and watch Noah walk over, but not in a straight line. *Shit*. No wonder he didn't text me to let me know he was coming over. He's wasted.

I open the door wider and wait for him with crossed arms and a glower.

"Hey, babe. I missed you." He opens his arms and pulls me into an alcohol-fueled embrace. I remain stiff, which he barely notices.

Then he throws his arm over my shoulders and steers me back into the apartment. "Do you have something to eat? I'm starving." He steps away from me and heads to the kitchen.

"I made popcorn. It's in my room. I was going to watch a movie."

"Sweet! What are we watching?"

"*Legally Blonde.*"

"Oh, that's a fun one."

He stumbles through the living room, barely avoiding a collision with the coffee table. I try to not judge or get exasperated about his condition. Something must have happened.

Noah dives onto my bed with his clothes and shoes on, dislodging the bowl of popcorn and getting it all over my comforter.

"Oops. Don't worry, I'll clean up." He scoops up a handful of popcorn and shoves it in his mouth. "Mmm… so good."

"Where have you been?" I sit next to him.

"Nowhere… everywhere."

"That's not an answer," I sigh.

"If you must know, I went to see your ex."

Shit on toast. "I didn't think you'd go through with that. Why didn't you tell me?"

He looks at me, squinting. "Why didn't you tell me he came looking for you today?"

Guilt warms my face. I break eye contact, focusing on the TV instead. "I didn't want to tell you over the phone or a text. Is that why you went after him?"

"No. I had no idea you'd met until he told me—with great smugness, by the way. Totally blindsided me. But don't worry, I didn't make a fool of myself."

"No, you just went and got drunk," I grumble.

"But not with *him*," he replies, indignant.

"With who then?"

He grabs another handful of popcorn and tosses it in his mouth. "Sean and Darren. Don't worry. I didn't tell them anything. I figured you didn't want to worry the guys."

I run my fingers over the stitching on my duvet cover, still avoiding looking into his eyes. I can't believe he had the foresight to keep my secret even when he was in this state of intoxication. I most definitely don't want to involve anyone else, especially after Ryder's ominous warning to keep Noah out of it.

"Are you mad at me?" he asks.

"Not really." I glance at him. "You told me you might ask for Ryder's help. What did he say?"

"He said we shouldn't worry about it. He already has 'people' looking into it."

"He told me the same thing and asked that we do nothing."

"He's one cocky motherfucker and is dead set on protecting you."

A sliver of apprehension punctures my chest. "He told you that?"

"Oh yeah."

I grow quiet, obsessing about my conversation with Ryder all over again.

"Are you having second thoughts?" Noah blurts out.

"About what?"

"About us."

I jerk back. "Why would you ask me that?"

His eyes have never shown more vulnerability than they do right now. "Ryder is still in love with you, and even though I don't like the guy, I have a feeling he made sacrifices to protect you. From what, I don't know."

"Even if you're right, I want to be with you. I'm in love with you. That's not going to change."

He reaches for the back of my head and pulls me toward him, pressing our foreheads together. "Thank you for saying that, sunshine. And I'm sorry I was feeling insecure and needed to drown my sorrows in beer."

I smile wryly, "At least it wasn't tequila."

"True." He pulls back. "Are you going to watch this movie or what?"

"I don't know. Are you going to clean up this mess or not?"

Noah jumps out of bed and gets rid of all the popcorn within seconds, sending half of it to the floor. I need to vacuum, but I'm not doing it now. Harper is probably already asleep.

He doesn't last ten minutes before he's snoring loudly next to me. I watch him sleep, and then put on noise-canceling headphones and connect them to the TV audio. I might love him, but I do *not* care for this symphony.

I try to concentrate on the movie, but our conversation made me more worried. Is the person harassing me doing it to get back at Ryder? Or are the two things not linked at all?

CHAPTER 57
GIA

FIVE WEEKS LATER

We don't hear anything from Ryder or the anonymous caller for five weeks straight. Talking to Blair yielded nothing, and even after she spied on Ryder and snooped around his things, she couldn't find a single clue. At first I was on pins and needles, waiting for something bad to happen. Noah pissed off my stalker, and I was sure the caller would retaliate, especially after Ryder implied Noah could get hurt if he got involved. But maybe Ryder followed through and "fixed" things, whatever that means.

But if he did, does that mean he knows who was calling me? I confess I was obsessed with that for a while, but in the end, I decided to let it go. Ryder will never tell me the truth anyway.

We visited the puppies at the farm a few times, and that helped me get my mind focused on better and brighter things. They're all thriving and growing by leaps and bounds. I'm so in love with Marshall, it's not even funny. I can't wait to bring him home.

I'm in the arena today, catching up on work for the Warriors. I shot a dance video last week with Noah and the twins. And for the first time, I broke away from my tradition of using only 80s and 90s songs in my videos. I think it's time for a change, a rebrand of sorts. For that video, I picked "Dynamite" by BTS. The song has an addictive beat, and the lyrics aren't controversial, meaning I can cross-post it safely on the Warriors' social media pages.

I'm almost done editing the video when a knock on my office's open door catches my attention.

"Hey, babe. Whatchu doing?" Noah's eyes crinkle and there's a hint of that sexy smile on his lips.

And there goes my heart, doing cartwheels in my chest. I didn't think it was possible, but every day I fall more in love with him.

"I'm about to finish editing our dance video. I thought you didn't have to be here until later."

"Training isn't until four, but Assistant Coach LaRue asked me to come earlier. Did he say anything to you?"

I pinch my eyebrows. "No, I haven't seen him today."

Alex and Logan join Noah in front of my office, crowding the door.

"What's up, guys?" I ask.

"Not much," Logan replies, squinting a little. "Is that our video?"

I close my laptop. "Yep, but it's not ready for your eyes yet."

"Did LaRue ask you to come early too?" Noah asks.

"Yep," they reply in unison.

"Strange. Maybe we should go look for him and see what it's all about." I get up from my chair and try to leave my office.

The twins walk away from my door, but Noah keeps blocking it and won't let me pass until he greets me properly. The kiss is a quick one and leaves me wanting more, like always.

"You look pretty today," he says.

I glance down at my clothes. "I'm wearing leggings and an oversize sweatshirt."

"Fine. You always look pretty no matter what."

I wrinkle my nose. "I don't know about that."

My cell phone rings, and I hate that I always tense when that happens. PTSD—it's a thing.

I check the screen, and relief washes over me when I read Blair's name. "Hello."

"Hey, I got a text from Derek asking if I could stop by the arena today."

I almost ask, *Derek who?* But then I remember that's Assistant Coach LaRue's first name. We never call him that, so it slipped my mind. Blair refuses to call him assistant coach. Her reasoning is that he isn't her coach.

Things become clear to me. The only link Blair has with him is the puppies.

"Are you coming?" I ask.

"I'm walking into the arena right now, but I need someone to come get me."

"Sure, I'll be right there."

I end the call and notice Noah is staring. "Did you hear all that?"

"Yep. I think Assistant Coach LaRue has been keeping a secret from us." He smirks.

"I think so too."

We didn't think we'd be able to get the puppies until after Thanksgiving. It seems LaRue wanted to surprise us.

We join the twins in the common room. Sean, Darren, and CJ are also already there.

"Did you find LaRue yet?" Noah asks.

Darren shakes his head. "He hasn't arrived."

"Blair is here, so you can guess what this is all about."

CJ's face lights up. "Puppies!"

We all look at him as if he's grown a second head. Realizing he sounded too chipper, he grows serious. "I mean, he must be bringing our puppies."

Noah and I trade a glance. He gives me a boyish shrug as if to say *CJ is weird*. I don't think he is. He just puts on an arrogant mask to hide his pain. I hope one day he realizes he can trust us. We're all family here.

"I'll be right back," I say.

Before I can step out of the Warriors zone to get Blair at the entrance of the arena, I see that she's already in and walking by the side of a pretty girl with pink hair. She looks familiar, and when they get closer, I recognize her. It's Micaela Bedford, Coach Bedford's daughter. I've never met her in person, but I've seen pictures of her in his office. Her hair is different now. She used to be blonde and wore big thick-rimmed glasses.

"Hey, Blair. I'm sorry it took so long to come get you."

"No worries. I ended up meeting Micaela, and she got me in."

"Hi." I wave. "You must be Coach Bedford's daughter."

"That's me. How do you know?"

"Your pictures are everywhere in his office." I smile.

Her face turns bright red. "Oh no. I don't photograph well, and Dad has the unique ability to choose the worst ones."

"I don't think they're bad. You have nothing to worry about."

She grimaces. "I don't know... but I'm glad I brought my oversize bag. I'll be raiding his office when he's busy and taking away any ugly picture he has of me."

"You're funny," Blair says. "What year are you in high school?"

Micaela tilts her head. "I've graduated already. I took this semester off to travel in Europe and hopefully figure out what I want to do with my life."

"Did you?" I ask.

She shrugs. "Not really. But I got to see beautiful places and eat amazing food. Now I'm back to reality. I start at Hannaford U next semester."

"You should join the Deltas," Blair says. "It's my sorority, and quite frankly, the only one worth rushing."

"I've never thought about joining a sorority, but I'm open to the idea."

"I can tell you more about Greek life if you want."

"Sure. You have my number already. Call me anytime."

I take a step back and listen to Blair and Micaela's conversation. There's a small smile on my face. Blair is not the easiest person to get to know, and very rarely does she like someone from the get-go. I love seeing her get along with someone right away.

When we get back to the common area, Assistant Coach LaRue is already there with the puppies.

Noah turns to me, holding a chubby Marshall in his hands. "Look how big he got, babe!"

The look of pure elation in his eyes gives me a rush of the most amazing feeling. My heart expands, overflowing with love for him and our new puppy. I don't care about anything now besides the cuddly new member of our family.

Marshall is full of energy and wiggles around when I hold him. "Oh my God. You're the cutest thing in the whole world."

He yaps, melting my heart a little more.

"I thought we had to wait another two weeks to get them." Blair takes her pup from the crate. He still wears the little bow she attached to him.

"My parents thought they were ready, and I wanted to surprise you."

"Wow. Did everyone on the team get a puppy? That's so sweet," Micaela pipes up.

LaRue notices her then and seems taken aback.

"Not everyone," I reply. "There were only seven puppies. Noah and I got one, Logan and Alex—"

"We got the only female. We named her Blair," Alex chimes in, smiling like a fiend.

"*You* named her Blair. Not me," Logan interjects. "Hi, I don't believe we've met yet. I'm Logan Kaminski, right winger." He smiles brightly at Micaela.

"Nice to meet you. I'm Micaela, but you can call me Mic."

I see Logan preparing to put on the moves, so I add. "She's Coach Bedford's daughter."

Like a balloon, he deflates. "Really? You look nothing like the pictures in his office."

She turns to me. "I *definitely* need to see what Dad has on display there."

"You could have warned us that you were bringing the puppies today," CJ complains to LaRue. "I'd have bought a crate and supplies. I have nothing in my apartment for a puppy."

The twins exchange a look. "Shit. We don't have anything either," Alex says.

Blair rolls her eyes. "Typical."

"Who's going to watch the pups?" CJ asks. "We have training in an hour."

The blank look on LaRue's face tells me he didn't think about that. He's in a tough spot now.

I open my mouth to offer to babysit the dogs, but Micaela speaks before I can. "I'm not doing anything. I can watch them."

"Really? That'd be a huge help," LaRue replies.

She smiles kindly at him. "It'll be my pleasure. I love puppies."

"I can help you once I finish work," I say.

"And I can go to the pet store and get food and supplies for the dumbasses who aren't prepared." Blair looks pointedly at Alex.

He wants to retort, I can tell, but there's really nothing he can say, and she's trying to help. "Make sure you keep your receipt."

She puts one hand on her hip while holding her puppy with the other. It's quite the image. "Why? Do you think I'm going to scam you?"

"I wouldn't put it past you."

"Bro, shut up." Logan elbows Alex in the stomach.

"Let's bring the puppies to my office before the boss shows up," LaRue cuts in. "I'd like to keep my job."

CJ stares at his pup and mumbles under his breath, "Maybe

he should have thought about that before bringing you guys here."

Lucky for him, Assistant Coach LaRue doesn't hear him. A comment like that from CJ is on brand, but unlike his other quips, this one doesn't have any bite. Maybe he's changing already.

I'm still holding Marshall when Noah throws an arm around my shoulders. "I'm so happy that our family is together again."

I giggle. "You're silly and cute. But I'm happy too."

For the first time in weeks, I feel the dark cloud over my head dissipate. I dare to hope that the worst is behind us.

CHAPTER 58
GIA

ONE WEEK LATER

I had plans to hit the gym after my classes, but I'm feeling so bone tired that I come home instead. Blair has Marshall today. She wanted the brothers to play together. Usually, Noah takes him to his classes since he can get away with it, and no one says a thing. It turns out, the school administration allowed the guys to have pets in the student halls, and it seems the request came from Coach Bedford.

My stomach is unsettled, and I feel dizzy. I didn't eat anything all day, and now I'm nauseated. When I enter the apartment, I'm hit by the scent of freshly baked chocolate chip cookies. That would usually make my mouth water. They're my favorite.

"Hey, Gia. You're here just in time. I made cookies."

Bile rises into my throat, and I cover my mouth with my hand. I run to my room, hoping I can make it to the toilet in time. I almost don't. I drop to my knees and hug the bowl as I throw up.

A moment later, Harper calls from outside the bathroom, "Are you okay?"

I sit on the balls of my feet and wipe my clammy forehead. "No. I just emptied the contents of my stomach."

"Did you eat anything at lunch that might have upset you?"

"No. I skipped lunch."

"That's strange."

"Yeah, I don't know what happened. I love the smell of freshly baked cookies, but today it made me hurl." I get back on my feet, flush the toilet, and brush my teeth.

When I walk out, Harper stares intently at me. "Is this the first time you've gotten sick over smells?"

I want to say yes, but when I think about it, I also got a little sick when a girl sitting next to me was wearing a vanilla-scented perfume.

"No, actually."

She crosses her arms and squints. "When was the last time you had your period?"

My heart skips a beat. "I... shit, I don't remember. I didn't take the week break from the pill, because I didn't feel like having my period last month. You know I get severe cramps."

"Do you think it's possible that you're pregnant?"

I get dizzy all of a sudden, which validates her suspicions. I stagger to my bed and sit on the edge of the mattress. "I'm not sure. I mean, I haven't forgotten to take a pill. How could that happen?"

"But you've been drinking on the weekends, right? Did you ever throw up after bingeing? That can impact the effectiveness of birth control."

"I did throw up the day after my birthday party." I rest my head in my hands. "Fuck. I need to take a pregnancy test ASAP."

"Hold on." She walks out of my room, leaving me reeling with the possibility that I might be pregnant. I've always wanted to have kids, but not while I'm still in college and my boyfriend is a freshman. We have our whole lives ahead of us, and I can't even picture what a baby would do to them. Marshall is already a handful.

Harper returns to my room and offers me a pregnancy test. I stare at the box for a couple beats and then I look up. "Why do you have a pregnancy test?"

"I had a scare last year, and this was left over. You know me, I had to be sure and bought a bazillion tests. It hasn't expired. I figured you'd want to know right away before Noah gets home."

With a shaking hand, I take the test from her. "Yes, I should probably do this now."

"Do you want me to wait here for you?"

"Would you?"

"Of course, hon."

In a daze, I lock myself in the bathroom and follow the instructions on the box. It's a straightforward test. Pee on the stick and wait for the result.

"How's it going?" Harper asks.

"I'll tell you in five minutes."

"Right. Is there anything I can do while we wait? I can tell you bad dad jokes."

I laugh despite myself. "I think that's a terrible idea, considering Noah might become one soon."

A lump forms in my throat and tears burn my eyes. Noah. He's *nineteen*. What are we going to do?

"Shit. I'm an idiot," Harper says.

"How about you tell me what's going on between you and Adrian? You've been avoiding the subject since that night we caught him here."

"Yes, but only because of what happened then. I didn't want to remind you of that phone call. Besides, there's nothing to tell."

"Really?"

"Fine. We drank too much wine, and we hooked up. That's it."

She's quick to dismiss it as nothing, but there's a slight tremor to her voice at the end.

"So it was a one-time thing?"

"Yep."

"Is he still acting like a jerk at work?"

"You betcha, and that's the reason I'll never sleep with a coworker again. That's why they say, 'Don't shit where you eat.'"

Adrian Steele is wild, the most reckless of Ryder's friends, and even though he's more than capable of doing douchey things, I don't think he's a purebred asshole.

"I know you don't want to hear this, but maybe you're exactly what he needs."

"Since when are you on his side? I thought you were drinking the Haterade too, after we had to prepare all those marketing boxes, thanks to him."

"Well yeah. It was a shitty move on his part, but maybe he was trying to get your attention."

"Are you serious right now?"

I shake my head. "Not really. I'm just saying shit to distract myself from the fact that my life might go completely off the rails."

"If you're pregnant, will you keep the baby?"

"Yes."

"Wow, no hesitation."

"No... not when it comes to this. I believe women have the right to decide whatever they want, but for me, that's the only way. I've always known it."

The timer I set on my phone goes off. The result is in. I look... and my breath catches. It takes me a moment to process what my eyes are showing me.

"What is it?" she asks.

I open the door, holding the test in my hand and showing it to her. Her eyes go round, and then she hugs me. "It's going to be okay, Gia. And I know Noah will be one hundred percent on board. He's so in love with you."

My chest feels so tight, I can barely breathe. She just exposed the crux of my problem. Noah will be totally on board with my decision, even though I'm about to implode his life.

✕ ✕ ✕

NOAH

"How's it going with Marshall?" Assistant Coach LaRue asks as we exit the gym building together.

Apparently, I didn't learn from my mistake and agreed to work out with him again. I'm not hurting as badly as I did the first time. Either he's gone soft, or I'm in better shape. Probably the latter. The guy is still a sadistic beast.

"It's going great. I'm sure it helps that I'm sharing the responsibility with Gia. How about you?" I watch him sideways.

"What about me?"

"How are you handling being a single parent?"

The easygoing demeanor vanishes from his face. He clenches his jaw and stares straight ahead. "It's fine. I've hired a dog walker."

"Cool," I reply and then decide to keep my mouth shut until I get to my truck. It seems I said something that upset him.

"Is that your truck?" he asks once we hit the parking lot.

"Yes, why?"

"You have a flat tire."

My gaze drops to the wheels. "Hell. How did that happen?"

I have a visual of only the left tire, but when I'm standing in front of my truck, I realize that *both* front tires are flat. LaRue circles around the back and then looks at me. "Someone slashed your tires."

My stomach drops. I mistakenly believed that I didn't have to worry about Gia's stalker anymore. It's clear he was biding his time, waiting for us to return to normalcy before he struck again.

"Do you know who could have done this?" he asks.

I hesitate. Gia doesn't want anyone to know about the phone calls, but it has come to the point where we can't keep this secret anymore.

"Yes."

He clenches his jaw. "We need to report this to campus police."

"I know." I look into the distance, letting rage consume me. "Fuck! This is the last thing Gia needs; to worry about me."

He taps me on the shoulder. "One more reason to report it. There are security cameras in front of the building. They could have caught the perpetrator in the act."

I stare at the building until I locate the cameras. My truck is parked too far away. It's out of range. I doubt they caught anything.

"Yeah. Maybe." I pull out my phone to make the call.

I let Ryder handle the situation before and he clearly has not. Now it's time to do things my way.

I get home about two hours later. *Home.* I don't know when I started thinking about Gia's apartment that way. Maybe when she gave me a key. I do spend most of my time here now that we're sharing custody of Marshall.

Everything is quiet when I walk in, and there's no light coming from her room. Marshall's crate isn't in the living room either. It's late, but it's not *that* late. Only ten past nine. Reporting the incident to campus police took a while, then I had to wait for roadside assistance to take my truck to the shop and wait again for them to fix my tires.

On tiptoe, I enter the bedroom, careful not to wake her. Marshall whines when he sees me. He wants to come out and play, but we're trying to train him, so I can't take him out of his crate while he's crying. It'd just reward bad behavior.

I use the bathroom quickly, then take off my clothes and slide into bed with Gia. She's lying on her side, so I spoon her.

"Hey," she says.

"Sorry, babe. I didn't mean to wake you."

"It's okay. I wasn't asleep yet."

"What time did you go to bed?"

"Just now. I'm tired. It was a long day."

I kiss her shoulder. "Go to sleep then."

I hold her for a while and notice she doesn't relax, which means she's not falling asleep. I can't relax either, not when I have this secret swirling in my chest. I have to tell her tomorrow. Someone might tell her before I have the chance, and she clearly doesn't need to deal with that tonight.

Maybe it's a sixth sense, but I don't think my girl is okay.

CHAPTER 59
NOAH

I wake up before my alarm goes off. I didn't sleep well at all, waking up every couple of hours, tormented by what happened last night and what it'll do to Gia when she finds out. Out of habit, I pull her closer to me and bury my nose in her hair. Her scent has the magic effect of calming me down. It also turns me on, and my morning wood is already pressing against her ass.

She stirs, making a sexy kitten sound in the back of her throat. Damn. Now I'm really horny. I wasn't planning on waking her to have sex, but since she's already up, why not? I run my hand down her stomach until I reach the edge of her panties. The tips of my fingers are already sliding under the fabric when she tenses and pushes my hand away.

"I have a headache."

Shit. That's usually code for *I'm not in the mood* or *I'm mad at you, so sex is off the table.* Besides not telling her that my truck got trashed last night, I don't believe I messed up. And I know LaRue didn't tell her what happened.

"Okay. Do you want me to get you painkillers?"

"I'll take them later." She keeps her back to me.

An uneasy feeling settles in the pit of my stomach like a

moldy loaf of bread. Something isn't right here, but I can't fathom what's going on with her. *Hell.* Maybe she received another anonymous call, and like me, she doesn't want to burden me with the bad news.

"Did something happen, babe?"

She becomes visibly tenser. "No. Nothing happened."

"Can you say that looking into my eyes?"

She lets out a heavy sigh, then turns to me. "Why are you making a big deal of me not wanting to have sex with you?"

My eyes widen. "That's not what I'm doing."

She stares at me for a couple seconds before turning her back once more. "I'm tired, Noah. Just let me be."

"Okay, babe. I'm sorry."

I get out of bed and go into the bathroom, confused and worried. That's not Gia acting cranky because she's tired or has a headache. Something happened to her; I know it in my bones. Why won't she trust me?

I take a quick shower and get dressed. Gia's eyes remain closed, but I know she isn't sleeping. Her body is too stiff. I take Marshall out of his crate and go for a quick walk. When I return, I bump into Harper in the kitchen.

"Hey, you're up early," she says.

"Yeah. I had to take Marshall for his morning walk. Gia isn't feeling well."

Harper gives me a quizzical look before asking, "What's wrong with her?"

"I don't know. She says she has a headache, but I think it's more than that. Did you talk to her yesterday? She was already in bed when I came home."

She averts her gaze. "I just spoke to her briefly. She seemed fine to me."

I watch her move around the kitchen with new jittery energy. The change in her demeanor is noticeable. *Fuck.* I'm almost sure she's lying, but I can't outright accuse her.

My instincts are rarely wrong. Something is going on with Gia, but there's little I can do until she's ready to talk to me.

GIA

I wait until Noah is gone to get out of bed. Then I just sit at my desk, staring at my laptop screen without seeing anything. I hurt Noah's feelings this morning, and I didn't mean to. I'm so scared that I've reset to default mode, blocking out everyone who cares about me.

My phone pings and I glance at the screen.

> I love you, sunshine. Always.

Punch me straight in the chest, why don't you, Noah? My eyes fill with tears. Everything seems to be closing in and ready to blow. I'm going to lose my mind if I stay in my room. My phone pings with another message. This time from Jaime.

> Have you told him yet?

He was the first person I called after the test came back positive. We spoke for hours. But I asked him to keep his mouth shut. I'll tell the rest of the family myself, and probably all at once, but not before I tell Noah.

> Not yet.

> Why not?

> I'm waiting for the right time.

> K. Call me after. Love you.

The tears finally fall. I wipe the ones that roll down my cheeks and decide I can't stay holed up in my room or I'll go crazy. I put on a jacket, shove my feet into running shoes without bothering with socks, and take Marshall with me. I know Noah already walked him earlier, but I don't want to leave him alone in the apartment. I don't have class until later anyway.

Once outside, I realize I'm underdressed for mid-November. I shiver as the cold wind blows against me, seeping through my clothes and chilling me to the bone. I could take my car, but perversely, I decide to brave the weather. I cross the street and head in the direction of the park across from our apartment. Marshall doesn't seem to mind that it's fucking cold and runs ahead as if this is all an adventure to him. He's on a leash, so he can't go far.

"Gia!" A male voice calls my name.

I look over my shoulder... and my stomach plummets. Martin is running toward me. *Hell.* The last thing I need right now is to deal with his bullshit.

"Nope. We aren't doing this." I resume my walk at a faster pace.

He grabs my arm and pushes something hard against my side. "Oh, but we are, my little whore."

I turn toward him slowly as my eyes grow wider. Then I drop my gaze to the object poking my ribs. A gun. My head snaps back up. "What the fuck!"

"You didn't think you'd get rid of me that easily, did you?"

My heart is beating so fast I might be having a heart attack. "What the hell do you think you're doing?"

"I watched you date that rich asshole, knowing he'd fuck up sooner or later. I knew that once he dumped you, you'd realize I was the guy for you. But then you had to go and start fucking the new hotshot. Then I knew you weren't special. You're just another puck bunny, spreading your legs for all the hockey players."

My stomach drops as I finally realize the truth. "*You* were the one calling me."

"That's right, bitch. And now I'm going to do with you what you let all those fuckboys do. Come on."

My survival instincts take over. Even shaking from head to toe, I plant my feet on the ground. "I'm not going anywhere with you, asshole."

He digs his fingers into my skin harder. "Do you think I'm messing around?"

"I think you're very confused, but deep down, you don't want to hurt me."

Marshall starts to yap when I won't let him keep running.

"Fine, I'll hurt your puppy then." He points the gun at Marshall.

My blood seems to freeze in my veins, and my heart keeps beating faster and faster, pushing against the barbed wire that's wrapped tight around it. I look around, hoping to see someone and catch their attention, but there isn't a soul in sight. It's too damn cold to be outside. I'm the only fool who had the brilliant idea to go for a walk.

"Please don't hurt him," I beg, tears forming in my eyes.

"Tie him to that tree and come with me quietly."

I do as he says with shaking hands. Martin drags me away in the next moment, and my heart breaks when Marshall begins to whine pitifully. I'm already sobbing, but I can't lose my wits.

"You don't really want to do this, Martin. Think about the consequences of your actions. You're a talented dancer. Your future is bright. Why are you going to throw it all away?"

"You don't get it. I'm only good because of *you*. No one cared about me before we started to collaborate. Everyone can see our undeniable chemistry. We belong together, Gia, but all you care about is fucking your puck boys."

"That's not true."

"It *is* true. You didn't post anything for weeks, and the next video you post is with those asshole twins and your little pup. I bet you're fucking all of them at once."

"You're insane." It comes out as a whisper.

"No, I'm not insane. I have eyes."

We cross the park and then the street, veering toward one of the alleyways. "Where are you taking me?"

"Somewhere where I can show you what a real man feels like. When I'm done with you, you won't ever want to fuck those asshole jocks again."

CHAPTER 60
NOAH

My chest feels heavy and achy, and no matter how many times I massage the area with my fist, I can't make the pain go away. Gia didn't reply to my text, even though she read it. But that's not the only reason I can't draw air into my lungs. My instincts are telling me something is really wrong, and they've never let me down before.

My phone vibrates on my desk. It's an unknown number—not anonymous, but it gets the same reaction from me. I answer fast. "What?"

"I was wrong before. Her stalker is Martin. It's Martin!" Ryder screams in my ear. He doesn't identify himself, but I recognize his voice.

I jump out of my seat, earning the professor's attention. "Am I boring you, Noah?"

"Sorry, sir. It's an emergency." With the phone still glued to my ear, I run out of the lecture hall without a backward glance.

"How did you find out?" I ask.

"It doesn't matter. I called her, and she didn't pick up. Is she with you?"

"No. I'm heading home now."

"I'm twenty minutes away. I'll see you there."

I don't question why he's coming. I don't care. All I'm worried about is getting to Gia as fast as I can. I don't stop running until I'm inside my truck. I couldn't have been more relieved that I spent the extra money to have all my tires replaced last night instead of waiting until today.

I peel out of my parking spot so fast I burn rubber, drawing the attention of some passersby. My heart is thundering in my chest as I go way over the speed limit, the drive back to Gia's apartment taking less than five minutes.

I get out of my truck like a bat straight from hell but stop suddenly when I hear barking nearby. I turn around and spot Marshall tied to a tree.

"What the fuck?"

I run toward him while I search for Gia in the vicinity. She wouldn't have left him here alone in the cold. But she's nowhere in sight. My hands are shaking as I untie the knotted leash, then I scream her name, but there's no answer.

I drop to a crouch and ask the puppy in a panicked voice, "Where is she, sweet boy? Where is she?"

He breaks into a run, barking as he goes. I hope he caught her scent. I follow him across the park and then across the street into a narrow alley. Marshall keeps yapping, and the sound echoes, matching the drumming in my chest. When I reach the other end of the alleyway, I see Gia down the street being manhandled by fucking Martin. He's trying to force her into his car.

"Gia!" I yell.

They both turn in my direction… and then Martin points a gun at me. *Fuck.*

If I'd known he was armed, I wouldn't have announced my presence. I prepare to dodge in case he fires, but Gia reaches for his arm, screwing with his aim. The shot rings in the open, but the bullet misses me by a lot, thanks to her interference. He shoves her to the side, and she hits the car and falls to the ground.

Rage erupts from the pit of my stomach and spreads through

my entire body like violence. I let go of Marshall's leash and don't stop running until I'm within striking distance. Before Martin has a chance to aim at me again, I punch his face. His head snaps back with the impact, and then his body follows. He collides with the car, stunned, and I use that moment to take the gun from his hand and make sure the safety is on before I tuck it in the back of my jeans. He shakes his head and then takes a swing at me. I dodge his attack and fire off a succession of quick jabs to his stomach before I toss him on the ground.

Breathing hard, I look for Gia. She's already back on her feet and clutching Marshall to her chest. Her face is red and tear-streaked. Her distressed appearance just makes me want to punch Martin's face all over again until every bone in it is broken.

"Are you hurt, sunshine?"

She shakes her head. "No."

Martin groans and attempts to get up. But I grab him by the lapel of his jacket and roll him onto his stomach, straddle him, and restrain his arms behind his back.

"Babe, do you have your phone?" I ask without glancing at her. I need to keep an eye on this sneaky bastard.

"Yes. I'm already calling 9-1-1."

"Good."

The gunshot must have alerted people in the vicinity, and soon a small circle of onlookers gathers around us. They all want to know what happened, but no one offers to help me. All I want is to hold Gia in my arms instead of keeping Martin from escaping. At least the cops don't take long to arrive. Within minutes several units are blocking the area, and there are enough cops to form a hockey team.

The moment Martin is in the hands of the police, I walk to Gia and engulf her in a bear hug, Marshall sandwiched between us.

Tremors rack my adrenaline-filled body. I kiss the top of her head, fighting tears that are turning my vision blurry. "Are you sure he didn't hurt you?"

In a shaky breath, she replies, "He might have bruised my arm from holding on too tight. Other than that, I'm okay. How did you find me?"

"Ryder called to tell me Martin was the stalker. I booked out of class to check on you. Then I saw Marshall tied to the tree all alone. He's the one that led me to you."

She whimpers. "I was so scared. He threatened to shoot Marshall if I didn't go with him."

"He's lucky I didn't pulverize his face."

"I can't believe he was the one calling me."

Another wave of fury hits me. I clench my teeth hard, trying to keep my feelings from spilling out. "I'm so sorry, sunshine."

One of the officers comes over and asks if we need medical assistance. We both decline and then we spend the next twenty minutes giving our statement. Now Gia knows about what happened last night too. Martin is out of sight, handcuffed and locked in one of the police cruisers. The cop tells us we'll need to come by the station later, but for now, he has everything he needs to put Martin behind bars.

"You're not going to let him out on bail, are you?" I ask.

"That's not up to me. The charges are severe enough though. The likelihood he'll get bail is small."

I don't like that answer, but it's the best I'll get now.

"Can I give you a ride back to your apartment?" the cop asks.

"I can do that, officer." Ryder appears suddenly, emerging from the crowd.

"Friend of yours?" the cop asks us.

"Yeah," I say, keeping my eyes locked with Gia's ex.

Ryder breaks the connection first when he focuses on her. Relief softens his features.

"Come on, babe." I steer her away from the cop, pulling her into a side hug, wishing there was more I could do.

Even if Martin spends the rest of his life rotting in jail, there's no punishment severe enough for what he put Gia through.

"Are you okay?" Ryder asks her in a soft tone.

"Not yet, but I will be. Thank you."

He studies her intently for a couple beats. "I'm sorry."

"For what? Didn't you warn Noah about Martin?"

"I was almost too late." He looks at me. "When you filed the report with the campus police about your slashed tires, I knew I was wrong about who I thought was behind those calls."

"How did you hear about last night's incident?"

He lifts his chin. "I'm a Westbrook."

An arrogant answer to fit an arrogant man, but today, I'll give him a pass. Not only because he saved Gia's life but also because, unlike the other times I met him, I don't think he believes what he's projecting.

Gia's quiet on the ride home, and I have to bite my tongue and not ask her every minute if she's okay. I know she's not. I'm not. Ryder doesn't speak either, but he keeps checking on her through the rearview mirror. For the first time, I don't mind that he's still in love with my girl.

He parks by the curb in front of her apartment and gets out of his SUV. He doesn't ask to come upstairs, but he does hug her goodbye.

"You'll be okay, Gia. And don't worry. Martin won't make bail. You have my word."

She just nods as she steps back.

I look Ryder in the eye, and a silent exchange happens. I don't like him, and I'm sure he doesn't like me, but we understand each other. Hell, I might even respect him a little despite not knowing exactly what made him betray the team.

"Take care of her, Kingsley."

"Don't worry. I will." I throw my arm around her shoulder

and steer her toward the building. A few seconds later, the rumble of a powerful engine tells me Ryder's gone.

Gia remains quiet during the entire elevator ride. As soon as we enter the apartment, she gives me Marshall and says, "I'm going to take a shower."

"Okay, babe." I watch her head to the bedroom, but before she disappears inside, I ask. "Do you want company?"

She freezes for a moment, then looks over her shoulder. "Yes."

I place Marshall back in his crate, then I take off my clothes and follow her into the bathroom. She's already in the shower, not moving as the water rains down on her. Her head is tilted back, and her eyes are closed. My heart bleeds for her, for the pain and trauma she's now carrying.

When I join her, she turns and looks at me without saying a thing, but her eyes are already telling me so much I don't need the words.

I reach for her face, cupping it gently. "I love you so damn much, Gia. If anything worse had happened today, I don't think I'd have survived. You're my whole world."

"You're my everything too, Noah." She steps closer, curling her arms around my waist and resting her face against my chest.

"It's going to be okay, sunshine. Not today, and not tomorrow, but one day, this will all be a hazy memory."

She leans back, tilting her chin up. "Make me forget now, Noah."

I kiss her gently. Loving her is the only way I know how to fulfill her request. Her soft lips part for mine, our tongues immediately giving and taking in a perfect dance. Our flame turns into a bonfire, bright and cleansing. I let it spread through my veins, scorching the pain and the fear.

She moans against my lips, then runs her fingers down my abs until she reaches my rock-hard erection. She wraps her hand around my shaft, making my desire burn ten times as hot. I grab her ass and lift her off the tiled floor. I need to be inside of her.

Taking a step forward, I press her back against the wall, wanting to be as close to her as possible. She guides my cock to her pussy, and I enter her with a single thrust, burying myself to the hilt. She gasps loudly, then grabs my face between her hands and kisses me harder. I match the tempo of my thrusts to the savagery of her tongue. I didn't think I'd take her in this wild manner, but it seems it's what we both need.

"Harder, Noah. Faster," she begs.

"I don't want to hurt you, babe."

"You won't."

Everything is slippery, the floor, her body, and yet, I dig my fingers harder into her skin and increase my pace, relinquishing my last trace of control. "Is this what you want, babe? Is it hard enough for you?"

"I want more."

I plow into her, driven mad by her pleas. "You take me so well, sunshine. You're made for me."

"Yes," she hisses.

"God... I'm so close, babe. I want you to come with me."

The next sound that comes out of her sweet mouth drives me off the edge. She's coming around me, her pussy clenching my cock as she shakes in my arms. I explode into her, pumping in and out faster than before.

I slow down after a moment, and her body relaxes against mine. She hides her face in the crook of my neck and then starts to tremble again. It's different now. I hold her tighter and say, "I got you, babe. I got you."

CHAPTER 61
GIA

I've never cried so much in one go as I did in Noah's arms. He held me close for as long as I needed. Now I'm sitting in my bed, wearing his jersey and some leggings while he brushes my hair. My eyes are still puffy, and I feel raw. My body is about to shut down, but I can't go to sleep until I tell him about the baby.

"There. All knots are gone," he says.

"Thank you." I turn around and kiss his cheek.

"You're welcome. Are you hungry? I can make you something to eat."

The idea of eating anything makes me feel sick again. I'm nervous as hell, and my throat is tightening. I don't know if I'll be able to speak.

"I'm not hungry." Dropping my gaze, I take his hands in mine and lace our fingers together. "I need to tell you something, but I don't know how."

He squeezes my hand. "Whatever it is, I'm here for you."

I lift my chin, and seeing the anguish shining in his eyes makes me want to cry again. "Why are you staring at me like that?"

"I don't know," he replies in a choked voice. "Maybe I'm afraid I'm going to lose you."

My brows furrow together. "You're not going to lose me. If anything, now you're really stuck with me, whether you want it or not."

His lips curl upward. "I'm okay with that. And to clarify, I do want that, very much so."

Nervous laughter escapes my lips. "Boy, you might regret saying that."

"I doubt it. What is it, sunshine?" He rubs his thumbs over my knuckles.

I take a deep breath, and blurt out, "I'm pregnant."

Noah's hands still in mine, and his face freezes as well. He doesn't blink, doesn't speak, and I don't even think he's breathing.

"I know it's crazy. I'm on the pill, and I haven't skipped a day, but they aren't one hundred percent effective, especially when you—"

He grabs my face between his hands and crushes his lips against mine, ending my word vomit.

He eases off a little and presses his forehead against mine. "We're going to have a baby? For real?"

"The home pregnancy test I took yesterday says so."

He kisses me again, more tenderly this time, making my body melt. But I can't succumb to him without knowing exactly how he feels about it. I push him back and look into his eyes. "You're not going to freak out?"

He narrows his gaze. "Do you want me to freak out?"

"No, but... why aren't you?"

"Because it's you. The moment I saw you in the crowd, I knew you were it. The search was over, and I wasn't even looking. You're my dream girl, Gia. Yes, I know there are a million reasons to panic, but oddly, I've never been calmer and surer of myself than I am now."

My vision turns blurry, and I'm a moment away from

bawling my eyes out. "How come you always know what to say?"

"I'm wise beyond my years." He smirks. "I knew something was bothering you this morning. Were you afraid to tell me?"

I nod. "Yeah. The fear hasn't left my body yet. Honestly, I'm waiting for the news to sink in for you, and when it does, you'll run away cartoon style, leaving a hole in the door in the shape of your body."

He laughs. "I'd never run away from you. I know what I have, and I'll treasure you and our child until the end of time."

The tears finally roll down my cheeks. I throw my arms around his neck and hug him tight. "I love you, Noah. More than you'll ever know."

"Bullshit. I'll always know."

I laugh. "Oh, I forgot how cocky you are."

We break apart, and he's now mock glowering at me. "How could you forget?"

I roll my eyes. "I know, right?"

"When do you want to tell everyone? Do you want to wait?"

"Harper and Jaime already know, and telling our family and friends the good news might shift the focus away from us almost getting killed by that psycho. I'd rather talk about the baby."

"Me too. Plus, it'd be so hard to not spill the secret. I'm terrible keeping them."

I raise an eyebrow. "You didn't tell anyone we were fake dating."

"Only because I didn't want our fake relationship to end before I made you fall in love with me."

I hit his arm playfully. "There's that cockiness I love."

He leans forward and kisses the corner of my mouth, sending tingles of desire down my back.

"Before we tell anyone, I have to ask something of you," I say.

"What?"

"You have to promise you won't propose."

His eyebrows shoot to the heavens. "What?"

"I don't want to get married only because I'm knocked up, and I don't want you thinking that's the right thing to do."

"What if I want to get married to you regardless?"

"Were you planning on proposing anytime soon?" I quirk an eyebrow.

"Well... no, but only because I didn't want to scare you."

"Exactly. The baby changes nothing. I'm not saying marriage is off the table, but not right now."

"When then?" He grins.

"Noah... I'm serious. Besides, maybe I want to propose to you instead."

His mouth makes a perfect O, then he smiles. "Don't get my hopes up, sunshine."

And just like that, he gives me an endless supply of teasing material. "Too late."

CHAPTER 62
NOAH

I'm going to be a dad. I still can't believe it, and it's been a week since Gia told me. I didn't freak out then, and I didn't freak out later. But I suspect it's not the same for her. Totally understandable. My only job for the next eight months is to be the best boyfriend in the world, which isn't a hard task. She's the one who has to carry our baby and give birth to them. But despite my suspicions that she's a little nervous, she's not letting it show.

We told our families the same day I found out. The news was too big to withhold from them. There was shock, then concern about how it will impact our lives, but in the end, everyone was over the moon, especially Gia's older sisters. If they have anything to say about it, our little one will be spoiled rotten. It was weird, meeting her parents for the first time over a video chat when I had to tell them I had knocked up their daughter. Definitely don't recommend it.

When it came to the team, we decided to tell everybody at the Thanksgiving dinner Assistant Coach LaRue was hosting. We figured that avoiding the Martin subject was impossible, and it was best to wait until that issue was taken care of before revealing the good news. Mercifully, the judge denied him bail.

He has to wait for his trial behind bars. Blair made a comment that the judge was a good friend of her family. Ryder did pull through, but I never doubted he would. As long as that motherfucker stays away from Gia and never hurts her again, I'm happy.

We have an out-of-town game the day after Thanksgiving, so LaRue warned us that dinner would be a low-key event, and everybody was expected to bring a dish because he couldn't cook. He'd provide the turkey, which I'm sure he ordered from a restaurant.

Thanks to a Marshall emergency—a.k.a. he got into the dog food and ate his weight before we caught him—we're the last to arrive. The poor thing was throwing up all over the apartment an hour before we were supposed to head out to LaRue's place.

Alex started texting us nonstop twenty minutes ago, asking where the hell we were. He's hungry, and Gia is the one bringing his favorite dish—a smoked chicken salad. The GPS tells us our final destination is at the end of the road. LaRue lives in a gated community, and judging by the houses we pass along the way, my guess is none of the homes here cost less than five million dollars. The guy is so laid back that it's easy to forget he's an NHL legend and made a lot of money while he was playing for the Boston Zodiacs.

LaRue told us to not bother with the doorbell and just come in. No sooner do we step foot inside his house than Alex bellows, "About time! What the hell were you doing?"

"I bet they don't want to tell you," CJ replies, keeping his focus on the massive TV in the living room.

"Why? Do you think they got a quickie in before they left the apartment?" Alex fires back.

"Hey!" I complain. "We had a dog emergency."

"Oh yeah, what happened?" CJ asks.

"I don't think we should tell you right before dinner," Gia replies.

"Or maybe we should only tell Alex and ruin his appetite." I drop into a crouch and remove the leash from Marshall's collar. He zooms through the entry foyer and joins his siblings in the living room.

Alex raises his hand. "No need. I get the picture."

"Well, welcome to my house." LaRue walks over. "You can set your dish on the kitchen island, Gia."

Without being distracted by Alex and his antics, I have a chance to look at my surroundings. LaRue's home is beautiful, and everything used in the construction is top-notch, but it lacks something, a spark of life. He obviously hired an interior designer to decorate the place. Everything goes with everything, but to me, what makes the perfect home is the chaos in the harmony.

Jesus, what do I know?

I suppose that's what I envision my forever home with Gia to be like.

Alex comes running into the open kitchen, already rubbing his hands together. "Finally."

"You're not touching it until we're all seated at the table," she tells him.

"Besides, he's not that hungry. He's been snacking since he got here," Sean pipes up.

I see only him, Darren, CJ, and Logan in the living room. "Where's the rest of the guys?"

"Oh, this is it. Everyone else had plans," LaRue replies.

Because we're an hour late, and the guys are all hungry despite their pre-dinner snacking, within fifteen minutes, we're seated at the table. LaRue sits at one end with the biggest turkey I've ever seen in front of him, and that's saying a lot coming from someone who grew up in a large family.

He clasps his hands together, drawing our attention. "Thanks so much for coming today. I know you all have busy schedules, and it means the world to me that you could spare a few hours to celebrate Thanksgiving with me."

"We're honored to be here," Gia replies.

"Yeah, man." Logan lifts his glass. "Thanks for having us."

Noah lifts his glass too. "A toast to Assistant Coach LaRue."

"And Gia's smoked chicken salad," Alex adds.

LaRue frowns, staring at her empty water glass. "Gia, do you want something to drink?"

She shakes her head. "No, I'm fine."

"Not even a mimosa?" CJ asks.

"Way to be sexist, dude." Logan laughs.

"How's that sexist? I like mimosas."

Alex rolls his eyes. "Of course you do."

I reach for her hand under the table and squeeze. If we don't tell these idiots now, they'll be bickering about her lack of beverage until all the food goes cold.

"I'm fine. I'm not really drinking alcohol these days," she says.

Logan snorts. "Why? Are you knocked up?"

We both remain quiet and wait to see who's going to figure it out first.

Sean leans back in his chair, his eyes growing wide. "No way. For real?"

Logan whips his attention to Sean and then back to us. "No shit. You're pregnant?"

"Yes," she says and looks at me, smiling. "We're pregnant."

I lean over and kiss her cheek.

"Holy shit! No way," Alex blurts out.

CJ shakes his head. "Oh my God. Your life is over."

"Hey! Our lives aren't over, jackass." I throw a dinner roll at him.

"Don't listen to them. That's amazing news. Congratulations." LaRue walks over and bends down to hug Gia.

Following his lead, everyone does the same, so Gia and I stand to make the hugging easier. After a few minutes or so, we're back in our seats, but all eyes remain on us.

"I can't believe the rookie got you preggers, girl," Logan says.

"Why is that so hard to believe?" I ask, faking being

offended.

He opens and shuts his mouth like a fish out of water.

"He probably figures if someone would get anyone pregnant, it'd be him." Alex laughs.

"Shut up."

LaRue shakes his head, but a smile is toying with the corners of his lips.

"I'm sorry about those dumbasses," Sean pipes up.

"No, it's fine. I missed this."

"What? Having stupid hockey players talking shit at your dining table?" CJ quips.

"Yes." He raises his glass. "It's been a long time since I felt... *thankful* for anything." He turns his attention to Gia and me. "And I *am* thankful that Noah and Gia are here with us today, healthy, and sharing this wonderful news with us." His voice cracks at the end, and his eyes become brighter.

Damn it. Who knew Derek LaRue was a softy?

"If you cry, I'm going to cry," I half joke.

"Nooo, there's no crying in hockey," Alex chimes in. "Can we eat now? Pretty please?"

"Dude, you're such a child." Darren shakes his head.

"Yes, let's feast," LaRue replies.

Am I ready for the go-ahead? I was a second away from crying like a baby, which would probably have resulted in weeks of teasing.

From the corner of my eye, I see that Gia put only a dinner roll on her plate. "What's the matter, babe? Not hungry?"

"The baby doesn't care for anything."

"Are you having any cravings? What can I get you?"

She places a hand on my arm. "I'm fine. I've got my eye on the pecan pie. You go ahead and eat." She takes the bread. "This will do for now."

Pecan pie. I make a mental note to add that to the list I started. Things baby Mancini-Kingsley likes to eat. I can't wait to meet them.

EPILOGUE

GIA

EIGHT MONTHS LATER

I'm due in five days, but nothing will keep me away from the arena this afternoon, not Noah, not this huge belly, not even Coach Bedford. It's media day at the arena, and I'm not missing it. I played a big part in putting the new marketing campaign for the Warriors together, and I won't be barred from the best part, which is shooting the video. I don't care that I have to leave the rink every ten minutes to pee.

I'm wobbling my way back to my seat, wearing more layers of clothes than necessary because Noah doesn't want me to be cold or to *catch* a cold. I rolled my eyes so hard in my head when he said it that I would have gotten a headache if I'd done that for real.

Zoey is on the ice, helping Noah and CJ with their choreography, while Sean watches, trying to not laugh. I purposely didn't schedule the twins to come until later, knowing nothing would get done with them around. When people ask if having a baby at my age scares me, all I have to do is point at the guys. Working for the Warriors has been a crash course in motherhood.

I won't deny it was an adjustment. I had to move out of the

apartment I shared with Harper, and that was sad. I loved living with her. But it's too small for three people, a baby, and a pup. My new place with Noah is still on campus, and much larger, with three bedrooms. It's reserved for students with families. Most residents aren't undergrads like Noah and me, but the important thing is, baby Mancini-Kingsley won't be the only child in the building. Hannaford U also has a daycare program, which will be a lifesaver. And my sister Robyn, who is recently single and works from home, decided to move to Fairbanks so she can help with the baby.

"Watch it," CJ complains when Noah hits him in the face by accident.

"What? You got in my way."

I shake my head. I was daydreaming and missed what happened, but I'm sure Noah did something wrong. I showed him the moves—off the ice, naturally—but the poor thing still can't dance. I thought if he tried the steps in his element, they'd be easier. Oh well, there's always plan B, which is to eliminate the most complicated parts of their program and focus on what they do well—hockey.

CJ isn't much better, which is beginning to frustrate Zoey.

"Ugh. You guys are hopeless." She throws her hands in the air.

I move closer to the ice and get Phil's attention. He's the videographer we hired for the job. This is an official video for the Warriors, so we needed a professional.

"Did you get anything we can use?" I ask.

He grimaces. "Eh... maybe. But hey, I'll have lots of funny BTS videos for you."

"I don't think showing how uncoordinated our center and D-man are will do us any favors."

"True."

"Sean, could you take over? I need a break," Zoey says, and then skates toward the bench without waiting for his reply.

Her face is beet red, and if she were a cartoon, there'd be

smoke coming out of her ears. "I'm about done with those two. I swear they're messing up the program on purpose."

"Maybe we should eliminate the part they're having trouble with. They aren't figure skaters."

"But if they could get their shit right, it'd be so good."

Suddenly, the baby kicks hard, and then I feel something give like a balloon popping. A second later, water trickles down my legs.

"Shit!" I place my hands over my belly. "I think my water just broke."

Zoey and Phil snap their attention to me.

"Are you serious?" she asks.

"Either that, or I just pissed my pants."

Zoey turns to the guys and yells, "Gia's water just broke."

I wince. *Thanks a lot, Zoey.*

Noah flies across the rink and chips ice when he stops in front of me. His eyes are panicked and his face whiter than usual. "Are you okay? Are you having any contractions?"

"I'm fine, and nothing yet." I start to get up, but Noah steps off the ice and reaches for my arms to help me.

"How long does she have?" CJ asks as he joins us. "Do we have time to take her to the hospital?"

"Calm down," Zoey chimes in. "She's not even having contractions yet."

"Oh, okay." He rubs the back of his neck. "I thought once the water breaks, then it's only a matter of minutes before the baby pops out."

"I'd be okay with that if it meant having the baby pain-free," I reply.

"Don't even joke about it." Noah furrows his brows. "You aren't having our baby in the arena."

Zoey turns to Phil. "Why are you recording this?"

"Maybe they want the moment captured."

"Great idea, man. Can you come to the hospital?" Noah asks.

"He wasn't hired for that," I say. "Besides, Alex and Logan are due for their turn in less than an hour."

Sean, who's also standing nearby, says, "I just told Coach Bedford you're in labor. He's canceling shooting for the day."

The news doesn't please me. "Why did you have to tell him? We're already behind schedule."

"Sorry but you know the twins would be pissed if they weren't at the hospital today."

"Why? They aren't coming into the delivery room," Zoey points out.

The muscles of my abdomen contract like menstrual cramps but ten times worse. I can't breathe for a moment.

"Ugh." I bend forward a little.

"Shit. Is that a contraction?" Noah massages my back.

I nod, unable to answer with words.

"Let's go." He tries to pick me up, but I stop him.

"I can walk, and you still have your skates on."

"Fuck!"

The pressure subsides, and I can breathe again. "Go change. I'll start walking to the truck."

"You can't go by yourself! What if you have another contraction?"

"She's not going by herself. Did you forget about me?" Zoey replies.

"No offense, but you can't carry her if she collapses."

Another contraction comes, but I still grit out, "I'm not going to collapse."

"I'll walk with her too," Phil offers.

Noah seems conflicted, so I add, "It's fine, Noah. Go change. You'll probably be done before we're even out of the Warriors area."

"Okay." He looks at Phil. "Don't let anything happen to her."

He then rushes to the tunnel toward the locker room with CJ and Sean close behind him. Zoey sits on the bench and undoes her laces. "Go on. I'll catch up with you in a second. I just have to put my shoes on."

Phil offers me his arm, and we make slow progress out of the rink. We've barely cleared the corridor when Zoey joins us and laces her arm with my other arm.

"How bad is it now?" she asks.

"Not terrible."

"You're doing great, Gia. My wife was screaming bloody murder from the very beginning."

"I'm pretty sure that's in my future if I don't get to the hospital soon."

As I predicted, Noah joins us before we even make it to the arena's entrance. "I'll take over from here."

Phil and Zoey step aside, and then Noah does sweep me off my feet. "Hey, I said I could walk."

"At this snail's pace, you *are* going to have our baby here."

CJ and Sean get the door for me, and then Noah sprints across the parking lot toward his truck.

"We'll see you at the hospital," Sean says.

Noah is too busy fussing with me to reply, so I give Sean a thumbs-up. Before Noah helps me inside the truck, I say. "We should probably cover the seat with a towel."

"Do you think I care about my stupid leather seat right now, sunshine?"

"Well, I care. There's one in the back seat."

He sets me on my feet and gets the towel for me. Then he fusses over me some more before running around the front of the truck and sliding behind the wheel.

"Okay. You're going to be fine. We can make it to the hospital in time." His voice trembles. I cover his hand with mine and make him look at me.

"Babe, we're okay. Just take a deep breath."

"I'm the one who's supposed to be saying that to you."

I laugh. "You're here with me. I don't need soothing words."

He captures my face between his hands and kisses me. "We're going to have a baby."

The emotion in his voice hits me straight in the chest. My vision becomes blurry, and I smile through the tears.

"We are, but if we don't get moving, they'll be born in this truck."

"Right. Let's do this."

NOAH

I'm in heaven and never more in love with Gia than I am now as I watch her nurse our daughter, Nora Jean. We chose to not find out the gender of our baby until we met her. We talked names, but Gia surprised me with Nora. She said our daughter looked like me, and Nora was the perfect name. Plus, it continues the Kingsley family tradition of first names starting with N. Jean is after Gia's grandmother who passed away a couple years ago.

"I can't believe we made her," I say in awe. "She's perfect."

Gia smiles at Nora. "She is. I don't think I've ever been this happy." She turns to me, eyes glistening with tears. "And to think it all started thanks to some crazy challenge."

"That was fate giving me a hand. But even if we hadn't had to fake date, I would have found a way to steal your heart. I've always known you were my forever girl."

A tear rolls down her cheek. "I think I've known you were the love of my life from the start as well. I just wasn't wise enough to recognize it."

I lean over and kiss her lips softly. "It's okay. I had fun showing you."

My phone vibrates in my pocket. I fish it out and see it's Nicole video calling. "Hey."

"I hear I have a niece," she says.

"Yeah. She's beautiful, Nikki."

"I can't wait to meet her. How long are you staying at the hospital?"

"I think we can go home later today."

"Great. I'll see her soon then."

My brows arch. "You're coming with Mom and Dad?"

She gives me a droll look. "Of course I'm coming, dumbass. Everyone is."

Shit.

"What's the matter, babe?" Gia gives me a quizzical look.

"I was hoping I'd have more time, but it seems you're meeting the rest of my family all at once. I'm sorry."

Gia laughs.

"Hey!" Nicole complains. "Stop scaring her. We aren't horrible."

"Whatever. When do you get here?"

"Soon." Nicole turns her camera around and shows my parents, my older siblings, and the twins chilling at the VIP lounge at the airport. "Everyone say hello to Noah."

They all look at the camera and wave. The twins run to Nicole's camera and begin to fight over it. "We want to see the baby," they say in unison.

I look at Gia. "Is it okay?"

She smiles. "Of course."

I turn the camera to her. "There they are."

"She's so small," Nash says.

"Duh! She's a newborn, silly," Neve retorts. "She's so cute. Will I be allowed to hold her?"

"Of course," Gia replies.

I turn the camera to myself. "I gotta go. Nora wants to take a nap. I'll see you soon."

They wave goodbye, and then Nash presses the end-call button before I can talk to Nicole again.

"The twins are so adorable," Gia says.

I snort. "Yeah, from far away. I'm really sorry that they're all coming."

She arches her brows. "Why? I was dying to meet the rest of your siblings in person."

I flatten my lips. "Because I'm afraid once you do, you'll run for the hills."

She giggles. "You're cute. I'd never do that, even if they were the worst, which I know they aren't. Besides, you've met *my* family, and you're still here."

"Ha, like you'd get rid of me that easily." I kiss the top of her head. "You're stuck with me now, sunshine. Forever."

"And ever." She smirks.

I tilt my head. "You're playing that Shakira song in your head, aren't you?"

"You know me too well."

"Now I'm thinking about her music video."

She narrows her eyes. "Is that so?"

"And wondering when you're going to dance like that for me?"

"Noah Kingsley, I just had your baby," she replies, feigning indignation.

"Okay, okay. Tomorrow then."

"You know we can't have sex for a while."

I press a hand against my chest. "Get your mind out of the gutter, will you? Who do you take me for? I'm not a horndog." She gives me a meaningful glance. "Fine. I am, but I have self-control."

She laughs. "We'll see how long it lasts."

"Well, can you blame me? Look what's in front of me, tempting me every day."

She scrunches her nose. "I don't think I'm tempting anyone right now."

"Sunshine, you've never looked hotter. Motherhood is a great look on you."

"You're lucky I'm holding Nora, or I'd smack you upside the head."

I smirk. "I know. And fair warning, the desire to do that to me will come many, many times in our lifetime together."

She watches me for a couple of beats without saying a word. "I'm okay with that. I love you, Noah. All of you."

Suddenly, the urge to cry hits me. I don't fight it. I sit at the edge of her mattress, tears sliding down my face, holding her closer. "I love you too, sunshine. Always have, always will."

THE END

ABOUT THE AUTHOR

USA Today Bestselling Author Michelle Hercules always knew creative arts were her calling but not in a million years did she think she would become an author. With a background in fashion design she thought she would follow that path. But one day, out of the blue, she had an idea for a book. One page turned into ten pages, ten pages turned into a hundred, and before she knew it, her first novel, The Prophecy of Arcadia, was born.

Michelle Hercules resides in Florida with her husband and daughter. She is currently working on the *Blueblood Vampires* series and the *Filthy Gods* series.

Sign-up for Michelle Hercules' Newsletter:
bit.ly/MichelleHerculesVIP

Join Michelle Hercules' Readers Group:
https://www.facebook.com/groups/mhsoars

Connect with Michelle Hercules:
www.michellehercules.com
books@mhsoars.com

- facebook.com/michelleherculesauthor
- instagram.com/michelleherculesauthor
- amazon.com/Michelle-Hercules/e/B075652M8M
- bookbub.com/authors/michelle-hercules
- tiktok.com/@michelleherculesauthor?
- youtube.com/@MichelleHerculesAuthor

Made in the USA
Las Vegas, NV
06 July 2023